I0671253

OVER THERE

A NOVEL

W. W. MONTGOMERY

Over There

Copyright © 2009 by W. W. Montgomery

All rights reserved.
No part of this book may be reproduced or utilized in any form or by any means,
electronic or mechanical, including photocopying, recording
or by any information storage and retrieval system
without permission in writing.
Inquiries should be addressed to

**BRYN
COLWYN
PRESS**

3390 Bob White Lane
Belton, Texas 76513
wmontgom@vvm.com

FIRST EDITION

ISBN 13: 978-0-9823643-1-4

This book is a work of fiction. Names, characters, places and events are
the product of the author's imagination or are used fictitiously, and any
resemblance to actual persons living or dead, events or locales is entirely
coincidental.

Cover design by Rebecca Bretz

ON THE COVER
LEFT: World War I Memorial of doughboy by sculptor Joseph P. Pollia. Dedicated
    30 May, 1927. Tarrytown, New York.
RIGHT: Civil War Monument, Sleepy Hollow Cemetery, by Johnson Marchant Mundy,
    1890. Sleepy Hollow, New York.
AIRPLANE: Curtiss JN-4D "Jenny" (model).
All photos from the author's private collection.

BACKGROUND: Breastworks on Little Round Top; Round Top in the distance.
Photo by Timothy O'Sullivan, July 1863. Courtesy of Library of Congress, Civil War
    Collection.

Printed in the United States of America
by Morgan Printing in Austin, Texas

To My Daughters
Lorie and Beth
And My Beloved Pets
Rebel and Bannock
Who Explored Virginia's Civil War
Campgrounds and Battlefields with Me

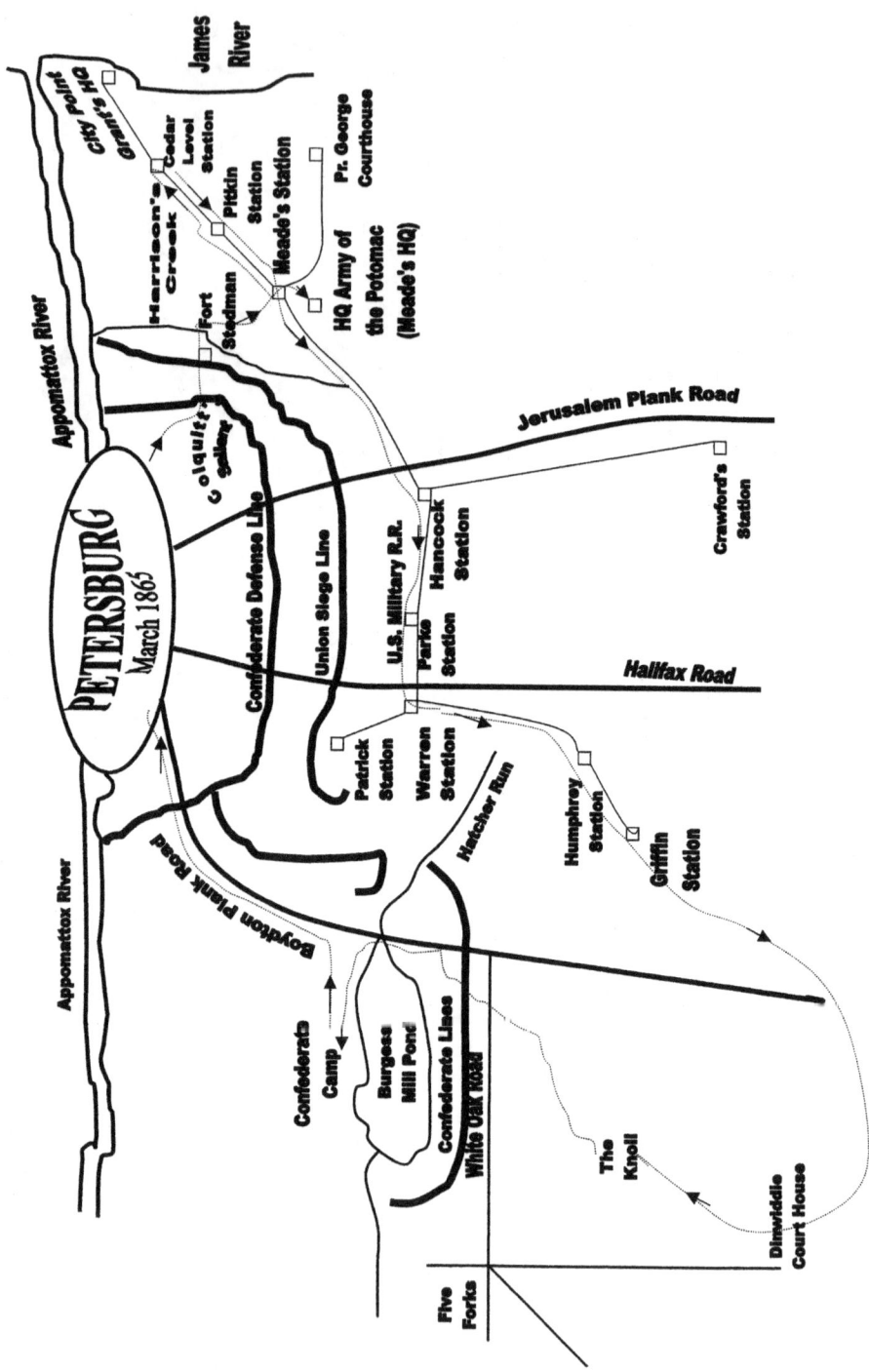

PROLOGUE

The truth of this story is anyone's guess considering I heard it from a 102-year-old World War I veteran locked away in the dementia ward of a local nursing home.

In 1994 I gave several lectures on the Civil War to various civic and elder hostel groups. At the conclusion of one particular presentation, as I was putting away the notes pertaining to my favorite topic, the siege of Petersburg 1864-1865, a distinguished-looking, gray-haired gentleman came up, and we chatted for several minutes. Mostly I answered his questions about some of the battlefield artifacts in my exhibits. Finally he broached what I later surmised was his real interest: would I be willing to visit his ailing uncle who shared a similar passion for the Petersburg campaign. "Sure, be glad too," I said, and he gave me the address. It was mid-November as I recall.

The following week I visited the ailing uncle; his name was Alex Wright. I found him sitting in a wheelchair gazing out the window in his semi-private room. I introduced myself and explained why I had come. The conversation went something like this:

"My nitwit nephew asked you to come?"

I smiled. "Your nephew says you're interested in the siege of Petersburg."

"And he told you that I'd *enjoy* hearing what you know about it. Well, okay. Just don't bore me to death with a tedious narration spanning the whole Petersburg campaign. Entertain me! Tell me what you know about the siege during the month of March, 1865. I'm all ears."

And so I began. For the next hour I lectured, throwing out every detail I could remember about Petersburg in March, 1865.

Mr. Wright didn't interrupt me a single time. He just sat there, prune-faced, unblinking, never taking his watery blue eyes off mine.

"Any questions?" I invited open handedly when I finished. Actually, I was quite pleased with myself, and the extent of my knowledge on the subject, and my ability to regurgitate the particulars without preparation or use of notes.

"Got all that from a history book, did you?" he said with more than a hint of sarcasm in his voice

"Several, actually," I replied evenly.

"Well sonny, you wasted your time, 'cause it's wrong," he chuckled contemptuously. "Come back tomorrow, and bring a notebook an' pen for note taking. I'm going to tell you a story that'll *blow your socks off*, as my great granddaughter likes to say."

"And what source will you be quoting from?" I inquired, trying to hide my annoyance and feeling as though I really had wasted my time.

"Me!" he answered with a fleeting expression that could have been either a grin or grimace. "I was there."

"Oh, I see," I nodded and smiled indulgently. Why should I have been surprised? After all, the old coot *was* locked up in a dementia ward with bolted doors.

As I rose from my chair thinking this was a good time to leave, I began making my excuses. "I'm sorry Mr. Wright, but tomorrow I have a busy day on campus, and the day after doesn't look very promising either, perhaps another time." I offered my hand to bid farewell and said in jest, "If you were at Petersburg in March 1865, I suppose that makes you the last surviving Civil War veteran, not to mention one of the oldest surviving World War I veterans. That's quite an accomplishment!"

There it was again, that grin or grimace.

"I'm locked up in this loony bin, sonny, but I'm not near as crazy as you think."

He regarded me for a moment with those watery blue eyes, and I hesitated as I turned to leave. In the swimming depths of those eyes I perceived intelligence and profound wisdom. "I don't have much time left," he said. "I have a story you will want to hear, one that I've never told another living soul—except my squirrelly nephew. That's how I ended up in here—for my own good, so he tells everyone. But

6

as I said, come see me tomorrow and be prepared to take notes. I promise to make it worth your while."

And so I did. I returned the following day, and the next, and the next. For more than a week I kept coming back, totally spellbound for hours as I listened to his incredible story. During that time I filled four notebooks with names, dates, places, and minute details.

The following week was Thanksgiving. I took a few days off to vacation with my family, but when I returned to Alex's room, he was gone. "Passed-away," they said.

My notes from his story gathered dust on a shelf in my den for years until I retired. Recently I dusted them off and organized them into a readable narrative, or as I prefer to call it—a novel.

CHAPTER 1

Langley Field, Virginia

1:00 P.M., NOVEMBER 10, 1917

First Lieutenant Steven Clarke, 119th Aero Squadron, U.S. Air Service, donned his leather cap and goggles and settled into the Curtiss JN-4D *Jenny's* cockpit.

A mechanic positioned himself in front of the wooden propeller, grasped the blade and gave it a half turn. "Contact, sir?" he inquired.

"Contact!" Clarke confirmed as he heard the *click* of the electric ignition switch.

The mechanic gave the propeller a sharp swing over then jumped back as the engine sputtered to life. It coughed once or twice, threatening to stall, then caught and reverberated smoothly as all cylinders fired in synch. Clarke gunned the engine until the revolutions reached 900 per minute, then throttled down to a gentle rumble. Satisfied, he signaled the mechanics to pull the chocks out from under the wheels.

The two-seater biplane with its long graceful wings taxied across the field then turned into the wind. The propeller whipped blue fumes of castor oil into Steve Clarke's face as the 90 horsepower engine propelled the fragile frame of wood and linen forward faster and faster until the tail lifted off the ground. The *Jenny* bounced across the field a few more seconds then soared into the air.

Steve circled Langley Field like a hawk riding the air currents in search of a prospective meal then turned eastward toward

CURTISS JN-4D JENNY, 1917, LANGLEY FIELD, VA

(Courtesy of Library of Congress)

A mechanic positioned himself in front of the wooden propeller, grasped the blade and gave it a half turn.

the James River. Just for the sake of logging in additional flying hours, he had laid out his flight plan in the shape of an elongated triangle that would take him up the river to City Point, then along the Appomattox River to Petersburg, then cross-country back to Langley.

An hour later he reached City Point, a promontory overlooking the confluence of the Appomattox and James Rivers. Having reached the terminus of the first leg of his flight plan, Steve changed to a new compass heading and followed the Appomattox's winding course. The *Jenny*'s long-winged shadow skipped along the bluffs overlooking the river.

Eight miles upriver, a white, wispy cloud of dust appeared off his left wingtip revealing the location of Camp Lee, a sprawling Army camp that had come into existence following America's entry into the war in Europe. Resisting the urge to have a closer look at the camp, Steve stayed on course and followed the river to the historic city of Petersburg.

The stately church steeples of Petersburg disappeared behind him as Steve completed the second leg of his flight plan. He glanced at his map then craned his neck over the side of the cockpit looking for landmarks. Below, the *Jenny*'s shadow skimmed over the patchwork landscape of Dinwiddie County with its foliage ablaze in fall colors. Far off to his left, the afternoon sun reflected mirror-bright on the James River.

Puffy white cumulous clouds began billowing up above and below him as though pulled from a magician's hat. Apprehensive, Steve climbed to 6,000 feet and leveled off. It was then that he observed the dark ominous-looking squall line stretching across the horizon.

Minutes later, his apprehension grew as the fast-moving storm descended on him. Boiling black clouds blotted out the sun, turning day into night while powerful downdrafts battered the *Jenny*, making her weave and bounce. Steve gripped the control stick with both hands, trying to keep the biplane level. Sweat beaded beneath his leather flying cap and goggles as he fought the turbulence and sensed vertigo setting in—the inability to distinguish up from down or upside down from right side up. Worse was the sense of something enormous whirling around him. A large shadowy object whizzed past his upper wing, but he was too focused on controlling the machine to see what it was.

The buffeting suddenly stopped, and the *Jenny* leveled off—except that it swayed strangely from side to side.

A terrible roaring filled his ears. It came and went, undulating in volume and intensity, seemingly rushing toward him then receding as though into a tunnel. He squinted through his goggles, searching for the source.

From the darkness evolved a whirling wall, like the torrent of a mighty flood. Cautiously, almost timidly, he craned his neck over the side of the fuselage and peered down.

A huge whirlpool-like thing coiled and whipped back and forth before ending in blackness far below him. "Oh My God! I'm inside it!" he mouthed the words, but heard only a hissing roar as the *Jenny* suddenly ceased swaying, hung suspended for a second, then nosed over and dropped like a stone into the swirling vortex.

Spiraling earthward, Steve felt a terrible pressure squeezing his chest, sucking the air from his lungs. He clenched his teeth and clutched the non-responding control stick in a death grip as he tottered on the brink of unconsciousness. The funnel cloud had matured into a full-blown twister that would soon be the ground where its cyclonic winds would grind to pieces anything in its path. Steve also knew that the debris sucked up by the twister would rip him and the *Jenny* to shreds. The multiple-colored quilted earth was quickly coming up to meet him when the *Jenny* suddenly tumbled out of the twister's mile-wide maw. But Steve was not yet out of danger. Behind his goggles his eyes popped open in panicky disbelief as the gnarled, ghostly white limbs of an enormous tree suddenly loomed in front of him. Before he could react, a flash of searing white light, like an exploding galaxy, blotted out the menacing limbs, the twister—and First Lieutenant Steven Clarke and his flying machine.

CHAPTER 2

U.S. Army Field Training Site
DINWIDDIE COUNTY, VIRGINIA
MARCH, 1918

"Uh-huh," Captain Alex Wright, Commanding Officer of "A" Company, 319th Infantry Regiment, 160th Infantry Brigade, 80th "Blue Ridge" Division, grunted appreciatively as he studied the knoll, a wooded hump almost two hundred feet high that dominated the low ridge on which it perched. "That's a good defensive position all right—real good. And you're *sure* this is the right place?" he asked for the second time in the five minutes since their arrival.

First Lieutenant Michael J. Dent, his executive officer, spread a topographic map on the fender of the lead truck in the convoy. "Yes, sir. I'm sure," he said, trying to hide his exasperation as his fingertip traced a terrain feature that clearly represented a long, low ridgeline bounded by a shallow ravine on its east and west slopes. "And we're standing right here," he tapped the map emphatically at a spot near the foot of the ridge.

"Uh-huh," Captain Wright grunted again, unconvinced. "That knoll is an impressive piece of real estate, but I don't see it on the map. Do you?"

"No, sir," Lieutenant Dent frowned. "I don't see how any Army topographical engineer worth his salt could have overlooked such a prominent terrain feature when he made this map. But if you look where we are in relation to these north-south and east-west roads," he pointed them out, "this is the only significant ridgeline in our quadrant. Knoll or no knoll, this *has* to be the right place!"

Dent looked up from his map as a figure emerged from the thicket alongside the road.

"It's Sergeant Pratt," Captain Wright said, stating the obvious but feeling relieved just the same. He had sent Pratt with a detail two days before to reconnoiter the area and set up camp.

Wright noted the black stubble of Pratt's beard as the sergeant approached. *I know what he didn't do for those two days*, Wright smiled indulgently. As a company supply sergeant, Pratt had the reputation of being the best in the division. Wright cut him a lot of slack as long as the sergeant delivered what he asked of him.

Pratt rendered his usual sloppy salute. "You picked a good'un, Cap'n," he grinned, jerking his thumb at the ridge behind him. "The Devil hisself couldn't take that position."

Alex lifted the brim of his campaign hat and gazed up at the craggy knoll. *It looks out of place,* he thought. As Pratt prattled on, Alex stopped him and pointed at the anomaly. "What about that knoll?"

Pratt closed his mouth and cocked a puzzled brow.

"Have you been up there?" Alex pressed, rephrasing the question.

"Uh…Yes, sir!" he nodded. "That knob's the best part of our defenses. It sits smack in the middle of the ridge like a big lookout tower—you can see for miles up there. Put a platoon of infantry among those boulders on its slope an' they could hold that hill 'til hell freezes over. By the way, Cap'n, there's a surprise waitin, for you when you an' the Lieutenant get up there."

Pratt grinned, expecting Captain Wright to nibble at the bait.

Instead, Wright turned to his executive officer. "Get these trucks unloaded, XO! The CO of the 329th Motor Truck Company wants them back by noon. So, unless you want to walk back to Camp Lee when the exercise ends, they better not be late."

"Yes, sir!" Lieutenant Dent saluted, then hustled down the line of trucks loaded with troops shouting "Dismount!"

When they finished checking the placement of the company's defensive positions along the ridge, Alex Wright and Mike Dent followed the faint traces of an old trail that wound steeply upward past rock outcroppings and jumbles of motor-car-size boulders to the top of the knoll. At the summit, they paused for breath and gaped in amazement. Before them, crowning the summit, a majestic grove of ancient oaks lifted their lofty canopies toward the sky. Alex and Mike stood transfixed, as firmly rooted as the trees themselves, staring up at the immense trunks and gnarled limbs sheathed in lichen and mold. Awed by the trees' incredible size and age, Alex whispered almost reverently "Holy Mackerel! Where did they come from?"

"Dunno," Mike wheezed, catching his breath from the exertion of the climb. "But I suspect this, and those over there," he said pointing to two wall tents pitched beneath the spreading limbs of an enormous oak, "is Sergeant Pratt's surprise."

That first night, and for many nights afterwards, Alex lay awake in his tent listening to the wind moaning through the canopy high above his head. He wasn't crazy about sleeping under the trees, but Sergeant Pratt and his men had worked hard pitching their tents and constructing an officers' latrine on the knoll, so he kept his mouth shut and tried to sleep.

Two weeks later, on the next to last day of the field exercise, Alex and Mike sat at a table in the company mess tent eating breakfast.

It was Mike who broached the subject. "I won't miss that knoll, Alex..." he paused, then lowered his voice upon noticing Sergeant Pratt sitting alone at the next table. "There's something really weird about those trees—y'know what I mean?"

"Yeah," Alex nodded as he took a sip of his coffee. "They give me the creeps too."

Sergeant Pratt poked at his scrambled eggs for a moment then got up and ducked out the back of the tent. Minutes later he returned carrying an old boot in one hand and a round canteen in the other.

"Didn't mean to eavesdrop, sirs, but I overheard you talkin' 'bout that knob. I found these up there when we was settin' up camp. 'Reckoned you might be interested."

Pratt dangled the canteen by its carrying strap. "Kinda looks like a Civil War canteen, don't it? But it can't be that old—see?" He swung the canteen back and forth by the strap like a pendulum. "Its still got a cloth cover an' strap on it. They would've rotted away 'fore now."

Alex lifted an eyebrow. Mike merely nodded in agreement.

"Then," Pratt held up the boot grasped in his other hand, "there's

14

this here boot. Looks like an old hip-length cavalry boot, but it shines like it was polished this mornin'.

Alex took the boot from Pratt and examined it. "There's a hole in the sole. 'Guess that's why it got thrown away." A well-worn steel heel tap caught his eye. "The trooper who wore this boot must have belonged to the Union 24th Corps," he said pointing at the tap where a heart had been cut out of it. "I saw one like this at the West Point museum. Union cavalrymen often wore heel taps incised with their corps or division crest."

Intriguing as the artifacts were, Alex agreed with Sergeant Pratt. *Equipment abandoned on a Civil War battlefield would have deteriorated by this time.* "Dunno," he shrugged, stumped for an explanation. "Maybe someone found these things in an attic or basement and dumped them."

Pratt nodded, a dubious look in his eyes. "Maybe so, but there's somethin' real strange 'bout that knob. I could've sworn someone was watchin' us when I had the work detail up there puttin' up your tents."

Now you tell us, Alex told himself as he and Mike exchanged frowns.

"Mind if I borrow the boot and canteen?" asked Alex, his curiosity piqued. "I can probably find someone in town who can tell me if they're authentic."

"Keep'em, Cap'n," Pratt shrugged. "I got no use for 'em."

"Thanks. I'll let you know what I find out."

Finishing his coffee, Alex pushed away from the table, exited the mess tent, then trudged up the knoll to his tent where he tossed the boot and canteen on his field desk.

After supper that evening, Alex met with his officers and senior NCOs in the mess tent to coordinate the next day's schedule and fix responsibility for the tear down of the camp. Satisfied with the arrangements, he left Mike and the others to work out the details. Outside he paused and took a deep breath, savoring the woodsy smell of dogwood blossoms, then set off in the direction of the knoll.

The sun had set and the sky was threateningly overcast, which further added to the eeriness of the grove as Alex reached the summit and headed to his tent. His scalp prickled under his cap, and he knew it wasn't the exertion of the climb that made his heart beat faster—he sensed *something* watching him. Groping in the dark, he found the box of matches lying on his field desk and lit the lantern suspended from the ridgepole. Calmer in the comforting glow of the lantern, he sat at his desk and for a moment contemplated the canteen and boot before pushing them aside and retrieving a box of stationary from one of the drawers. He took a deep breath, collected his thoughts, and began writing a letter home.

In the wee hours of the night, a thunderstorm seemed to spring from nowhere. Alex lay on his cot in the dark listening to the howling wind. The hair stood up on the back of his neck as tree limbs snapped and crashed to earth around him. Lightning arced across the heavens revealing the shadows of wind-whipped boughs dancing wildly on the roof of his tent. Rain pelted the canvas, and the rumble of thunder grew louder and more intense.

After a quarter of an hour the wind gradually subsided, and the thunder diminished to a low distant rumble. Alex dozed, lulled by the patter of rain dripping from the overhead branches.

A high-pitched wailing woke Alex out of a sound sleep. "What the hell...?" he grumbled sleepily as he propped himself up on one elbow and squinted into the darkness of his tent.

A storm, more violent than the first, struck the knoll, shaking the ground beneath his cot. Slashing rain and shrieking wind pummeled the tent threatening any moment to collapse it. The crash of thunder and jagged lightning ripped the night apart, and all the while the wailing grew louder.

"That sound!" Alex groaned as he clamped his hands over his ears. His frontal lobe throbbed like a dozen migraines rolled into one. *Good God! What is that?*

Alex momentarily forgot his pain as he became aware of the boot and canteen on his field desk starting to glow and pulsate eerily.

Suddenly a brilliant flash of light filled the tent and the the knoll heaved beneath his cot. He gasped for breath and stars exploded in his head. A crushing weight bore down on his chest as he lost consciousness—then, *nothing*.

CHAPTER 3

Dinwiddie County, Virginia

The pain in his sinuses had begun to subside. Alex sat on the edge of his cot massaging his temples, reflecting that he hadn't slept well—thanks to the storm. Twilight glimmered outside his tent; the nocturnal serenade of crickets had given way to a scolding chorus of jays among the overhead branches.

Retrieving his towel and shaving kit from his field pack, Alex pushed aside his tent flap and stepped outside. He paused to gaze up at the grove of magnificent trees, then glanced at Mike's tent, noting the absence of sound or movement. *He's probably already up and about*, he concluded as he made his way through the grove to the washstand erected beneath one of the giant oaks.

After living in the field all this time, Alex had grown accustomed to the sounds of voices and camp noises; however, this morning something was oddly different. An oppressive stillness hung in the air; even the birds had stopped singing. He picked up the water can stored under the washstand and filled the metal basin. Taking his razor from his shaving kit, he carefully extracted the finely honed blade, laid the razor next to the basin, then lathered his face with his shaving brush. Reaching for the razor, he studied his reflection in the mirror attached to the tree by the washstand, then deftly began shaving his neck and the underside of his jaw with smooth upward strokes.

"They're gone!" rasped a breathless voice, practically in his ear.

Alex flinched, nicking his Adam's apple and drawing a thin trickle of blood.

"Jeee-sus!" Alex hissed through clinched teeth. "I nearly slit my throat, Mike! Why're you sneaking around like that?" He dabbed the cut with his towel to staunch the bleeding. "Who's gone?" he snapped, sensing that whatever Mike had to say, it wasn't going to make his day.

"The whole company," Mike puffed, still catching his breath from the climb up the trail.

"It's a bit early for April Fool, isn't it?"

"For real, Alex! Everyone's gone—the equipment too! The only tents left are ours."

"Yeah. Right," Alex replied, the tone of his voice mirroring the skepticism in his eyes.

"Go see for yourself," Mike prodded impatiently, pointing to the trail leading down to the ridge.

"I'll just do that," Alex growled, toweling off his shaving cream and slipping his arms into the sleeves of his tunic.

Mike led the way down the fog-shrouded slope to the foot of the knoll.

"Move aside, Hawkeye!" Alex said sarcatically brushing past Mike and taking the lead, "I'll show you the way to the mess tent—" The sarcasm died on his lips.

The ground mist lifted revealing a broad, wooded ridgeline void of habitation.

Alex stopped and stared at the pristine woodland thick with holly and flowering dogwood.

"Believe me now?" Mike said, taking small consolation at being proven right.

Ignoring him, Alex cupped his hands to his mouth. "Hello-o! Can anyone hear me?" The empty woods magnified the sound of his voice; the only response was a startled deer fleeing through the underbrush at the base of the ridge.

"Maybe the trucks from camp picked up the company last night," Mike ventured, "and the boys thought it would be a great prank to leave us out here—y' know, like a snipe hunt."

Alex shook his head. "I don't think so, Mike. Look around. They couldn't have broken camp in the dark without leaving something behind. I don't see anything. Even the leaves on the ground aren't disturbed."

Mike ran his eyes over the area. "Weird, all right," he nodded.

"I'll tell you something else that's weird," Alex continued, "besides the knoll and those Civil War relics Sergeant Pratt found up there. Do you remember Private Rizzo?"

Mike shook his head. "He left before I arrived, but I heard the story."

"Well, I can tell you a thing or two that you didn't hear. Last fall, Camp Lee sent out search teams to look for an Army aviator who reportedly crashed in this area. We sent Rizzo and three other men from our company. While they were scouring these woods for the missing flyer, a thunderstorm suddenly popped up, and everyone scattered. When the teams reassembled, Rizzo came up missing too. The search teams combed these woods for two days but never found a trace of the pilot or his plane—or Rizzo. I brought the whole company out here to help in the search. About a mile from where we're standing, we finally found him. Hiding. Yeah, that's what I said, *hiding*. He was babbling about soldiers in blue uniforms trying to kill him, and something, too, about trees and lightning. That's what I wrote in the investigation report: he had been struck by lightning. But I really don't think that was it. I believe something out here literally scared Rizzo out of his mind. The last I heard he's cutting out paper dolls in a loony bin in Iowa."

"If you're trying to cheer me up, it's not working," Mike smiled wanly.

"Well, now you know as much as I do about this place," said Alex. "Let's split up and look around, then meet back here in thirty minutes. Keep your eyes open."

"Don't worry!" Mike called over his shoulder as he set off toward the ravine. "You'll be the first to know if I find anything. You do the same."

"Yeah," Alex grunted, then struck out to reconnoiter the crest of the ridge.

They were still within sight of each other when a deep voice rang through the woods. "Hello-o!"

Alex and Mike exchanged startled glances.

Mike cupped his hand to his mouth: "Hey-y! Where are you?"

"Here!" the reply echoed in the silent woods.

19

A man suddenly appeared on the far side of the ridge and quickly strode toward them. Alex recognized him as Sergeant Thomas Hill, one of his squad leaders.

Hill promptly saluted when he reached them; he wore a relieved smile.

"Where's your squad, Sergeant?" Alex asked, returning his salute.

"I've no idea, sir." Hill's smile faded. "I've been looking for them."

Alex and Mike exchanged gloomy glances.

"So you got left behind too," Alex sighed dejectedly. "Okay. Go get your gear, Sergeant, while we get ours. Meet us at the foot of the knoll in fifteen minutes. Looks like we'll have to hike back to camp."

"I'm ready now, sir. When the company left, they took my tent and field gear, too."

"Then where did you sleep last night?" Alex asked, curious.

"Up there," Hill replied, pointing up at the knoll. "There's a small shelter cave just below the crest. My tent collapsed during the storm, so I grabbed my blanket, climbed the knoll, and crawled inside the cave where it was nice and dry. Odd thing, that storm," Hill scrunched his face meditatively. "Just when I thought it couldn't get any worse, it suddenly stopped—just like that," he snapped his fingers. "'Never seen anything like it!"

"Yeah, I noticed," Alex nodded, remembering all too well the excruciating pain and the wailing. "Mike, let's go pack our gear. I'll send someone back later for our tents and other equipment."

Alex dragged his backpack from beneath his cot, then quickly packed some clothing and a few personal items: letters from home, a notebook, a photograph of his parents and his two sisters, and another of himself with his golden retriever, Jake, together on the front steps of his Charleston home.

Giving the tent a final scrutiny, his eyes fell on the field safe tucked away in a corner. The company officers carried the standard issue 1911 Colt .45 automatic pistol; however, for safety reasons, Alex kept the ammunition in the field safe under his personal supervision. Squinting at the numbers in the dim light, Alex rotated the dial on the combination lock and opened the safe revealing a stack of cartridge boxes inside. Acting on premonition, he stuffed a box into his tunic pocket, then dumped a partial box on his cot and loaded three pistol clips: one he inserted into his .45; the other two he slipped into the magazine pouch on his pistol belt.

Alex locked the safe, regretting leaving it unprotected. *It took four strong men to carry it up here, so it's not like someone's going to walk off with it,* he reassured himself.

As he pushed the tent flap aside to step outside, he suddenly stopped, cocked his head to one side, and listened. Off to the east came a distant noise, like the muffled sound of corn popping inside a kettle. *What is that?* he wondered as the sounds grew louder, then receded, and now and then were accompanied by a loud *thump.*

Dry leaves rustled nearby. Alex saw Mike and Sergeant Tom Hill coming toward him.

"Every soldier at Camp Lee must be on the rifle range this morning," Tom opined, squinting in the direction of the firing.

"Yeah," Mike frowned as he listened, "but it sounds different."

Alex nodded. "It *is* different. That occasional loud *bang* you hear is artillery—some really big guns, too, judging from the sound. Last I heard, the 80th Division just had 75 and 155 caliber artillery batteries. The guns we're hearing sound a lot bigger than that." Alex looked perplexed as he stared off in the direction of Petersburg for a few more seconds. "Well, the sooner we get started, the sooner we'll find out. Let's move out."

CHAPTER 4

Dinwiddie County, Virginia

From the base of the knoll the ancient trail traversed the deserted ridge then plunged into a narrow ravine.

"This is where the trucks dropped us off," Alex said, pointing to the spot as they came upon a narrow track winding through the wooded ravine.

"I don't think so," Mike said, shaking his head. "I don't see any signs of recent traffic."

Alex unfolded his map and oriented it on the surrounding terrain features. "Well, this looks to be the right road even if it hasn't been used lately. And seeing that it's the only road around, let's follow it."

Half an hour later they came to a creek bottom where another road intersected the one they had been following.

"Huh?" Alex grunted, perplexed, as he studied his map again. "I see the creek, but I don't see this other road."

"Take a look at this, Captain," Tom called to him a few yards away where he squatted on his heels examining the intersecting road. "There are lots of fresh footprints, horse tracks and wheel ruts, most of which head off in a westerly direction along the creek."

Alex scratched the back of his head as he studied the tracks. "For a road that's not on the map, this one seems to be a popular thoroughfare. In any case the Boydton Plank Road is only a mile or two to the east of us, and I bet if we follow these tracks, they'll lead us right to it. Then, with a little luck, maybe we can hitch a ride into town."

"Sounds good," Mike nodded.

As they turned with a more brisk pace onto the new road, Alex silently pondered some worrisome questions: *Why so many men and horses, and where were they going?*

At a ford where the road crossed the creek, they came upon the stark silhouettes of four blackened chimneys against a bright blue sky—all that remained of the main house of what had been a prosperous farm. Acres of fields lay fallow behind the ruins; the few tobacco plants that remained were brown and trampled. A jumble of charred timbers filled the void between the chimneys, and conspicuous gaps in the brick foundation bore evidence of someone helping himself to the bricks.

This was a grand place before it burned, Alex thought as he gazed at the ruins. *Strange, though, that a farm house this size didn't have some outbuildings around it. No barns, sheds or—Wait! Looks like something in the woods further down the road.*

Mike and Tom were already exploring the grounds.

"See if you can find a well or spring," Alex said, "where we can fill our canteens. Meanwhile, there's something down the road I want to check out…. be back in a minute."

In the woods away from the road, Alex counted what appeared to be over a dozen tobacco sheds, a common sight on many Virginia farms. However, these were constructed of logs and were lower and smaller than the sheds he remembered. Each possessed a chimney at one end fabricated out of wooden barrels, sticks and mud. *Maybe they're smokehouses, but then—why so many?* He noted, too, the symmetry of their dimensions; each was about eight by ten feet in area by seven feet in height.

Curious, Alex went over to the nearest structure and lifted the door latch. Crafted from hand-hewn planks, the door creaked open on rusting hinges. Alex ducked under the low doorsill and stepped inside.

As his eyes adjusted to the dark interior, curiosity yielded to disbelief.

For a long time he stood in the doorway gazing at the interior. Boyhood memories came flooding back—of his grandfather sitting in his rocking chair by the hearth recounting the winter of '62 near Fredericksburg, Virginia. *Well, by late fall the Yankees had had their fill of fighten' an' retreatin',* then he would get that far away look in his eyes and smile, *an' they settled down in winter quarters. We South Carolina boys settled down for the winter, too, in regimental camps. Four men would usually go together an' build a log hut to live in during the winter. Those of us in my hut found some boards an' built us some comfortable bunks. With a little more ingenuity, we built us a dandy chimney an' fireplace out of barrels an' bricks. We were snug as bedbugs by the first snow—but that's probably stretchin' the truth every which way but straight.* He would pause, then lean over and look me squarely in the eye, as though taking me into his confidence. *Truth is, it weren't really all that comfortable. The hut was always full of smoke. Sometimes it was so thick you'd swear your eyeballs was on fire, an' it was hard on your lungs. I near always had a cough. And we still got cold. Sickness in winter was terrible bad. My company lost more men to pneumonia an' measles than we ever did to bullets an' cannon fire—"*

The scene inside the cabin matched to the smallest detail his grandfather's portrayal of camp life during the Civil War. Two crudely constructed sleeping platforms, each padded with straw, occupied two of the interior walls. In the middle of the hut stood a table fashioned from the lid of a wooden crate and four railing balusters scavenged from a front porch. The uneven floor, he noted, was paved with bricks laid end to end without mortar. A fireplace constructed of brick and stone encompassed one whole end wall. A horseshoe twisted in the shape of a letter **S** formed a double-ended hook from which a blackened kettle hung from an iron bar inside the fireplace. Above the fireplace a rough plank served as a mantel. Iron spikes studded the mantel from which wet clothing could be hung and dried. A dust covered coat hung from one of the spikes. It appeared to be homemade; the right sleeve was ripped at the shoulder. The buttons were tarnished brass and bore a familiar motif—a large letter "I."

The pieces in this puzzle of mysterious events were quickly coming together. The final piece caught Alex's eye just as the sound of galloping hooves echoed in the woods outside.

Chapter 5

Dinwiddie County, Virginia

Alex dashed out of the open doorway into the brilliant sunlight.

Mike and Tom had also heard the drumming of hooves and stood in the middle of the road looking back in the direction from which they had come.

"Take cover!" Alex yelled. In the same instant, two horsemen riding at full gallop suddenly burst into view around a curve in the road.

Startled, the riders promptly reined in their horses and slowed their pace. At a safe distance, they stopped and leaned forward in their saddles quietly studying the uniformed men barring their path. The one on the left, a heavily bearded fellow, casually surveyed the ruins and the terrain on either side of the road, obviously sizing up the situation. Apparently having decided that the strangers were few and posed little danger, he nodded to his companion. As if by mutual assent, they suddenly spurred their mounts and galloped forward.

Paralyzed by indecision, Mike and Tom stood in the middle of the road and stared as the riders drew carbines from their saddle scabbards and leveled their weapons at them.

As the horsemen emerged from the shadows of the woods into the sunlight, Alex was startled by their appearance. Both riders wore dark blue uniforms.

"Hold up! Don't shoot!" he yelled, waving his arms, trying to get their attention.

The riders came on, side by side, quickly closing the distance between them and the *doughboys*.

Smoke suddenly spouted from the carbine in the hands of the rider on the right. A bullet whistled harmlessly past Mike's head.

Roused from their lethargy, Mike and Tom scrambled for cover on opposite sides of the road.

The other rider, however, had Tom squarely in his sights as he closed in on his quarry.

Alex heard the sharp crack of the carbine as the horseman pulled the trigger.

The bullet struck Tom, spinning him around with its force. Still on his feet, Tom staggered drunkenly a few more steps until the iron-hard shoulder of his assailant's horse smashed into him, sending him sprawling in the dirt.

With undiminished speed, the horsemen hurtled on.

A three-foot-high tree stump at the edge of the road offered the only concealment Alex had any hope of reaching before the riders reached him. Bullets from the two carbines whined and ricocheted around him as he darted across the road and slid unscathed behind the stump. Alex drew his Colt .45 caliber, Model 1911 pistol from his holster, slid the barrel assembly rearward, released it, and felt it spring forward, chambering a cartridge from the seven-round magazine. Alex stood up and assumed the stance he customarily used on the pistol range. Holding the .45 in his right hand, he raised his arm, aligned the front and rear sights on the nearest horseman, took a breath and held it. Carbine bullets continued to whine past him. Fortunately, neither of his attackers had mastered the art of shooting accurately from a galloping horse.

Alex held his aim and slowly squeezed the trigger. The heavy .45 bucked in his hand and his ears rang from the blast. A powerful handgun, the .45 was designed to stop an assailant in his tracks at short range. Alex frowned as his first shot missed his intended target. The riders were still too far away.

He clenched his teeth. "Wait 'til they're closer," he muttered to himself.

His attackers came on, seemingly unimpressed by his returned fire.

Alex quickly kneeled, propped his elbows on top of the stump's flat surface for support, and again took aim at the same rider. Steadying the Colt with both hands, he took a deep breath, slowly exhaled, and squeezed off three quick shots.

His bullets struck with terrible effect. Both horse and rider tumbled in an animated cloud of flying dirt, flailing arms, and splaying hooves.

Without so much as a backward glance at his fallen comrade, the second rider dug his spurs into his horse's flanks, urging greater speed, and bore down on the stranger in the brown uniform.

His attention now focused entirely on the second horseman, Alex noted that he had exchanged his empty carbine for a revolver.

Stretched low over his horse's neck, the rider leveled his pistol at Alex, his thumb and index finger alternately cocking the hammer and pulling the trigger of his long-barreled, single-action, cap and ball revolver. The pistol flashed four times in quick succession; Alex heard the peculiar whir of the bullets whizzing past him. With the horse and rider almost on top of him, he no longer had time for carefully aimed shots. For the first time, Alex clearly saw his assailant's face—a snarling, bearded mask with piercing, deep set eyes glaring at him over the sights of his long-barreled revolver.

Alex's .45 roared three times as he quickly squeezed the trigger. At least one of the slugs found its mark. His attacker catapulted backwards from his saddle as though he had struck an invisible wall. His body bounced and rolled, then lay unmoving in the middle of the road, while his horse, eyes wide with fear, bolted past Alex and kept going.

Except for the pounding of the horse's hooves fading into the woods, it had suddenly become very quiet.

Quickly ejecting the empty ammunition clip and inserting a new one, Alex kept his pistol pointed at the motionless body lying in the road as he stepped out from behind the stump. Shaking, his face bathed in sweat, he warily approached the fallen rider, half expecting the man to jump to his feet and resume shooting. But his assailant lay quite still, staring up at him with unseeing eyes from under his crumpled slouch hat.

A few yards up the road, the other rider and his horse lay heaped together; neither showed signs of life.

Alex had never killed a man before, yet within the space of seconds, he had taken two lives. Dazed, he stared at the bodies. *Their deaths were their own doing*, he told himself, offsetting remorse with moral justification. *It's only luck that I'm still alive.*

As the numbness wore off, Alex took another look at the body nearest him. His bearded assailant was clad in a dark blue uniform adorned with gold, eagle-embossed buttons. A one-inch wide yellow stripe ran down the side of each trouser leg and disappeared into the top of black knee-length riding boots.

"Union cavalryman," Alex whispered, awed by his grim discovery.

The man's revolver lay in the dirt, still clutched in his outstretched hand.

Curious, Alex holstered his own weapon and pried the trooper's stiffening fingers from the pistol's handgrip. His grandfather had once shown him a similar but smaller handgun he had brought home from the war. The pistol Alex now held in his hand was a Colt New Model Army 1860 revolver, .44 caliber, a standard sidearm issued to the United States cavalry during the Civil War. The handsome brass frame supported a round steel barrel and a revolving fluted cylinder containing six chambers. Each chamber held a single ball and a powder charge that took time to load. Alex noted, too, that like other handguns of the period, the revolver was single-action; the hammer had to be cocked each time the weapon was fired.

"Alex! You okay?" he heard Mike shout from up the road.

"Yeah, I'm fine," he replied. "How about you?"

"I'm okay, but Tom wasn't so lucky. He got hit in the shoulder."

Alex tucked the revolver in his pistol belt and started up the road.

Beyond the bodies of the first rider and his horse, he found Mike kneeling beside Tom in a thin strip of woods between the road and the creek. Tom sat against a tree grimacing in pain.

"Got any idea who those guys were?" Mike asked, pulling out his pocketknife and cutting away Tom's blood-soaked uniform from his shoulder.

"Uh-huh," Alex grunted with a nod. "Union cavalry."

Mike paused at his task and stared at Alex. "That doesn't make any sense! What're they doing here? The Civil War ended over fifty years ago!"

"You've got it wrong, Mike. Think about all that's happened since last night: the disappearance of our company; the rifle and artillery fire; roads that should be on our map but aren't; wagon ruts and horse tracks but no tire tracks; a burned plantation; an attack by Union cavalry." Alex paused to let his words sink in. "Maybe the question you should be asking is: What're *we* doing here?"

Despite his pain, Tom gaped open-mouthed at Alex.

"If you want more proof," Alex continued, "take a look in those huts down the road. Until recently, they were home to some Confederate troops. There's an infantry soldier's coat in the nearest one, but the real clincher is hanging on the wall—a calendar, showing the month and year as *March, 1865*. And that firing we've been hearing all morning? Well, I'm pretty sure it's coming from the fighting around Petersburg."

Mike folded the blade and slipped his pocketknife back into his pocket as he listened. "Well, I suppose that explains it then," he said with a frown and a shake of his head as he peeled the sodden tunic fragment away from Tom's shoulder exposing an ugly hole below his left collarbone. Mike winced at the blood flowing in rivulets down his chest. Tom's face was ashen.

"I think he's going into shock," Alex said, desperately trying to remember what he had learned about basic first aid at the Academy.

As they gently stretched Tom out on the ground, Alex noticed blood on the bark of the tree that he had been sitting against. "We won't have to dig that bullet out of him," Alex said, pointing to the blood on the tree trunk. "It came out through his back."

They rolled Tom onto his right side, revealing a gaping hole in his back just above his shoulder blade where the bullet had exited.

Mike blanched at the size of the wound. "Gawd! What did they shoot him with—a cannon?"

"Spencer carbine," Alex replied matter-of-factly as he removed Tom's tunic and shirt. He tore the shirt into strips, then retrieved the two gauze dressings from the metal first aid kit on his pistol belt. "Hold this," he said, handing Mike one of the dressings. He pressed the other dressing over the entry wound, using a cloth strip to hold it in place; then Mike handed him the second dressing, and he repeated the procedure with the exit wound.

"The bleeding is slowing," Alex said, re-examining his handiwork, "but he needs a doctor. We also need to keep him warm. I'll get the saddle blanket off the horse and see what else our uninvited guests were carrying."

"I'll come along," Mike offered. "You're going to need some help."

Mike had been right. Alex did need an extra hand. Even in death, the young cavalryman and his horse remained bonded together. Still sitting more or less astride his saddle, the trooper's left leg was pinned beneath his horse. Retrieving the saddle blanket would require removing the body and the saddle.

"Grab an arm," Alex said. "Maybe we can drag him out from under the horse."

The loose sandy soil made the task easier than expected as, together, they pulled the trooper's leg out from under his horse. Alex tried not to look at the boyish face as they then dragged the young cavalryman over to the side of the road.

"What's that hanging from his shoulder?" Mike asked as they laid the body on the ground.

The small, flat leather case had escaped Alex's attention. "Dunno," he shrugged. "Let's have a look."

Alex slipped the strap of the case from around the soldier's neck.

"Looks like a dispatch case," he said, unsnapping the brass clasp securing the flap.

Mike moved closer and peered over his shoulder as Alex reached inside and pulled out a sealed brown envelope bearing a bold cursive script. "Hmm! This *is* interesting," Alex said, raising an eyebrow. "It's addressed: *Major-General John G. Parke, Commanding IX Corps.* Intriguing, to say the least—I wonder what's inside." Alex pulled out his pocketknife; ignoring the wax seal, he inserted the blade under the envelope flap and slit it open. Inside were several folded documents which he unfolded, studied briefly, and then read aloud:

Headquarters, Army of the Potomac
March 22, 1865–8:10 A.M.
General Parke,
Commanding Ninth Corps

The enclosed dispatches are provided for your information. In accordance with instructions from Major-General Meade, a review of troops of one division of your corps will be held in honor of the President. The review will be held at 9 o'clock on the morning of the 25th instant in the vicinity of Meade Station on the Military Railroad. The Major-General Commanding further directs that you send a staff officer to this headquarters to obtain details concerning the review. The President will attend a dinner in his honor at this headquarters at 7 o'clock on the 24th instant. Your presence at the dinner is requested if your duties permit.

Geo D. Ruggles
Assistant Adjutant-General

The second page had been folded and the edges were soiled from someone's dirty fingers; however, it was neatly typed in large block letters. Alex continued reading aloud:

```
WASHINGTON D.C.
MARCH 20, 1865 - 6 P.M.
LIEUTENANT-GENERAL GRANT
CITY POINT, VIRGINIA
YOUR KIND INVITATION RECEIVED. HAD ALREADY THOUGHT
OF GOING IMMEDIATELY AFTER THE NEXT RAIN. WILL
GO SOONER IF ANY REASON FOR IT. MRS L AND A FEW
OTHERS WILL PROBABLY ACCOMPANY ME. WILL NOTIFY
YOU OF EXACT TIME, ONCE IT SHALL BE FIXED UPON.
A. LINCOLN" *
```

Pinned to the telegram dispatch was a third page.

City Point
March 21, 1865-4 P.M.
Major General Meade
Commanding, Army of the Potomac

During his previous visit, the President expressed an interest in making a tour of the lines and visiting some of the camps. I anticipate that he will want to carry out this plan during his upcoming visit; therefore, I have made the following tentative schedule. I will accompany him to your Headquarters at 3 o'clock on the afternoon of the 24th instant and remain overnight. I desire that you arrange a review of troops nearby at 9 o'clock the following morning. At 10 o'clock we will board a train and proceed as far as the Jerusalem Plank Road. We will dismount at that point, visit some of the camps along the road, and dine at an officer's mess of your selection. I suggest that you invite a number of your division and brigade commanders to join us for lunch. At 3 o'clock we will again board the train and return directly to City Point, stopping enroute,

*(Note: Author's transcription of historically accurate correspondence.)

> *of course, for you to dismount at your headquarters.*
> *Such a journey as this causes me much anxiety over*
> *his safety. Confide this information only as you must in*
> *order to complete the arrangements for his visit. Take*
> *all precautionary measures you think proper under the*
> *circumstances.*
>
> *Respectfully, yours, e.c.*
> *U.S. Grant*
> *Lieutenant-General*

"I think we'd be smart to hang onto these," Alex concluded after he had finished reading the dispatches. "They just might come in real handy later on." He placed the dispatches back into the envelope, then stuffed it inside the top of his boot. "However, in case we're captured, we don't want to be caught with that dispatch case."

"No problem," Mike said, reaching for the case, whereupon he swung it over his head by its strap three or four times, then let go. The case landed in the middle of the swirling creek, floated for a moment, then gradually disappeared beneath its muddy surface.

"Satisfied?" Mike asked.

Alex nodded, but his thoughts were elsewhere—mulling over the implications of the intercepted dispatches. *The dispatches confirm where we are in time, and their importance explains why we were fired upon—the couriers mistook us for Confederate soldiers.*

Mike returned to the dead horse and loosened its saddle cinch.

"Too bad the other horse ran off," Alex said as he jerked the blanket out from under the saddle. "He could have carried Tom."

"We've got to get him to a doctor, Alex, which means we'll have to do some tall explaining. Got any ideas?"

Before he could answer, Alex felt the nudge of a rifle muzzle between his shoulder blades.

"Don't look now, Mike, but I think we have company."

CHAPTER 6

Executive Mansion, Washington D.C.

8:45 A.M., MARCH 23, 1865

A lone in the Oval Office, President Lincoln slumped in his high-backed, padded leather chair contemplating the stack of documents on his desk. He had just finished breakfast with Mary and their son Tad, but the grumbling in the pit of his stomach told him that the meal, or more likely his wife's company, had not agreed with him. Mary had complained, as she often did, that he was spending too much time working and not enough time with his family. Breakfast had not been pleasant. Mary was in another of her sour moods. He had quickly eaten and excused himself on the pretext of needing to attend to some pressing matters—which only exacerbated Mary's complaint. Sifting through the pile of papers, he pulled out a single sheet and adjusted his spectacles to better read the small print:

> City Point, Va
> March 20, 1865, 10 A.M.
> His Excellency A. Lincoln
> President of the United States
>
> Can you not visit City Pt. for a day or two? I would like very much to see you, and I think the rest would do you good.
>
> Respectfully, yours, ec.,
> U.S. Grant
> Lieutenant-General *

Although he had received and read this message several days earlier, he had placed it back in the stack to wait until Mary was in one of her better moods to tell her about Grant's invitation. When he finally broached the subject, she had turned on him like a scalded cat;

*(Note: Author's transcription of historically accurate correspondence.)

33

however, Abe patiently and lovingly endured her scathing temper. After the death of their son Willie a cloud of gloom had descended on the White House, and Mary had become reclusive and irreconcilable in her grief which was bad enough, but then began the unexpected rages and unreasonable jealousy. The latter, unfortunately, did not long escape the notice of the press and Washington society. No, he reflected, Mary hadn't liked what he had proposed. However, after two days of his gentle and persuasive coaxing, she had finally acquiesced.

Sunlight streamed through the window behind his desk as he read the message again. On the surface, it was simply an invitation from General Grant to visit him at his headquarters at City Point, Virginia. Mary's reaction notwithstanding, he had already telegraphed his acceptance. Abe chuckled at Grant's wry humor; they both knew that *rest* was the last thing on either of their minds. Abe reflected a moment on the real reason for the visit. On one hand the Confederacy was crumbling on all fronts except on the Petersburg-Richmond line; even there the Union armies' relentless pressure was beginning to have the desired effect. But on the other hand, a war-weary nation that had bled and sacrificed for so long was beginning to yield to the groundswell of sentiment favoring ending the conflict and allowing the South to go its own way. It was now a race against time—for both his administration and the Confederacy. His hopes for the future of the Union rested on this trip to City Point. Only Grant and a handful of his most trusted officers knew the secret behind his visit. Not even Secretary of War Stanton had been brought in. Abe knew only too well from bitter experience that secret plans had a way of becoming common knowledge in Washington and beyond.

Abe leaned back in his chair and smiled. If things went as planned, Grant would have good news to share with him when he arrived. He looked forward to the long boat ride down the Potomac River to the Chesapeake Bay, then up the James River to Grant's headquarters at City Point. Strategically situated on a high bluff at the confluence of the Appomattox and James Rivers, City Point was a perfect base from which to operate against the defenses of Petersburg and Richmond. The building and gradual extension of the U.S. military railroad from City Point to the Union forces besieging Petersburg was a brilliant innovation, and he wanted to see it. Then, too, his re-election was in no small part due to the support he had received from the valiant men occupying the trenches around Petersburg. The military railroad would enable him to visit some of the camps and allow him to personally convey his appreciation to these brave soldiers for their confidence and for their sacrifices. The newspaper reporters would be told that this was the purpose of the presidential visit.

Abe shifted uncomfortably in his chair as the first pangs of indigestion began gnawing at his stomach. Dismissing the malady as nervous anticipation of his upcoming trip to City Point, he took out a sheet of foolscap from his top desk drawer and began writing:

Executive Mansion
Washington, March 23, 1865 - Noon

Lt. Gen. Grant,
City Point, Va.
We start to you at 1 PM today. May lie over during the dark hours of the night. Very small party of us.

A. Lincoln*

When he finished, he folded the stationary, then rang for his secretary. The door to an adjoining room promptly opened, and a frail, pygmy-size man entered carrying a notebook.

"Yes, Mr. President?" he asked in a raspy voice.

Over the years Abe had developed a fondness for this extraordinarily efficient and intelligent member of his personal staff. He was also a frequent source of amusement, for whenever he became excited or stressed, the little secretary's nose twitched, giving his face a rodent-like quality. Abe had once confided to his First Lady over a cup of tea, "Mary, put whiskers and a tail on that fellow and he would be the perfect dormouse!" Mary giggled so hard she spattered tea down the front of her dress. That had been an earlier and happier time. Neither Abe nor Mary found much to laugh about these days.

"Ah, Hiram!" Abe smiled as his thoughts returned to the business at hand. "Please see to it that this message is dispatched to General

*(Note: Author's transcription of historically accurate correspondence.)

Grant at City Point at once. Send it by telegraph without enciphering it. Also, the family and I will board the packet *River Queen* this evening and, barring any delays, should arrive at City Point tomorrow night. Advise Secretary of War Stanton that I will keep him informed as to our progress and arrival. I anticipate being there for two days but will remain longer if there is a need for it."

Hiram took the document from the President's hand and read the contents. His nose twitched slightly. "Mr. President, are you sure you want to send this message to General Grant without encoding it? It's common knowledge that the Rebels have been tapping the telegraph lines along the James River. Your message could be intercepted."

"I appreciate your concern, Hiram, but send it by telegraph anyway, just the way I wrote it and without encoding it."

"I'm confused, Mr. President," the little secretary frowned. "You say that you and the family are boarding the *River Queen* this evening; however, your message to General Grant says you will be leaving at 1:00 P.M. today. I already have you booked on the packet *Greyhound* which embarks at 1:00 P.M. today, per the instructions you gave me two days ago. Do you want me to change your bookings? I didn't know until now that you intend to sail on the *River Queen*."

"No. That won't be necessary. One of my security agents made the sailing changes. I know you normally coordinate my traveling arrangements, Hiram. I'm entirely satisfied with the manner in which you have attended to such matters in the past; however, this is a slightly different situation. Please don't take offense."

"None taken, Mr. President," said Hiram, his nose twitching furiously. "However, won't General Grant be expecting you to arrive on the *Greyhound* tomorrow afternoon when he receives this message?"

Becoming exasperated, the President gazed at his secretary from beneath heavy brooding eyebrows, his customary smile fading. "Hiram, don't worry about it! Send the message—just the way it's written." Then as an afterthought he added, "Tell no one about the change in my sailing plans. Officially, if you receive any inquiries, I'm sailing on the *Greyhound* at 1:00 P.M. Security, and all that, you know," said Abe, forcing a smile.

"Yes, Mr. President, I understand. Will there be anything else?"

Leaning back in his chair Abe reflected a moment. "Yes, there is one more thing. Mrs. Lincoln has exacted a pound of flesh for agreeing to make this trip with me. She wants to see a new play next month at Ford's Theater, *Our American Cousin* I think it's called. I agreed to take her. Check my calendar and pick a night when I'm not otherwise engaged and make the necessary arrangements."

Hiram looked up expectantly as he finished taking notes. His nose still twitched.

Abe smiled and shook his head. "That's all, Hiram. Thank you."

The little secretary scurried out of the office, closing the door behind him.

I guess we all have our little crosses to bear, Abe mused, gazing down at his oversized feet.

CHAPTER 7

Dinwiddie County, Virginia
12:23 P.M., MARCH 23, 1865

L ike apparitions, the soldiers materialized from the woods. They stood silently, rifles pointed at the three men.

Alex counted four soldiers within a 30-foot radius, but he had a feeling more were hidden and watching from the woods. Slowly he rose to his feet, resisting the impulse to reach for his pistol.

Mike wasn't aware of the two soldiers standing behind him with rifles pointed at his back; his right hand crept to his holster flap. Alex quickly raised his hands and nodded to Mike to do the same.

Mike frowned, then reluctantly complied.

Tom pushed himself up on one elbow to better see their visitors.

"Don't move," the soldier nearest Alex growled, squinting over the sights of his rifle. He kept his voice low but loud enough for his companions to hear, "I'm goin' to check them for guns. If any of 'em move—shoot 'em."

The soldier's gaze never wavered from Alex's face as he shoved his rifle barrel into Alex's belly.

At 6-foot-2, Alex towered above the other man who, due to his gaunt features and a scraggly black beard, appeared to be much older than he probably was. His baggy butternut uniform failed to hide a wasted body that most likely hadn't seen a good meal in months. Piercingly dark and hawkish, his sunken eyes peered up at Alex from beneath a shabby slouch hat. Two brass buttons on his grimed and tattered coat were embossed with a large letter that Alex presumed stood for *Infantry*; the other buttons appeared to be homemade, fashioned from either bone or wood. A leather strap, cracked and worn, supported a cartridge box on his right hip, and on his left, a wooden canteen swung from a canvas shoulder strap. The rifle he poked into Alex's ribcage appeared to be a single-shot, British Enfield. On his leather waist belt a large oval brass buckle bore the letters *CS*, leaving no doubt as to the allegiance of their captors.

Hands raised above his head, Alex stood quietly as the Confederate soldier lifted his .45 from his holster. The sleek design of the handgun elicited no curiosity—not even a blink—as the soldier tossed the pistol to a young boy who looked barely old enough to shave.

The soldier backed away, then turned and confronted Mike. "Don't do nuthin' foolish, boy," he drawled, pointing his rifle at Mike's chest. "This thing's gotta hair-trigger, an' my hand gits the tremors real easy. So don't give me no cause to fret. Hear?"

"Yeah, I get the idea," Mike scowled and raised his hands higher.

The soldier repeated the same drill he had with Alex and relieved Mike of his pistol, then looked down at Tom who had pushed himself into a sitting position.

"How 'bout you, Mister?" he snapped. "Whar's your gun?"

"Don't have one," Tom growled. "I must have left it at home."

The soldier merely stared at him.

"What? You don't believe me?" Tom gibed. "Well, wait here and I'll go get it for you."

Seemingly satisfied that the injured man was telling the truth, the soldier backed away and joined the kid who was curiously examining the two pistols.

"Lemme see one of them guns," the older soldier demanded.

"Ever see anythin' like this, Sergeant?" the boy asked, handing him one of the pistols. "Its got **U.S.** stamped on the barrel. Must be somethin' new, like them Spencer carbines an' Henry rifles."

"Uh-huh," the sergeant grunted, turning the deep metallic blue pistol over in his hands. "It's made by Colt Firearms—see that there horse?" he pointed a grubby finger at the barrel. "But it ain't got no cylinder to put bullets in."

Baffled, he pointed the weapon at Alex. "This thing got bullets in it?"

"Care for a demonstration?" Alex offered, smiling.

"A whut?"

"Would you like me to show you?" Alex tried again.

"Nah! Jus' stay where yo're at. I'll figger it out for maself," he drawled, sticking the .45 in his waist belt. "Wes, hang on to the other one 'til we git back to camp. The Provost Marshal'll want to see it an' talk to these prisoners."

"It's in my haversack," the boy replied, gazing at the prisoners with renewed interest. "I've never seen Yankees dressed like these fellas befo. D'ya suppose they're ferineerss? I heard the Yankee pickets 'cross the crick from our lines say they had some Prussian officers visit their camp recently. 'Said they couldn't understand much of whut they said on account of their accent, but they sure wore dandy uniforms."

"These here look to be Yankees," the sergeant replied with an air of authority. "They're jest dressed diff'rent is all."

As Alex listened to this exchange, several more soldiers came out of the woods and stood around curiously studying them.

"We aren't Yankees," Alex said. "We're on our way to meet with General Gordon. We have important information for him."

Astonished, everyone stared at Alex—including Mike and Tom.

"Well if that don't beat all!" the sergeant slapped his thigh and guffawed. "Mister, tell that to the Provost Marshal when you see'im. Maybe he can get you invited to supper with the General."

Snickers from unseen faces.

"What's your outfit?" Alex casually asked, turning to the kid.

Without thinking, the young soldier smiled proudly and blurted "Hill's Corps."

"Shut your trap, Wes!" the sergeant rebuked him, then glared at Alex. "We'll be the ones askin' the questions 'round here!"

The young private had already confirmed what Alex suspected.

These men belonged to General A. P. Hill's Corps, Army of Northern Virginia.

From the direction of the huts, two more members of the patrol came up the road and joined the sergeant and the private. One was tall, about Alex's height; the other, short and heavyset. Like the others, their uniforms were threadbare, and they were armed with Enfields.

The taller man eyed Alex warily as he spoke to the sergeant. "Got a another dead Yankee cavalryman down the road apiece."

"'That your doin'?" the sergeant asked, squinting hard at Alex.

Alex nodded. "They fired on us first—didn't leave us much choice."

"How many were there?"

"Two," Alex answered without elaborating.

"'Could be they thought you was thievin', murderin', bushwackin' deserters tryin' to rob 'em," the tall man said pointedly. "There's lots of deserters roamin' the woods hereabouts, preyin' on soldiers an' innocent civilians. So, if that's whatcha are, we'll take you back to camp, give you a fair trial, then hang you."

"We're not deserters," Alex said, regarding the man icily. "I shot those men in self-defense. My men had no part in it."

Alex knew their uniforms and weapons had aroused their captors' suspicions, and he needed a plausible explanation. "I'm Captain Wright of Mosby's Rangers. I suppose you've heard of Colonel Mosby?"

The sergeant and his men nodded, waiting for Alex to continue.

"We operate behind the Union lines as guerrillas—although we prefer the term *partisans*. Each band of partisans equips itself with whatever it captures from the enemy. The uniforms we're wearing and the weapons you took from us, for example, we liberated from a group of New England industrialists who were on a train bound for Washington. They were hoping to interest the War Department in some new firearms and uniform designs; however, we offered to try them out first." Alex grinned, noting the nods and approving smiles from among his listeners.

"If you're with Mosby, how come you're so far from Northern Virginia?" the sergeant asked perceptively, a brown stream of tobacco juice dripping from the corner of his mouth. "Mosby's command don't operate this far south."

"That's true," Alex nodded affably, "however, Colonel Mosby recently intercepted some intelligence that must be delivered to General Lee or one of his corps commanders. That's why we're here. The country between here and Washington is crawling with Yankees, so we came a roundabout way through the mountains. Our horses played out about fifty miles west of here, and we've been on foot ever since."

The sergeant listened, staring hard at Alex all the while until he finished. "That's an interestin' story, Captain, but you best tell it to the Provost Marshal—he's the one you need to convince."

Signaling an end to the discussion, the sergeant turned to his men. "Wes, find a couple of fence railin's an' make a litter for the wounded man. Monk an' Shorty, strip those dead Yankees of everythin' useful, check their pockets for papers an' letters—the Provost Marshal is always lookin' for information— then bury'em."

Mike looked at Alex questioningly.

Alex shook his head, *no*, warning Mike not to say anything about the dispatches.

The exchange did not go unnoticed. The sergeant cocked his head, eyeing the pair suspiciously, obviously wondering what *that* was all about. Finally, he said "Seein' as how you've walked this far, I reckon you won't mind carryin' your wounded friend a bit further."

The drumming of horse hooves suddenly reverberated through the woods. A single rider burst from the underbrush and onto the road where he reined up in front of the sergeant. "Found this horse down the road apiece, Sarge."

Alex recognized the roan-colored mare as the one the second Union cavalryman had been riding.

"Good!" the sergeant smiled approvingly. "She can carry the extra saddle and maybe some meat for the stew pot back at camp. Give Monk an' Shorty a hand butcherin' some choice cuts from that dead horse."

The sergeant contemplated his wounded prisoner for a moment; then looked away, apparently discarding whatever he had been mulling over in his mind.

Altogether, Alex counted ten men in the patrol. Two were detailed to guarding the prisoners while a third led the horse, which now carried an extra saddle, bridle, two sabers, two carbines in their scabbards, two pairs of boots, and two bundles of meat wrapped in rubberized blankets. Alex knew from his grandfather's stories that the Confederate Army was desperately short of everything at this stage of the war and resorted to battlefield scavenging to augment its dwindling supplies. A Confederate cavalry regiment would undoubtedly welcome the horse and the recovered equipment, and the horse meat would fill many an empty belly around the campfires.

The patrol fanned out in a circle, keeping the prisoners in the center as they herded them toward the Confederate lines. The sergeant and two of his men led the way while Alex and Mike followed, carrying Tom on a crude litter fashioned from two fence railings and a blanket. Despite the jolting, Tom maintained a stoic silence as they struggled through the seemingly endless tangle of foot-snagging vines and uneven ground.

Alex's arms grew numb. Both he and Mike were sweating profusely and tripping with increasing frequency. Although they had actually come only two or three miles, the steep ravines and dense thickets through which they passed made it seem much further. Dehydrated and exhausted, Alex was about to demand a break, when they suddenly stumbled out of the wilderness into a vast clearing dotted with stumps. In front of them stood an immense earthen work nearly eight feet high stretching like a red scar across the land. At a number of places along the top of the parapet, heads turned in their direction.

CHAPTER 8

Vicinity of Burgess Mill Pond

2:00 P.M., MARCH 23, 1865

As the Confederate patrol herded their prisoners through a breach in the earthworks, clusters of curious soldiers gathered to gawk at the men in the strange uniforms and the horse loaded with captured equipment.

Guffaws and ribald comments from some of the onlookers reached the prisoners' ears as they passed by: "*Brown!* Never seen Yankees wearin' *brown* before!"

"Hey Yank!" a voice in the crowd called out. "Wisht I had me a hat like your'ne! Wanna trade?"

Alex and Mike looked straight ahead, ignoring the jeers from the throng lining the roadway as they shuffled along carrying Tom on the litter. Even so, they couldn't help but notice the general shabbiness and physical deterioration of the soldiers they passed.

With our well-fed appearance and natty uniforms, we present a startling contrast, Alex mused—*and that has to be demoralizing to these soldiers. There's hardly a man among them who isn't wearing a ragged or incomplete uniform. But on the other hand, every one of them is armed or is within an arm's reach of his weapon.*

Despite the taunts of a few, Alex observed that most of the Confederates stood quietly and watched as the prisoners paraded past them.

A quarter mile beyond the earthworks, they crossed a bridge that spanned a creek below the spillway of a large millpond. Beyond it, on a bluff overlooking the pond, they were startled to see a large encampment with orderly rows of white canvas tents and crude huts of every size and description spread out before them. Teams of horses hitched to canvas-covered wagons rumbled through the camp raising choking clouds of dust in their wake. In a sun-parched field at the edge of the camp, a regiment drilled, their burnished muskets with fixed bayonets gleaming in the sunlight. Men on horseback watched the marching troops or ambled along the rutted streets on other business.

The rhythmic *clang* of metal striking metal came from an open-sided structure where sweating blacksmiths pumped air from giant bellows into the roaring forges or labored at anvils, hammering the bright-molten iron into horseshoes and wagon wheel rims.

The Confederate patrol marched their prisoners around the camp's periphery onto a dirt road teeming with traffic. Dust churned up by freight wagons, artillery, and long columns of marching troops rose into the air, then settled as fine white powder on everything and everyone on or near the road.

"What road's this?" Alex said to the guard nearest him.

"Hsst! Keep your voice down," the soldier hissed. "Sergeant McFadden don't want us talkin' to prisoners." The guard glanced back to make sure the sergeant wasn't looking in their direction, then replied, "This here's the Boydton Plank Road."

The soldier didn't elaborate, but for Alex it was enough. He was familiar with this road, or at least with the road it would eventually become. It bore little resemblance now to the road he had traveled in 1918. Remembering the wooden bridge they had crossed and the large millpond below the camp, sudden realization jolted him. "Of course!" he said, thinking aloud.

"What?" the soldier gave Alex a quizzical frown.

"That you're right about this being the Boydton Plank Road," Alex smiled affably. "It just doesn't look the way I remember it."

"That so?" the soldier threw him a curious look. "You from around here?"

"No, I came this way once to visit some folks who lived near the millpond," Alex replied truthfully.

"Burgess' Millpond?"

"Yeah. That's what they called it."

"That's the millpond you saw back there by the bridge. If the people you visited are still around maybe they can vouch for you."

"I'm sure they aren't. That was a different time." Alex said whimsically. *Yeah, about fifty years from now.*

"The war's been hard on folks—especially here," the soldier nodded sadly at the surrounding landscape. "What with the constant fightin', most people have packed up and left for safer places. I heard that Mr. Burgess, who owns the mill and the pond, went over to the enemy with his family. I met him once. Loyal as any Southerner, but livin' where he was with the fightin' goin' on around his mill, he was havin' a hard go of it. Can't say I blame him. If it were my family, I'd take 'em some place safer too."

"Are you from this area?" Alex asked.

"Nah. I'm from Georgia, but the war's there too. There's no place you can go to escape it, I guess. My brothers an' I will be glad when it's finally over," he said gloomily.

"Brothers?"

"Yeah. I've got two—both with the Troup Artillery in Longstreet's Corps on the Bermuda Hundred line."

Alex and the guard walked on in silence, each thinking his own thoughts.

Burgess' Millpond! Alex savored the words, for the name conjured up pleasant memories. In the spring of 1918 he had driven his Hudson Super-6 south from Petersburg on the Boydton Plank Road to attend a shad bake at Burgess' Millpond hosted by the Gilliams, Boisseaus, and other prominent families living in the area.

His thoughts drifted back to the weekend before the picnic, which was actually when it all began. To escape the drab confines of Camp Lee, he had attended the Sunday morning service at the Methodist Church in Petersburg. He arrived late. Unable to park his motorcar on South Sycamore Street in front of the church, he drove around the block and found space on Fillmore Street adjacent to Poplar Lawn Park. He took a shortcut through the park to the church and hurried up the steps to the entrance.

As the heavy oak door swung shut behind him, Alex found himself inside a dank vestibule, ripe with the musty smell of the ages. In hushed tones an usher greeted him. Not having a proper suit to wear, Alex had worn his Army uniform. The usher shook his hand warmly, smiled profusely, then led him like a prize bull down the long center aisle of the sanctuary to the very front pew. Alex felt every eye in the congregation on him and heard whispering as he self-consciously took his seat.

The service began with an administrative announcement inviting the congregation to a shad bake the next Saturday. Following the announcement the reverend welcomed the visitors, asking them to stand and introduce themselves.

Being the only visitor in the front pew, Alex was first to be called upon. He stood and awkwardly turned to face the congregation.

"I'm Captain Alex Wright from Charleston, South Carolina. I'm stationed at Camp Lee. Thank you for welcoming me this morning."

Two pews behind him a lovely young girl gazed up at him with the prettiest blue eyes he had ever seen. Golden ringlets framed her exquisite face. Her eyes sparkled and the corners of her mouth tilted slightly upward, giving her an angelic aura. Alex was captivated. He smiled; then she smiled with just a hint of shyness. He continued to gaze at her, totally oblivious to everything around him, until she blushed and looked away.

A far away voice broke the spell. "You may sit down now, Captain—that is, should you wish to," the reverend said, humor in his voice.

Alex awoke from his trance aware of the whole congregation watching him. His cheeks burned hotly as he took his seat amidst scattered giggles and muffled laughter. He didn't remember a word of the sermon, so focused were his thoughts on the lovely girl sitting behind him.

Just before the benediction, Mr. Gilliam, the usher, approached the altar and handed the reverend a note. He read it and nodded.

"Just one more announcement before we conclude this morning's service," the reverend smiled broadly. "We wish to extend a cordial invitation to our visitors this morning, especially our visitors in uniform, to join our church family for the shad bake at Burgess' Millpond this coming Saturday. Directions for getting there are available in the vestibule."

After the benediction Alex remained standing, politely waiting for the pews behind him to empty before going up the aisle. Trying not to appear obvious, he allowed his eyes to stray to the third pew where the girl chatted with an older woman as they moved between the narrow pews toward the center aisle. The woman smiled at him as she turned and headed toward the vestibule. The girl, too, flashed him a pretty smile. Her eyes danced merrily, and Alex suspected that he had been the topic of conversation between the woman and the girl.

The reverend stood by the exit smiling as Alex approached. "I'm Reverend Shryock," he said, greeting Alex warmly and shaking his hand. "Visitors from Camp Lee are especially welcome at Trinity Methodist Church. We hope you will consider making us your church family while you're here." He winked at Alex as he continued, "I think you would like our congregation. You seemed to enjoy being here this morning."

"Yes, sir. I did, and I really liked your sermon, too," Alex half-lied, hoping the reverend wouldn't ask him which part he liked best.

"And I suspect that wasn't all you liked, Reverend Shryock smiled knowingly. "Why don't you join us for the shad bake next Saturday?"

Before Alex could think of a good excuse to get out of it, Shryock turned to Mr. Gilliam who was standing by the door talking to one of the male members of the congregation. "Aaron, give this young man a copy of the directions to next Saturday's shad bake. I imagine we'll see him there."

Mr. Gilliam held a stack of directions in his hand and handed one to Alex.

"I hope you'll join us," Mr. Gilliam smiled. "It's a beautiful place; you'll have a great time; and I think you'll like the company."

Alex noted a slight inflection on the word: *company*.

"If the Army doesn't have other plans for me, I'll be there," Alex replied giving himself a way out should he change his mind. "By the way, Mr. Gilliam, a pretty girl was sitting two pews behind me. Would you happen to know her name?"

"Blond ringlets and *very* pretty?"

"Yes, sir."

"Well now, let me see if I remember. Hmmm…two pews behind you, you say. Well, I guess that would be my daughter Marian." Gilliam's smile vanished, and his eyes took on a steely glint as though censuring Alex's audacity.

Embarrassed, Alex was at a complete loss for words.

Like a passing shadow, Gilliam's scowl faded and his grin re-emerged. "Had you there for a minute, didn't I?" his wide-set eyes crinkling in amusement at Alex's discomfiture.

"Yes, sir! I'm afraid you did!" Alex admitted, vastly relieved. "I didn't mean anything by it. I just thought she was the prettiest girl I had ever seen!"

"Do you have a girl already?"

"No, sir."

"Why not? Something wrong with you?" Gilliam taunted.

"Uh…No, sir! It's just that, being in the Army, I don't have much of a social life," Alex stretched the truth for the second time that morning.

"Is that a fact? Well, think about coming to the shad bake next weekend. Meanwhile, I'll think about whether or not I want you to meet my daughter." Gilliam's expression was unfathomable; Alex wasn't sure if he was toying with him again or not.

"Maybe we'll see you there." Gilliam gave him a two-fingered salute, then turned away and ambled over to a group of women conversing on the sidewalk. The woman and Marian were in the group. Marian was smiling, pretending not to notice him, but Alex sensed she had been watching him out of the corner of her eye.

Wonder what shad tastes like?—not that it matters. I'll like it just fine! In high spirits, Alex took the long way back to his car following the cobblestone walk along South Sycamore Street.

The following Saturday was warm and sunny as he drove south from Petersburg on the Boydton Plank Road. He promptly decelerated after crossing the wooden bridge spanning Hatcher's Run. Off to his right he glimpsed the millpond with the sun reflecting brightly on the water. Glancing at the sheet of paper with the directions to the shad bake, Alex watched for the first dirt track on the right past the bridge, found it, then pulled off the road onto a trace that wound through the woods toward the pond. The trace, carpeted with pine needles, ended in a clearing where Alex found an assortment of automobiles, trucks, and horse-drawn wagons. Several women were busily removing baskets of food from the back seat of a big touring car as he pulled up alongside and parked. A few yards away, men in bib overalls were busily unloading the bed of a truck crammed with tables and chairs. He recognized one of the three men in the back of the truck handing down chairs to the others.

A swarthy, barrel-chested man with huge hands and ham-like forearms, Mr. Gilliam's physical appearance bore testimony to a lifetime of hard work. Behind the weathered face and craggy eyebrows, Alex sensed, dwelt a shrewd mind and strong intellect. The previous Sunday, Gilliam had been like a cat toying with a mouse. Alex didn't think he missed much either and suspected Gilliam had seen him drive into the clearing. As he walked up to the truck the older man never looked in his direction.

"Need some help?" Alex asked.

Gilliam hesitated and looked down at the visitor. "Alex Wright, isn't it?"

Alex took that as a good sign. He had remembered his name. "Yes, sir. It is," his throat felt suddenly dry.

Gilliam grinned. "Good! Glad you could come! I guess it's only proper to introduce you before we put you to work."

The unloading stopped momentarily as the men paused to look at their visitor.

"Friends and neighbors, this is Captain Alex Wright. He's stationed at Camp Lee and came to our church service last Sunday as some of you may remember. Although he accepted our invitation to the shad bake, I think he's more interested in my daughter Marian than the fish."

The men laughed.

Alex just smiled and tried not to look embarrassed.

One by one, the men shook his hand and, amid knowing winks and grins, welcomed him to the picnic. With the introductions over, Gilliam handed Alex two light cane-bottom chairs, then climbed down. Lifting two heavier chairs off the back of the truck, one under each arm, he strode toward a well-worn path leading into the woods.

"If everyone will follow me, I'll show you where these go."

Carrying an assortment of chairs and tables, Alex and the other men followed Gilliam through the woods toward the millpond. Moments later, they entered a park-like setting where, beyond the trees, the pond shimmered in the afternoon sun. Alex gazed around, admiring the magnificent stands of oak and pine and flowering dogwood. Reverend Shryrock had been right; it was a beautiful place.

In the center of the clearing a group of women were at work spreading tablecloths over tables placed end to end to form a serving line. Other women busily emptied the contents of large wicker baskets and arranged an assortment of salads, cakes, pies and home cooked dishes on the tables. Two little girls half-heartedly waved tea towels over the exposed sliced tomatoes, pickles and jams in an effort to shoo away the flies. Frequently they looked wistfully over their shoulders at the other children playing games and wading along the shoreline. The flies buzzing among the delicacies appeared only slightly intimidated.

Mr. Gilliam walked up to two women wearing sunbonnets. They had their backs turned to him and were unloading serving dishes and plates from a large square wicker basket. "Ma, where do you want us to put these tables and chairs?"

Neither woman looked up as they rummaged about in the depths of the basket. Mr. Gilliam heard a muffled: "We don't need any more tables for the serving line, Aaron, so just place the rest of the tables and chairs out under the trees for people to sit at. Save a table an' three chairs for us."

"Better make that four chairs, Ma. We have company," Gilliam said, winking at Alex.

"Ohhh? Who?" Mrs. Gilliam crooned, lifting her head from the basket and giving her husband a questioning look.

Mr. Gilliam didn't answer. He just nodded his head in Alex's direction.

Mrs Gilliam's gaze shifted from her husband to the handsome young man standing next to him holding two cane-bottom chairs. A smile of recognition flashed across her face, and she laughed softly. As though she had just betrayed a secret, she clamped her hands over her mouth, then placed a finger to her lips signaling Alex and Mr. Gilliam to keep quiet. She went up to Alex and placed both hands on his arm. "We're so pleased you could come!" she whispered excitedly. "There's someone I'd like to introduce you to."

Taking him by the arm, Mrs. Gilliam led Alex toward the table where her daughter was struggling to lift a heavy ironstone platter from the bottom of the basket.

"Who is it, Mama? I could really use an extra hand with this heavy platter. I don't know why you insisted on bringing it. It's as heavy as sin!"

Alex was immediately caught up in the ploy Mrs. Gilliam was instigating. Setting the chairs on the ground, he tiptoed up to the young lady whose sunbonnet had slipped off her head and was now dangling unceremoniously between her neck and shoulder.

"May I be of assistance, Miss Gilliam?" Alex asked. Before she could reply, he reached around her and lifted the platter from the bottom of the basket.

Marian's head suddenly popped up—her eyes instantly fixing on Alex's.

Her cheeks flushed bright crimson, and Alex was instantly captivated with the way the corners of her mouth lilted upwards as she smiled up at him.

"Oh, my…" she said, catching her breath in that first moment of recognition. Suddenly conscious that she was staring at the young man in the same way he had stared at her in church, she caught herself and managed to whisper huskily, "Yes, thank you."

She took the platter from him and set it in the middle of the table.

"Ahem!" someone cleared his throat, breaking the spell. "We hate to be a bother, Mrs. Gilliam, but these tables an' chairs are gettin' a mite heavy. Is it okay if we put 'em down sooner rather than later?"

Mrs. Gilliam reluctantly turned her attention from the couple and frowned at the men standing around gripping chairs and tables. "You men! You wouldn't recognize romance if it bit you!"

"Oh, yes, M'am, I would for a fact," answered a sweating middle-aged man lugging a table. "Ten years ago one ran out from under the front porch and bit me on the leg! Now I'm married to her!"

All the men guffawed.

Mrs. Gilliam placed her hands on her hips and scowled at him. "Leroy, I've a good mind to tell Emma what you just said 'bout her—she'd fix your wagon good if she knew you were goin' aroun' talkin' 'bout her like that! Aaron show these Romeos where to put the tables an' chairs before I do some bitin' of my own!"

"Best be movin' along now," Gilliam grinned, signaling the men to follow him.

"Not you, Captain," Mrs. Gilliam commanded as Alex bent to pick up the chair he had been carrying. "You haven't been properly introduced to my daughter. Miss Marian Gilliam, may I present Captain Alexander Wright? My husband should, of course, make these introductions; however, as you can see, he's engaged in other matters."

"May I say, Miss Gilliam, how delighted I am to make your acquaintance," said Alex formally, but his smile and the twinkle in his eyes conveyed a much warmer greeting.

"I'm pleased to make your acquaintance, sir, as well," Marian replied evenly, but her eyes danced merrily belying the protocol.

Alex turned to Mrs. Gilliam who seemed amused by this awkwardness. "Ma'am, would you object if I invited your daughter to walk with me along the shore?" Then, directing the question to Marian, "Assuming, of course, Miss Gilliam would be willing to accompany me, and I wouldn't be taking her away at a time when you need her assistance." That would give either lady a graceful way of refusing his offer, Alex reasoned.

The awkwardness instantly evaporated as Marian blurted out most unladylike, "Oh, yes! I'd love to! May I, Mama? The serving tables are all set, and I'll be back in time to help you serve the food. Besides, it'll be a few minutes yet before they finish cooking the shad."

Mrs. Gilliam shook her head in mock disapproval of her daughter's unseemly behavior. "Well Captain Wright, I suppose I could spare my daughter for a few minutes. It appears that she might be somewhat amenable to accompanying you. She has my permission; however, please remain in sight so I can signal you when we're ready to serve the food."

Not waiting for any further instructions, Marian grabbed Alex's hand and pulled him in the direction of the shoreline. "Thank you, Mama!" Marian shouted excitedly over her shoulder. "Don't worry, I'll be back in time to help!"

"Yes, thank you, Mrs. Gilliam," Alex stammered, not believing his good fortune, as Marian tugged his arm.

"That girl!" Mrs. Gilliam clucked as she watched the young couple hurrying toward the shore. "Anyone would think I was raising a hussy instead of a proper Christian daughter!"

Alex found himself completely enchanted by Marian's beauty and vivacity. She no longer held his hand, yet the memory of her touch still lingered in his thoughts. Strolling together along the shore of the pond, Marian steered the course of their conversation. Responding to her glib and constant prattle and unobtrusive way of questioning, Alex found himself talking easily about himself and his family. The discomfort he usually experienced when making conversation with a girl for the first time didn't apply to Marian. He felt he had known her all his life. Whenever he said something she found amusing, Alex's heart skipped a beat as she looked up at him with the glitter of laughter in her eyes and that incredibly beautiful smile that lit up her whole face. Each time he looked at her, Alex felt a pleasurable warmth course through his body.

"You don't think I'm too impulsive, do you, Alex? I fear Mama thinks me so."

"Oh no, Marian!" Alex replied instantly, shaking his head emphatically. "On the contrary! Please don't think me too brash if I confess that I find you totally refreshing and wonderfully charming—not to mention incredibly beautiful. I wouldn't want you to be any other way than the way you are just this minute."

Marian blushed prettily but went on, "You don't think me too bold and"—she paused, searching for the right phrase—"and too unladylike then?"

"Hell no!" Alex blurted out then quickly corrected himself. "I mean, heck no!"

"I feel comfortable with you, Alex," Marian smiled demurely, giving him a sidelong glance. "I also like the sound of your voice; maybe it has something to do with your lovely South Carolinian accent."

Alex grinned modestly, unsure how to respond. "Well, no one has ever complimented my accent before, but I'm relieved to know you don't find me too objectionable."

Marian laughed. "I suppose there's worse," she teased.

"Well then," said Alex, getting up his courage, "would I be too impetuous if I asked if I might call on you?"

Marian smiled coyly and seemed to ponder the matter for several seconds before answering.

Alex held his breath.

"Yes, I suppose so," Marian finally replied, rolling her eyes with a ho-hum expression.

"Then I have your permission to call on you?" Alex asked, sounding cautiously hopeful."

"No! I meant that you're too impetuous!"

"Oh," Alex said deflated, not knowing what else to say.

Marian laughed. "Alex, I'm just teasing! Of course! Please do call on me!"

Alex's face beamed like the sun coming out from behind a cloud. "You have your father's sense of humor, all right," he nodded. That's the kind of stunt he pulled on me at church last Sunday. I can't tell when he's serious and when he's not, the same as you!"

"You'll know if and when you get to know him better. He's slow to anger, but when it's aroused, he has a terrible temper. I suggest getting his approval, and Mama's too, before you come calling. You'll have no problem with Mama; I can tell she likes you. Winning Mama over is most of the battle because Papa is really a big teddy bear who pretty much goes along with anything my heart is set on doing."

"If they won't think I'm too forward, I'd like to ask them today, Marian. I leave Monday with my company for a field training exercise, but I'll be back in a couple of weeks."

And it happened just the way Marian said it would, Alex reflected, as he marched along beside the Georgia private, their feet kicking up little puffs of powdery dust along the roadside. He had her father's conditional approval to call on her. "Any funny business" he said, "and you won't have to worry about the Germans. It's me you'll have to fear! Understand?"

Yeah, I got the message, Alex smiled inwardly as he replayed the scene in his mind. *How ironic, to be here and, yet, be separated from Marian by a gulf of over fifty years. What will she think of my disappearance? Will she think I don't have feelings for her?*

His melancholy thoughts were interrupted as the Confederate patrol veered off the plank road onto a lesser dirt track for a short distance; then the patrol halted in front of a long palisade constructed of pine logs with an eight-foot-high double gate. The gate was closed.

Alex looked at Mike and shrugged.

Sergeant McFadden went to the gate and peered through the gaps in the logs. Seeing no activity inside the compound, he pounded on the gate with his rifle butt. "Hey!" he shouted. "We've got some prisoners for the Provost Marshal. Open up!"

A long minute passed before a head appeared in one of the two palisade guard towers. A bearded face peered down at them from behind a long rifle barrel. "State your business!" the soldier challenged.

"I'm Sergeant McFadden, Company C, 44th Georgia Infantry," McFadden growled." I've got three prisoners for the Provost Marshal."

"Show me your pass!" the sentry growled back.

McFadden stared at him, blankly. "What pass? I don't got no pass! I just want rid of these here prisoners!"

"I can't open the gate 'til you show me a pass. Orders an' all that, y'know. Go see the Provost Sergeant Major, an' maybe he'll give you one."

"Where do I find'im?" McFadden demanded, seething at the bureaucracy.

"Look in that hut over there," the sentry gestured with his rifle barrel. "Do y'know Sergeant Major O'Leary?"

"Can't say I've ever had the pleasure!" McFadden scowled.

"Well, you can't miss'im! He's a charmin' fellow, that one!" the sentry chuckled.

McFadden glared at the man, then, shaking his head and muttering obscenities, turned and stomped off toward the hut on the side of the road. "Wait here!" he growled as he stalked past his men and the prisoners.

Alex sighed wearily over his shoulder, "Looks like this may take awhile."

Without asking permission, they set the stretcher on the ground in the shade of the gate. Alex massaged his aching arms and shoulders as he studied the stockade's exterior walls and watchtowers.

McFadden disappeared into a canvas-roofed hut a stone's throw away, then re-emerged a minute later accompanied by a lumbering, pot-bellied soldier wearing a gray kepi with a battered visor, faded cavalry trousers, suspenders, and a dirty union suit unbuttoned at the neck revealing a course mat of chest hair. He shuffled along stiffly dragging one leg as if he had a bad knee. He and McFadden stopped outside the doorway, arguing and gesturing angrily toward the prisoners.

An occasional word floated their way, but the two men were too far away for Alex to get the gist of what was being said. The other man finally turned away from McFadden and hobbled over to a wall-tent, stuck his head inside, and growled something unintelligible. Two young soldiers immediately rushed out and stood ramrod straight in front of the older man who dwarfed them in height and weight. He glared at the two of them for a second then loosed a verbal barrage in a strong Irish brogue. Alex had no trouble hearing what was said. The Irishman's voice boomed like thunder.

"Well, me dahlin's, didja have a good nap now? I know ya both are new here, an' I hate to be a botherin' ya, I really do, but there's a small matter that's come up, ya see, an' I need a wee bit o' your time. That is, iv I wouldn't be imposin' on ya."

The younger, and clearly less intelligent of the two youths, took the Irishman's fatherly inflection at face value. "Sure, Sarge! We'd be glad to help. Just say the word."

The Irishman's cheeks and bulbous nose turned beet-red. Alex thought he was going to have a stroke. "Ya impudent, snot-nosed, fatherless, son of a jack-ass, did I ask ya to say anythin'? Did I?"

"No, suh, you didn't," the soldier replied, his brow knotted, obviously confused.

"Well, what're ya jabberin' for, lad? You're supposed to be at *attenshun* an' not a flappin' your lips. Keep your trap shut when you're at *attenshun*. When I want your chicken droppin's, I'll unscrew your head an' dip some out!" The Irishman stood nose to nose with the soldier who was now ramrod straight and looking very pale. Beads of sweat trickled down the boy's temples.

The Irishman took a step back, tucked his thumbs under his suspenders, and gazed at the boys for a moment. A tender, fatherly smile spread over his face. "Now, lads, seein' as we've cleared the air an' got that behind us, here's what I need ya to do. D' ya see that wee group o' prisoners standin' at the gate? Let me point'em out to ya, so there's no mistakin'. The ones without guns are the prisoners. Now if ya look closely that would be those two standin' next to that stretcher with another prisoner lyin' on it. Are ya with me so far, lads?"

"Yes, Sergeant!" they replied in unison.

"Good!" he beamed angelically. "Now why d'ya suppose that other prisoner is lyin' on that stretcher?"

The boys glanced at each other out of the corners of their eyes, but neither offered an opinion. They stood ramrod straight and looked straight ahead.

"Well now, it's not because he's a bit tired. It's because he's had the misfortune o' bein' shot. Prisoners who've been shot (pause), an'

56

are still breathin' (pause) can't go into the *bull pen*, that's what we call that stockade that's holdin' all those soldiers on holiday from the Union army. Now what I want ya to do is to carry that prisoner on the stretcher over to the field hospital just up the road an' stay with him 'til someone from the hospital takes 'im off your hands. Be sure to tell 'em that he's a prisoner, then report back to me when the job's done. D'ya suppose you can do that on your own?"

"Yes, Sergeant!"

"Splendid, lads! I knew the Confederacy could count on ya!"

The boys smiled from ear to ear but remained at attention.

"Now, me dahlin's, there's just one more wee thing I want to tell ya before I send ya on your way. Don't take it personal, 'cause I wouldn't want to bruise your tender feelin's...."

The Irishman paused to see if they were paying attention then smiled as he observed the same silly smiles on their faces.

In a booming voice suggestive of a displeased Lord Almighty, he fired a verbal broadside that made passersby on the plank road stop and look around, wondering. "My name is Sergeant Major O'Leary! The next time ya call me Sarge or Sergeant, I'll kick your arses up between your shoulder blades after which ya'll need to take off your shirts to shit! D'ya understand?"

Alex saw two Adam's apples bob in unison, "Yes, Sergeant Major O'Leary!"

"Good! Be off with ya! An' don't forget, I expect ya back here in an hour."

The two privates saluted smartly, then hurried over to the prisoners.

Alex was surprised by their youth. *Incredible, they can't be more than fifteen or sixteen years old! They should be home with their mothers!*

The older boy stopped in front of Alex and pointed at Tom on the stretcher. "We got orders from the Provost Marshal Sergeant Major to take this man to the division hospital."

Alex looked down at the peach fuzz on his cheeks. A wisp of blond hair protruded from under the bill of his faded cap, but the blue eyes were cool and business-like. Alex suppressed a smile and kept his voice low and stern. "For the moment I'm a prisoner, but I don't expect to be one by this time tomorrow. See to it that you give this soldier the same care and respect you would give your own father. If any harm comes to him through your neglect, I will personally wring your scrawny neck." Then mimicking the Irishman's voice and accent, "D'ya understand, lad?"

"Yes."

"Yes, what?" Alex snapped.

"I don't know what to call you. After all—you *are* a prisoner."

"Son, my last name is Wright, but you can call me by my first name, Captain, or if you prefer, you can just call me 'sir.' Okay?"

"Yes, sir."

"That's better," Alex said, stepping aside.

The boys promptly picked up the stretcher.

Alex put a restraining hand on the boy's shoulder at the head of the stretcher, "Just a minute, I want a word with this man before you take him away."

Alex noted Tom's face was drawn and pale. He was conscious, but the suffering in his eyes betrayed the pain he tried to hide. Alex gripped his hand to say farewell, noting it was hot and dry to the touch.

"Do me a favor in case I don't make it," Tom whispered in short, painful gasps as he lifted his head from the stretcher. "If you find your way home, tell my wife, Sarah, I love her and the children." He slipped a gold ring off his right hand and pressed it into Alex's palm. "Please give her this ring to pass on to my son when he's old enough to wear it. It belonged to my father and his father before him. She knows I'd never take it off if I were alive."

"You have my word on it," Alex assured him, placing the ring inside his breast pocket. "The doctors will fix you up, Tom. Then as soon as you're well enough, we'll find a way back—all three of us. Count on it."

"Yeah, sure. Count on it," Tom smiled wanly. "I'll see ya later." A tear rolled down his cheek as he closed his eyes.

Alex tapped the soldier on the shoulder and nodded.

The private looked at him with the same steady gaze as before. "He'll be cared for the same as our own; it's just that we don't have much these days. You understand, I hope?" There was a sympathetic pleading in the boy's voice.

"Yeah, I understand how it is," Alex nodded somberly.

A few minutes later, Sergeant McFadden returned with a piece of paper clutched in his hand. He walked up to the gate and shook it again. "Hey you, inside the gate!" he shouted. "Here's our pass for these prisoners!"

"Shove it under the gate, then step back," replied a voice from inside.

McFadden did as he was told. He backed away and joined his men.

As the gate swung open, a tall Confederate officer in an immaculate gray uniform and bearing a drawn sword appeared inside the gate leading a squad armed with rifles and attached bayonets. From beneath the brim of his cap his steel blue eyes bore straight through Alex and Mike as though they were invisible. A handsome face, long aquiline nose, blond mustache and goatee further enhanced his appearance.

"Send forth the prisoners!" the officer commanded.

"Well, I guess this is where we leave you," whispered the private from Georgia. "They won't let us inside the stockade. I was wounded at Gettysburg, then got captured during Lee's retreat and imprisoned at Point Lookout, Maryland. I was finally exchanged last year. I hope you have better luck. If you like, I can try to send word to your family so they'll know you're alive and well."

Alex shook his hand. "Thanks for offering, but that would be pretty hard to do. By the way, what's your name?"

"Private William Montgomery. My friends just call me Billy. I'm from Watkinsville, Georgia, just south of Athens."

"You're a good man, Billy. I hope you and your brothers get home safely."

"I wish you luck too, sir," Billy smiled.

Sergeant McFadden suddenly appeared alongside Billy and elbowed him in the ribs, "Stop jawin'! The lieutenant ordered you prisoners to march forward. You best step lively."

Alex's cool blue eyes fixed on McFadden. "Take good care of our weapons, sergeant. I expect to get them back."

"You needn't fret 'bout your pistols," McFadden growled. "I turned 'em over to the Provost Marshal Sergeant Major."

Alex wondered if he was lying.

"Prisoners! Fo'ward, March!" McFadden ordered.

Shoulder to shoulder, Alex and Mike marched through the open gate, passed the phalanx of infantry on either side, and crossed the parade ground toward the Confederate lieutenant.

Alex noted that the squad of infantry repositioned themselves as soon as they passed by—four had fallen in behind them and the rest were on either flank. No verbal commands had been given. Apparently the detail had performed this little maneuver so routinely that commands were unnecessary. Behind them the gate swung shut, and Alex heard the cross bar slide home. He suddenly felt like a trapped animal.

"Prisoners, Halt!" ordered the Confederate officer when Alex and Mike approached within six paces of him. "By order of the General commanding, all prisoners of war are to be interrogated by the Provost Marshal, Army of Northern Virginia, or members of his staff in order to determine the prisoners' status and privileges according to rank. State your names and rank."

"We're not Union soldiers," Alex replied, wondering if that was, technically, a true statement under the circumstances. "Allow me to introduce ourselves. I'm Captain Wright, and my friend here is Lieutenant Dent. We were on our way to report to General Gordon when we were intercepted by a patrol from A. P. Hill's Corps."

"I see," the lieutenant nodded with the utmost gravity. "Nonetheless, I must insist you remain with us for awhile as our guests. As for obtaining an audience with General Gordon, hmmm…worst luck I'm afraid. He's a trifle busy at the moment fighting battles and that sort of thing. I will, of course, schedule you in at the earliest opportunity. Is there anything else I can do for you chaps?"

Alex and Mike stared in surprise.

"What's an Englishman doing in the Confederate Army," Alex said, "if you don't mind my asking?"

"Not at all!" the officer replied. "I was born in Charlottesville, Virginia of American parentage but raised and educated in England by my uncle. I'm a graduate of Oxford, too, I might add. The faculty and my classmates considered me something of a rebel, and so it seems they were proved quite right, wouldn't you say?" he smiled pleasantly.

"So, if you good fellows don't mind waiting here for a moment, I will just step over to that tent—the one over there—," he said, pointing with the tip of his sword, "to announce your arrival. Ta!" The lieutenant smiled showing very white, even teeth. Sheathing his sword, he strode off in the direction of the tent.

Mike nudged Alex with his elbow. "Can you believe this? First an Irishman, and now a blooming Englishman! I always thought the Confederate Army was made up of Southerners!"

As promised, the lieutenant returned a minute later. "How thoughtless of me," he apologized, "not to introduce myself to you chaps. I'm Lieutenant Nevill Anderson, 24th Virginia Infantry. As for the business at hand, I'm afraid I can't get you in to see General Gordon; however, the Provost Marshal and his staff did express an immediate interest in speaking with you; perhaps they can be of more service. So, if you will be good enough to follow me, I will take you to them: *Prisoners, Left Wheel! Prisoners, Forward March!*"

Alex and Mike just shuffled along after Anderson, making no attempt to stay in step.

Mike chuckled.

"What's so funny?" Alex asked, failing to see the humor in the situation.

"What's a Left Wheel?" Mike asked, stifling a snicker.

"That's a British thing. It's the opposite of Right Wheel."

"Oh? Well that helps," Mike nodded sagely. "Thanks for clearing that up for me."

"Any time."

Alex and Mike followed Lieutenant Anderson to the tent noting that the four guards were still following close on their heels like silent shadows.

At the tent's entrance Anderson commanded, *"Prisoners, Halt!"*

Alex and Mike promptly halted, clicking their heels together Prussian style and kicking up a cloud of powdery dust.

Anderson grimaced at the tomfoolery but said nothing as he ducked his 6-foot, 2-inch frame under the entrance flap and reported to someone inside.

His voice carried to Alex and Mike waiting outside. "Sir! Lieutenant Anderson reporting with the prisoners as ordered!"

"Enter!" a deep voice answered from within the tent.

"This is one time I'm glad you outrank me!" Mike flourished his hat for Alex to enter first.

Alex rolled his eyes, stepped past Mike, and entered. Anderson stood to his right inside the entrance, and in front of him, three men in splendid Confederate uniforms sat at a long table in the center of the tent facing him.

Judging from the gold braid on their sleeves and collars, Alex assumed they were officers, but as to their rank, he didn't have a clue. Alex saluted and stood at attention in front of the table, looking straight ahead, his face expressionless. Mike snapped his best West Point salute and stood at attention beside Alex. Like shadows, the four guards quietly entered the tent and stood behind the prisoners.

The Confederate officers studied Alex and Mike's uniforms with obvious interest.

From his peripheral vision, Alex noted their inquisitiveness as their eyes flicked from his short hair and clean-shaven face to the crossed-rifles infantry insignia on his collar. The officer seated in the middle leaned to his right, raised his hand to mask his lips, and whispered something in the ear of an older man sitting next to him. The man nodded in apparent agreement or understanding as he looked first at Alex and then at Mike.

Finally the older officer demanded brusquely: "Names?"

"Captain Alexander Wright," Alex answered without hesitation.

"First Lieutenant Michael Dent!" Mike replied, more loudly than was necessary.

"Company, regiment, and division?"

"And who are you gentlemen?" Alex said, ignoring the question.

Unused to being so addressed by enemy prisoners of war, the officer drew back and scowled at Alex.

The man seated in the middle again leaned over and whispered in the older officer's ear.

From beneath bushy eyebrows his deep-set eyes studied Alex contemplatively for a moment, then his face softened.

"Very well," he nodded, "I'm Colonel Thompson, Provost Marshal,

Hill's Corps, Army of Northern Virginia. The gentleman to my left is Captain Kincaid, my deputy, and the young man on the end is my adjutant, Lieutenant Henry. Now that we're introduced, perhaps you'll be kind enough to enlighten us about yourselves. This is the first time we've seen the uniform you're wearing, so naturally we're interested in knowing the identity of your unit. We've been told that you were captured near the White Oak Road a mile or two outside our lines. How is it that you came to be there?" The Colonel lifted a questioning eyebrow, inviting Alex to respond.

Well here goes, Alex took a deep breath. *Hope I can pull this off.* "As much as I'd like to satisfy your curiosity, sir, the only thing that I'm at liberty to disclose is that we belong to Mosby's Rangers. We have verbal orders from Colonel Mosby to report to General Gordon—that's where we were heading when the patrol from General A.P. Hill's Corps found us."

The two junior officers were clearly astonished. Thompson, on the other hand, didn't even blink.

Alex was playing a high stakes game, and he knew he had better play this hand well if he didn't want to spend the rest of the war in a prisoner of war camp. For what seemed an eternity, Alex held his breath and returned the Colonel's stare.

Like a venomous snake slowly uncoiling, Thompson leaned back in his chair, but his cold brooding stare never wavered from Alex's face. "Very interesting." The Colonel's tone was flat and emotionless. "You do, of course, have some proof?"

"No disrespect intended, sir, but Colonel Mosby has entrusted me to deliver a message of time sensitive importance to no one but General Gordon."

"Time sensitive? I would think such an important message would be delivered to General Lee. Why General Gordon?"

"General Lee has delegated to General Gordon responsibility for certain military matters. And General Gordon will need the intelligence report that Colonel Mosby is sending him."

"I suppose Colonel Mosby will vouch for you if we contact him?" Thompson countered, arching an eyebrow.

Alex shook his head. "Colonel, under present conditions, you know as well as I do that it would take too long to obtain confirmation from Colonel Mosby. If we had been captured on the way here, the enemy would have shot us as spies or partisans, so obviously I have no written proof to show you."

Realizing he was getting nowhere, Alex decided on a different tack. "Sir, in your position as Provost Marshal, you are entrusted with gathering timely military intelligence. Arrange for us to see General Gordon today and you will have done your duty. I just pray that we're not already too late."

Thompson unbuttoned his tunic, reached inside, and withdrew a large gold pocket watch and chain from his vest pocket. The gold case popped open in his hand exposing a glass face. In an accent that Alex had already recognized as South Carolinian, Thompson drawled, "It's now six o'clock. It's a little late in the day to call on General Gordon."

Thompson stared at Alex for a long time as if trying to make up his mind.

"Another question or two, if you please," Thompson drawled.

Alex tensed.

"I note your accent is similar to mine. Are you a South Carolinian as well?"

"Yes, sir, I was a former resident of that state. I was born and raised in Charleston. Just before the war I moved to Alexandria, Virginia and worked in my uncle's dry goods business." What Alex had said about Charleston was true, but the rest was pure fabrication. He knew he was going further out on a limb with each falsehood. Even so, he correctly anticipated the Colonel's next comment.

"I see," Thompson said, scrunching up his face sourly as if suffering from indigestion. "But one must assume that Colonel Mosby's men would be from northern Virginia. Neither your speech nor your appearance fits the image I have of his rangers—and I find that unsettling."

Alex shrugged and smiled. "Well they do make sport of my accent, but I'm treated like a close cousin."

Thompson gave Alex a fake tight-lipped smile, but there was no thaw in his icy stare.

Thompson suddenly turned to Mike, putting the same question to him. "And you, Lieutenant aah…?"

"Dent, sir."

"Yes, of course—*Dent*—my apologies. And where are you from, sir?"

"Fairfax, Virginia, sir," Mike answered without hesitation.

Alex knew Mike was from Fredrick, Maryland, but Thompson would have thought it suspiciously odd that neither of them was a native of Northern Virginia. *Good thinking, Mike.*

"I understand the third member of your party was severely wounded and has been sent to our field hospital," Thompson continued, shifting his gaze back to Alex. "How did he come to be wounded?"

"We encountered two Union cavalrymen at the place where your patrol found us," Alex explained. "During the exchange of gunfire, I killed them both, but Sergeant Hill was hit in the shoulder. Your patrol can verify my story; they saw the bodies."

Apparently satisfied, Colonel Thompson looked to his left, "Captain Kincaid and Lieutenant Henry, do either of you have any questions?"

"I don't," the captain replied.

"Nor I, sir," shrugged the lieutenant.

"Lieutenant Henry, a pen and some paper please," ordered Thompson, sliding his chair closer to the table.

The adjutant opened a leather case on the table in front of him and slid a sheet of parchment, an envelope, an inkwell, and a pen to the captain who in turn passed them to the colonel.

Thompson wrote quickly, the scratching of his pen clearly audible as everyone quietly looked on. Signing his name with a flourish when he finished, Thompson folded the parchment, stuffed it in the envelope, and addressed it to *Major General Gordon, Eyes Only, URGENT.* Thompson handed the envelope to Captain Kincaid. "Rather than entrust this to one of the couriers, I'd prefer that you delivered this message to General Gordon's adjutant personally. However, before you leave I want to speak with you privately."

Thompson and Kincaid stepped outside the tent.

Alex glanced at Mike apprehensively, wondering what the two officers were discussing.

Thompson returned a few minutes later and took his seat at the table. He looked at Alex for a moment as if deliberating. "Well, so *I have done my duty*," he said finally. "Now it's up to General Gordon as to whether or not he'll see you. We may receive a reply from him sometime tonight—it's rumored that he never sleeps. In the meantime, I imagine you both are a bit hungry. When did you eat last?"

"Oh, about fifty years ago," Alex replied as if joking, "wouldn't you say, Mike?"

"At least," Mike said with a smile, then frowned at Alex when Thompson looked away.

"Well, we'll have to do something about that," Thompson continued, dismissing what he perceived as Alex's peculiar sense of humor. "We're having beans and cornbread for dinner tonight."

"Sounds mighty good to us, Colonel!" Alex replied gratefully, the pangs in his stomach already reminding him that he and Mike hadn't eaten since yesterday.

"That's good, because that's what we're having for breakfast and supper tomorrow too—we generally skip lunch. As you've probably seen from the condition of our men, we're on pretty slim rations these days."

Thompson leaned back in his chair and gazed around the tent vainly searching for someone. Finally, he growled, "Lieutenant Anderson! Report!"

Anderson had been standing outside, listening to the proceedings. Hearing his name, he promptly stepped back inside, brushed between Alex and Mike, and appeared in front of Thompson. He saluted smartly, "Lieutenant Anderson reporting, sir!"

Thompson returned the salute, then shifted in his chair and looked thoughtfully at Alex and Mike standing behind Anderson. "If I release you into Lieutenant Anderson's custody, do I have your word that you won't wander off?"

"Yes, sir," Alex nodded. "You have our word."

"All right then. Lieutenant Anderson, dismiss the guards. These gentlemen are your responsibility until I hear from General Gordon. See that they're fed, after which, find a suitable place for them to sleep tonight."

"Yes, sir. I'll see to it."

Before Thompson could dismiss them, Alex quickly interjected,

"Colonel, may I make one more request?"

Thompson looked at him warily. "What is it?"

"We'd like to know how Sergeant Hill is being treated. The hospital staff has been told that he's a prisoner of war. Could you inform them otherwise?"

Thompson nodded. "I'll send an orderly to check on his condition and notify the field hospital commander of his change in status. We'll keep you posted."

"Thank you, sir," Alex smiled appreciatively, saluted, then turned and followed Mike and Anderson outside.

CHAPTER 9

General Lee's Headquarters
Petersburg, Virginia,
7:00 P.M., MARCH 23, 1865

Major General John B. Gordon paused on the steps of the Turnbull House to gaze at the brilliant full moon rising above the pasture across the road. He drew a deep breath of crisp, cold air and exhaled slowly, watching the vapor of his breath drift away in the moonlight. The landscape reminded him of other evenings when he and his wife enjoyed carriage rides together on brisk evenings under the same brilliant moon. The war forgotten, the scenery by moonlight was beautiful as they laughed and enjoyed their closeness under the heavy lap robe. Because their time together was always brief, these were cherished memories, bought with the passion of lovers in wartime. Despite his objections, she insisted on staying with him in Petersburg, exposing herself and the baby in her womb to the enemy's constant shelling.

"That's sweet, John," she countered as he argued with her to leave, "but it's utter nonsense, really. What with marauding Yankee cavalry and deserters from both armies pillaging the countryside, the baby and I are much safer here in Petersburg—with you." He couldn't refute her logic and, in the end, relented.

His orderly emerged from the shadows mounted on a fine-looking chestnut mare and rode up to the foot of the steps leading Gordon's horse. Taking the reins from the orderly's hand, Gordon mounted; the oiled leather creaked pleasingly as he settled in the saddle.

Having served with Gordon through most of the war, the sergeant had learned to recognize his moods and sensed this was one of those times when the General wished to be alone with his thoughts. He rode alongside Gordon and did not attempt to engage him in conversation.

Gordon allowed his mare to set her own gait as they ambled toward Petersburg. Incredibly brilliant, the moonlight illuminated the countryside and flickered through the barren branches of the row of sycamores lining the sides of the road.

Occasional flashes of light arced across the heavens as artillery batteries dueled along the lines. *The enemy has been shelling Petersburg and its defenders for almost a year now without let up,* Gordon reflected as he gazed at the fiery missiles. *It's a wonder that I can still find an occasional moment of peace and solitude with the enemy pounding at the gates of the city.* Gordon's thoughts strayed to his private meeting with General Lee and remembered, too, an earlier meeting in February when Gordon had been summoned to Lee's headquarters, a ride of several miles in the wee hours of a bitterly cold night. When he arrived at Lee's headquarters on the outskirts of Petersburg, Gordon found him alone in the parlor, standing before a fireplace gazing at the flames in the grate. Appearing worn and tired, Lee turned around when he heard Gordon enter the room. Gordon inquired about his health to which Lee waved a hand in casual dismissal of the question. "Physically, I'm sound. I wish I could say as much for our army, which is why I sent for you. Read those," he said pointing at an assortment of reports scattered across a long table in the center of the room. "Those are command status reports describing conditions throughout the army—some I just received tonight. Have a seat," he said, offering Gordon his choice of several chairs at the table. As Gordon pulled one up, Lee did likewise, sitting opposite him across the table. "When you're finished, I'd like your opinion."

Gordon was appalled by the deplorable conditions existing in every portion of the army as he hurriedly scanned the reports. He had, of course, skipped over his own report in which he had detailed shortages of rations and supplies of every description and the effect on morale and the physical well-being of his men. As dire as he had depicted the needs and physical condition of his own troops, they were on a whole, much better off than other commands where men were actually starving and were without shoes, warm clothing, or blankets. "I had no idea it was this bad," Gordon said solemnly as he dropped the last report on the table, the one from A.P. Hill's Corps. "We have about 50,000 men, of which only 35,000 are fit for duty, against Grant's 200,000 well-provisioned soldiers. In contrast, General A.P. Hill reports that 600 of his men are compelled to subsist on less food than what 100 of their adversaries receive. As I see it, we have but three choices: Surrender and get the best terms we can. Retreat and abandon Richmond and Petersburg to link up with General Johnston in North Carolina. Or attack and do it now while we still can."

Lee listened thoughtfully until Gordon finished, then slowly nodded. "That's the way I see it too. As for surrender, only the Confederate government has the lawful authority to ask for terms from the United States. Quite frankly, I don't see that happening; consequently surrender is not an option we can put on the table for consideration.

Retreat hardly merits consideration. To evacuate Richmond and Petersburg with our skin intact would be perilous at best." Lee seemed to play the scenario in his mind for a moment then shook his head. "Neither President Davis nor the Confederate government would consent to such a move. And Grant's cavalry would be nipping at our heels the minute we left our trenches. We have only half the horses needed to evacuate our artillery and munitions, and most of those are in pitiful condition. Grant is dangerously close to severing the South Side Railroad. A.P. Hill is protecting it, but his corps is stretched to the breaking point. If Grant keeps extending his lines westward parallel to the railroad, in a very short time he'll put us in a position where we can no longer defend it. He's getting fresh troops daily, and General Sheridan will add ten thousand more when his command arrives here from the Valley. Logistically, Grant's military railroad ensures a continuous supply of ammunition, supplies, and reinforcements along his entire front regardless of the weather. We, on the other hand, continue to grow weaker through disease, desertion, and a shortage of everything. If we lose the South Side Railroad, our supplies will be cut off, and that will signify the beginning of the end for us.

So, as you correctly concluded, the only realistic option left to us is to attack and force Grant to shorten his lines and abandon his efforts to seize the railroad." Lee pointed a finger at Gordon; the fatigue had vanished from his face, and his eyes had taken on a startling fierceness. "I'm giving that job to you, John. As you have seen from those reports, your troops are in the best condition to carry it off successfully. I need you to find Grant's weakness, devise a plan to exploit it, and report back to me when you're ready."

It was still dark when Gordon, ignoring the cold and deep in thought, rode away from Lee's headquarters.

Today, almost six weeks later, Gordon had returned to the Turnbull House to present his plan to General Lee.

"Well General, what can you do?" Lee asked.

"I can punch a big hole in Grant's siege line by taking Fort Stedman, sir," Gordon replied confidently. "Then I can roll up his flanks and capture everything between Fort Stedman and the Appomattox River. I can also penetrate deep enough into his rear to cut his military railroad and communications—all of which will force Grant to shorten his lines and take the pressure off the South Side Railroad. My plan is bold and risky, just the kind of thing Grant won't expect. I have capable, energetic officers who will jump at the chance to get out of the trenches and carry the fight to the enemy. On the other hand, the physical condition of my men is my greatest concern in carrying out the assault. Many are sick or weak. After the initial break-through, they may not have the stamina to sustain the momentum needed to take and hold the enemy lines to the extent I envision. I will need more troops than I have now and a much heavier concentration of artillery than is presently on my front."

Lee listened, his expression solemn, as Gordon briefed the details of his plan.

GENERAL JOHN B. GORDON, C.S.A.

(Courtesy of National Archives)

"I can punch a big hole in Grant's siege line by taking Fort Stedman, sir,"
Gordon replied confidently.

"It's a given," Gordon concluded, "that Grant is well apprised of our numerical strength. He'll know we stripped our defenses of troops and artillery to make an attack of this magnitude. And if we fail in this endeavor, he'll most assuredly order a general assault upon the whole twenty-two-mile length of our defenses with the direst consequences."

"You have assessed the stakes very astutely," Lee said when he had finished. "Very well then," he nodded, accepting Gordon's plan. "I'll issue orders tonight to provide you the additional troops and artillery support you'll require. Your total force will be approximately ten thousand. I will, of course, order demonstrations elsewhere along our lines to dissuade Grant from reinforcing his lines in your front as well as to disguise our real intentions."

Gordon nodded. "I anticipate having all preparations completed tomorrow and will assault Fort Stedman at 4:00 A.M. the following morning, March 25th."

The discussion continued until both men were satisfied that the essential details were understood. Gordon then bade farewell and summoned his orderly.

As Gordon rode towards Petersburg, two things troubled him. The first had to do with the Federal deserters from whom much valuable information had been gleaned about Fort Stedman and its defenses. Twenty-eight percent of the Union soldiers deserting to the Confederate lines in the past month had shown up along Colquitt's Salient—the closest Confederate position to Fort Stedman. It wasn't the high percentage that puzzled him. *Why were so many Union soldiers deserting along that segment of the line when Grant's ultimate victory seemed so assured?* He shook his head; maybe it was just one of those conundrums that defied logic.

The other *thing* weighed heavily on his conscience. He had kept part of his plan from Lee. Twice during their meeting he had reached for the message in his pocket that had been tapped from the Union telegraph lines along the James River between City Point and Fort Monroe. Each time, he had withdrawn his hand, leaving the message in his pocket. He knew Lee for the honorable soldier and the gentleman that he was—chivalry was ingrained in him. And it was because of that that

Gordon chose not to be totally forthcoming. He saw in the intercepted message a chance to win the war in a single stroke, but, because it would violate his code of ethics, Gordon knew that Lee would never consent to what he proposed to do. His plan went far beyond battlefield tactics, and the consequences of carrying it out would be wholly on his own shoulders—*as it should be*, he told himself.

CHAPTER 10

General Gordon's Headquarters
Petersburg, Virginia
8:00 P.M., MARCH 23, 1865

An hour after his meeting with General Lee, Gordon arrived back at his own headquarters, a stately Georgian-style mansion below Blandford Cemetery whose owners had fled at the beginning of the siege. As he entered the immense but dimly lit foyer with its elegant marble floors and graceful spiral staircase, Gordon heard voices coming from the library where his Secretary of the General Staff had set up his office. An exceptionally large room, it was also the place of duty for the Officer of the Day during his twenty-four hour shift.

Inside, he found two officers sitting and conversing. They immediately stood as Gordon entered the room. He recognized Major Hollis, the Officer of the Day; but the other officer was a new face to him.

"Good evening, sir!" greeted Hollis, and without waiting to be asked, promptly introduced his visitor. "This is Captain Kincaid. He just arrived with an urgent dispatch from Colonel Thompson, Provost Marshal for General Hill's Corps, with instructions to deliver it to your adjutant. Perhaps you would prefer to receive the message directly?" Hollis suggested, then added as an afterthought. "Colonel Thompson told Captain Kincaid to wait for your reply."

Gordon was tired and had a lot on his mind. Never a patient man, he regarded Kincaid with a look of exasperation. "Is it really so important that you need an answer tonight, Captain?"

"Colonel Thompson thinks it is, sir," Kincaid replied, stepping forward and handing him an envelope.

"I hope so," Gordon grumbled as he tore open the envelope and unfolded the enclosed note. He held it close to the oil lamp on the table to read:

March 23, 1865, 6:00 P.M.
Major General Gordon

I have detained two men alleging to be officers (a captain and a lieutenant) from Colonel Mosby's command. A patrol apprehended them near White Oak Road west of the Boydton Plank Road. They profess to have been sent by Colonel Mosby bearing urgent intelligence for your ears only. It may be a ruse but in light of other factors, I think it worth your time to see them. They insist on meeting with you immediately. My deputy, Captain Kincaid, can provide additional details and has in his possession one of two side arms taken from these men. I have the other weapon. Their uniforms and weapons are unlike any I have seen previously.

I will send these men to you if you wish to see them. They are not under guard.

Your Obedient Servant,
Colonel Chas. Thompson

Despite his weariness, Gordon was suddenly intrigued. "Colonel Thompson says you have more to add," he said, glancing up from the note at Kincaid.

"Yes, sir.

"Let's hear it."

Kincaid began to recite. "The senior ranking man, Captain Wright, claims to have important information for you from Colonel Mosby.

Of course, there's no immediate way to verify that. There is also a wounded enlisted man who has been sent to our field hospital. The sergeant in charge of the patrol that found them reported that these men had engaged and killed two Union cavalrymen. The enlisted man was allegedly wounded in that engagement. They are wearing unusual uniforms, wool and olive drab in color. Although different from what we are accustomed to seeing, the insignia on their uniforms is clearly United States issue."

"Tell me about their side arms," Gordon interjected, his curiosity aroused. "I understand you have one with you."

"Yes, sir. Both officers were armed with handguns manufactured by the Colt Firearms Company in Springfield, Massachusetts. They appear to be either highly advanced or experimental firearms. What's puzzling is the date of manufacture. The date on the barrel of both weapons is incorrectly stamped *November 19, 1917*. I have one with me and the holster and belt worn with it. I was instructed to deliver it to you for whatever disposition you care to make. Colonel Thompson has the other sidearm and will send it also if you desire it."

Kincaid opened a small black valise he'd been carrying, took a khaki-colored bundle from it, and handed it to Gordon.

Gordon unrolled the bundle on the table revealing a fabric belt with an interconnecting brass buckle and numerous brass eyelets. Attached to the belt was a brown leather holster with a cover flap embossed with two distinctive initials. Gordon stared at the bold *US* as he opened the flap and lifted from the holster the most unusual and exquisitely crafted handgun he had ever seen. Its sleek design and deep blue metallic tint fascinated him as he examined the weapon under the soft glow of the oil lamp. Gordon noted the date of manufacture error that Captain Kincaid had mentioned. Holding the pistol in his right hand, Gordon squinted as he took aim at a portrait hanging above the fireplace mantle.

"Is it loaded?"

"I don't know, sir. No one has tried to fire it."

Gordon considered squeezing the trigger but thought better of it. Instead, he slipped the pistol back into the holster, fastened the leather flap, and wrapped the belt around the holster. "Tell Colonel Thompson that I wish to see these two men right away—tonight.

And I want the other pistol and holster delivered to me personally. Please thank him for his astuteness in bringing this matter to my attention so promptly."

"Yes, sir!" Kincaid replied, saluting smartly.

As the Captain reached the doorway, he encountered Major Moore, Gordon's Secretary of the General Staff. Kincaid stepped aside, smiled an acknowledgment, then hurried down the hall.

"Ahh, Major Moore," Gordon greeted him, "I was just about to send for you. Please notify all division commanders and the Chief of Artillery that I will be conducting a briefing tonight at 10:00 P.M."

"Yes, sir. May I tell them the purpose of the briefing in the event they should ask?"

Gordon suspected that the query was more to satisfy Moore's curiosity than for the reason stated.

"No. Just tell them to be here. In the event any of the division commanders can't be here on time, tell the division duty officers that I want the next highest-ranking officer available. Got that?"

"Yes, sir!" Moore promptly retreated to his desk to write the required dispatches.

Gordon wasn't concerned. Moore had plenty of time to write the dispatches and have them delivered. Six couriers with mounts were always at the ready in the carriage house where the adjutant had his office.

Finishing the last dispatch, Moore turned to the Officer of the Day who, with little to do, sat looking ill at ease as the General quietly paced back and forth. "Major Hollis, please deliver these dispatches to the adjutant in the carriage house. Tell him they're to be delivered to the addressees within the hour."

"Right away," Hollis said, taking the dispatches from Moore and heading toward the door.

"One more thing, Major Moore," said Gordon, still pacing the floor, "sometime this evening I'm expecting two visitors who are presently guests of General Hill's Provost Marshal. If they arrive during my meeting, make them comfortable in the carriage house until it's over."

Gordon retrieved the pistol and holster from the table and started for the hallway. "I'll be upstairs in my quarters. Let me know if anything important arises; otherwise I'll be down for the briefing."

CHAPTER 11

Provost Marshal's Camp, A.P. Hill's Corps Near Boydton Plank Road, Petersburg, Virginia

7:00 P.M., MARCH 23, 1865

In the growing dusk, Lieutenant Anderson escorted his two charges across the parade ground toward one of the palisades. "We call our quaint little dining establishment *Chez Le Trots* for reasons you will soon fathom for yourselves; however, some say that it offers the best food this side of Petersburg. Imagine that!"

A large rectangular tent loomed ahead of them. Anderson led them around it to the opposite side where a ten-foot square piece of canvas had been stretched between the palisade and two supporting poles. The makeshift shelter provided a degree of protection from the elements for the cooks and servants who were busily cleaning up after the evening meal. Steam billowed from an iron kettle suspended over the grate of a stone fireplace and chimney, all that remained of a house that had once occupied the site.

Seated at a table near the fire, two men played cards. One player, of immense girth with jowls proportionately too large for his mouth, puffed on a clay pipe as he squinted at the cards in his hand. The other, a scrawny, consumptive-looking man, rocked backward on the rear two legs of his chair, idly scratching his scraggly beard as he waited for his partner to call his bet or fold his cards. In the middle of the table lay a half-dozen poker chip-size Liberty head pennies.

Obviously a high stakes poker game, Alex chuckled; however, the use of Yankee pennies as valued currency did not go unnoticed.

Anderson promptly got the attention of the bigger man. "Sergeant MacIntyre, I brought you two more dinner guests. Hope there's something left in your cook pot?"

Both men promptly pushed back from the table and stood up as Anderson ducked his head under the canvas. In height, MacIntyre matched Anderson inch for inch, but his girth was every bit three times larger, and his arms were big as hams.

"Uh-huh," MacIntyre grunted before he remembered he was addressing an officer. "Yes, sir," he corrected himself, taking the pipe out of his mouth. "There ain't much, but I can rustle up some cornpone to go with the bit o' beans that's left in the pot."

"Good!" Anderson smiled amiably. "Please seat these gentlemen at your best table and serve them tonight's house special."

"Yes, sir," MacIntyre grinned, revealing a dark gap where two front teeth should have been. "Two *specials* comin' right up!"

"After Sergeant Mac dishes you up a plate, you can eat over there," Anderson said, pointing at the adjacent tent where several long tables and benches were visible. "While you're treating your palettes to an incredible experience, I really must duck out for a few minutes to check on my other duties. I'll be back in a flash. Ta!"

Alex and Mike sat across from each other at a trestle table that wobbled irritatingly under the weight of their elbows. Two swaying kerosene lanterns suspended from the ridge pole played upon their faces as they spooned down a tin plate of beans flavored with a little fatback that had found its way into the kettle. The thin, oval cornpone cakes possessed a gritty texture as if the dust and sand from the plank road had been added to the ingredients.

"'May not look like much to you, Alex, but this is the best grub I've had since I joined this war," Mike said glibly, flicking off a baked weevil before biting into his cornpone.

"I'm so happy for you," Alex muttered distractedly as he picked through his plate, skimming off anything with legs before spooning the beans into his mouth. "A condemned man deserves a good meal before he's executed."

Mike choked on his cornpone. "Just so you know," he sputtered, sending flecks of cornmeal across the table, "I'm not excited about

78

being the honored guest at a public execution, so why don't you tell me about this plan of yours."

Alex sopped his plate with his last piece of cornpone before stuffing it in his mouth. Brushing the crumbs from his fingers, he puckered his lips and squinted at the lantern suspended above the table as if contemplating something. "Guess maybe I better," he nodded. He leaned over the table, looked around to see if anyone was listening, then lowered his voice conspiratorily. "I don't know how we got here—or how we're going to get back to 1918—but I *do* know this much: I grew up on a diet of Civil War stories, and I studied the siege of Petersburg extensively at West Point. I know in considerable detail the events that will take place here during the next two weeks—and, Mike, we can use that knowledge to our advantage." Alex tapped the table top with his index finger to emphasize the point he was making. "The war is going to end April 9th, 1865, with the surrender of Lee at Appomattox Court House. Today is March 23rd, 1865. The end is near. I don't want to sit out the last few weeks of the war in some pest hole of a prisoner of war camp, so I concocted that story about us belonging to Mosby's Rangers. With the Confederacy fast crumbling, I figure there's little chance of anyone proving otherwise."

"Wasn't Colonel John S. Mosby called the *Gray Ghost*?" Mike interjected.

"That's right. He was a flamboyant figure who led a band of partisans in Northern Virginia and was famous for his daring exploits. The area where he operated was often referred to as Mosby's Confederacy."

Mike picked up the last bean from his plate, put it in his mouth, and chewed it thoughtfully. "And what role does General Gordon play in this?"

"Major General John B. Gordon is a Corps Commander in the Army of Northern Virginia. The day after tomorrow, March 25th to be exact, he will launch the last major Confederate offensive action of the war. The attack will fail. Confederate losses in killed and captured will be substantial, and General Lee will be forced to abandon his defenses around Richmond and Petersburg.

Now I'll digress for a moment and tell you what's really at stake on March 25th. Many historians agree, and it's my belief as well, that President Lincoln represented the best hope for healing the nation's wounds and reuniting the country; however, in a few short weeks he'll be assassinated. Vindictive Republicans will have their way and will take their revenge on a defeated and impoverished South. The North will call it *Reconstruction*, but for the South it will be another name for *Hell*. The wounds inflicted by it and the war will fester for decades. Reconstruction will go down as one of the most bitter and disgraceful chapters in American history. Had Lincoln lived, he would have pursued a more reconciliatory course to reunite the nation, and the evils of Reconstruction would have been avoided.

Now let me ask a hypothetical question: What would have happened if Lincoln had not been assassinated but had been captured instead? By this time in 1865, the South was all but finished, and those in authority had pretty much abandoned any hope for independence. But had Lincoln fallen into Confederate hands during the final weeks of the war, I think it would have broken the back of Northern resolve. I think, too, that the war-weary North would have accepted a negotiated settlement without retribution, and the South would have reluctantly, but willingly, rejoined the Union."

"Fascinating," Mike smiled indulgently, "and you're telling me all this because...?"

"I'm getting there," Alex gestured for Mike to be patient. "You must admit that our being here is pretty *miraculous*—I don't know what else to call it. Knowing what we do, maybe Providence is replaying this piece of history and wants us to help end this war differently from the way it did."

Alex paused as two soldiers, laughing and talking loudly, ambled past the tent.

The laughter suddenly stopped as the soldiers passed the strangers in their olive-drab uniforms sitting in the open-sided tent. Stealing curious glances over their shoulders at the strange pair, they hurried on whispering between themselves.

Alex watched the soldiers disappear into the darkness, then leaned forward and continued talking in a lower voice, conscious now that someone might be listening. "Mike, during the next thirty-six to forty-eight hours we have an opportunity to change the course of history for the better. In the pre-dawn hours of March 25th General Gordon's troops will initially capture several strong Union positions. The Confederate breakthrough will occur near Meade Station on the U.S. Military Railroad. It just so happens that the headquarters of the Army of the Potomac, commanded by Major General George G. Meade, is only a quarter of a mile from there. If you remember, one of those dispatches we found on that Union courier stated that Lincoln would layover at Meade's headquarters on the night of March 24th. That's only a mile from where the Confederate breakthrough will occur. If we offer our services to General Gordon during the attack on the Union lines, with a bit of luck we just might succeed in capturing Lincoln."

"That's it?" Mike stared at Alex with an incredulous expression. "That's *The Plan*—capture Lincoln? Does insanity run in your family, Alex? Your cockamamie scheme could get us both killed! You know that?"

"Yeah, I suppose," Alex shrugged. "You have something better to do on March 25th?"

"I've got one question."

"Just one?"

"Yeah. Do you own a crystal ball or something—how do you know all this?"

"Got it from my grandfather," Alex smiled.

"Your grandfather!" Mike rolled his eyes. "Care to elaborate?"

Alex nodded, then began: "Granddad was here at Petersburg during the siege—as a matter of fact, he was a private in Gordon's Corps. Once, when he had had a little too much of his homemade brandy, he told me a wierd story about the Confederate attack on Fort Stedman. He said that during the battle, he was in a company of hand-picked infantry that infiltrated behind the Federal lines with the mission of capturing General Meade's headquarters. Before the assault began, General Gordon gave a rousing speech to Granddad's company and, in essence, told them that they might very well win the war for the Confederacy. Gordon didn't elaborate beyond that. However, something went terribly wrong after the company got behind the Union lines. They ran into a large enemy force and were surrounded. Every man in his company, except Granddad, was killed in the battle. A bullet grazed his head and knocked him unconscious. Later, he crawled off into the brush and hid for two days. Dazed and weak from loss of blood, he wandered about until he was captured by a Union patrol. He was evacuated to a hospital at City Point and remained there until the war ended."

"Is he still living?" Mike asked, wondering where Alex was going with this story.

Alex shook his head. "During my senior year at West Point I received a telegram from my folks saying that he was dying. I hadn't seen him in almost four years, so I got nine days compassionate leave to go home. When he saw me standing at the foot of his bed in my uniform, his eyes suddenly popped open. 'You!' he yelled, pointing at me. 'It was you, Alex! I saw you at Meade's headquarters!' Of course I thought he was hallucinating; then his eyes gradually became fixed, and he died staring at me. I'll never forget it." Alex shook his head as though trying to purge the memory from his mind. "I spent hours and hours researching the records and the personal accounts describing the Confederate offensive on March 25, 1865 and found nothing about an attack on General Meade's headquarters. I finally concluded that the old soldier had just made up a fanciful war story. Well, that is, until today when I read those dispatches."

"So, if I understand what you're getting at, you think Gordon was really after President Lincoln and not just General Meade. Is that it?"

"Yeah, "Alex nodded. "Looks that way to me."

"Let's say by some miracle we even find Lincoln, much less take him prisoner, just how will you persuade him to come along with us—invite him over for a cup of coffee?"

"Dunno. I'll have to think about that."

"This is totally preposterous," Mike laughed, "but since this is all just a bad dream, and I'm going to wake up any minute, you can count me in. So? Where do we go from here?"

"We can't do anything until we see General Gordon. He's the key to the whole thing."

"Looks like we're about to find out the likelihood of that happening," said Mike, gesturing with his thumb toward the other end of the tent.

Anderson strode toward them with Captain Kincaid close on his heels.

"Glad to see you chaps are still breathing after eating Mac's grub," Anderson gibed as he reached their table. "Captain Kincaid here has seen General Gordon and has some interesting news for you."

"Good, we hope," Alex said, offering Kincaid a seat on his bench.

"Yes, quite," Anderson confirmed as he plopped down on the bench next to Mike, "based on what the Captain reported just now to Colonel Thompson."

"Thank you, Lieutenant," Kincaid said icily, glaring at Anderson. "I think I can handle the rest of it from here."

Anderson flushed at the rebuke and looked appropriately contrite.

Kincaid turned to Alex and Mike. "I met with General Gordon briefly and conveyed your urgent request to speak with him. Apparently, Colonel Thompson's note piqued his curiosity as did the handgun I showed him."

Noting the sudden concern in Alex's eyes, Kincaid quickly added, "I left the weapon with General Gordon. He seemed quite taken with it. In any event, he directed Colonel Thompson to deliver you to his headquarters tonight, along with the other sidearm. So, if you gentlemen have finished your meal, your transportation is waiting outside the gate. Lieutenant Anderson and I will accompany you to ensure you find your way without mishap."

'…To ensure you find your way without mishap.' Alex digested Kincaid's words, finding them distasteful. *Still smacks of house arrest to me.*

"Thank you, Captain, for your hospitality and for interceding on our behalf," Alex said, shaking his hand and offering an appreciative smile.

Kincaid shrugged modestly as though it had just been a routine matter for him.

"Then, if you will please come with me…" he said, getting to his feet and ducking out the open side of the tent.

Alex and Mike quickly pushed away from the table and followed him across the parade ground to the barred gate. Anderson brought up the rear.

"Sergeant of the Guard! Open the gate!" Kincaid ordered loudly as they approached the guard tower.

A face peered down at them from high in the tower. Recognizing the two Confederate officers, the Sergeant of the Guard complied instantly. "Open the gate!" he yelled.

Two soldiers sprang from the shadows and promptly slid the heavy oak bar through the iron brackets securing the gate.

As the gate swung open, Alex observed a mule-drawn freight wagon in the moonlight beyond the opening. A colored man and a small boy sat on the wagon seat. Nearby, a soldier stood holding the reins of two saddled horses.

As he led them to the wagon, Kincaid pointed at the man and boy perched on the seat, "This is Big Joe and his son Little Joe; they'll give you a ride to General Gordon's headquarters in Petersburg."

Big Joe merely nodded, then looked away.

Taking the reins of one of the horses from the soldier, Kincaid swung easily into the saddle. "Big Joe," he called to the teamster, "Lieutenant Anderson and I will lead the way. Follow us, but not too close; my horse will kick your mules if they don't keep a proper distance."

"Yas, suh," Big Joe drawled.

Alex nudged Mike with his elbow. "Our coach awaits!"

They hoisted themselves onto the back of the wagon.

With his passengers stowed as comfortably as they were going to get on the hard floorboards behind the wagon seat, Big Joe waited for Kincaid and Anderson to ride ahead, then shouted "Ha!" and flicked his whip at the mules' hindquarters. Jarringly, the freight wagon began rolling along the rutted road. Brilliant moonlight flooded the denuded landscape, and ahead of them, the powdery surface of the plank road glowed like a ribbon of white sandy beach.

Alex found himself enjoying the surreal scenery as the wagon rumbled noisily towards Petersburg.

Twenty minutes into the ride without a word being spoken, Alex decided to strike up a conversation with the driver. "Big Joe, mind if I ask you a few questions?"

"No, suh," Big Joe replied but the words were uttered with little enthusiasm.

"How is it that you and your son are working for the Confederate Army?"

"We works fo' our freedom."

"You're slaves?"

"Yas, suh."

"Someone in Petersburg owns you?"

"No, suh. We comes up fum Georgia wit' Massah when he comes ta fight in Marse Robert's army. Massah hires me 'n Little Joe out ta work fo' de army. Massah say if we help Marse Robert win de war, den he free us."

"President Lincoln has already freed all the slaves—haven't you heard?"

"Tha's so?" Big Joe grunted, pulling out a corncob pipe from his shirt pocket and sticking the stem in his mouth. "I don' tink Massah got de word yet. I be sure ta tell'im when I see'im."

Alex heard a familiar metallic clicking sound. A little flame suddenly illuminated Big Joe's face. Fascinated, Alex watched Big Joe's cheeks pucker as he inhaled through the pipe stem, drawing the flame down into the pipe-bowl. Then again he heard the metallic click, and the flame disappeared.

Alex and Mike looked at each other.

"Whataya got there, Big Joe?" Alex asked, keeping his voice pleasantly inquisitive.

Big Joe looked perplexed for a moment. "Yo mean dis?" he asked, holding up a small silver object that reflected the moonlight.

"Yeah. What's that?"

"It be my fire maker."

"May I see it? 'Promise I'll give it back to you."

Alex sensed reluctance on the man's part, but Big Joe handed him his *fire maker* without comment.

"Is that what I think it is?" Mike whispered.

"Uh-huh," Alex grunted, holding the object up and examining it in the moonlight. "It's a cigarette lighter."

"I didn't know they had cigarette lighters in the Civil War," Mike said, keeping his voice low so Big Joe and his son couldn't overhear their conversation.

"Not like this, they didn't." Alex handed it to him. "This one's custom made—check the engraving on the case."

Mike squinted at the inscription on the silver case, and read it aloud: *"Get a Hun!"* Mike's breath suddenly caught in his throat as he scanned the artwork below the inscription. "Holy cow!" he gasped. "There's an engraving of a German biplane crashing in flames! I can make out the Iron Crosses on its wings and tail!

Obviously, it's not ours or Tom's, so where did Big Joe get this?" Mike wondered aloud, handing it back to Alex.

"Let's find out." Alex reached up and tapped Big Joe on the shoulder with the lighter.

Sitting hunched over on the wagon seat, Big Joe glimpsed the *fire maker* in Alex's hand. Assuming it was being returned as promised, he snatched the lighter without a word and stuffed it into his pants pocket.

"Can you read, Big Joe?" Alex asked.

"No, suh," he answered perfunctorily without taking his eyes off the team of mules.

"That's a nice *fire maker*, Big Joe," Alex nodded appreciatively. "Did you buy it in Petersburg? I'd like one for myself."

"No, suh. I don' buy it. Ma boy, Li'l Joe, fin' it in de woods den gib it ta me."

"In the woods where?" Alex pursued casually, looking from Big Joe to Little Joe.

"I don' know. He fin' dat t'ing lon' time ago. May be he 'member whar he fin' dat, eh Li'l Joe?"

Little Joe nodded, then shyly looked down at his feet.

"Yo' go'n haf do bettah den dat, boy. Dese men can't hear yo' head rattle back dere! Speak up!"

Little Joe was a skinny kid, about thirteen years old, and a head shorter than his father. He shrugged his shoulders, then turned on his seat and gave Alex a sidelong glance.

Alex saw fear in his eyes as the boy peered down at him.

"Don't be afraid, son. We don't want the *fire maker* you found. It's finder's keepers. Someone lost it; then you found it, so now it's yours and your daddy's. Okay?"

The boy nodded but avoided his gaze.

Alex reached into his pocket and pulled out a pearl-handled

penknife. "Little Joe, I'll make you a deal. Tell me where and when you found the *fire maker*, and I'll give you this real pretty penknife."

Little Joe's eyes opened wide with astonishment. Taking the penknife from Alex's hand, the boy's face glowed with wonder as he ran his fingers over the mother-of-pearl handle.

"I fin' dat t'ing on top o' de hill where'n Papa n' me stay when we come here from Georgia."

"And where would that be?" Alex coaxed.

"He mean de Boisseau farm 'tween White Oak Road 'n de Boydton Plank Road," Big Joe interjected. "Massah 'n Marse Boisseau ol' friends. We stay dere 'bout six months ago 'til de soldiers come n' toll us ta leabe. Den de soldiers burn de house. Li'l Joe n' de udder chilluns play in de woods on de high hill by de creek dey call Grably Run. Ders some big ol' trees on top o' de hill. De chilluns climb in dose trees all de time."

Mike gave Alex a quizzical look. "Sounds familiar, doesn't it?"

"Yeah, and if that's the same hill where Little Joe found the lighter, it got up there before we did. Our being here has something to do with that knoll, Mike, I'm sure of it. I remember reading a magazine article a few years ago about Britain's early inhabitants. The Celts and their Druid priests believed that certain groves of ancient oaks possessed magical powers. They were centers of pagan worship. The isle of Anglesey off the northern coast of Wales was where the Druids had their most sacred grove. The article went on to say that the Romans put the Druids out of business by cutting down the sacred oaks on the island. But Patricus, a Roman Centurion, in his account of the incident contended that the destruction of the oaks never happened; the story had been fabricated by the Druids to stir up opposition to Roman rule. According to Patricus, the Romans found no such grove of trees when they arrived on the island, and when questioned, the inhabitants claimed that the oaks had suddenly vanished. There may have been something to the Druid belief in the ancient groves possessing magical power. *And*, we both know there's something weird about those old oaks on the knoll where we camped. Maybe they're magical too—whatdoya think?"

"Beats me," Mike shrugged wearily. "This just gets *curiouser and curiouser*."

The conversation tapered off as they reached the outskirts of Petersburg. The Plank Road evolved into a thoroughfare that Alex and Mike vaguely recognized as Washington Street. A scene of utter desolation greeted them when they entered the heart of the city. No lights shone in any of the windows or doorways of homes and shops lining the streets. The only sounds were theirs—the clatter of shod hooves and iron wheel rims echoing through winding canyons of dark and deserted cobblestone streets.

Anderson reined his horse aside and waited for Big Joe to catch up. As he rode alongside the wagon, his voice echoed off the vacant three and four-story buildings towering above Bollingbrook Street. "Not much to see in the city at night I'm afraid. As you might expect, many of the townspeople fled when Grant began shelling the city, but there's still a surprising number going about their business during the day despite an occasional cannonball dropping in. A shell fired from *The Dictator* generally gets more attention than most. People scramble for shelter when they hear it coming."

"What's *The Dictator*?" Mike asked.

"Oh, you haven't heard of it?" Anderson seemed surprised. "Well, it's a monster seacoast mortar that the Yankees have on a railroad flatcar in the vicinity of Battery 5. It hurls a 13-inch shell into the city on a regular basis. Fortunately, most of them don't do much damage; the townspeople view them as more of a nuisance than a danger."

Just before eleven o'clock, Big Joe turned his mules onto a side street and stopped in front of a stuccoed two-story mansion on the southeast side of the city. The clatter of hooves suddenly greeted them as a half-dozen mounted Confederate officers entered the cobblestone street from a narrow lane leading from the rear of the house. Only one or two bothered to glance at the escorted wagon as they rode past into the darkness.

Kincaid and Anderson stopped and dismounted. Two sentries stood at their posts on either side of the steps leading up to the mansion's front door; both saluted.

Kincaid returned the salutes then handed his horse's reins to Anderson. "Lieutenant, how about remaining here with the horses. I'll be inside just long enough to introduce our guests and give this valise to General Gordon; then we'll head back to camp."

"Uh...yes, sir," Alex heard the disappointment in Anderson's voice as he and Mike climbed down from the wagon.

Kincaid turned to one of the sentries. "I'm Captain Kincaid, Deputy Provost Marshal, Hill's Corps. General Gordon sent for these two gentlemen."

"Yes, sir," the sentry replied. "You may go in. We were told to expect you."

Alex noted the small leather valise gripped in Kincaid's left hand as they followed him up the steps—he had a pretty good idea what it contained.

Beyond the grand entryway, Alex and Mike found themselves inside a dark foyer.

"This way, please," Kincaid said in a hushed voice as he led them into a hallway and turned into the first doorway.

Seated at a table where he was writing in a ledger, Major Moore looked up when the three men entered the room. He promptly closed the ledger, pushed his chair back from the table, and crossed the room to greet them. "Ahh, Captain Kincaid," he smiled, offering his hand "You made good time! You're back sooner than I expected!"

Kincaid shook his hand, but Moore's eyes had now strayed to the strange uniforms of his other visitors.

"And these are the gentlemen General Gordon is expecting?" he said, although it was more of a statement than a question.

"Yes, sir. Allow me to introduce Captain Wright and Lieutenant Dent."

Moore shook their hands heartily. "Good! Good! General Gordon's expecting you in the study. Your arrival is timely. The command briefing just broke up."

"Isn't it a little late for a command briefing?" Kincaid asked, his curiosity piqued.

"Yes. I suppose it is," Moore replied without further explanation. "So, if you'll come with me, I'll take you to the study. It's late, and we don't want to keep the General waiting."

Moore led them to the end of the dimly lit hallway to a closed mahogany double door. He rapped gently and waited.

"Enter!" answered a deep, resonant voice.

Alex looked around as he followed Moore into the study but saw little of interest aside from an abundance of cane bottom chairs and a long oak table.

Movement at the far side of the room caught his eye. A high-backed leather swivel chair in front of a fireplace turned slightly, and Alex glimpsed the profile of a thin, stern-looking man in his shirtsleeves studying a sheath of papers lying in his lap. He appeared to be in his mid-forties with a severely receding hairline and a thick, bushy mustache and goatee.

Kincaid entered last, pausing by the doorway as Moore strode to the middle of the room to announce the visitors. "Sir, Captain Kincaid has returned with the two… ah… gentlemen you sent for."

Alex noted Moore's reluctance to refer to them as *officers*.

General Gordon finished reading the document in his hand before looking at them. "Did you bring the other handgun as I instructed, Captain Kincaid?"

"Yes, sir. It's in this valise."

"Thank you. Leave it on the table; then I'd prefer to speak with these gentlemen privately."

Moore promptly retraced his steps to the doorway.

Kincaid strode forward, placed the valise on the table, then hesitated. "Sir, will these gentlemen be leaving with me?"

"Are they prisoners of war?"

"No, sir. They aren't, unless you decide otherwise."

Gordon was silent for a moment as he read another document. "Then, Captain, I don't see any reason for you to remain. Thank you for your diligence, and convey my appreciation to Colonel Thompson. You may tell him that he's relieved of further responsibility for these gentlemen. I'll see to their subsistence and lodging."

"Yes, sir." Kincaid saluted smartly, did an about face, and nodded to Moore as he left the room.

Moore then stepped into the hallway and closed the double wooden doors behind him.

Alex and Mike stood by the table, waiting.

General Gordon continued his perusal of the papers in his lap, ignoring his visitors.

A long minute passed with Alex and Mike exchanging uncomfortable glances.

"Unless you fellows like standing, why don't you have a seat," the general said, pointing to a couple of chairs near the fireplace. "While you're at it, bring that valise on the table over here with you."

Being closest to it, Alex picked up the valise and carried it over to where Gordon was sitting. Alex held the valise in his outstretched hand; however, still absorbed in his papers Gordon ignored him.

After a long hellish day, Alex was tired and irritable and rapidly developing a dislike for the man. "As you know, General, there's a gun in this bag. Aren't you worried I might use it?"

Gordon gave the valise a cursory glance, then looked up at Alex.

"You plan to shoot me?"

"No, sir."

"Then I'm not worried."

Alex dropped the valise on the floor by Gordon's foot. It made a loud *thud* as it struck the marble tiled floor.

"I'll take that seat now, General," Alex said, pulling up one of the cane bottom chairs.

Gordon frowned as he tossed the sheath of papers onto the hearth in front of the fireplace, then leaned back in his chair and contemplated his visitors.

"Okay. Let's have it. Who are you and what are you doing here?" Gordon demanded. "And don't give me that rot about being from Mosby's command. I have neither the time nor the patience for games. Lie to me and I'll have you strung up as spies."

Gordon caught the nervous glance the one named Dent gave his companion.

"Well?" Gordon growled, already beginning to lose his small store of patience.

"And if you still don't believe us?" Alex treaded cautiously.

"I'll let you know," Gordon said with an icy smile. "Seems you boys are stuck between a rock and a hard place. Try telling the truth and let's see how it fits."

"Okay," Alex nodded. "I'll tell you some things, and you can draw your own conclusions."

Gordon's eyes narrowed as he waited for Alex to continue.

"Have you seen our side arms?"

"Captain Kincaid brought one to me earlier in the day. I examined it."

"I suggest you look at the one in the bag as well."

Gordon reached down, opened the valise, and withdrew a leather holster with a pistol belt wrapped around it. He unwrapped the belt, then pointed at the bold *U.S.* letters embossed on the holster's flap. He raised an eyebrow as if to say: *Care to explain this?* Next, he unsnapped the holster's flap and gingerly withdrew the pistol with his fingertips. He gazed at it admiringly as he examined it by the light of the fire. "Looks just like the other one," he said finally, rendering his verdict

Alex noted the magazine inserted in the .45's hand grip. *Most likely it's still loaded.*

"I assure you, General, no one living today has ever seen a handgun like this one. Look at the barrel, see the date stamped on it?"

Gordon held the pistol so the light from the fireplace played on the barrel. "Patented *August 19, 1911*," he read aloud. "I noticed the same dating error on the other weapon."

Mike started to interject that the dates weren't errors; however, a darting glance and an almost imperceptible shake of the head from Alex told him to keep his mouth shut, so he just leaned back in his chair and continued listening.

For the moment, Alex chose to ignore Gordon's observation about the dating error. "The handgun you're holding is semi-automatic, meaning it will fire each time you pull the trigger."

Gordon didn't appear impressed. "Similar innovations have been applied to carbines and rifles manufactured in the North, including those produced by Mr. Colt. We've captured a few Spencer carbines and Henry rifles, but the South can't reproduce them or manufacture ammunition for those we've recovered on the battlefield. So," he shrugged, "it was only a matter of time before the North produced superior pistols using the same technology."

"Don't look for these to be in the hands of Union troops any time soon," Mike joined in, no longer able to restrain himself.

Failing to understand Mike's meaning, Gordon queried "If this is an experimental firearm, how did you acquire it?"

Instead of answering, Alex decided to change tack. "General, you held a meeting tonight with your division and brigade commanders to present your plan for an attack on Fort Stedman before dawn on March 25th. *Ostensibly*, your plan is to envelop Grant's right flank between Fort Stedman and the Appomattox River, then destroy his lines of communication."

Gordon's eyes betrayed the alarm bells Alex had just set off.

"Shall I continue?" Alex smiled confidently.

Shifting uncomfortably in his chair, Gordon re-crossed his legs. "Go on," he nodded.

"For your plan to succeed, General Lee must strip his defenses elsewhere to support your attack. Under cover of darkness your troops will move forward from Colquitt's Salient and remove the obstructions separating your lines from the enemy's, a distance of about 150 yards. When you give the signal—a rifle shot—the assault will begin. Disguised as Union soldiers, 300 of your troops will rush to the rear of the Union works pretending they're pickets being driven back by the enemy. Your reasoning is based on the premise that when one sparrow flies, the whole flock usually flies." Alex paused and nodded his admiration.

"As I was saying," he continued, "three companies of 100 men each will push on to the Union rear and capture the garrisons and cannon in three small forts overlooking Fort Stedman. The captured cannon will then be turned against the Union works, subjecting them to artillery fire from both front and rear. After securing the breach in the Union line, Confederate cavalry will push through and destroy Grant's lines of communication—rail, telegraph, and bridges."

Alex leaned back in his chair and folded his arms. "So, General, have I correctly outlined your plan?"

"How in the hell do you know all that?" Gordon demanded, squinting hard at Alex. "Some of those details weren't worked out until tonight! Just who are you?"

"It doesn't matter, General. It's too difficult to explain, and you wouldn't believe me if I told you."

Anger simmered in Gordon's eyes. "I hate to spoil the evening for you boys, but your future just took a turn for the worst. Like I said, we execute spies in this army."

Gordon suddenly snatched up the .45 in his lap and pointed it at Alex. "I was a bit premature telling Captain Kincaid not to wait for you. It appears you'll be returning to the Provost Marshal's stockade tonight after all, although I must admit this meeting has been entertaining."

Alex smiled and shook his head. "You don't want to do that, General. Not if you want your *real* plan to succeed. If you remember, I prefaced my summary of your battle plan with the word *ostensibly*?"

Gordon squinted narrowly over the pistol sights but kept the .45 pointed squarely between Alex's eyes. "Yes, I remember," he nodded. "Go on."

Mike sat quietly, watching Gordon and Alex as though they were performers in a Shakespearean drama.

"Don't keep me in suspense, sir," Gordon glowered at Alex. "Continue!"

"It's really President Lincoln you're after, isn't it?"

Gordon slumped back in his chair, a stunned expression on his face—the hand holding the pistol dropped to his lap.

"How...?" Gordon hesitated, grasping for words. "How could you have known?"

"It doesn't matter how we know or who we are," Alex said, leaning forward in his chair and looking Gordon in the eye. "What matters is: we're here to help you. If you fail, the future will take a direction that will prolong the misery of this war."

Gordon contemplated his visitors for several seconds. "And just how do you intend to help me?" he asked warily, cutting straight to the chase.

Alex was prepared for the question. "As we both know, sir, only two of your hand-picked companies will be sent to take the three small forts in the enemy's rear. The third company will be assigned the task of capturing General Meade's headquarters. If they get through, they stand a good chance of capturing not only President Lincoln but possibly Grant and Meade as well. Such an event would be disastrous to the Union cause."

Gordon paled noticeably, shaken by Alex's revelation.

"Y'know, General, I was baffled at first as to how you knew Lincoln would be at Meade's headquarters. Then this morning the answer literally landed in my lap. I knew the moment I saw it that Lincoln was your real quarry."

Gordon looked puzzled. "You've lost me. What are you talking about?"

Alex withdrew a packet of paper from the top of one of his leggings and handed it to Gordon. "This morning we encountered a Union courier and his escort who, unfortunately for them, decided to shoot it out with us. I found these messages in the courier's dispatch case. As you can see, they clearly reveal the arrangements for Lincoln's forthcoming visit to the Union army. Confederate agents have been tapping the Union telegraph lines along the James River for months, so you knew of Lincoln's upcoming visit almost as soon as Grant did."

Gordon gave the messages a cursory glance then tossed them on the pile of the papers he had dropped on the hearth, confirming Alex's assertion that the General already knew what they contained.

Gordon merely looked at Alex and shrugged "Yes, so...?"

"Hate to rain on your parade some more, General, but you won't capture Lincoln or anyone else of importance for the simple reason that your troops won't be able to find Meade's headquarters in the dark. By daylight, Lincoln and everyone with him will be beyond your grasp. So, that's where Lieutenant Dent and I enter the picture. To fix the problem, you need us to act as guides for your company. We know the exact location of Meade's headquarters."

Gordon appeared dubious. "And why should I believe you?"

"Could it be because our lives depend on it?" Alex reluctantly reminded him.

Gordon contemplated him for a moment without commenting; then shifted his gaze to Mike. "And you, sir? What have you to say?"

Mike opened his mouth but all that came out was a rasping sound, like a dog with a hair up his nose. He swallowed and cleared his throat. "Captain Wright speaks for me as well, sir."

"I see," Gordon grunted, unimpressed, and turned back to Alex. "I'm a sensible man who deals in logic and hard facts; ergo, I don't put any store in fortune-tellers, mind readers, seances, and the like. Nothing I've seen or heard tonight makes any sense; however, it's impossible for you to have known my plans for attacking Fort Stedman before I shared them with anyone. To even entertain the possibility of where you might have come from is unsettling—" Gordon paused as he considered the disturbing notion in spite of himself. "Uh...I don't suppose you'd mind telling me when you were born?"

Alex smiled and shook his head. "I really don't think you want to know, sir."

Gordon nodded, beginning to understand more than he wanted to admit, yet sensing how little he really understood. "Let's say I buy your story—where do we go from here?"

"Suppose we start with you returning our side arms, General," Alex said. "Secondly, we'd appreciate knowing the condition of our comrade, Sergeant Thomas Hill. As you probably know, he was wounded this morning, and the Provost Marshal sent him to a field hospital. I'm confident he'll receive more attentive care if you express interest in his welfare."

"I'll have Major Moore inquire into his condition. As for your weapons—" Gordon's eyes registered a thin veil of understanding as he holstered the .45 and handed it to Alex. "—just be careful you don't shoot your father or grandfather by mistake."

Alex slid the weapon out of the holster and checked the serial number. "This one's yours," he said, handing it to Mike. Alex looked at Gordon expectantly.

Gordon reached down and picked up a bundle wrapped in paper and tied with string lying on the floor between his chair and the hearth. As he untied the string, the wrapping fell away revealing another identical holster belt. "Must be yours," he said, handing it to Alex.

Alex slipped the .45 from its holster, inspected it thoroughly, then removed the magazine and counted the bullets. The magazine still held seven rounds, confirming it had not been fired. Next, he slid the barrel assembly back and forth twice—the action worked smoothly. Satisfied no one had tampered with it, Alex returned the weapon to its holster.

Mike made a similar inspection of his .45, after which they both buckled on their pistol belts.

Gordon rose from his chair, watched quietly until they finished, then led them to the door of the study. "I'll have Major Moore make arrangements for your lodging in the carriage house. I think you'll find it satisfactory. Get some sleep then join me here for breakfast at 7 o'clock. Tomorrow will be a busy day; we have a lot of details yet to work out."

In the hallway Gordon left his guests with Major Moore, bid them all a pleasant night, and started up the staircase to his quarters. On the third step he paused. "Oh, one more thing, Major Moore; please issue them a couple of passes. They'll be joining me for breakfast and will probably be in and out of the headquarters during the day." He cast a glance at Alex then added as an apparent afterthought, "You'll need the passes to get past my sentries and for other places as well. Keep them on you at all times."

"Yes, sir. Good night, sir!" Alex said, watching Gordon's shadowy figure disappear up the dark staircase.

Major Moore returned to his office, took a ring of keys and a couple of passes from a desk drawer, and handed them to the Officer of the Day. "Major Hollis, please be kind enough to show these gentlemen to the General's guest room."

Alex and Mike trudged wearily behind Major Hollis out the back door, across a cobblestoned courtyard, then up an exterior staircase to the carriage house's second-story level. As they climbed the stairs, Hollis explained that the lower level had been converted into billets for the headquarters' sentries and couriers. When they reached the landing at the top, Alex and Mike listened patiently to the jangle of keys as Hollis fumbled with them in the dark. Finally; they heard a distinctive *click* as he found the right one then pushed the door open. "The privy is behind the carriage house," Hollis resumed, pointing in the general direction, "but you'll find a crock under the washstand if it's too cold or wet to go outside. You both look pretty ragged—get some sleep. 'Anything else you need?"

"Thanks, but no," Alex said, eyeing the closest bed. He couldn't remember ever being so totally drained. "A soft clean bed will do just fine."

Chapter 12

Headquarters, Gordon's Corps, Army of Northern Virginia
7:00 A.M., MARCH 24, 1865

Two aged, black male servants rapped on their door just after daylight. "Mornin', gen'men," they announced cheerfully as they opened the door and entered the room without invitation. One carried a washbasin and pitcher of hot water; the other bore towels, a shaving mug and brush, and a straight-edged razor.

"Compliments of Major Moore, I suppose?" Alex asked as he sat up in bed and rubbed his eyes.

"Yas, suh! De Major, he tink may be yo might wanna wash up befo' yo eats wit de Gen'ral."

"Yeah," Alex nodded sleepily as he listened to Mike groan. "Tell Major Moore we're much obliged for his hospitality."

"Yas, suh! We sho will," one of them said as they set everything on the table, then hurriedly left the room.

An hour later, the sun shone brightly on the wet cobblestones as Alex and Mike crossed the courtyard between the carriage house and Gordon's headquarters. The elevation on which the property stood offered a dazzling view of a brilliant sunrise and church spires silhouetted against the city's skyline.

At the rear entrance to the mansion, they showed their passes to the lone sentry, a mountain of a man in butternut homespun who stood in the doorway brandishing a bayonet-tipped rifle. Giving their passes only a cursory glance, the sentry surveyed them from head to toe with obvious contempt and continued to bar their path.

"The General's expecting us," Mike insisted, waving his pass in front of the sentry's nose.

"That so?" the sentry sneered through cracked, puffy lips revealing a black void where a front tooth should have been. He spat a brown stream of tobacco juice at Mike's feet then wiped the spittle off his beard with the back of his hand. "You jaybirds best be on your way, 'cause you ain't gettin' in here to see squat."

Mike caught a whiff of the sentry's foul breath as the tobacco wad *splat* on the cobblestone beside his boot. He stuffed the pass into his tunic breast pocket with his left hand while with his right, he unsnapped the flap on his holster and slipped his fingers around the wooden grips of his .45.

The movement didn't go unnoticed; the sentry cocked his rifle and stared down at Mike like a rattlesnake ready to strike.

"Mike!" Alex snapped impatiently. "Quit playing around! The General's waiting for us!"

In the blink of an eye, Alex's fist flew past Mike's nose and connected with the sentry's windpipe.

The sentry dropped his rifle and clutched his throat. Eyes bulging, he slowly sank to his knees, but whether the effect was caused by the sudden interruption of his air supply or having swallowed his tobacco plug, neither Alex nor Mike could say for certain.

"After you," Alex said, smiling smugly as he stooped to pick up the sentry's rifle.

"Really, Alex! I'm embarrassed to be seen in public with you! Must you always cause a scene?" Mike gibed as he stepped toward the door.

Inside, Alex stuck his head inside the open doorway of Major Moore's office. Moore wasn't in; a captain sat at his desk with his nose stuck in a newspaper. "Captain Wright and Lieutenant Dent to see General Gordon," Alex said loudly, to get his attention.

Startled, the captain looked up and stared at them blankly for a moment. "He's through those doors," he said, pointing in the direction of the closed double doors at the end of the hall. "The General's expecting you, but I'll announce you if you like."

"That's okay," Alex waved him off as he started to rise from his chair. "We know the way."

Alex and Mike found Gordon seated at the table in the study. He smiled and gestured for them to have a seat. "Help yourselves to the biscuits, preserves, and tea. There's porridge of sorts in the covered dish if you really want something that'll stick to your ribs. It's a meager breakfast, but it's a damn sight better than the fare most of our boys are having this morning."

Alex leaned the rifle against the table and took a seat facing his host.

Gordon sipped hot tea from a cup cradled in his hands and curiously eyed the rifle with its long, thin bayonet as Alex unfolded his napkin and placed it on his lap. "Going hunting this morning?" he asked casually.

Alex reached for a biscuit from the white linen-covered basket in the center of the table before answering. "Possibly. The rifle belongs to your friendly sentry guarding the back door. He didn't object to my borrowing it for awhile."

"Oh?" Gordon blew gently on his tea to cool it before taking another sip.

"Yes, sir. Just a prince of a fellow, wasn't he, Mike?"

"Oh, yeah!" Mike chimed in. "And a gifted conversationalist as well."

Gordon smiled, obviously amused. "I'm rather surprised he was so accommodating—especially since I told him to pick a fight with you."

"Well, you can give him an 'A' for that!" Mike laughed, "But why sic him on us?"

"To test your mettle before I put you to work."

"Did we pass?" Alex asked, reaching for the bowl of preserves.

Gordon nodded his approval. "I trust you didn't injure my sergeant. He's been with me since the beginning of the war; there's never been a better or braver soldier."

"He's okay," Alex replied as he smeared peach preserves on his biscuit, "but it might be a day or two before he feels like singing."

"Good," Gordon chuckled, apparently satisfied, "so let's move on to other matters. I invited another guest to join us this morning. He should be along any minute. He's a native of Petersburg and is well-acquainted with the area where we'll launch our assault. I've decided to use the three of you as guides for the company I've assigned to capture Meade's headquarters. With so much at stake, there can be no margin for error, so I'm sending you on a little scouting mission before we begin the assault. If everything goes well, I anticipate all of you meeting at the rendezvous point to link up with the company. If not, then I'm counting on at least one of you reaching the rendezvous point to complete the job."

A soft knock at the door interrupted Gordon's discourse. Excusing himself, he went to the door while Alex and Mike continued eating.

"Ahh, you're just in time! We were just talking about you!" Gordon greeted his visitor who remained out of view in the hall.

"Nothing too loathsome I hope, sir!" a familiar voice said from beyond the doorway.

"Not at all! I mentioned only your redeeming qualities," Gordon answered jovially.

"Then I haven't missed much, have I?" the voice countered in fine humor.

Recognizing the voice, Alex and Mike exchanged surprised glances as Lieutenant Anderson's tall figure entered the room.

"Allow me to introduce my other guests," Gordon said, closing the door behind Anderson.

"That won't be necessary, sir," Alex interjected. "We had the pleasure of Lieutenant Anderson's company yesterday afternoon."

Anderson paused, an astonished grin on his face. "Well! Well! I must say, this really is a bit much, but I'm delighted to see the two of you again! When we dropped you off here last night, I had no idea I would see you again so soon. They're splendid chaps, don't you think, sir?"

"Oh, yes! I have never met anyone quite like them," Gordon responded tongue in cheek. "Come! Pull up a chair and join us. Help yourself to whatever is left on the table."

Anderson eased into the remaining vacant chair, then did a double take at the rifle leaning against the table next to Alex. "Trouble?" he asked, nodding at the weapon.

"No thanks. Already had some," Alex replied, savoring another bite of buttermilk biscuit and preserves.

"That's jolly good!" Anderson chuckled as he helped himself to a bowl of porridge. Putting a spoonful in his mouth, he grimaced, "Good God, what is this?"

"Porridge or possum tail soup, I forget which—tastes about the same," Alex answered.

Anderson set the bowl aside and reached for a biscuit instead.

After a few minutes of pleasantries, Gordon pushed his chair away from the table and cleared his throat to get everyone's attention. "Lieutenant Anderson, when I brought you into my confidence, I told you that I planned to send three hundred men disguised as Union soldiers behind the enemy's main line to capture three small forts. That much is true; however, I must confess that I wasn't entirely forthcoming. I trust you will forgive me."

Anderson raised a puzzled brow but gave the expected reply, "Yes, sir."

"As these other gentlemen already know," Gordon continued, "Fort Stedman and the three forts in the Union rear are only intermediate objectives. Our primary objective is to capture the Headquarters of the Army of the Potomac."

Anderson made a low whistle, registering his surprise.

Gordon observed that his breakfast guests had stopped eating and were listening attentively. "Based on intercepted dispatches, I'm convinced that President Lincoln and possibly other cabinet and senior military leaders will be staying over tonight as guests of General Meade at his headquarters. Lincoln is at this moment making a good-will tour of the Petersburg and Richmond encampments. Just imagine the implications if we capture Lincoln and possibly Grant and Meade as well."

Alex nodded his appreciation of the far-reaching consequences of such an event. "Are General Lee and President Davis aware of Lincoln's overnight stay?" he asked, hoping Gordon would provide the answer to such an historical question. "And have they approved your plan to capture Meade's headquarters?"

Gordon regarded Alex with a glassy smile. "For someone possessing so much *hindsight*, Captain Wright, I'm surprised you're asking me that. I hope you won't take it personally if I tell you that it's *none of your business*. We both must keep our little secrets, mustn't we?"

Alex immediately realized his error in asking such a question. This assault would be *the last hurrah* for the Confederacy—a final roll-of-the-dice win or lose gamble. If Gordon failed to capture Lincoln or Grant, or if either were killed in the attempt, the game would be over. Anticipating the adverse Union reaction to either eventuality, Gordon was taking extraordinary measures to shield the Confederate top leadership from what might later be perceived as a kidnapping or assassination plot. In a worse case scenario, he would accept all responsibility for the outcome and simply attribute it to the misfortunes of war.

Gordon pushed aside a curtain covering a section of the wall revealing a large map of Petersburg and its extensive fortifications and trench lines. Pausing to detach the bayonet from the rifle propped against the table, Gordon used it as a pointer as he started to brief the key elements of his plan.

"Feel free to ask questions at any time," he began. "Here is the phased sequence of events in preparation for the attack: Phase 1 will commence at 8:00 P.M. tonight with our engineers removing the obstacles in front of Colquitt's Salient from here to here," Gordon explained, drawing the bayonet tip across the map.

Alex was acquainted with this particular area. In 1918 it had been a popular weekend destination for the *doughboys* training at Camp Lee. During his first few weeks at the camp he had explored the ground that Gordon now described.

"Won't the enemy pickets hear the noise and sound the alarm?" Anderson asked, already warming to the discussion.

Gordon shook his head. "Their picket line is stretched thin, and most of the pickets are usually napping or playing cards. Their officers rarely inspect them. If they do hear anything, they'll probably assume it's our boys scavenging for food in the cornfields between the lines—a common practice. It's generally understood and agreed to by their pickets and ours to live and let live in this sector. I'm told there's a lot of unauthorized visiting and fraternization between the two picket lines."

Picking up where he had left off, Gordon pointed the bayonet tip at them. "You gentlemen represent Phase 2. At 10:00 P.M. the three of you will slip across the area cleared by our engineers. You will avoid the enemy pickets, then sidestep around Fort Stedman and proceed to the vicinity of Meade's headquarters."

"And just how do we *sidestep around Fort Stedman*, General?" Alex asked with a perplexed frown. "There are at least a thousand soldiers in and around that fort."

"You'll be disguised as Union staff officers, and if you use your head and your instincts, you should be able to bluff your way through," Gordon answered matter-of-factly. "I'm confident of your ability to pull it off."

"Your confidence in us is reassuring," Alex replied with more cynicism in his tone than he intended. "Just what is it you would like us to do after, that is, we slip through and around Meade's army and arrive at his headquarters?"

Gordon stifled a laugh. *By God! This irascible young pup is amusing!* "Above all," he replied, "I want you to get there without letting the cat out of the bag, so to speak. The three of you will scout the area around Meade's headquarters taking note of fortifications, obstacles, disposition of troop, roads and trails, and the *exact* location of Meade's headquarters tent.

Phase 3 begins at 4:00 A.M. at which time our picket line will advance and seize and silence the Union pickets in front of Fort Stedman. Fifty strong men, capable of doing quick and efficient work with sharp axes, will then rush across the open ground and cut a passage through the enemy's defensive barrier in front of the fort. Behind them will come a supporting column of massed infantry who will assault the fort and the adjacent earthworks. They will overrun the garrison before they can react, then turn the captured cannon on the flanking enemy works on both sides of the fort. Concurrently with the assault on Fort Stedman, a regimental-size force consisting of three hand-picked companies of one hundred men each, disguised as Union infantry, will enter the enemy's main line of works as though driven in by Confederate fire. Pretending to be retreating in panic, the companies will continue to the rear of Fort Stedman, pass through the line of Union infantry support, then advance to this bridge," he tapped the spot on the map with the tip of the bayonet, "over Harrison's Creek where they will link up with you.

Company A, commanded by Major Jonas, has the mission of capturing Meade's headquarters. He will depend on you to guide him there. Companies B and C, under the command of General Lewis, will follow Major Jonas' company to the high ground beyond the creek. Once he has gained the high ground, General Lewis' detachment will overpower the garrisons in three small forts overlooking Fort Stedman and employ the forts' cannon to prevent Union reinforcements from reaching Fort Stedman.

As quickly as possible, Major Jonas with Company A will converge on Meade's headquarters from three directions, surround it, and take as many prisoners as they can.

"And how much time do we have to do this?" Alex asked.

"Just be patient. I'll get to that in a moment," Gordon said with a taut smile, then continued. "You must finish scouting the area around Meade's headquarters and return to the bridge over Harrison's Creek behind Fort Stedman by 4:00 A.M. Each of you will wear a strip of white cloth around your neck so you can be distinguished from the enemy—Lewis and Jonas' commands will also be wearing strips of white cloth. All commanders participating in the attack tomorrow morning will instruct their troops not to fire on anyone wearing white scarves or white strips of cloth tied across their upper bodies. Of course, y'all realize that if you're captured wearing Union uniforms, you run the risk of being executed as spies?"

Gordon paused, letting this last remark sink in; however, he observed no hint of apprehension on their faces.

Satisfied, he continued: "I'll have my Quartermaster fit you up with Union officer uniforms this afternoon in the carriage house. I trust he can find some without noticeable bullet holes." Gordon smiled thinly, then picked up an envelope from the table and removed its contents. "These are passes bearing General Parke's forged signature. He commands the Union 9th Corps; you'll be operating in his area. If you're stopped for any reason, show your passes and identify yourselves as Inspector General staff officers from the 9th Corps Headquarters out inspecting encampments. There's a universal fear of Inspector Generals, so you probably won't be detained long.

Incidentally, I'm conducting a briefing here at 9:00 A.M. for General Lewis and Major Jonas. Plan on attending so you can meet and later recognize these officers. Except for them and the four of us, no one else participating in the attack tomorrow will know about this special phase of the plan. If Major Jonas should be killed, wounded, or captured, then whichever of you is the senior ranking survivor will assume command of his company. No one, repeat *no one*, else is to be told about the objective of this phase of the assault.

When the morning briefing is completed, I want you to accompany me to Colquitt's Salient—the ridge from which the attack will be launched. You'll want to familiarize yourselves with the lay of the land during daylight and conduct any coordination you may require with Lewis and Jonas.

Finally, Phase 4 will be a general assault by our infantry on the heels of the three companies. Supported by artillery, they'll seize Fort Stedman then roll up the Union flanks. By dawn they must also have seized the two forts immediately south and north of Fort Stedman—Fort Haskell and Fort McGilvray, respectively. Failure to take those forts will allow the enemy to concentrate their fire on Fort Stedman, making it untenable and forcing us to withdraw." Gordon frowned fleetingly as he contemplated the grim consequences, then moved on.

"When you capture Meade's headquarters, you must hold it until our cavalry or other reinforcements arrive. I will push a strong force through to relieve you by daylight.

Now for the most important point: under no circumstances is Lincoln to be harmed or endangered. If the enemy perceives our assault on Fort Stedman as a pretext to kill Lincoln, be assured if they win this war, that they will exact a terrible price from the South. Better not to attack at all than succeed and have Lincoln killed in the process. Am I clear on that point? Any questions?"

"Yes, sir," Mike volunteered. "I have one. Are any women accompanying Lincoln and his entourage?"

Gordon thought about it before answering. "The answer is: I don't know, but it's unlikely. A battlefield isn't a pretty sight; I wouldn't want my wife to see it. If it turns out I'm wrong, then use your best judgment in handling the matter within the bounds of gentlemanly decorum. Are there any other questions?"

Alex nodded. "If our detachment is challenged en route to Meade's headquarters, what do we do?"

"By that time all hell will have broken loose on the enemy's front lines. The detachment commanders will assume the identities of two Union officers who are connected with Fort Stedman. Show your pass if asked for it and say your detachment is being sent to protect

Meade's headquarters. Be pro-active; be pushy as hell. Tell'em to get out of the way; the Rebels have broken through. Everything has gone to hell, and the Army of the Potomac headquarters is in danger." Gordon flashed a sardonic grin. "Nothing's better than spreading panic in the enemy's rear!"

Alex smiled, appreciating the stratagem. "Not many men would be willing to shoulder the blame for delaying the detachment under those circumstances."

"Exactly," Gordon nodded, acknowledging the plan's simplicity and audacity.

CHAPTER 13

City Point, Virginia
9:00 P.M., MARCH 24, 1865

Lanterns mounted atop the pilings along the edge of the wharf glowed and flickered as Lieutenant General and Mrs. Ulysses S. Grant and Major General George G. Meade watched the *River Queen* prepare to dock. As the vessel eased within four or five feet of the wharf, deck hands tossed mooring lines to the waiting stevedores then ran a gangway out to the landing.

Grant and Meade waited at the foot of the gangway, while on board at the other end, the *River Queen's* officers hastily lined up along the ship's railing. Farther down the wharf, a small group of curious onlookers gathered at a respectful distance, gawking at Grant and his entourage.

A voice from on deck, presumably the ship's Captain, alerted Grant and Meade that their visitors were about to disembark. "Good evening, Mr. President. I trust you and Mrs. Lincoln found the voyage pleasant?"

"Yes, quite restful, thank you, Captain. We appreciate all that you and your splendid crew did to ensure our comfort and safety."

"Glad to be of service, Mr. President. Good night, sir."

The President held the First Lady's arm and steadied her as they descended the gangway. When they stepped onto the wharf, Grant and his wife received them with warm smiles.

Meade, tall, thin, and scholarly in appearance, stood politely aside, not wishing to intrude on so special an occasion.

Grant saluted his commander-in-chief and greeted the couple with genuine relish. "Welcome to City Point, Mr. President and Mrs. Lincoln!"

Lincoln smiled as Grant shook his proffered hand. The two wives embraced, then moved aside and engaged in pleasantries while their husbands conversed.

"General Grant, I can't tell you how pleased I was to receive your invitation," the jovial tone of Lincoln's voice masked the gravity in his eyes. "We have much to discuss."

Taking a nod from Grant as his cue, Meade stepped forward to welcome the President and the First Lady.

"Ahh! General Meade!" Lincoln said, turning to Meade and shaking his hand. "It's a pleasure to see you again, sir."

"The pleasure is mine, Mr. President. You timed your arrival perfectly; great things appear to be in the offing."

"Yes, I'm most anxious to hear about them."

"I realize the hour is late, Mr. President; however, there's a pressing matter that warrants your attention. I hope you're up to a meeting after your long voyage?" Grant sounded apologetic, but he got his message across.

"By all means, General. I'm quite rested and at your disposal!"

"Then with your approval, sir, Mrs. Grant and some of my officers' spouses will entertain Mrs. Lincoln while we attend to matters at my headquarters. I also made arrangements for you to stay at Appomattox Manor while you are here. As you may recall from your previous visit, it's that beautiful old home on the bluff adjacent to my headquarters. General Ingalls, my Chief Quartermaster who runs the City Point supply base, has been using the parlor for his office, but this morning he cheerfully vacated the premises so you and Mrs. Lincoln wouldn't be disturbed by the coming and going of his staff."

"That's very gracious of you and Mrs. Grant as well as considerate of General Ingalls," Lincoln replied, "however, our luggage is unpacked in our cabin aboard the *River Queen,* and I think it would be easier on everyone if we retained our accommodations aboard ship."

"Wherever you and Mrs. Lincoln will be most comfortable, Mr. President," Grant nodded his understanding, but the tone of his voice betrayed his disappointment. "However, should shipboard living become too snug for your liking, by all means let me know, and we'll make more suitable arrangements for you."

"As little time as we'll stay aboard the *River Queen* during our visit, I'm sure our stateroom will prove satisfactory. If Mary changes my mind about that, I'll let you know," Lincoln jested, rolling his eyes.

Grant smiled in commiseration, the crows' feet about his eyes crinkling jovially.

"My aide is waiting with transportation to take us up the hill to my headquarters," Grant said loudly enough for his wife and Mrs. Lincoln to hear.

The men strode across the wharf toward an ambulance wagon hitched to a six-horse team. The two women prattled congenially as they followed along several paces behind the men.

Lincoln gazed about as they strolled along the wharf. "I couldn't see much of the port facilities in the dark, General Grant, but they seem more extensive than I remember from my last visit."

"When that ammunition barge blew up a few months ago, it destroyed a large section of the wharf and storehouses." Grant pointed to the general area where the barge had been moored. "The Army Engineers did a commendable job repairing the damage and expanding the facilities. The wharf and storehouses now occupy nearly a half-mile of the City Point waterfront. The ammunition dock has been extended offshore for safety, but off-loading has been expedited by running a rail spur out to it. However the bulk of the ammunition and siege artillery is unloaded at Broadway Landing a few miles up the Appomattox River from here."

"Impressive," Lincoln said, squinting at some of the shadowy structures looming in the dark along the water's edge. "I hope to see more of City Point in daylight."

"Of course, Mr. President. A lot of changes have taken place since your last visit, and General Ingalls would be honored to show you his supply operations. However, I suggest waiting a day or two before touring the base. The way things are shaping up, I think tomorrow will be a busy and rewarding day for you elsewhere on the Petersburg front." Grant gave his Commander-in-Chief an emphatic nod communicating a meaning mutually understood.

The former ambulance had been converted to accommodate the steady flow of distinguished visitors to City Point. Beneath its white canvas roof, soft leather benches had been constructed along the interior walls of the wagon bed, and a set of fold-down steps permitted passengers to enter and exit the conveyance with minimum effort.

When everyone was comfortably seated, Grant's aide-de-camp secured the steps and latched the tailgate, then climbed aboard and seated himself next to the driver. With a crack of a coach whip the horses were set in motion, the iron-rimmed wheels rumbled noisily over the wharf's washboard-rough planks. Upon crossing from the wharf to the riverbank, the passengers were treated to more uncomfortable jarring as the ambulance lurched across three sets of railroad tracks and began ascending a steep, unevenly-paved incline that led to the heights above the river.

Lincoln launched into one of his humorous anecdotes as the ambulance's momentum slowed to a crawl. The horses leaned into their traces, their steel-shod hooves slipping alarmingly and frequently against the smooth cobblestone paving as they plodded toward the top of the grade.

Grant noticed the women didn't laugh or giggle—even dutifully—when Lincoln got to the punch line of his story and glanced in their direction to deduce the reason. Mrs. Lincoln had suddenly paled as she clutched the cushioned back support in a death grip and stared fearfully at the *River Queen* far below. Eyes closed, Mrs. Grant also appeared more than just a bit queasy. Grant knew she was afraid of heights and remembered laughing at her when she clasped her hands over her eyes on the downhill trek in the ambulance to meet the President's ship. Having taken seats opposite each other in the wagon, Grant was suddenly concerned that Mrs. Grant might become ill all over the First Lady's lap, or vice-versa, seeing that the First Lady wasn't exactly in the pink either. *Now that would be a story to*

CITY POINT DOCKS

(Courtesy of National Archives)

...the iron-rimmed wheels rumbled noisily
over the wharf's washboard-rough planks.

tell our grandchildren! Grant told himself, stifling a chuckle.

Cresting the summit without incident, the ambulance turned onto a long straight drive at the end of which stood a lovely one-and-a-half-story plantation house. Beautiful dormer windows and a wide, white-columned verandah offered a spectacular view of the confluence of the James and the Appomattox Rivers.

Candlelight and kerosene lamps glowed invitingly in the windows as they approached the stately home. Abe regretted turning down Grant's offer of comfortable accommodations in this beautiful home with its panoramic view of the rivers. The decision, of course, had been Mary's. She believed their stateroom aboard the *River Queen* would offer a better refuge from the hordes of journalists and curiosity-seekers than they would find in an army camp. *Another trip or two up and down that precipice to the boat and Mary will begin to look more favorably upon the company of journalists and curiosity-seekers,* Abe smiled inwardly.

A long row of cabins stood to the right of the drive where it formed a little loop in front of the manor house. Arrayed perpendicularly to the others, three additional cabins stood at either end of the longer row, giving the whole a western frontier-fort effect with a grassy parade ground in the center. Abe recalled that, on his previous visit, one of these cabins had served as Grant's headquarters in preference to Appomattox Manor or some other large dwelling in City Point. He was also aware that the Grant family lived in one of the cabins, while Grant's staff and their families occupied several of the others.

Mrs. Grant took Mrs. Lincoln in tow, steering her toward their small, Spartan-furnished quarters. In a matter of minutes, word of Mrs. Lincoln's arrival had traveled throughout the close-knit community of Army wives, who were soon knocking on Mrs. Grant's door bearing fresh-baked pies and cookies.

Abe ducked his six-foot, four-inch frame under the transom of the small, one-room cabin that served as Grant's headquarters. Inside, a half-dozen senior officers stood at attention. A few faces were familiar; most were new. Abe smiled affably, shaking hands as Grant introduced them. He knew they shared Grant's confidence or else they wouldn't be here. Behind them stood a square drop-leaf table with three low-backed chairs. Grant invited him to take the middle

GENERAL GRANT'S HEADQUARTERS AT CITY POINT

(Courtesy of National Archives)

A few faces were familiar; most were new.

chair. Benches along the back wall accommodated Grant's staff.

Anxious to get started, Abe took the initiative as he sat down. "Please accept my apologies for arriving at such a late hour, Gentlemen, and for keeping you waiting. Perhaps by this time tomorrow we will find that the wait was well worthwhile." He nodded to Grant, "So, let's get started, shall we?"

"Everything is in place, Mr. President," Grant responded, exuding confidence, "and according to the latest intelligence we received tonight from 9th Corps, it looks as though the bait is about to be snapped up."

"Good!" Lincoln beamed. "How long before we know if Lee has gone for it?"

"Soon, Mr. President, very soon," Grant said. "My staff will brief you on the details after General Meade updates you on what has transpired since the arrival of your Presidential impostor at noon today."

"That part went well I hope?" Lincoln asked, his eyes belying the calmness of his voice.

"It couldn't have gone better, Mr. President," Meade replied, wearing one of his rare smiles. "I'll start at the beginning..."

CHAPTER 14

Colquitt's Salient

Confederate Defense Line, Petersburg, Virginia

9:00 P.M., MARCH 24, 1865

Clothed in Union officer uniforms, Alex and Mike sat in a cold, dank, underground bombproof waiting impatiently for Lieutenant Anderson to join them. A candle sat on an upended cracker box, giving off a sooty trail of smoke that stung their eyes and throats in the close, unventilated shelter. Feeling like moles, Alex and Mike sat on wooden kegs, which substituted for chairs, inspecting their burrow in the flickering candlelight. Dug into an embankment, the eight by ten foot bombproof with its low ceiling of six-inch logs and two-foot earth overburden, could easily shelter a dozen men from artillery fire or inclement weather.

"In here, sir," one of their infantry escorts announced outside.

The canvas strip covering the entrance was suddenly swept aside.

Lieutenant Anderson wrinkled his nose as he stepped inside and got a whiff of urine and rotting garbage. "Good Gawd! It's enough to gag a buzzard! How can you chaps stand it?" He doffed his cap and waved it in front of his nose like a fan as he shuffled with stooped shoulders over to a keg next to Alex and sat down.

"Nice of you to join us," Alex groused good-naturedly. "We were just worried sick about you!"

"If you were *worried sick*, Old Man, I'll wager it wasn't over me," he grinned. "More likely, it was over what's going to happen if you get captured dressed in those crisp new Yankee uniforms."

"I'm curious, Nevil," Alex said. "What made you suddenly volunteer for this mission?"

"Well, I couldn't very well let you *doughboys* corner all the glory for yourselves, could I?" Anderson replied, enunciating his words very British-like.

Alex stared at him. "What did you call us?"

"*Doughboys*. I say, aren't you chaps in the wrong war? If you intend to fight in this one, the very least you can do is arrive properly dressed for the occasion. You looked positively ridiculous yesterday in those 1917 form-fitting uniforms!"

Alex and Mike gaped open-mouthed.

"Who are you?" Alex finally managed to ask.

"Before I became Lieutenant Nevil Anderson, Confederate States Army, I was Lieutenant Stephen Clarke, United States Army Air Service. Late one afternoon in November 1917 while flying over Dinwiddie County, I encountered a bit of bad weather. I was forced to land in a field where I spent the night. It rained during the night, making the field too muddy for a safe take-off the next morning, so I rolled the *Jenny*—that's its nickname—into a strip of woods and covered it with brush. The rest of the morning I wandered around, thinking it strange that I hadn't seen anyone, not even a house. I climbed a knoll with lots of big oaks on top, hoping to see something from the higher elevation. But when I reached the summit, I discovered I wasn't alone—and that I had gone back in time!

I found some Union army deserters camped in the grove on the knoll. They were a pretty scruffy-looking bunch. Fortunately I saw them first and hid behind a log. When it was safe, I crawled away."

"So how did you become a lieutenant in the Confederate Army?" Mike asked, fascinated by Anderson's story.

"I thought you'd never ask!" Anderson laughed. "The next day I stumbled onto a farm owned by a man named James Anderson. He and his wife had just buried their oldest son who had been a lieutenant in General Mahone's division. Brought home to die, he had been mortally wounded at the Battle of the Crater in July of 1864.

Anyway, the Andersons took me in, no questions asked. I guess they figured me for a deserter, sick of the war—like so many others. Having lost a son to the war, they wanted it to be over before their younger boys became old enough for military service. I spent a month helping out on the farm, but we all knew it was just a matter of time before someone reported me to the authorities. The Andersons were kind, generous people and offered to help me get home. Of course, I couldn't begin to explain to them how difficult that would be.

My only alternative was to set about creating a new life for myself. Their son, Nevil, had an extra uniform in his wardrobe. I asked them if I could borrow it. Thinking I had decided to return to the Army, they gave it to me as a farewell gift. The next day Mr. Anderson hitched his horses to his wagon and took me into Petersburg where I reported to the Confederate authorities. I concocted a yarn about being Lieutenant Nevil Anderson who had miraculously recovered from his wound..." Noticing Alex's bemused expression, Anderson paused. "Don't laugh! It's been known to happen! Nevil Anderson had just returned from four years of schooling in England and had been in Mahone's Division less than a month when he was wounded. Most of his company was captured up in the Shenandoah Valley. I figured it was a pretty safe bet that no one would remember the real Nevil Anderson. When a Colonel on Lee's staff found out that

I had been educated in England and was a superb writer, I was assigned to the Army staff and served as military liaison to various headquarters—the latest being the Provost Marshal's staff in Hill's Corps. As you can see, I play this role splendidly!"

"What about the English accent?" Alex asked, curious.

"Nevil Anderson had spent so much time in England that he had acquired an English accent. Luckily, I was a ham actor in college and played lots of Shakespeare roles, so faking an English accent was a piece of cake! What! What!" he said, mimicking a speech mannerism of King George III who was the British monarch during the American Revolution.

Alex frowned. "Gordon thinks you know this area like the palm of your hand. You may jeopardize his plan—and ours."

Anderson grinned from ear to ear, revealing a set of exceptionally white and even teeth. "Ah, but you see, Old Man, I really do know this area—I was born and raised in Petersburg! I graduated from Washington and Lee College in 1914 and volunteered for the French Lafayette Escadrelle where I flew combat missions until the United States entered the war. I then accepted a lieutenant's commission in the Army Air Service and was sent to Langley Field, Virginia to train pilots. Then I made the mistake of flying a *Jenny* biplane up here to get a birds-eye view of my hometown and, like I said, on the way back to Langley, I ran into some nasty weather and made a forced landing somewhere in Dinwiddie County—in the year 1864.

So, that's my story. You can call me Steve, but I'm *Nevil Anderson* whenever Gordon or any other Confederate officers are around. Understand? It wouldn't do to get tripped up on names. Gordon doesn't miss much.

Now, tell me about you two—especially the part about how you got involved in Gordon's mad scheme to capture Lincoln."

Alex looked at Mike to see if he wanted the honor.

Mike shook his head. "You tell it. You fantasize better than I do."

"Well, we're really who we claim to be..." Alex began.

Steve listened intently for the next few minutes as Alex told their story.

"...And then we encountered a Confederate patrol," Alex said, keeping the narrative as brief as possible. "They took us prisoner and turned us over to the Provost Marshal. From that point on, you know the rest."

"Yes, of course," Steve nodded thoughtfully, "but why did you insist on seeing General Gordon when we first met? I was intrigued by that at the time, and I still am—you, an officer from the 1918-era of the War to End All Wars, demanding to see General Gordon on the eve of the last great Confederate offensive. *What could they possibly have in common?* I asked myself. Very intriguing indeed, I'd say!"

Alex contemplated the smoking candle for a moment as he probed the recesses of his mind for a memory from the distant past. "For a course in U.S. Military History at West Point, I wrote a research paper on the last great Confederate offensive. After weeks of sifting through and digesting all the library's material on the subject, I felt something significant had been omitted or overlooked in the accounts of the battle. It seemed illogical that Lee and Gordon would risk so much for nothing more than interrupting Grant's lines of supply and communication. There had to be something more—something that had escaped the attention of military historians. I speculated that it might have had something to do with President Lincoln's visit to City Point on the eve of the battle. The timing of his visit seemed a little too coincidental. But until yesterday, I couldn't find any documentation corroborating that theory."

"Yesterday?" Steve said, mystified. "What happened yesterday?"

"We stumbled upon a dispatch from General Meade to General Parke informing him that Lincoln would be an overnight guest at Meade's headquarters on March 24th. His headquarters is just a mile from Fort Stedman, which Gordon intends to assault in the pre-dawn hours of March 25th. This was the written proof I had searched for at West Point, which, inexplicably, didn't appear in *The Official Records of the War of the Rebellion*. Union Army correspondence frequently mentioned telegraph lines between Grant's headquarters and Washington being tapped or cut, so Lee and Gordon probably knew Lincoln's itinerary for his visit to the Union camps around Petersburg. Doubtless, a Confederate spy or two at City Point was also keeping them informed. I was certain that President Lincoln was Gordon's real quarry, but I needed to confront him with the evidence and see his reaction."

"And what part do you play in this scheme?" Steve asked. "Are you now embracing the Confederate cause?"

"I'll ask you the same question," Alex countered. "After all, you *were* wearing a Confederate uniform when we met."

"My allegiance is to the Stars and Stripes, not the Stars and Bars," Steve said, keeping his voice low. "I would never want to see this great country divided."

"Good answer," Alex said, "but inconsistent, considering we just might inadvertently bring about the very thing you profess to be against—Southern independence. So why are you here?"

"I met Gordon informally some months back, and in the course of our conversation I happened to mention that I was from this area. Apparently he remembered it, because he sent for me a few days ago—said he needed an officer acquainted with this area for a special mission, and would I be interested? Of course I said 'Yes.' That's when he brought me into his confidence about his plan to attack Fort Stedman. He made no mention of Lincoln. That came later."

"And do you intend to carry out your part in this?" Alex prompted.

"Do I have a choice? Steve shrugged. "I can't find my way to the outhouse in the dark, and Gordon wants me to guide his troops to Meade's headquarters at night? That's pretty dicey at best. What're you going to do?"

Alex mulled the question over before answering. The flickering candlelight reflected eerily in his eyes and imbued his angular features with a grim and cadaverous quality. "Do my best to complete the mission just the way Gordon planned it. The United States will be better served if Lincoln becomes a reluctant guest of the Confederacy instead of allowing him to be assassinated before his plans for reuniting the country can be carried out. The Confederate leaders know their cause is lost. All they can hope for is a negotiated settlement followed by reunification with dignity and malice toward none. With Lincoln's murder, all his hopes for a quick healing of the nation's wounds will die with him. Mike and I believe we have been given a chance to prevent a monstrous evil that will haunt this nation for generations to come. That's what we intend to do, Steve—change the course of history by saving Lincoln's life. We think it's worth the risk. How about you?"

Steve stared into the flame of the candle as he weighed Alex's reasoning. "Yeah," he finally nodded. "I think it's worth the risk. Count me in," he said, extending his hand.

As Alex and Mike shook Steve's hand, sealing the pact, the solemnity of the moment was short-lived. The murmur of voices outside heralded the arrival of visitors.

An invisible hand probed the ragged piece of canvas stretched over the entrance, then pushed it aside revealing the silhouette of a phantom-like figure against the night beyond. Heads bobbed close behind him as they, too, ducked beneath the low entranceway.

"I see you're ready," a familiar voice came from the darkness, the accent unmistakably Georgian.

Gordon moved into the light, followed by the three company commanders whom Alex remembered from the morning briefing. The commanders were now clad in well-fitted Union officer uniforms with thin white scarves tied around their necks.

A fourth man emerged into the light wearing a rumpled and threadbare Confederate officer's uniform. Alex and Mike didn't recognize him, but Steve promptly stepped forward in friendly greeting.

"Nice to see you, sir!" Steve said, shaking his hand.

"And you, sir!" the officer smiled in recognition.

"I don't believe everyone here has met Major Arnold," Gordon interjected, quickly making the introductions before continuing.

"As soon as Fort Stedman falls into our hands, Major Arnold will garrison it with a large force of infantry and turn the fort's artillery against the enemy. He will be responsible for the safe passage of all prisoners through our lines," Gordon added poignantly.

Gordon paused and looked at Alex, Mike, and Steve for a long moment as though suddenly at a loss for words. "And now, I suppose it's time to set events in motion." A pocket watch suddenly seemed to materialize in his hand; he glanced at the Roman numerals then nodded, "It's eight o'clock. Remember, you have only eight hours to accomplish a great deal before the assault begins."

"Yes, sir," Alex replied, trying to sound confident.

"I know you'll do your best," Gordon said somberly. "Let's pray that the sacrifice of so many brave and gallant men will not be in vain."

Gordon hesitated, as if there were something else on his mind. "Captain Wright and Lieutenant Dent, I don't know if I should tell you now or wait until after tomorrow."

"If it's bad news, General, it won't improve with time," Alex said. "Better we hear it now."

"I thought that would be the case," Gordon nodded, looking Alex straight in the eye. "Your companion, Sergeant Hill, is dead—and I'm partly to blame. His wound was infected and, on the recommendation of the surgeon at the field hospital, I approved his evacuation to Richmond where he would receive better care. Unfortunately, the Union cavalry raided the Boydton Plank Road this morning while he was being evacuated. During the exchange of gunfire, some of the wounded in the wagons were killed. He was among them. I'm sorry."

"Thank you for telling us, General," Alex replied hoarsely. "We know you tried to help."

Gordon nodded uncomfortably, then returned to the immediate matter at hand. "Gentlemen, I wish I could stay to see you off, but as you can imagine, I have much to check on and coordinate before the main assault begins. Major Arnold will provide you his best guide to get you to and through the Union picket line. May God bless and reward you in this endeavor," he shook each of their hands, then turned and disappeared into the darkness.

Major Arnold broke the silence that followed Gordon's departure. "Lieutenant Anderson, whenever you and your fellow officers are ready, I have one of my men outside to guide you through the Union picket line. By now our engineers should be finished removing the obstacles in front of our works, so I suggest you get started before the moon comes up."

They followed Major Arnold out into the chill night air head on into an impenetrable wall of darkness, forcing them to grope across the uneven ground.

Alex heard voices conversing in subdued tones, then realized Arnold had stopped a few paces ahead of him to talk to someone. As his night vision improved, Alex distinguished the outlines of two men. One was Arnold; the other, a soldier in butternut homespun. Alex observed that he had a blanket roll draped over his shoulder, a well-worn slouch hat with a floppy brim that hid his face, and a Spencer carbine cradled in the crook of his arm.

Arnold turned around and whispered in a low voice: "Gentlemen, this is Corporal Horn. There's not a better scout, tracker, or guide in the Confederate army. He's full-blooded Cherokee, and there isn't much over there on the enemy side that he hasn't seen. He'll get you through their picket line, but afterwards you're on your own."

Mike whispered just loud enough for Alex to hear. "If you ask me, he's the one Gordon should be sending on this mission instead of us. He can probably tell you what General Grant had for breakfast and what he reads in the outhouse. With Indians scouting for him, why does Gordon need us? I bet Corporal Horn even has a few Yankee scalps tucked away!"

"Well, there's your answer," Alex replied. "Gordon wants to capture Lincoln, not scalp him."

"Why didn't I think of that?" Mike said, smacking his forehead with the heel of his palm. "I guess that's why you're a Captain!"

"Wonder if he speaks English?" Steve whispered.

"Probably educated in England—at Oxford," Alex chuckled.

"I bloody well doubt that!" Steve scoffed. "I say, Old Man, are you pulling my leg?"

Alex just smiled.

As if he had heard the remarks, Corporal Horn suddenly strode over to Alex. Two luminescent slits below his broad brimmed hat were the only discernible facial features Alex could see. Horn seemed to be studying him. As dark as it was Alex wondered what Horn could possibly see of interest.

"Why no hair on face?" Horn asked. "Look 'em more like Blue Coat with hair on face."

"Too young to grow any, I suppose," Alex grinned, too surprised by the question to think of anything better to say.

The two slits under Horn's hat brim neither wavered nor blinked, reminding Alex of an owl sizing up his prey.

"Then more better you dress like drummer boy," Horn replied, obviously not amused.

Properly rebuked by a corporal, Alex felt the blood surge up his neck to his face. *Guess I asked for that*, he told himself.

Horn's head pivoted to the left and his owlish gaze settled on Mike.

Uncomfortable under Horn's close scrutiny, Mike reached up and tapped the pencil thin mustache on his upper lip with his finger. "See? I have hair on my face."

"Look'em better in dress," Horn grunted, as he turned away and returned to stand beside Major Arnold.

"Stay close, no talk, no noise," Horn snapped, leaving no doubt in anyone's mind that irrespective of rank, he was in charge. "You first," he said, tapping Alex on the arm. "Then you, an' then you," pointing at Mike and Steve, respectively. After lining them up single file, he turned to Major Arnold. "We go now!"

In the darkness they descended an earthen ramp into an eight-foot-deep trench where groups of soldiers silently waited.

Alex glimpsed armbands or neckerchiefs of white cloth and knew these men were the volunteers he would later lead to Meade's headquarters.

A quarter mile later, Horn stopped at a ladder propped against the side of the trench. "We go up," he said, grasping a rung and starting to climb.

Alex did as he was told and scaled the ladder after him. When he reached the top rung, he spied Horn a few yards away crouching behind a low earthwork. Alex ducked low, ran the short distance, and dropped to his knees beside him. While they waited for Mike and Steve to join them, Alex gazed around. What he saw was appalling. The terrain in and around Colquitt's Salient was a virtual desert totally void of trees, grass, and animal life. Beyond, as far as he could see, it was the same—total desolation.

The moon had not yet risen; however, the composite yellow clay and white loamy soil mirrored enough starlight to provide visibility for nearly thirty yards. Alex squinted at the landscape and made his own assessment. *Crossing this barren terrain under a full moon at night would be just about as dangerous as it would be in broad daylight.*

As if reading his thoughts, Horn grunted, "Moon up soon. Move fast!"

With his charges in tow, Horn darted toward a long meandering breastwork behind which hundreds of soldiers sat or crouched in idle anticipation of the upcoming assault. At the base of the breastwork they found a small open space where a group of soldiers were playing cards by candlelight.

One of the players looked up from his cards long enough to recognize the Union uniforms in their midst. "You Yankees lost? Ain't ya supposed to be over there?" he queried casually, pointing over his shoulder in the direction of the Union lines beyond the breastwork. "I'll see your two cents and raise ya two cents more," he whispered hoarsely, the three *Yankees* crouching beside him already forgotten.

Alex turned back to Horn, then realized too late that their guide had not intended for them to stop. Horn had scrambled up the steep slope and now lay atop the breastwork gesturing impatiently for them to follow him.

Alex tried to imitate Horn's agility, but for every two feet he gained crawling up the slope, he slid back one. With little consolation, he noted that Mike and Steve weren't faring any better. Their dark blue coats were chalked with dust, and the dirt they were kicking loose was tumbling down onto the card players, producing a furor of profanity.

"Let's give these damn Yankees a boost," grumbled a disgruntled player, "so they kin get back to where they belong and we kin get back to playin' cards—'specially since I'm winnin'."

Alex was suddenly aware that someone had shoved a rifle butt under his left foot for support. "Thanks," he panted over his shoulder to his unseen benefactor as he painfully crawled to the top of the breastwork.

Alex lay face down gasping for air.

Horn tapped his arm to get his attention, then pointed down the opposite slope.

Cautiously, Alex peered over the edge, then quickly drew back. The reverse slope of the breastwork was at least three times higher and much steeper than the one he had just climbed. The precipitous slope dropped away into a deep moat at the bottom of which stood a formidable obstruction of eight-foot-high sharpened stakes.

FENCE RAIL BARRIER IN FRONT OF FORTIFICATIONS

(Courtesy of Library of Congress)

The precipitous slope dropped away into a deep moat at the bottom of which stood a formidable obstruction of eight-foot-high sharpened stakes.

Again Horn poked his arm and again pointed down the slope.

Puzzled, Alex peered over the edge and squinted at the barrier below. Being in the breastwork's shadow, he nearly missed seeing them, but a closer look revealed holes cut into the barrier. As part of his obstruction removal plan, Gordon's engineers had removed several three-foot-wide sections of the stakes at selected points in preparation for the attack on Fort Stedman. One of these gaps appeared in the fence rail barrier directly below them. Alex nodded, indicating that he understood.

"Stay close," Horn whispered; then in the blink of an eye, he disappeared over the edge of the breastwork.

Alex was right behind him, practically in a free fall as he plunged down the slope.

Fortunately, the deadly stakes angled outward, away from the slope; otherwise, he and Horn would have been impaled on them. As it was, the stakes checked their precipitous slide into the muddy moat then served as an elevated, albeit slanting, walkway to the hole they had seen from atop the breastwork.

As he climbed through the hole, Alex was grateful that the engineer who had cut this opening had selected one of the few spots with access to firm, dry ground instead of making them wade across the moat in knee deep mud.

Reaching the far side of the moat, Horn paused momentarily, then set off in a low-crouched run for another twenty yards to a defensive line of chavaux-de-frise extending to the left and right in front of the Confederate breastworks.

The barrier consisted of twelve-foot-long logs through which holes had been drilled a foot apart at right angles. Sharpened stakes had then been inserted into the holes. The finished product resembled a wooden hedgehog. Placed end to end and secured in place by tying them together or chaining them to stumps or stakes driven into the ground, they formed a formidable defense against infantry or cavalry assaults.

Horn led them through an opening in the line of chevaux-de-frise created by Gordon's engineers within the past hour; however, a short distance beyond, he suddenly held up a hand, signaling them

**PETERSBURG, VA. SECTIONS OF CHEVAUX-DE-FRISE
BEFORE CONFEDERATE MAIN WORKS**

(Courtesy of Library of Congress)

The finished product resembled a wooden hedgehog.

to stop, then squatted on his heels.

Strung out behind him, his charges stopped and followed his example.

Long seconds passed. Alex found squatting to be uncomfortable and decided to kneel instead—a dry rustling noise pierced the night.

Horn heard it and peered in Alex's direction.

Alex couldn't see his face but knew disapproval was stamped across it. Wondering what had caused the disturbance, he glanced down and saw his knee resting atop a withered corn stalk.

Horn again raised his hand and motioned for them to move forward.

Alex looked to his left and right and noticed that they were crossing an abandoned cornfield. The combined effect of shot and shell and countless tramping feet had devastated some farmer's crop leaving only a ruin of dry and shattered stalks.

Again, Horn stuck up his hand.

Everyone stopped and squatted on their heels as before.

Horn appeared to be talking to someone in low whispers.

A slight movement at the edge of the cornfield caught Alex's eye. What appeared to be a cornstalk leaning at an angle a foot or two above the ground moved a second time. Alex now recognized it as a rifle barrel, and it was pointed directly at Horn.

For several more seconds Horn and the invisible owner of the rifle exchanged words too low for Alex to hear. Abruptly, the rifle barrel disappeared.

Horn turned his head in Alex's direction. Pointing at the spot where the rifle barrel had appeared, he whispered, "Gray Coat picket line here." Then pointing at some indiscernible place beyond the dark and featureless cornfield, he said, "Blue Coat picket line there. We go now. Stay close. *No noise.*"

The slits under Horn's hat brim were fixed on Alex.

Alex nodded and smiled sheepishly.

Crouching low, Horn moved forward again.

Where the rifle barrel had appeared, Alex saw nothing as they passed the picket post whose lonely vigil protected the main Confederate defense line from surprise attack. He sensed a pair of eyes intently watching him over the sights of the rifle and resisted the temptation to look back over his shoulder.

Horn moved more cautiously now, carefully stepping over and around cornstalks and the pieces of an artillery caisson that littered the ground. Casualties of war, the scattered bones of horses lay ghastly white strewn amidst the wreckage.

Advancing another forty yards, they came to the edge of the cornfield beyond which lay an area overgrown with weeds and scrub pine.

Horn suddenly paused in mid-stride, sniffed the air, then dropped to the ground.

Alex and the others did the same. Behind them the upper edge of a brilliant full moon gradually crept above the horizon.

Lying in a furrow that offered little concealment, Horn started crawling toward the brush at the edge of the cornfield. Close behind him, three bodies inched forward, trying to avoid the dry, brittle stalks in their path.

With sweat dripping down his forehead and into his eyes, Alex welcomed the cool breeze that first stirred the tall grass along the edge of the field, then swept lightly over him. Taking a deep breath, he held it for a moment, savoring the fragrance of grass and pine— then something else less agreeable. He sniffed the air again. His eyes widened with alarm as he identified the other odor wafting in the breeze—tobacco smoke.

Horn must have smelled it first which explained why they were now playing inchworm. At the edge of the field, Horn stopped again to listen and sniff the air; then changing direction, crawled off at an angle across three or four furrows before disappearing into the cover of weeds bordering the cornfield.

Alex scrambled after Horn on his belly, following his trail of flattened vegetation.

The moon rising into the evening sky bathed the landscape in soft illumination. Improved visibility had a calming effect on Alex, and the soft plant growth under his knees and elbows made crawling less painful. He slithered forward, his eyes fixed on the alternating rhythm of Horn's feet ahead of him as they dug into the earth and pushed forward.

The guide's feet suddenly stopped moving.

Alex raised his head a few inches and glimpsed Horn looking back at him, index finger pressed against his lips.

Horn pointed to his right, then repeating the finger to his lips gesture, slowly crawled off into the undergrowth to his left.

Alex crawled to the spot where Horn had been a moment before. He glanced to his right—then froze. A mound of red earth, like a giant anthill, suddenly appeared an arm's length away; two long rifle barrels jutted out from the top of the mound just inches above his head.

Picket post!

A low resonance, like someone snoring, came from the Union dugout or foxhole.

Alex heaved an inaudible sigh of relief, alerted Mike to the danger, then crawled off after Horn.

Twenty yards beyond the picket post they came to an obstruction of fence rails that stretched into the night to his right and left as far as he could see. Alex had seen photographs of these barriers, the forerunners of barbed wire entanglements that would appear on the battlefields of France a half century later. He was impressed by the obstruction's simple but effective construction. The base of the fence rail was buried in the earth with the pointed upper end angled chest high toward the enemy. Spaced six to eight inches apart, the rails were lashed together with telegraph wire and supporting horizontal poles.

Horn stopped at the rail barrier. Crawling up alongside him, Alex was surprised at the extent of the barrier's disrepair. Many of the rails were rotten or broken, and gaps occurred at frequent intervals where the well-trodden trails of the Union pickets passed through it.

Maybe this is why Gordon picked this section of the Union line to assault. Alex was gaining increased respect for Gordon's insight. *The distance between the Confederate and Union forces at this point is only about two hundred yards. Anyone attempting to repair or improve Fort Stedman's outer defenses would probably get a sharpshooter's bullet through the head.*

The laxity of the pickets, obscured avenues of approach to the main line of fortifications, and the disrepair of the outer defenses were an invitation to attack.

Curious to see the condition of the Union defenses in and around Fort Stedman, Alex started to slither through the closest gap in the obstruction.

Horn placed a restraining hand on Alex's arm and pointed at a wall of earth some twenty yards away. This was as far as Horn was told to accompany these men. "Stedman," he whispered.

By now Mike and Steve had crawled up alongside them and were gazing at the formidable fortification with a mixture of anticipation and awe.

Horn had no idea why these men were posing as Blue Coat little chiefs or what they were hoping to accomplish here. They were brave but foolish and unknowing in the ways of waging war. He did not believe he would see them again, and that was well, for it was not his wish that they should meet again.

"Die well, my brothers," Horn whispered, then turned around and crawled away.

"Humph! A bit melodramatic if you ask me," Steve whispered angrily as Horn disappeared into the brush. "Personally, I would have preferred a chipper 'Cheerio' or 'Keep a stiff upper lip, lads' instead of 'Die well.' You noticed that he didn't offer to stick around to die with us. Bloody savage! Good riddance, I say!"

"Don't be too hard on him," Alex said, coming to Horn's defense. "He's just following orders. Can't imagine what it must be like to be an Indian fighting in a white man's war—I wouldn't want to trade places with him." Alex decided to change the subject. "From here on we're on our own. We'll need to keep our wits about us if we're going to get through the Union line."

"Three officers traveling together may strike someone as a bit unusual," Steve interjected. "Maybe we should split up and infiltrate individually."

"That would be even more risky," Alex replied, "but I think I have a solution to the problem." Reaching inside his coat, Alex withdrew three small leather bound notebooks and a small bundle of pencils.

"I asked Major Moore for these notebooks along with a map of the area, thinking we might need to take notes and make sketches of what we observe in and around Meade's headquarters. However, they may also help us get through the Union lines."

"Okay, I'll bite," Mike said. "Just how do you plan to use them?"

"Simple. We're wearing Union engineer officer uniforms," Alex grinned. "There's nothing so officious-looking as an engineer officer walking around recording observations in a notebook. So here's what we do…"

CHAPTER 15

Fort Stedman
9th Army Corps, Union Siege Line
9:45 P.M., MARCH 24, 1865

Privates Phillip Mason and Fritz Goebel, Company B, 48th Pennsylvania Volunteer Infantry Regiment sat on cracker boxes behind Fort Stedman's parapet gazing out over the desolate landscape, the moon so bright they could clearly see the rebel breastworks two hundred yards away.

"I swear," Mason grumbled, "watching my Aunt Molly knit doilies back home was more exciting than this."

"I wouldn't know about that," Fritz chuckled. "I had better things to do than watch my aunt knit doilies."

Mason punched his arm. "You know what I mean, Turkey! Nuthin' ever happens on guard duty. We just sit and wait, then sit and wait some more. At least the boys in Fort McGilvray up the line see an occasional Reb deserter come over. Hell, our pickets and the Reb pickets over there are on a first name basis. That tells you just how exciting the action is on this part of the siege line!"

"Well, it ain't all bad, Phil. That's pretty good whiskey the Johnny

FORT STEDMAN

(Courtesy of National Archives)

*Privates Phillip Mason and Fritz Goebel . . . sat on cracker boxes
behind Fort Stedman's parapet . . .*

Rebs make over there, which they trade with our pickets for coffee an' tobacco. An' we get a share of what gets traded just for keepin' our mouths shut an' lookin' the other way while on guard duty. Can't say I'd want to trade places with anyone else on the siege line—bored to death is a lot better'n shot to death! But right now, I'm dyin' of thirst. Get out that whiskey bottle hid in that box you're sittin' on."

Mason reached between his legs, lifted the cracker box lid and fished out a shiny black bottle of freshly distilled Reb whiskey. "This is better'n the last batch," Mason said, handing the bottle to Goebel. "This one's had a chance to age a week or two."

"Yep," Goebel nodded in anticipation as he uncorked the bottle, "I think that last stuff was pure alcohol. I was afraid to smoke an' drink at the same time!"

Goebel tilted the bottle up and took a long swig. The fiery liquid seared his throat and settled warmly in the pit of his stomach. His eyes rolled in blissful ecstasy, tears running down his cheeks and into his bushy black beard. "Tha's really smooth!" he gasped, handing the bottle back to Mason.

As Mason took a long pull from the bottle, he mindlessly scanned the scarred landscape in front of the fort, then choked as his eyes came to rest on a solitary figure walking along the rail obstruction.

He wiped his mouth and nudged Goebel with his elbow. "Who's that?"

Goebel squinted at the distant figure. Whoever he was, he appeared to be writing in a notebook. "Dunno. What in blazes is he doin' out there?"

Mason set the bottle down on the parapet and reached for his rifle.

"Wait!" Goebel placed a restraining hand on Mason's rifle barrel. "There's someone else out there with him."

Mason looked where Goebel was pointing and observed two more figures about ten yards apart casually walking along the inside of the barrier.

"Think we ought to call the Sergeant of the Guard?" Mason queried anxiously.

"Nah, let's find out who they are an' what they're doin' before we get Mad Dog Howlin excited." Like almost everyone else in the company, Goebel didn't like the Sergeant of the Guard—a mean-tempered man when sober and infinitely worse when drunk. Behind his back, everyone referred to him as *Mad Dog Howlin*. Goebel had never seen Howlin when he wasn't disagreeable, so he never knew for certain what state of sobriety he was in. "I don't want him mad at us for wakin' him if it turns out to be nuthin'."

"Hey you! Who goes there?" Goebel whispered loudly at the nearest of the three figures.

The shadowy figure paused and looked in Goebel's direction. "Lieutenant Farris, Corps of Engineers, with a survey detail," came the reply.

"What're you surveyin'?" Goebel demanded suspiciously.

"Allow me to approach," the voice replied gruffly, "and I'll tell you. If we keep yelling like this, we're going to attract the attention of some Reb sharpshooter."

Mason and Goebel exchanged questioning glances, but they were now more curious than cautious.

"Okay," Goebel answered, lowering his voice. "Approach. But tell your detail to stay put 'til we check you out. There's a gap in the breast-works. Jus' follow the trail in front of you an' it'll take you there. Don't try nuthin' funny; we'll have you in our rifle sights all the way."

As the figure approached, Mason and Goebel, good to their word, monitored his progress over the sights of their rifles. In the moonlight they noted that his uniform was indeed that of a Union officer.

A dozen feet from where they waited, Goebel hissed "That's close enough! State your business—" Goebel knew that officers weren't gods, but in this army they were pretty damn close, he quickly added the obligatory "—sir" at the end of his challenge.

"I'm Lieutenant Farris, Corps of Engineers," Alex repeated imperiously. "By order of the Army Inspector General, I'm surveying the adequacy and serviceability of the defenses between Fort Stedman and Fort Haskell."

"Humph! 'Bout time," Mason muttered, just loud enough for Goebel to hear. "It don't take no damn engineer to see that the rail obstruction out there is in sorry shape, an' the weeds are takin' over the place."

"So why're you doin' this at night—sir?" Goebel demanded

suspiciously.

Alex shook his head as though he were dealing with a couple of imbeciles. "With the Rebs being only two hundred yards away, how far do you think we'd get in broad daylight before a sniper put a bullet through us?"

"Makes sense to me, sir," Mason agreed as he glowered at Goebel for asking such a dumb question. "However, we weren't told that you'd be in our area tonight. We'll have to send for the Sergeant of the Guard who will need to obtain a clearance for you from the Duty Officer."

"That will take awhile I suppose?"

"Yes, sir. It probably will, an' we'll need a copy of your orders."

"Yes, of course," Alex sighed consignedly as he stepped forward into the opening.

Mason and Goebel stood on either side, still pointing their rifles at him.

Alex stuck his hand inside his coat pocket as if to retrieve a copy of his orders, then paused and scowled. "Are you men drinking on guard duty?" he demanded, pointing at the whiskey bottle that Mason had left in plain view atop the parapet. "Phew! Don't bother answering; I can smell the whiskey on you from here. Don't you know drinking on guard duty is a courts-martial offense? You could be executed for endangering the lives of your comrades. This is exactly the kind of misconduct the Army Inspector General ordered me to look for and include in my report concerning the adequacy of Fort Stedman's defenses."

Alex flipped open his notebook. "Guards at Fort Stedman drunk on duty," he said aloud as he began scribbling. "Give me your names and unit!"

Mason and Goebel paled and lowered their rifles.

"N-now hold on, sir!" Mason stammered. He was beginning to perspire despite the chill in the air. "It ain't as bad as all that. Me an' Fritz here had a couple of snorts, but we ain't drunk by a long shot."

"No, sir! We ain't for a fact," Goebel chimed in. "It was just for medicipal, uh, medicional purposes, sir."

Alex made an effort not to smile. "You mean *medicinal purposes*?"

"Yeah! I mean…. Yes, sir! Tha's what I mean," Goebel slurred the words uncertainly.

"I suppose the Inspector General's Board of Inquiry and the Courts-Martial Convening Authority will have to be the judge of that," Alex shrugged, "unless…"

"Unless what, sir?" Goebel pursued anxiously.

"Well, it seems we both have a problem." Alex paused and frowned for effect. "If I'm to finish this survey before daylight, I don't have time for delays. But having caught the two of you drinking on guard duty, by regulation, I'm supposed to report you immediately to your commanding officer. Of course, he'll want a written statement from me to include in the charges he'll bring against you, and that will take more of my time. See the awkward position you've put me in?"

"Yes, sir. We do," Mason nodded with just a glimmer of understanding.

"On the other hand," Alex continued, "if you didn't see me, and I didn't see you, then I would have no reason to put you in my report, and you would have no reason to involve the Sergeant of the Guard or the Duty Officer. Maybe it would be better to try and work this out among ourselves."

Stroking his beard and mustache, Mason looked up at the stars reflectively. "As you suggest, sir, maybe we *can* work this out amongst ourselves." Mason glanced at Goebel for affirmation and saw him nodding enthusiastically.

"What if we never had this little talk," Mason continued, "and allowed you to get on with your survey without any more delays, would you be willin' to forget you ever laid eyes on us?"

Alex looked pensive, as if considering the matter. Finally, he nodded. "Private, I'm impressed with your astute perception and problem solving ability! Well done! Yes, I believe that's a proposal I can accept with a clear conscience."

Mason beamed at the compliment and puffed out his chest.

"But just one more thing," Alex's voice was stern. "You seem to be good men, but *John Barleycorn* has clouded your judgment. I'd be guilty of dereliction of duty if I didn't confiscate that bottle of whiskey. Being sober on guard duty tonight is far better than being dead drunk. Trust me, I'm doing you a favor."

Mason picked up the bottle and handed it to Alex with a happy grin.

Goebel looked as though he were parting with a dear friend. Alex thought he saw tears welling in the soldier's eyes.

"Good night, gentlemen," Alex turned away and waved for Mike and Steve to come forward.

CHAPTER 16

Vicinity of Harrison's Creek in Rear of Fort Stedman

10:00 P.M., MARCH 24, 1865

His arms draped over their shoulders as Alex and Steve supported his weight between them, Mike lustily sang the *Battle Hymn of the Republic*. In his left hand he clutched the neck of a whiskey bottle, waving it in time with his singing. To any passerby, they appeared to be two friends helping a drunken comrade home after a night of drinking in one of the sutler tents—except, this comrade hadn't drunk a drop.

"Mike, you can stop singing now," Alex growled. "I don't see anyone else ahead of us, and I don't think I can take another verse of the *Battle Hymn of the Republic*. Don't you know any other songs?"

"It's the only Civil War song I can remember, except *Dixie*. Would you prefer I sing that or...Say! How 'bout it I sing the one that's all the rage back home? You know the one!" Terribly off key, Mike began singing the refrain: "*Over there! Over there!*"

Suddenly two Union officers on horseback emerged from the shadows of an intersecting wagon road. They politely reined their horses off to one side to let the three dismounted men pass.

"God, that's awful!" one of the riders complained. "Why don't you just shoot him and put him out of his misery."

"If they don't, I might," said his companion. "He's scaring the bejesus out of my horse!"

"No taste for good music, tha's your problem," Mike roared drunkenly as the riders disappeared into the night behind them.

The road they were on led away from the regimental camps behind Fort Stedman and gradually descended into a creek bottom. Alex was pleased with their progress. "So far, so good," he said as they stepped onto the wooden bridge across Harrison's Creek.

"Remember how to get back to this bridge. We meet Major Jonas and his troops here in six hours. You can drop the drunk act, Mike. It served to get us through the Union camps around Fort Stedman, but it might look odd to someone this far away from the camps."

Beyond the bridge, the road snaked up and down a series of ridges and gullies. Campfires flickered here and there, which they avoided as they also avoided the occasional freight wagon that rumbled toward them in the dark.

As they crested a long spur of cleared land above the creek, the road leveled off and meandered in the direction of a distant camp where lanterns glowed and campfires flickered.

"Let's give that camp a wide berth," Alex suggested, "and stay on the high ground above Harrison's Creek. When we reach the first tributary that flows into it, we'll follow it upstream, which should take us to Meade Station on the U.S. Military Railroad."

Steve studied the distant camp through his field glasses as he listened to Alex.

"I think you should take a look at this, Alex," he said, handing him his field glasses. "Seems to be a lot going on in that camp this late at night."

Alex pressed the field glasses to his eyes and viewed the moving lanterns and activity in the camp. "You're right," he said, his face mirroring his concern. "It's a beehive of activity all right. Two infantry columns are leaving camp, one marching south, the other coming this way with lots of horse-drawn artillery." Alex squinted harder into the eyepieces. "I estimate at least one brigade on the march— wonder where they're going this hour of the night? I don't like the looks of this. Let's get off the road and put some distance between them and us. We're lucky we didn't run head on into them!"

Fifteen minutes later, as they worked their way up the slope of a deep ravine, Steve tapped Alex on the shoulder. "Must be close to the Military Railroad," he whispered. "I hear a steam engine."

They sprinted the last few yards up to the head of the ravine, then stepped out onto a flat expanse of land that had once been cultivated.

Startled by the sight that greeted them, they stopped and stared.

Spread out across the plain in the moonlight lay row upon row of white canvas tents. They had not expected to find so large a camp here.

Through the heart of the encampment ran twin ribbons of steel that gleamed in the light of lanterns hanging from the entrances of a hundred tents alongside the railroad. Nearby, a steam engine squatted on a siding like some medieval dragon, hissing mightily and belching forth great clouds of white steam.

Steve studied the scene through his field glasses. A swarm of men were busy unloading rail cars and stacking the supplies near the siding. He looked perplexed as he handed the field glasses to Alex. "I don't have any idea where we are. I thought I knew this area, but everything looks different at night. We could be on the moon for all I know."

Alex grunted as he peered through the glasses. "Uh-huh! Where that steam engine is parked is called Meade Station, so named because of its proximity to Meade's headquarters. If you look close, you'll see a road intersection a short distance southeast of it. Fifty years from now that will be the intersection of Mahone Avenue and Avenue A on Camp Lee. I know exactly where we are. About a half mile south of Meade Station there's a shallow ravine. Meade's headquarters is on the high ground beyond the ravine near the Prince George Court House Road."

"And you know all that because...?" Steve asked.

"Because," Alex smiled, "fifty-three years from now, Mike and I will be working in a building just south of where Meade's headquarters is presently located."

"But that's over half a mile from here," Mike interjected, "with a lot of Union troops in between. How do you plan to get there?"

"By riding mostly, I hope," Alex grinned. "Still got that bottle of whiskey?"

"Yep," Mike answered, patting the bulge in his coat pocket. "I kept it in case I got snake bit."

"Well keep it handy. I have a better use for it."

From the head of the ravine they chose a northwesterly route that bypassed most of the Union encampment. But to save time and distance, Alex decided to take a chance and led them through the middle of a company bivouac. Most of the men appeared to be asleep or at work unloading the train. They encountered no one except a camp guard who eyed them warily as they trooped by.

They pressed on until they reached a wagon road that ran parallel to the railroad tracks, then followed it toward Meade Station.

A burly sergeant stood on the edge of the loading dock with his arms folded, watching three officers—obviously intoxicated—staggering down the road toward him.

"You gentlemen lost?" he asked in a deep bullhorn voice.

"Nope! Jus' a teensy bit turned aroun'. Tha's all!" slurred one of the two tall officers who, with much effort, was supporting a shorter one between them.

The short one belched loudly.

Laughter rippled up and down the loading dock as workers paused to watch.

"Jus' tryin' to help our frien' here fin' his way to his headquarters," the other officer chimed in. "He jus' arrived an' needs to report to his new commander. Anyhow, I think we tooka left somewheres when we shoulda taken a right." He frowned and looked at his companion. "Or was it a right when we shoulda taken a left?" His friend shook his head stupidly, equally confused. "Well whichever, it was the wrong one!"

"Which headquarters? I'm the railroad freightmaster here. Maybe I can point you in the right direction."

"Tha's mos' kind of you! The Lieu...Lieutenant here is assigned to Gen'l Meade's staff. He's suppose' to report to the Gen'l by the end of the day."

Guffaws erupted from the onlookers at this news.

The freightmaster grinned. "Well, wouldn't we like to be a fly on the wall when he reports to General Meade! *More laughter.* Luckily for your friend, I saw the General board a train for City Point just after dark, so he's probably not coming back tonight.

On the other hand, the rumor is Ol' Abe himself arrived late this afternoon and is staying overnight at Meade's headquarters. Don't know if it's true. Seems a mite odd that Meade would suddenly leave when he has the President as his guest. But if it *is* true, why don't you have your friend report to Ol' Abe? After all, he's the top man here, being Commander-in-Chief and all."

"I'll do it!" Mike roared, then launched into the refrain for *The Battle Hymn of the Republic.*

"Tell you what I'll do," the freightmaster shouted over Mike's singing. "To keep your friend from scaring these mules to death, I'll put you on the next wagon going that way. Tell Abe I said hello when you see him."

"I'll do it!" Mike slurred drunkenly, saluting the sergeant with the neck of the whiskey bottle clutched in his hand as he resumed singing: *Oh, he is stamping out the vintage where the grapes of wrath are stored...!*

The steam engine hissed loudly and belched forth a cloud of super-heated steam as the mule-drawn freight wagon rumbled past. Three men sat atop the bales of hay stacked in the bed of the wagon.

"You're delivering forage this late at night?" Steve asked, trying to make conversation with their aged driver who bore a striking resemblance to the *Grim Reaper* with his sunken eyes, cadaver pale flesh that covered his cheekbones like thin parchment, and a mane of greasy white hair that spilled from beneath his dirty blue kepi.

"Ayep," the driver drawled in his New England twang. "Deliverin' this load to the First District of Columbia Cavalry camped at

Prince George Court House. They're pullin' out 'fore daylight, so they need it pretty quick. I'll drop you off at the cutoff to Meade's headquarters. From there, tain't far to walk—'bout two hundred yards is all." Squinting, the teamster pointed up the road. "See that gully up ahead? You'll find the Headquarters of the Army of the Potomac just past it a short ways to the right of this road. It's got a fence of hedgehogs 'round it, so you'll need to stay on the road to the entrance gate."

A few minutes later, the teamster grunted, "This is it!" The wagon creaked to a stop on the high ground beyond the gully. The teamster sat patiently, waiting for his passengers to climb down.

"Thanks for the ride," Alex smiled and waved as he stepped off onto the side of the road.

The teamster tossed him a two-fingered salute, then with a *haw* coaxed his mules into motion.

Taking advantage of the dust churned up by the mules and the freight wagon, the *doughboys* hid behind an embankment across the road from a barrier of chevaux-de-frise—*hedgehogs*, the teamster had called them.

"So, Alex, what do you make of General Meade's departure for City Point just when the President of the United States drops in as his overnight guest?" Mike whispered as they watched the wagon disappear into the darkness.

"I doubt he would have left," Alex shrugged. "The freightmaster said he saw him leave after dark, so maybe it was someone he mistook for Meade."

"At least he confirmed that Lincoln is here," Steve said, "but I'm baffled by all the activity we've seen tonight. Something's afoot."

"Sure looks that way," Alex nodded. "It may have something to do with Lincoln's visit. I wonder how much security Lincoln has around him. Normally one Honor Company would be assigned to a Corps or Army headquarters. However, with Lincoln as his guest, Meade might very well have doubled or tripled that number. Major Jonas' force will be sufficient to defeat one company, maybe two, but any more than that, the odds will turn against him."

Alex withdrew a gold pocket watch from his coat pocket and opened the handsomely engraved cover. "It's now 11:45 P.M. Let's split up and scout the area. Steve, you check the south and east sides of the headquarters' perimeter. Mike, you take the north side; that will put you between the headquarters and the camp at Meade Station, so be careful."

"I'll do it!" Mike slurred, affecting his drunken guise.

"Whatever you do, don't sing," Alex chuckled. "We don't want to start a stampede!"

"And just what are you going to do while Steve and I are risking life and limb for the Confederacy? Did you bring a good book?"

"Don't worry, pal. Just keep an eye out for me. I'll be inside the headquarters encampment."

Steve whistled through his teeth. "That's a bit risky, isn't it?"

"Yeah, but we need to know where Lincoln's sleeping. Unless he suffers from insomnia, we're not likely to find him wandering around in his stove pipe hat in the middle of the night."

"Where and when do we link up when we finish?" Mike asked, checking his wristwatch.

Alex thought a moment before answering. "I'd prefer to rendezvous on the other side of the headquarters encampment, but we don't know what might be over there. Our safest option is to meet back here at 2:00 A.M., which will allow us plenty of time to link up with Major Jonas at the bridge over Harrison's Creek. In the event any of us, including me, doesn't make it back here by 2:00 A.M., wait ten more minutes then go on. If we get split up, meet at the bridge. Two hours should be sufficient to scout the area. We need to know the Federal troop strength; where they're positioned; what roads and trails lead into and out of the area; and, lastly, where Lincoln is sleeping. Any questions?"

Mike and Steve shook their heads.

"Okay, let's get going. Keep your eyes and ears open."

Mike and Steve departed, heading in opposite directions along the Prince George Court House Road, then dashed across it and disappeared into the weeds and scrub pine on the opposite side.

CHAPTER 17

Perimeter

Headquarters, Army of the Potomac

MIDNIGHT, MARCH 24, 1865

Alex crouched in the brush beside the Prince George Court House Road. Confronting him was the problem of crossing the road and getting through the defensive barrier—a double row of chevaux-de-frise—that encircled Meade's headquarters, and he had already spotted a pair of sentries patrolling the space between the rows.

He waited until another freight wagon passed by then sprinted across the road behind it, using the wagon's plume of dust to cover his movement. Concealed in the brush on the opposite side, Alex crept toward the narrow track that led to the entrance of Meade's encampment.

Ten minutes and a hundred yards later, Alex still hadn't figured out how he was going to get through the obstruction and past the sentries. He lay in the weeds along the edge of the track studying the well-guarded gate through his field glasses. *Nothing to do but to do it, I suppose,* he thought, trying to screw up his courage to make a dash for the first line of chevaux-de-frise. *I'll have to play this by ear and hope I don't get shot by some trigger-happy sentry.*

Like a sprinter at the starting line, Alex was about to spring forward—then paused as a faint disturbance carried to his ears. *What the hell is that?* Puzzled, he squatted on his heels in the tall weeds and gazed up and down the track.

Moments later, the distinctive, pleasing chords of a banjo and the deep, melodious voice of a Negro singing in accompaniment became clearly audible. A canvas-topped freight wagon rolled into view along the nearby Prince George Court House Road, the steady *clip clopping* of its four mules and the creaking of their leather

145

harnesses clashing discordantly with the music. The white canvas top shimmered in the moonlight, and even at a hundred yards Alex could distinguish the large Corps insignia—a black Iron Cross—stenciled on the side of it.

To Alex's surprise, the wagon suddenly turned onto the narrow track leading to the encampment's guarded entrance. A plan quickly took form in his mind, and his lips curled into a smile at the simplicity of it.

Alex ducked low in the brush and waited until the wagon rolled past him before springing to his feet and scrambling after it. Unseen by its occupants, he grabbed hold of the tailgate and flung himself over it into the wagon bed.

Suddenly, all hell broke loose.

A crescendo of squawks filled the wagon's interior as Alex toppled onto a crate of panicked chickens. His heart skipped a beat. Any second he expected the wagon to stop and find someone peering over the tailgate to determine the cause of the ruckus.

Seconds passed. The mules continued their plodding.

Alex listened to the Negro teamsters exchanging verbal barbs and laughing.

"Rosco, I tol' you yo' singin' was bad 'nuff to wake the dead! Now look wha' you gone an' done! You has scared dose chickens back dere to death! Lord ha' mercy! Listen to dat squawkin'!"

Well fo' sure it ain't my singin' wha' got dem birds to sqawkin'; it' be yo' playin' on dat banjo. Dem birds ain't gonna lay no eggs fo' a month after dis! Wha' de Gen'l gonna say when he ain't got no eggs fo' breakfast? I'll tell'im ya banjo'd dem to death! Dat's wha'!

We comin' up to de gate, so ya bettah stop playin' dat t'ing 'fo ya wakes up de whole camp, de chickens is bad 'nuff!"

Scrunched into a ball in the wagon bed, Alex lay listening to the good-natured bantering.

"Halt!" came a sudden shout.

"It jus' us, Corp'l. Jus' Rosco an' Nap."

Through a crack in the wagon's sideboards Alex saw a corporal standing beside the wagon brandishing a rifle. Three more similarly armed soldiers stood behind him.

"What're you two doin' out so late?" the corporal growled as he recognized the Negroes and lowered his rifle. "You been to a cockfight? I hear chickens squawkin' in the back of your wagon. I hope you ain't plannin' to hold a cockfight around the headquarters. General Meade or his Chief of Staff will skin you alive if either catches you at it!"

"No, suh! Dems jus' egg layin' chickens back dere," Rosco said hurriedly. "De train wit de food fo' de headquarters folks dun come late. We wait fo' four hours fo' it to come. We jus' now gettin' back."

"Okay! Okay!" the corporal nodded impatiently. "Spare me the details, Rosco. Just show me your pass."

"Wha' fo', Corp'l? You knows who we is."

"Yeah, I know you and Nap. But I have orders to check everyone for passes. I need to see your pass too."

"Here 'tis, Corp'l. But dem chickens ain't got none. You gonna let dem in?"

"I suppose so, Rosco," the corporal chuckled. "So what else is in the wagon?"

"Jus' boxes o' can' meat an' fruit. Dere's some fresh veg'tbles an' some barrels o' flour fo' de Boss Gen'l mess. Oh, an' de chickens so de Boss Gen'l can hab eggs wit' his breakfast. Wanna see?"

"Nah!" the corporal wrinkled his nose, scorning the offer. "This is close enough. I can smell those chickens from here. Get on outta here!"

The corporal of the guard stood aside and waved the wagon through the gate. The other soldiers leaned on their rifles and casually watched the mules and wagon pass them by.

Alex waited until the wagon was out of view of the gate guards before peering over the tailgate. The wagon rocked from side to side, like a ship tossed on a stormy sea, as it snaked through a grove of pines towering above the encampment. The pine boughs blocked out most of the moonlight, creating an impenetrable gloom that made it difficult for Alex to see beyond the trees that lined both sides of the road. *But that isn't all bad. If I can't see them, they can't see me either.*

Alex climbed over the tailgate and dropped to the ground, pleased to find it carpeted with soft pine needles. He picked himself up, scrambled to the side of the road, then moved stealthily among the trees, continuing to follow the wagon at a safe distance. *If the wagon's loaded with rations destined for Meade's mess tent, then it's a reasonable assumption that his headquarters must be close by.*

As the mules plodded by a row of circular Sibley tents, a voice from the wagon rang out, "*Whoa!*" The wagon slowed to a stop in front of the second tent.

Across the road from the wagon, a light glowed from under a canvas tarp stretched over an open-sided framework of beams and posts.

Alex crept closer for a better look.

The tarp sheltered an assortment of trestle tables, benches, and chairs. Light came from a scattering of lanterns placed on various tables.

Looks like a mess hall, Alex surmised, noting movement inside.

At a corner table two young soldiers sat quietly drinking coffee; otherwise the place appeared empty. He studied them for a moment. *This late at night, they're probably coming on or going off guard duty.*

Alex was about to retreat into the relative security of the trees when an idea occurred to him. Straightening his cap and coat and untying the white scarf from around his neck and stuffing it into his pocket, he stepped boldly out into the road. He gave the two teamsters unloading the freight wagon a casual nod as he walked past them.

For their part, the teamsters scarcely glanced in his direction.

Alex turned off the road and followed the well-worn path leading to the mess hall.

On a trestle table a few feet inside the entrance sat a steaming pot of coffee with a pyramid of tin cups stacked next to it. Alex stopped and filled one of the coffee cups, all the while feeling the weight of the soldiers' eyes on his back.

He turned around to find the two soldiers looking at him.

"Evening," he said calmly, taking a cautious sip of the steaming coffee.

The men started to rise, but Alex waved for them to keep their seats.

"Good evening, sir," they answered, almost in unison.

One of the soldiers frowned as his eyes wandered over Alex's uniform. "What happened to you, sir? Your uniform's a mess."

Surprised by the question, Alex took stock of his uniform, noting in the dim light that it was spattered with mud and leaves, two buttons were missing from his coat, and his boots were scuffed and muddy. He shrugged and smiled, seemingly unconcerned. "I took a tumble finding my way over here in the dark. Being a new kid on the block, I'm still learning my way around."

"You're up awfully late or awfully early, Lieutenant," his friend said. "Are you on duty?"

"Nope. Just the occupational hazard of being an Engineer Officer. I'm writing a report that's due tomorrow morning."

They smiled and nodded their understanding of such things.

"Are you coming off duty or going on?" Alex asked, shifting the topic of conversation away from him.

"Getting off, I suppose, sir," one replied glumly, "but we go back on again in three hours, so we're just sitting around killing time until then."

"Why so little time between shifts?" Alex asked, genuinely curious. He blew on his coffee to cool it as he waited for the answer.

"With the President here, the Headquarters Honor Company is stretched doubly thin providing for his security as well as for the headquarters."

"I'm surprised to hear that," Alex said, wiping the coffee from his lips with the back of his hand. "I'd have thought General Meade's staff would have brought in another company or two to beef up security—at least for tonight."

"You'd think so," the private nodded, then added, "but according to the scuttlebutt, something big is in the works. The 9th Corps, to which we're assigned, is sleeping on their weapons tonight and can't spare any additional troops for security duty."

"Well, you can't put too much store on camp rumors," Alex said, consolingly. "They're more often wrong than right. I overheard two of Meade's staff officers at dinner tonight say that the President and General Meade had boarded a train enroute to Grant's headquarters at City Point."

The two privates looked at each other and laughed. "Well, there you go, sir! Another false rumor or at least *partly* false."

"You know about this?" Alex asked, appearing surprised.

"Yes, sir," one grinned knowingly. "General Meade did in fact leave his headquarters earlier this evening. We saw him ride out the gate while we were pulling guard duty. Don't know where he was going, but for sure, President Lincoln wasn't with him. We got a glimpse of the President later while he was palavering with some officers on the porch of the cabin where he's spending the night."

"You're sure it was Lincoln you saw?"

"Oh, yes, sir! As sure as I'm sitting here talking to you," the private grinned. "It was him for sure—tall and thin and wearing his famous stovepipe hat!"

"Well, there's no one else around here who looks like that," Alex shrugged, "so it must have been him all right. Obviously, you two know your way around this place in the dark—wish I did." Alex frowned as he waved a hand over his ruined uniform. "I'm afraid this coat is beyond repair after my fall. Could I persuade one of you to give me some directions so I don't fall into a privy on the way back to my desk? Better yet, how about drawing me a sketch of the area. I have a terrible sense of direction," Alex smiled sheepishly, taking the leather-bound notebook out of his pocket.

"Yes, sir, be glad to," one of the privates offered.

Handing him the notebook and pencil, Alex pulled up a chair and moved the lantern closer for better light.

In two minutes the soldier had drawn a detailed map of the encampment, including Meade's headquarters tent and the location of Lincoln's cabin.

"I don't suppose they built that cabin just for his visit?" Alex inquired.

"No, sir. It's called the *Honeymoon Hut*. General Meade had it constructed to accommodate distinguished visitors and officers' wives visiting their husbands."

"I suppose it must be occupied all the time then. Wonder how Mrs. Lincoln likes it?"

"She didn't accompany him on this part of his visit, sir. He's by himself, except for the four Pinkerton agents who came with him—bodyguards, I suppose. They stay as close to him as stink on a skunk, if you will pardon my putting it so crudely."

"Well that must make for cozy sleeping arrangements," Alex laughed.

The private also laughed. "Not *that* cozy, sir! There's a smaller cabin next door to the President's. Two agents are sleeping there while the other two have made themselves comfortable on the covered porch of the President's cabin. They spell each other during the night, two agents on and two off every four hours."

"I don't suppose it would be a good idea for me to drop by and ask the President for his autograph," Alex said, amazed at how much sensitive information the young soldier was readily imparting to a total stranger.

"No, sir. Not unless you want a fatal dose of lead poisoning. His Pinkerton bodyguards take their work seriously."

"Speaking of work, I guess it's time I got back and did some more myself," Alex said, getting to his feet. "I enjoyed the coffee and the pleasant company. Thanks for the directions. You've been more than helpful."

"Glad to be of assistance, sir," the soldier who had drawn the map smiled.

"See you lads around," Alex said in parting.

Straightening his cap, he started for the entrance when one of the soldiers called out to him. "Hold on, sir!"

Alex hesitated, afraid for a moment that they were on to him. He glanced apprehensively over his shoulder.

"That map won't do you a bit of good, sir, if you can't see it. Here, take this lantern with you," he said, picking up the lantern from their table. "No one will mind as long as you bring it back tomorrow; besides it may save you from another nasty tumble."

"Yes, thank you!" Alex smiled appreciatively. "That's an excellent idea."

"It's time for us to report for duty, sir. Would you like us to escort you back to headquarters?"

"I appreciate the offer, but that's not necessary. I need to stop off at my tent on the way and clean up. Somebody might mistake me for a Reb from the way I look."

The privates laughed at Alex's little joke. "Then good night, sir!" they said, saluting smartly as they left him outside the mess hall entrance.

Alex watched them disappear into the darkness, relieved that they were heading in the opposite direction. Holding the lantern high to light the way, he walked back to the road. The freight wagon and the harnessed mules still stood in front of the Sibley tents. A light shone in one of them, the silhouettes of the two teamsters moving about inside as they carried and stacked boxes.

Alex checked his watch—12:30 A.M. *Getting into the encampment was an easy matter and obtaining the information we needed proved even easier; however, getting out of here undetected might be far more difficult. Maybe if I follow the road back to the gate I'll get an inspiration along the way.*

Alex held the lantern higher to see the road more clearly as he walked past the freight wagon. Roused by the sudden light, the chickens in the back of the wagon began clucking nervously.

Those blasted chickens are going to be my undoing yet, Alex scowled as he lowered the lantern and dimmed the light. Suddenly an idea occurred to him. He stopped and looked back at the wagon. *There's my inspiration!* The scowl gave way to a devious grin. *Now if the mules and chickens will just cooperate.*

Alex climbed onto the wagon seat, set the lantern on the floorboard at his feet, then released the wheel brake and picked up the reins and whip. He flicked the tip of the whip lightly at the rumps of the mules and said softly, "Yay!"

The mules leaned forward in their traces, and the wagon rolled noiselessly over the thick carpet of pine needles.

A short distance beyond the mess hall, Alex found a clearing wide enough to turn the team and wagon around. Having spent several hours riding in mule-drawn wagons, he had picked up some of the basic mechanics and language needed to turn them. So as not to alert the two teamsters, Alex gave a muted "Haw!"

The team promptly responded by pulling left in a tight turn until they were again on the dirt track heading back in the opposite direction. As the wagon rolled past the line of tents, Alex saw the teamsters still silhouetted against the tent wall and heard the tinny plunking of Rosco's banjo.

So far, so good. Now let's head for the gate, he told himself, giving the mules free rein to retrace the wagon's earlier route through the pine grove. In the glow of two kerosene lanterns suspended on either side of the gate, Alex counted four guards standing in the middle of the road.

"Whoa," he said softly.

The mules plodded to a stop.

Alex didn't bother setting the wheel brake before climbing over the seat into the back of the wagon. Retrieving the lantern from where he had stowed it under the seat, he unscrewed the fueling cap on the base of the lantern, sloshed kerosene around the wagon's interior, then opened the door on the chicken cage.

The chickens clucked nervously and crowded together protectively in the back of the cage as Alex, still clutching the lantern, climbed over the tailgate, dropped to the ground, then lifted the lantern's glass globe and let the flame from the wick lap against the wagon's canvas top. As tongues of fire greedily licked their way up the canvas, Alex tossed the lantern into the wagon bed and heard the sound of glass shattering against the wooden flooring. Flames quickly engulfed the wagon's interior.

Alex sprinted into the woods, away from the wagon and the road, but had gone only a few dozen yards when the wagon suddenly burst into a raging inferno.

Panicking, the mules reared in their traces, then charged toward the gate with the freight wagon swaying and pitching behind them, leaving a shower of sparks and a trail of burning canvas in its wake.

The mules made straight for the gate where the sound of men's laughter over a shared joke was suddenly drowned in a flood of terrified squawks and braying.

All but one of the gate guards promptly scrambled out of the path of the run-away wagon. The corporal, however, stood his ground, whisked off his cap and waved it at the onrushing mules.

The mules, balking at the waving arms and flashing hat in front of them, veered off the road just short of the gate and went crashing off through the pine grove scattering squawking chickens and flaming debris among rows of tents and their slumbering occupants.

Alex stood behind a tree as the gate guards disappeared into the darkness in pursuit of the wagon and the run-away mules. He contemplated the clamor of angry and frightened men suddenly and rudely awakened from sound sleep and the shower of sparks cascading up into the night sky, then strolled toward the unguarded gate.

On a wooden bench beside the gate, smoke curled from a fine-looking pipe one of the guards had left behind. Alex picked it up, stuck the stem in the corner of his mouth, and smiled as he savored the cherry-blend aroma of the pipe tobacco. *I think this properly falls under the classification of spoils of war, not petty larceny.* Gratified, he strolled unhurriedly through the open gate. Behind him, a hubbub of angry shouts, squawks, and braying filled the night—punctuated by the occasional discharge of a firearm. Alex puffed contentedly on his new pipe as he glanced at the formidable line of chevaux-de-frise on either side of the gate and wondered what Lincoln must be thinking. "Guess it's one of those nights, Mr. President," Alex chuckled, "and it ain't over yet."

At the intersection with the Prince George Court House Road, Alex checked his pocket watch—*1:03 A.M., no sign of Mike or Steve.* He walked across the road to the appointed rendezvous location. *I still have almost an hour to kill. Might be a good idea to see what lies in that direction,* he told himself, peering down the Court House Road in the direction the forage wagon had gone earlier. *Besides, it's cold, and moving about is better than sitting.*

Alex walked an unproductive half-mile, the road before him being of a talcum powder consistency that resembled a thin white ribbon stretching into infinity. He had barely begun to retrace his footsteps when a vibration disturbed the stillness of the night: the steady drumming of hooves on hard earth.

Heads of mounted riders suddenly emerged behind him. Alex darted into the scrub and hid, scarcely daring to breathe as a long column of Union cavalry trooped past. A battery of six 12-pound Napoleons rolled by in their wake, followed by an equal number of caissons and ammunition limbers.

When the column had vanished into the night, Alex cautiously stepped out into the road. *Why are they out and about at this late hour with artillery,* he wondered, then remembered the forage teamster's earlier comments about the 1st District of Columbia Cavalry at Prince

George Court House preparing to pull out early in the morning. *There must be a connection, but where are they going in the dead of night?*

CHAPTER 18

Prince George Court House Road
Near Meade's Headquarters
1:50 A.M., MARCH 25, 1865

When Alex reached the spot where he was to meet Mike and Steve, he heard a *"Psst!"* from a thicket at the edge of the road. He stopped and looked around, then ducked into the undergrowth.

Mike and Steve crouched in the shadows.

"Glad to see you're both on time," Alex said. "I was afraid that column of cavalry might delay you."

"What cavalry?" Mike asked, giving him a puzzled look. "We didn't see any cavalry."

"A whole regiment rode past me about a half-mile down this road a few minutes ago, Alex said, perplexed. "They were headed in this direction with six artillery pieces in tow. They must have turned off the road between here and there."

"Wonder where they're going at this hour?" Steve mused. "Seems to be a lot of activity tonight."

"Yeah," Mike nodded, "especially when you factor in the two infantry regiments I saw detraining in the woods west of Meade Station just after midnight."

"Two regiments?" Alex said, surprised. "You're sure?"

"It was hard to miss the two big Pennsylvania regimental colors they were carrying."

"The colors weren't cased?"

"Nope. After they got off the train, they assembled and marched off

155

toward Harrison's Creek with their flags flapping in the breeze. They were obviously in a hurry to get to wherever they were headed. No talking or horseplay in the ranks—seemed like a real serious bunch."

"Let's compare notes," Alex said, pulling his notebook from his coat pocket. "I'll go first."

Alex opened his notebook to the page where the Union private had so painstakingly sketched in neat and elaborate detail the location of every important feature inside the headquarters' perimeter.

Steve made his peculiar little whistle when he saw the map. "You've been busy tonight, Bubba!" he said, exchanging his British accent for a Southern drawl. "How'd you git holt of all that information? An' looky here! You even got Lincoln's cabin drawn on here. How'd you do it?"

"Nothing to it, really," Alex replied smugly. "While you were crawling about in the muck and poison ivy, I was having a cup of coffee with a couple of friendly Union sentries. They told me everything I wanted to know and more."

"I don't suppose you had anything to do with that fire and the hubbub inside the perimeter a little while ago?" Mike asked. "I sensed your finesse and unobtrusive imprint."

"Well, yeah, I did have a little something to do with that. I'll tell you all about it over a beer when this is over."

For the next few minutes Mike and Steve took turns adding their respective knowledge of the terrain, roads, trails, and the disposition of Union troops to Alex's sketch map. When they finished, Alex made copies of the map, then tore the pages from his notebook and gave them each one.

"To get back to the rendezvous point, I think it would be safer to circle around south of Meade's headquarters," Alex said as he looked at his pocket watch—2:05 A.M.

"It may be safer," Steve admitted, "but it's the long way back to Harrison's Creek Bridge. Going around the north side is quicker, and besides, that's the way we'll be bringing Major Jonas and his troops in a few hours. It's better if we're all familiar with the lay of the land on the approach route."

Alex thought about that for a moment, then nodded. "Makes sense to me. What d'ya think, Mike?"

"Okay by me," Mike said, shrugging his shoulders.

"We'll do it your way then," Alex gave Steve a thumbs up. "However, the Union army is up to something. With all the movement we've seen tonight, they either know of Gordon's preparations, or they're planning an attack of their own."

"If they've been tipped off, I wouldn't think the President of the United States would be this close to the front lines," Mike countered.

"Yes. Quite right," Alex agreed. "In neither event would Lincoln be here. So what's going on in the Union camp? If Lincoln is visiting, then why isn't Meade or Grant, or both, with him?"

"Well, whatever's afoot," Steve interjected, "Gordon needs to be told."

"We'll get word to him when we link up with Major Jonas. Speaking of whom," Alex said, tapping the ornate gold cover on his watch, "it's time we headed back to the bridge."

Alex led the way, initially following the Prince George Road a short distance, then ducking into the protective shelter of the scrub pine between the encampment's northern perimeter and Meade Station. Safely past the encampment, they emerged from the dense scrub onto the double ribbons of track of the City Point and Military Railroad.

"Meade Station is about a quarter mile that way," Alex whispered, pointing up the track. "If we keep going the way we have been, we'll reach Harrison's Creek in a few minutes. Then all we have to do is follow it downstream to the road that leads to the bridge—we're practically home free."

"Piece of cake," Mike chuckled, "except for the little problem of a few thousand Yankees standing between us and the bridge."

"Did I neglect to mention that?" Alex grinned. "Silly me!"

"Lord, what have I gotten myself into?" Steve smiled, shaking his head. "I was better off being the only fighter pilot in the Confederate States Army."

"Welcome to the pantheon of unsung heroes, my friend!" Mike said, slapping him on the back. "How does it feel to know your name will never appear in a history book?"

"Doesn't bother me at all. Actually, I'm only in this for the money!"

Alex couldn't resist. "Well, that's what I'd expect from a guy who makes a living flying a coffin with a propeller."

The friendly bantering took their minds off the dangers confronting them, but the humor quickly faded as they crossed the tracks and plunged headlong into a nightmare labyrinth of felled trees and lopped limbs amid jumbles of briars and blackberry thickets. The sounds of cracking limbs, crashing trees, and ripping briars threatened to betray their presence to any enemy patrols that might be in the area.

Alex floundered through the morass in the dark, cursing under his breath the unseen briars that ripped his flesh and snagged his feet. For the next ten minutes he struggled through an almost impenetrable tangle of underbrush, then suddenly stumbled into a clearing.

A dozen blue-clad soldiers lounged around the glowing embers of a dying campfire in the middle of the clearing studying him with a mixture of curiosity and amusement.

Alex froze in his tracks, like a bird dog spotting a covey of quail, and stared.

Then, with the sound of briars ripping away from trouser legs and coat sleeves, Mike nearly collided with him as he stumbled free of a clutching blackberry patch. As he extricated himself from a clinging briar, Mike glimpsed the Union soldiers gathered around the campfire. "Uh-oh" he whispered.

Behind them, Mike and Alex heard Steve's familiar low whistle noting surprise.

For what seemed endless seconds, the two groups stared at each other in silence.

"Well now," a voice with a thick Irish brogue finally broke the stillness, "leave it to an officer to get to his thumb by goin' around his elbow."

"That's enough, Hagerty," a seated figure admonished from the far side of the flickering fire. Getting on his feet, the man strolled toward them; the embers flared brightly as a light breeze suddenly stirred them, revealing the uniform of an infantry captain.

"But I have to admit, you *do* have a point," he acknowledged as he came face to face with Alex. "Instead of thrashing around in that briar patch in the dark, why didn't you just go down the tracks another fifty yards and come through on the main road?"

Mike glowered at Alex as he pulled a piece of prickly briar off his sleeve.

A slow, sheepish grin settled over Alex's face as he surveyed the cluster of armed soldiers in front of him. "Made the mistake of listening to my friend here," he answered jerking a thumb in Mike's direction. "Said he knew a shortcut. Actually, this is one of his better ones—no sprains, broken bones or snake bites this time!"

Shifting their gaze to Mike, the soldiers guffawed heartily.

Mike pretended to appear properly chagrined as he muttered under his breath just loud enough for Alex to hear. "Keep'em laughing. That's a good sign."

"Where're you boys heading this time of night?" the captain asked in his unmistakable New York City accent.

"The Chief of Engineers, Army of the Potomac sent us to check the condition of the bridge over Harrison's Creek," Alex answered casually.

"You're Engineer officers?" the captain laughed, obviously finding their predicament uproariously funny.

Alex heard the derisive snickers around him as the soldiers picked up on the humor. *I suppose encountering three lost Engineer officers from Army headquarters in the middle of the night is kind of funny,* he had to admit.

"Yep, believe it or not," Alex shrugged.

"Which bridge?" the captain asked, still chuckling.

Alex hesitated. It hadn't occurred to him there might be more than one bridge over the creek. "The one behind Fort Stedman," he replied, hoping the description would suffice.

"Keep going the way you have been and you'll get there—" the captain turned and winked at his men—"next week."

More snickers.

"If you could just point us in the right direction, we'd be much obliged," Alex smiled contritely as he handed the captain a folded copy of his phony orders.

The grin promptly faded from the captain's face as he unfolded the paper, revealing the bold letterhead of the Office of the Inspector General of the Army of the Potomac. Studying the smaller print in the glow of the campfire, the Union officer glanced up at Alex with a puzzled expression. "Do you work for the Chief of Engineers or the Inspector General?"

"We're assigned to the Chief of Engineers but detailed to the Inspector General," Alex replied matter-of-factly. "We were ordered to inspect the bridge tonight, which is why we're out here in the dark taking ill-advised shortcuts."

The captain nodded in sympathetic understanding as he handed the orders back to Alex. He picked up a twig and began drawing lines in the earth by the campfire. "We're here, and this is the creek flowing north in this direction." He made the quick, decisive strokes of someone intimately familiar with the surrounding area. "You'll find a trail of sorts over there," he continued, pointing the end of the stick at the edge of the clearing. "It will take you to the creek and intersects with a wagon road at this point." He tapped the end of the twig at the spot on the crude map he had drawn in the dirt. "The wagon road generally winds south to north following the high ground above the creek. About a mile north, it intersects with another wagon road—here—that descends into the creek bottom. You'll find the bridge at this spot," he said, tapping the end of the twig at an imaginary point on the dirt map.

"If we were to follow the wagon road south, will it lead us back to our headquarters?" Alex inquired, looking to pick up some useful intelligence.

"Hmm...No, not quite. But it will take you within a few hundred yards of it, and it's an easy walk from the wagon road through the woods to the headquarters."

Alex smiled, looking suitably grateful. "I can't tell you how much we appreciate your help, Captain...?"

"Deveraux. Captain Matt Deveraux."

"Thanks, Matt. I'm Alex Wright. Incidentally, what brings you and your men out here tonight?"

"Like you," Deveraux shrugged impassively, "just following orders."

"Lots of infantry and cavalry moving about tonight." Alex hoped Deveraux might volunteer an explanation.

"That so?" he replied, arching his eyebrows. "Probably has something to do with the President's review tomorrow. You know, heightened security and all that, which is why we're here."

"Yeah, I guess that's it," Alex nodded. "We were concerned that we might wind up in the middle of a battle."

"If that happens we'll all be unpleasantly surprised," Deveraux laughed. "I don't want to hold you up, Alex. Just be careful—there are a lot of patrols out tonight. You'll be okay if you stay on the roads and don't take any more shortcuts through the brush."

Alex smiled, gave the Union officer a casual salute, then turned toward the trail at the edge of the clearing. Mike and Steve closed in behind him.

CHAPTER 19

Harrison's Creek Bridge
4:00 A.M., MARCH 25, 1865

For twenty minutes they had been squatting on the bone chilling ground beneath the Harrison's Creek bridge, a rifle shot distance from Fort Stedman. The cold sapped the warmth from their bodies through their light layers of clothing. They shivered as they waited impatiently for the Confederate attack to begin.

For the fifth time since arriving at the bridge Alex pulled out his pocket watch and checked the time—*4:02 A.M.*—then frowned again as he stuffed it back into his vest.

Mike and Steve exchanged worried glances.

Alex sighed impatiently as he folded his arms across his chest and shoved his hands under his armpits for warmth.

Suddenly the ragged rattle of musketry and the heavy booming of cannon carried to their ears. As they sat up and listened, artillery shells began bursting on the high ground behind them. The musketry grew more intense, and so did the cannonade as Confederate gunners shifted their fire from the fortifications on the Union line to the camp on the reverse slope behind Fort Stedman.

Under the bridge, Alex cursed as the rain of exploding shells from mortars, field guns, and heavy siege cannon shook the earth around him.

Once more the Confederate gunners shifted their deadly barrage to the hillside beyond the bridge. Alex lifted his head and gazed around. Not much was visible due to the drifts of fog that had suddenly materialized. Not until the acrid odor of cordite wafted into his sinuses did he realize that it wasn't fog but smoke produced by the exploding shells and the discharge of countless rifles and cannon.

As the artillery exchanges subsided into isolated duels between Union and Confederate gunners, the sounds of voices carried down the slope from the direction of Fort Stedman.

Alex heard the tramping of feet running in their direction punctuated by an occasional command. "That may be our three assault columns," he yelled above the din of the battlefield.

Mike and Steve nodded.

"Let's check it out," Steve suggested, pointing to the bridge above them.

Cautiously they crept up the creek bank and peered over the bridge abutment.

The swirling smoke parted momentarily permitting them to see the sloping ground behind Fort Stedman.

Before the drifting smoke swallowed them up again, Alex glimpsed a ragged formation of blue-clad soldiers running hell-bent toward the bridge. He held his breath, straining to see if the approaching phantoms had white scarves tied around their necks.

Alex's hand wandered to his neck as he suddenly remembered that he had taken off his scarf inside Meade's encampment. He fumbled in his coat pockets for the scarf, but his fingers were too numb to feel the material. As he pulled his notebook from his pocket, a ball of white cloth tumbled out with it. He quickly picked up the scarf and tied it around his neck.

Meanwhile, the onrushing infantry reached the bridge. Alex

looked up to see them charging through the swirling smoke, but in the same instant, the soldiers in the forefront saw the doughboys and were immediately upon them.

As Alex got on his feet, he felt the sharp prick of a bayonet pressed against his throat. His eyes traveled up the length of the bayonet to the rifle barrel, then to the blue uniform of the soldier brandishing the weapon. Tied around his neck, Alex happily noted, was a strip of white cloth.

Alex pointed to his own scarf. "'Bout time!" he said, pushing the bayonet aside.

"Sorry," the soldier smiled apologetically as Major Jonas pushed through the mass of soldiers toward him.

"It's okay, boys," Jonas said, recognizing Steve and Alex. "These are our guides."

"Glad to see you, Alex," he said, clapping a hand on Alex's shoulder. "Hope you have good news."

"Nice to see you too, Major," Alex nodded and smiled as they stepped off to the side of the road to talk privately. "I managed to get inside Meade's camp. I didn't see Lincoln with my own eyes, but I met a couple of sentries who claimed to have seen him tonight. They also said General Meade left on a train going to City Point earlier in the evening. That's most unusual for someone who's entertaining such a distinguished visitor. General Gordon should also be informed that the area between Fort Stedman and Meade's headquarters is fairly crawling with Union troops. We observed two infantry regiments and one cavalry regiment moving towards Harrison's Creek after midnight. I recommend we move fast. I've got a bad feeling about all this."

"We're ready. I'll let General Gordon know what you've learned."

Major Jonas quickly scribbled a short message, handed it to a courier, then signaled the column to move forward.

In a column two abreast, the Confederate raiders broke into an easy jog; Alex fell in step beside the Major at the head of the column with Mike and Steve following on their heels. Behind them the battle raged unabated as they crossed the bridge then followed the tortuous wagon road winding upward out of the creek bottom.

On the heights above the creek, the wagon road straightened and stretched away across open, level land that had once been cultivated fields. It was a pretty scene to behold in the moonlight—except for the distant line of rising dust heralding the rapid approach of Union infantry.

"Good thing we got here before they did, Major," Alex said, puffing slightly from the uphill exertion. "There's a road intersection just ahead. Turn right when we reach it and don't slow down. We'll just barely make the turnoff ahead of those Union troops. And of course, they'll be wondering why we're high-tailing it away from the fighting, so let's put as much distance between them and us as we can."

Alex was well aware of the heavy, raspy breathing behind him, a warning that most of the men in the column were in poor physical shape and couldn't keep up this pace much longer. *Losing men will put the mission at risk, but it's a race against time. We have to get to Meade's headquarters before they move Lincoln to safer ground.*

"We can't afford to wait for the stragglers to catch up, Major," Alex said, noting that Major Jonas was looking over his shoulder more frequently now. From his worried expression, Alex knew he shared the same concern. "There's only one company—less than a hundred men—guarding Meade's headquarters. We still have the element of surprise in our favor and enough men to do the job; however, our window of opportunity is slipping away. We need to move fast before they send reinforcements."

A short distance beyond the road intersection, the second and third detachments of the Confederate column suddenly dropped out of sight. Alex wondered if they had stopped to wait for stragglers contrary to Jonas' orders but then remembered their mission was to capture the three redoubts thought to be overlooking Fort Stedman on this side of the creek. The first detachment, under Major Jonas' command, continued to follow the road south.

"Uh-oh," Jonas grunted as they rounded a curve and saw a small column of blue-clad soldiers rushing toward them. "I think we've just encountered our first snag."

The officer in charge of the column had spotted the disguised Confederates and promptly halted his troops. Alex couldn't hear the orders the officer was issuing, but it wasn't necessary; the marching movements of his troops told the story. With drilled precision, the Union column turned sharply, exposing their flank momentarily to the approaching Confederates, then stopped and executed a left face. The front rank quickly kneeled and raised their weapons to their shoulders.

As the Confederates drew closer, Alex suddenly recognized the officer commanding the small Union force. He charged ahead of Major Jonas, shouting as he ran, "Matt! Don't shoot! Don't shoot!"

The distant officer stood on high ground behind the rear rank of his troops, his sword poised, about to give the order to fire.

Captain Deveraux hesitated. Shouting and waving, a lone figure had suddenly darted out ahead of the approaching column. As the figure closed within a dozen yards, Deveraux breathed again, not realizing that he had been holding his breath for long, anxious moments, then lowered his sword. "Ground your weapons, boys! They're our troops!" he laughed as he pushed through the ranks of his men and stepped out in front of the formation to greet the approaching visitor.

"You have more lives than a cat, Alex!" Deveraux grinned as Alex slowed to a walk. "This makes twice tonight we came close to shooting you! You lost again?"

The men behind him chuckled as they stood at ease, leaning on their rifles.

"Looks like you brought company with you this time." Deveraux nodded at the distant column of troops stopped on the road as he held out a welcoming hand.

"Hello, Matt," Alex smiled, shaking the proffered hand. "I didn't expect to see you again so soon!"

"I'm guessing you reached that bridge just in time to get swept up in the fighting. Got any idea what's happening?" Deveraux asked anxiously, the sound of musketry drawing ominously closer.

"It looks real bad," Alex grimaced as though it pained him to share the news. "Just after we reached the bridge on Harrison's Creek, the Rebs attacked and overran Fort Stedman. The garrison surrendered without so much as a whimper, and we came within a hair of getting captured ourselves. Seems like everything's come unglued; most of the 9th Corps has been routed; and there's no organized resistance between here and Fort Stedman. General Parke believes the President is in danger and sent that infantry detachment to reinforce whatever security he already has assigned to him. The Major commanding the detachment is unfamiliar with the area, so I'm guiding him to General Meade's headquarters taking the route you showed me. The Rebs were right on our heels when we crossed the bridge at Harrison's Creek a few minutes ago." Alex noticed that the laughter had stopped, and Deveraux's men were now exchanging nervous looks as they digested this last bit of news.

Deveraux drew himself up ramrod straight. "Well, the Rebs haven't run up against the 96th New York yet. They'll pay a heavy price getting past us. Tell your Major we'll let him pass. We'll dig in here and protect his rear."

Alex waved to Jonas that it was safe to proceed.

The detachment moved forward, resuming its former shuffling gait.

Deveraux saluted Major Jonas, then stood beside Alex watching the long column of disguised Confederates stream past. "What outfit is this, Alex?" Deveraux asked, frowning at the deplorable condition of the men. "And what does the white scarf tied around their necks signify?"

Alex didn't answer.

"Alex, I said—" Deveraux started again, then hesitated as he turned and gave the other man a puzzled look. He noticed for the first time the white scarf tucked inside his collar. Then his gaze dropped to Alex's right hand. It held a sleek-looking pistol pointed directly at Deveraux's ribcage.

"Sorry, Matt. You were about to figure it out, so I might as well show my colors."

"I wouldn't have guessed you for a Reb," Deveraux said, eyeing the strange pistol in Alex's hand with more curiosity than alarm.

"Lucky for me," Alex acceded with a smile. "I wouldn't be here now if you had thought that earlier,"

"Behind us are thirty armed men, Alex. I think your luck just ran out. All I have to do is say the word and you're a dead man, so why don't you just hand over that pistol."

"Would you do that knowing you'd be a dead man too?" Alex cocked the hammer of his .45, hoping Deveraux wouldn't call his bluff.

Deveraux raised an eyebrow then flashed a taunting smile. "Just watch me," he said as he turned away from Alex and shouted an order.

Alex didn't need to look over his shoulder to know there were thirty rifles pointed at his back. He held his pistol at arm's length, inches from Deveraux's head.

Deveraux squinted at him, and Alex saw rock hard determination and fearlessness in his eyes. In quick succession Deveraux snapped his orders. "Ready! Aim!—"

Beneath his uniform, Alex felt the cold sweat from his armpits running down his arms. *Well, I guess this is it,* he told himself. *I never expected that Matt Deveraux's face would be the last thing I'd see in this life.*

CHAPTER 20

Between Harrison's Creek And Meade's Headquarters

4:40 A.M., MARCH 25, 1865

"Surrender!" A voice suddenly rang from the woods. Alex turned halfway around and stared in amazement. Almost a hundred of Major Jonas' men had enveloped the right flank and rear of the smaller Federal force. Shoulder to shoulder the Confederate infantry held the enemy in their rifle sights, waiting for the command to fire.

Deveraux's defiance faded in the face of such overwhelming odds. Reluctantly, he gave the order: "Okay, boys, lay down your weapons.

They got the jump on us."

With some grumbling, they reluctantly obeyed and, one by one, dropped their rifles.

Deveraux presented his sword to Alex.

Seeing the pain in his eyes, Alex shook his head. "Keep your sword, Matt. It means nothing to me—" Deveraux's grim expression softened perceptibly—"but I'll take your pistol."

The other shrugged resignedly as he lifted his holster flap. "I intend to get this back," Deveraux said, handing over his side arm butt first. He gave Alex a cold smile, then turned on his heel to join his men who were being herded into a wooded ravine.

Alex watched him go with a premonition that he hadn't yet seen the last of Matt Deveraux. He put the thought aside as he walked over to Major Jonas who was busy reorganizing his straggler-thinned ranks.

"Coming to thank me for rescuing you, I suppose?" Jonas grinned as he caught sight of Alex. "Well, I hate to disillusion you, Old Man, but the truth of the matter is: those Yankees might have blocked the relief force that Gordon will be sending later. I had to eliminate that possibility."

On the face of it, Jonas' explanation seemed plausible, but Alex wasn't buying it. This encounter had cost Jonas precious minutes he could ill-afford to lose. They both knew that every minute of delay increased disproportionately the probability that Federal reinforcements would reach Meade's headquarters before the Confederates. Alex merely smiled. "Right on, sir!"

At 5:00 A.M. the detachment reached the tracks of the U.S. Military Railroad between Meade Station and Harrison's Creek.

Jonas summoned his guides and team leaders. "I'll be located with the first platoon. Alex—Captain Wright," he corrected himself, "will be our guide. We'll take the south and east sides of the headquarters' perimeter. Second platoon—Lieutenant Anderson will be your guide, and you will approach the perimeter from the west. Third platoon—your guide will be Lieutenant Dent. Since you have the shortest distance to travel, remain in place until the other teams are in position, then approach the perimeter from the north. We'll attack at 5:25 A.M. Watch for my red flare."

The moon hung low on the horizon. First platoon stealthily moved into an area of new growth pine and tall brush within sight of the chevaux-de-frise. Alex was pleased. All was quiet along the Headquarters, Army of the Potomac perimeter, despite the sounds of battle rumbling ominously around Fort Stedman a scant mile away.

Major Jonas also had good reason to be pleased. He had reached his objective with most of his detachment intact. He had dispatched a small holding force of ten men, less than half the number his plan originally called for, to set up a blocking position on the Courthouse Road to engage any Union cavalry that might come from Prince George Courthouse. Likewise, the third platoon had a similar task of establishing a blocking position to thwart reinforcements sent from Meade Station.

Jonas held a pocket watch in his palm. At precisely 5:25 A.M., he pointed a naval flare gun at the stars above the silent camp and pulled the trigger. A bright red flare arced across the night sky. Like ghosts rising from the ground, eighty men sprang toward the dark perimeter and quickly scaled the chevaux-de-frise.

Alex and Jonas drew their pistols and, together with four men, leaped from the brush onto the road and dashed toward the encampment gate.

The lanterns on either side of the gate glowed brightly, but nowhere within their lighted circumference did Alex see any sign of the half-dozen guards on duty earlier. *It appears they've been caught literally napping;* the thought sent his spirits soaring.

Their headlong rush slowed to a cautious walk when they reached the gate. Alex's euphoria was short lived as uneasiness, dark and ominous, settled over him. The woods shut out the moonlight making whatever lay beyond the gate an impenetrable black veil. Alex stared into the darkness, half-expecting to see flashes of gunfire erupt from the concealed guards lying in ambush.

Alex and Jonas exchanged anxious glances as they passed through the gate. A short distance away, the rattle of musketry and the booming of cannon raged as the struggle for Fort Stedman continued. But here, less than a mile behind the Union siege line, an eerie stillness hung in the air as Alex led the Major and his men down a series of winding trails inside the silent camp. Having committed to memory the map that the Union sentry had drawn for him, Alex was confident he could lead them to Lincoln's cabin, but he had a gnawing feeling in the pit of his stomach that something was terribly wrong. They passed through the middle of the encampment of tents and wooden structures without encountering a single Union soldier. *What's going on here? We haven't heard a shot or a voice since we entered the camp.*

On the left side of the trail, under the limbs of two magnificent oaks, three small cabins came into view that matched the description the Union sentry had given him. He remembered, too, that Lincoln's cabin was the one closest to them.

Alex stopped and pointed at the cabin.

Like silent phantoms, the Confederate raiders fanned out and surrounded it.

Jonas and Alex crept onto the cabin's covered porch. Light shone through the bottom of the door, but no sound came from within.

Alex carefully lifted the latch, gave the door a slight shove, and watched it swing open noiselessly on well-oiled hinges.

The cabin's interior was bathed in a soft luminescence that came from an oil lamp on a table in the back of the room. A chair was placed conspicuously in the center of the room. Equally conspicuous was the handwritten message on a large sheet of parchment left on the seat. From the doorway, Alex and Jonas easily read the large bold text:

> *Sorry to have missed you*
> *Please convey my regards to Jeff Davis*
> *A. Lincoln*

Jonas and Alex gaped at the sign.

"They've either skedaddled or we've walked into a trap!" Alex said, his voice quavering as foreboding wrapped its icy tentacles around his heart and squeezed.

Jonas strode angrily into the room, snatched up the parchment, and stuffed it into his coat pocket. His eyes roamed the room searching for a clue that might explain the mystery. Finding none, he returned to the porch where he confronted Alex. "You've led us into a trap, Captain!"

Alex bristled at the accusation. "I don't know what happened, Major, but for damn sure I didn't have a hand in it. Five hours ago the camp appeared normal, and three eyewitnesses told me that Lincoln was here."

Jonas gave Alex a long hard, penetrating look, then after a moment he said quietly, "I was wrong to blame you, Alex—you did your best. Whatever is going on here is being directed by someone with his own agenda."

"You think we've been set up?" Alex asked.

"Yeah, I do, and I think we'd better get out of here *now*."

They were interrupted by Mike and Steve. Both appeared worried.

"We captured our sector of the camp without firing a shot," Steve said, then added, "We encountered no opposition whatsoever, sir."

"No opposition?" Jonas repeated dully.

"Yes, sir," Steve nodded, wondering if it was a question or a statement. "The camp's deserted."

"Same in my area," Mike added. "We didn't see anyone."

Jonas chewed his lower lip as he stared thoughtfully at the cabin where he had expected to find Lincoln. He nodded, as if reaching a decision, then turned to Anderson and Dent. "Go back to your platoon leaders. Tell them the detachment is to reassemble here immediately. We've been lured into a trap. Have the men throw away anything that will slow them down, except weapons, ammunition, and canteens."

Eighty men—all that were left of the initial hundred-man company—formed up in the little clearing in front of the cabin. The platoon leaders made a final headcount as the first streaks of dawn appeared on the horizon.

Jonas waited patiently for the platoon leaders to make their reports. He knew—they all knew—they might have to fight their way out of here. Reorganizing the detachment was important if they hoped to beat off an attack.

Alex pulled out his pocket watch; a bright gold Masonic fob danced on the end of the heavy gold chain as the engraved case popped open in his hand—*6:04 A.M. An odd hour to launch an attack,* he thought as he listened to the peculiar whir of an in-coming cannonball.

A plume of brown earth suddenly erupted skyward in the center of the encampment thirty yards from the detachment. If anyone flinched, Alex didn't see it—every man remained rigidly at attention. Well…almost everyone. Mike and Steve most certainly flinched but didn't permit themselves to be disgraced in front of Jonas' battle-hardened veterans by dashing for cover.

Before the dirt and debris finished falling around them from the first shell, the telltale whine of two more incoming rounds filled the air. Alex held his breath.

The first struck a giant pine—the blast shattering its trunk ten feet above the ground and showering the detachment with a deadly rain of shrapnel and splintered wood.

Two men in Steve's platoon were felled, one from a two-foot-long chunk of wood through his chest, the other from shrapnel in the head, killing him instantly.

The second cannonball plowed a furrow in front of two of the cabins before detonating under the porch of the third one. The explosion lifted the porch in a cloud of matchwood and timbers, some of which rained down on the tightly packed formations.

Jonas smiled, seemingly oblivious to the shelling and the falling debris. "If it's a fight they want, boys, then let's give'em one! *Forward, March!*"

The three small formations marched forward two ranks deep toward the edge of the deserted camp. They had gone only a dozen yards when the next salvo from the unseen cannon landed in their rear among the headquarters tents and camp equipage. Hot shrapnel sliced through the camp, setting fire to many of the tents.

Jonas halted the company a few yards from the chevaux-de-frise on the camp's perimeter, then sent an axe-wielding detail forward to cut away a section of it. Beyond the barrier, a low-lying mist blanketed the field as it sloped gently uphill for two hundred yards to a line of woods.

While the detail cut through the chevaux-de-frise, a grim silence settled over the company as a light southerly breeze suddenly lifted the veil of mist, revealing along the high ground in front of the woods a regiment of blue-clad infantry formed up in a line of battle. On their left, the crews of a two-gun section of artillery were busily reloading their brass 12-pound Napoleons.

Their escape blocked by the larger enemy force, the Confederates appeared dazed and uncertain. "Lieutenants Dent and Anderson! *Front and Center!*" Major Jonas ordered. Mike and Steve marched to the front of the company and halted in front of the Major.

"Scout the rest of the perimeter and see if you can find another way out of here. Make it snappy. Report back to me in ten minutes."

"Yes, sir," they said in unison, saluted, then turned and set off at a run in opposite directions along the camp's perimeter.

It occurred to Alex that it had suddenly become strangely quiet. The cannonade had stopped. The only audible sound was the desultory cannon fire and ragged musketry from Fort Stedman where the fighting seemed to be abating.

Mike and Steve quickly returned with more bad news. Another Union regiment was positioned north and east of the perimeter while a large body of cavalry with supporting artillery occupied the open area south of the encampment.

There's no hope of escape, Alex thought glumly. *So, is this it? To come so far and through so much just to die or be taken prisoner?*

Movement within the Confederate ranks caught his eye. One after another, as if in response to an unspoken command, the soldiers began shedding their Union headgear and the dark blue coats and jackets in favor of their own caps and scraps of Confederate uniforms which they had stuffed in their pockets or worn under the enemy uniforms.

A sergeant picked up a pole and attached a Confederate battle flag that he had secreted away.

Alex saw no fear in their eyes as the men checked their rifles and attached their bayonets. Some shook hands or shared a plug of tobacco or just stood quietly squinting at the distant line of Union infantry with their regimental colors waving brightly in the first rays of the morning sun. He knew these battle-hardened veterans possessed no allusions about the probable outcome of their predicament. They had volunteered for this dangerous duty and were now prepared to give their last full measure for the cause they had so valiantly defended for so long.

Alex watched as Major Jonas positioned himself in front of his troops with the sergeant bearing the Confederate battle flag standing beside him. He wondered what Jonas had decided to do—*attack, defend, or surrender?* Alex glanced at Mike and Steve. They wore the same stubborn expressions as the other men.

CHAPTER 21

Union Rear Area Defense Force

6:20 A.M., MARCH 25, 1865

Brigadier General Dorsett knew he had the Rebels trapped. Hopefully the Reb commander would see the hopelessness of his situation and agree to end the matter without further bloodshed. After quietly eliminating the two small enemy blocking forces on the Prince George Courthouse Road, he had given the order to his artillery to fire a few rounds into the camp. Until a few hours ago it had been Major General Meade's headquarters, more generally referred to as Headquarters, Army of the Potomac.

Taking advantage of the current lull, the Union commander pulled a white handkerchief from his pocket and allowed it to flutter in the breeze as he held it above his head. He gently nudged his horse with his spurs and rode out onto the open ground between the two opposing forces.

CHAPTER 22

Confederate Detachment

6:20 A.M., MARCH 25, 1865

Alex watched the two approaching riders through his field glasses. "Major," he shouted. "Looks like a General Officer coming over under a flag of truce. Doesn't take a genius to figure out what he wants to talk about."

"He could just as easily have stayed safely behind his troops and let his artillery blow us away," Jonas grunted in grudging respect for the man's courage as he studied him through his binoculars. "I'll listen to what he has to say.

Hold your fire, boys," Jonas shouted. "I'm going out to talk with him."

"You gonna surrender, Major?" a soldier asked.

"We'll fight our way outta here, an' to hell an' back, if'n you was to ask us," another voice piped up.

A chorus of assenting "Ayes" rose from the ranks.

Jonas doffed his hat, and with a flourish, bowed humbly.

"Most of you boys know me or know me by reputation. You know I never left a battlefield unless I was ordered to withdraw. You also know I would never risk your lives unless I believed we had a good chance of winning a fight, and I thought the gain was worth the sacrifice—that holds true here as well. I'll let you know the score after I talk to that Yankee General. He's waving a white handkerchief, so maybe *he* wants to surrender." Jonas flashed them a grin.

"Kin I have his saddle an' bridle if'n he does, Major?" a soldier shouted in the rear rank, eliciting loud guffaws from his comrades.

"Hell, I'll even throw in his horse if he does," the Major laughed as he turned away and strode through the opening in the chevaux-de-frise.

Like the officer riding toward him, Jonas too, held up a white handkerchief signaling his willingness to parlay.

Alex was suddenly aware of Mike standing beside him.

"My guess is we're going to surrender," Mike ventured, his voice emotionless.

"No matter. We've lost the game either way," Alex said bitterly. "So much for changing history."

"Well, if they get their hands on our pistols, history could still change—possibly for the worst," Mike rationalized. "We need to hide them someplace before the Major gets back. Got any ideas?"

"As a matter of fact I do, but we need to hurry."

With everyone's eyes on Jonas, Alex and Mike slipped away among the trees, then raced along the footpath back to the three cabins.

Mike followed close behind as Alex carefully picked his way through the debris littering the ground to a small wooden structure standing behind the damaged cabin. An overpowering stench greeted them as Alex opened the flimsy wooden door. A swarm of flies and gnats buzzed inside the dark interior. Mimicking the Major, Alex doffed his hat with a flourish. "Please enter my office!"

Mike recognized the structure as a privy, or out house, as they called it back home. "You're forgetting," he said nasally, holding his nose, "I've seen your office. This is an improvement!"

Unbuckling his pistol belt, Alex dangled it over the black hole inside the privy for a second or two then let it go. It made a satisfying *plop* as it struck the thick liquid ooze at the bottom of the pit.

Alex stepped aside and held the privy door open as Mike tossed his weapon and holster into the hole under the wooden seat. "Phew! So this is the Presidential privy." Mike wrinkled his nose in disgust. "Lincoln must have had an upset stomach. It's really foul in there! Y' know, Alex, if we ever get home, they're going to make us pay for those pistols."

"And I'd be happy to," Alex said wistfully

"Good!" Mike nodded affably. "Then I'll just have the Regimental Quartermaster deduct mine out of your pay too."

"Fine! I can afford it," Alex grinned. "The way I figure it, the Army owes me back pay for fifty-three years."

"Oh?" Mike looked at him with a raised eyebrow. "Aren't you forgetting?—you're in the *Confederate* army. You'll be lucky they don't shoot you for desertion— if and when you get home!"

"Nah!" Alex shrugged. "They'll just ship me off to France hoping some Boche will save them the trouble."

"That's what I like about you, Alex: your optimism."

No one seemed to have missed them. Everyone's attention was focused on the two officers conversing on the distant slope. The Union General had dismounted; the broad brim of his hat hid his face, but he seemed to be listening as well as talking.

"I saw you and Mike wander off a few minutes ago," Steve said as he walked up from behind and joined them. "I thought maybe you were deserting."

"Sorry. Didn't mean to worry you," Alex replied. "We were in need of a privy. I remembered seeing one behind the cabins back there."

"Unless you messed your pants when the artillery opened up on us, it's a rather odd time to go looking for a privy, isn't it?" Steve said with a questioning smile. "However, it might be a convenient place to dispose of a pistol."

"That obvious—huh?" Alex said, impressed with Steve's astuteness.

"Maybe it's because everyone else is armed and you aren't. Tsk! Tsk!" Steve clucked with mock disdain, "But your secret is safe with me."

A sudden stirring and muttering came from the group of soldiers nearest them.

Alex peered across the field to see what was happening. Major Jonas strode toward the opening in the chevaux-de-frise while the Union General and his orderly were, in leisurely fashion, urging their horses up the slope toward their own lines.

Alex studied the Major as he approached, noting the bowed head and the lack of vigor in his step. His men, too, had detected the despondency in his bearing.

Alex made a quick decision. He strode to a position directly in front of the detachment, executed an *About Face*, clicked his heels together, and commanded—*Detachment! Atten-shun!*

Thin and ragged as scarecrows most of them were, but every man and boy pulled himself up tall and proud and stared straight ahead. His voice choked with emotion, Alex commanded—*Present, Arms!* then did another *About Face* and saluted Major Jonas.

Jonas' face reflected surprise as every man snapped his rifle smartly in his honor, but his eyes betrayed the sadness in his heart. With precise and slow deliberation, he returned Alex's salute.

Alex let his arm drop slowly to his side, whereupon he executed another *About Face* and gave the order to the detachment—*Order, Arms!*

The men promptly grounded their weapons at their sides while Alex marched to the left flank of the formation.

"*At ease*, men," Jonas said softly. The words sounded more like a paternal request than a command yet were loud enough for all to hear.

The men relaxed; most leaned casually on their rifles as though they were walking staffs. They stood in respectful silence, anticipating what he was about to say.

Jonas paused for a long moment to gaze at them. He remembered so many of those faces from shared campfires, marches, and battles through four terrible years of war. These men and boys had asked little in return but had always been willing to do whatever he asked of them. There were none better than these brave soldiers or those of earlier times who now lay in unmarked graves on a score of battlefields, or those with broken health and shattered bodies, yet steadfast in their beliefs and in their love of home and country. Most were mountain men, descendants of the flood of intrepid Ulster Scots who settled the Appalachian frontier two generations earlier. Their ancestors, with little love in their hearts for the English whose tyranny had forced them from their homes in Northern Ireland, had been in the forefront of those who fought in the American Revolution. Few owned slaves, and the notion expressed in the North that the war was being waged over slavery was absurd to their way of thinking. They weren't putting their lives on the line, nor were their families enduring hardship and privation just so a landed few could keep, buy, and sell slaves. Instead, that which incited their forefathers to take up arms against the British had also motivated them: defense of their homes, their communities, and their state against foreign invaders.

Jonas, himself, represented the warrior-leader of old. He had earned the love and steadfast loyalty of his men through his bravery, charismatic leadership, genuine humility, and his concern for their individual and collective well-being. If he asked them to storm the gates of Hell, they would follow him.

He spoke with a knot in his throat, but his voice rang clear and strong without betraying his emotions. "As you can easily see, we're completely surrounded. They outnumber us; they have artillery; they have the high ground, and we're caught out in the open within easy range of their cannon. Other than that, we have the upper hand."

Hoots, laughter, and some elbowing in the ranks.

Jonas paused and grinned, letting his little joke sink in. Then his face turned solemn.

"From what I can make of the fighting around Fort Stedman, I'm afraid General Gordon's attack has failed. That means no one will be coming to our rescue. With thousands of Yankees between Petersburg and here, that leaves us only one choice that makes any sense…"

"Beggin' yo'r pardon, Major."

Jonas eyed the man who had so brazenly interrupted him, wondering what he had to say.

With a long white beard that made him appear of Biblical age, a private stood in the front rank contemplating him with dark brooding eyes. He spat a stream of brown tobacco juice, then continued. "Whut do we do with all them Yankees after we capture'em?"

Grins and nodding of heads within the ranks.

Jonas laughed, acknowledging the soldier's bravado. "You are to be commended, Private Laird, and all of you, for your spirit and courage. However that Yankee General over there has given us ten minutes to lay down our arms and surrender. We both want to avoid further loss of valiant lives. If we surrender, he has agreed to overlook the fact that many of us are wearing Union uniforms. As most of you know, being captured in the wrong uniform could mean a death sentence. Under the circumstances, I thought his terms were acceptable, if not generous. In a few more weeks or months, I believe as many of you do, the war will end, and we can all return to our homes and families. In the little time remaining, I want you to stack your weapons, furl the flag, and then follow me up that slope to give ourselves up."

Before Jonas could say anything further, the senior sergeant stepped forward and saluted. "Major, me and the boys talked among ourselves whilst you were out there palavering with that Yankee General. We decided we'd rather fight than lay down and give up like whipped dogs. If you'll lead us, sir, we'll take those pretty regimental colors and those cannon up there home with us as souvenirs from this little foray."

Jonas returned the sergeant's salute. "Well, I can't say I'm surprised. I guess we've been together for so long, I pretty much expected this. It's just—" Jonas paused as he groped for the right words, "—having cheated death for so long, and now with the end of the war in sight, I can't ask you to keep on sacrificing—not against these odds. You have families waiting for you, and they've been waiting for four long years. We all know the Confederacy is dying, and each day it suffers and dies a little more. If it were your favorite hunting dog, you'd end its pain and suffering. Can you do no less for your country? You've done your duty. You can't save it, and to throw your lives away won't change that. The Yankees are giving you a chance of returning home to your loved ones—alive. Take it!"

"We've been down this road already, Major," the sergeant replied, loud enough for everyone to hear. "We're not budging. If the South falls, then we'll fall with her. We'd rather die on our feet as free men than live on our knees under Yankee tyranny. Our families back home feel the same way. We think all the world of you, Major, and you know we'd do whatever you ask of us, but not this. We'll not surrender. Either you lead us, or we respectfully ask that you step aside for someone who will."

Jonas stood silent, his head bowed for a long time. When he looked up, tears were welling in his eyes. "I'll lead you," he nodded, his voice choked with emotion. "If this is to be our last hurrah, boys, then let's go out with a roar!"

Major Jonas drew himself up straight and tall and took a deep breath. *Detachment! Atten-shun!*

The detachment snapped to attention. There would be no surrender today—or any day.

No one seemed to notice the group of officers standing off to one side. Alex, Mike, and Steve simply watched as the long double column trooped past them.

Alex studied their faces. Some were young boys, maybe eighteen or nineteen. If they were afraid, they didn't show it. *Do they share the same passion and loyalty as their older comrades-in-arms, or are they simply reacting to the emotions of the moment?* Most were kin or life-long neighbors from the same mountain communities. As descendants of a warrior-society, their deeds on the battlefield were borne home as badges of honor and courage to be revered and passed on from one generation to the next. Conversely, cowardice and dishonorable conduct would forever be remembered with shame and scorn.

To the Appalachian Mountain men who marched out onto the field of battle, it mattered little that the three officers had not joined them—after all, they *were* outsiders. If these strangers preferred to kneel in subservience to their oppressors, it was their business; however, to the mountain men, honor and love of country were all that mattered.

One young soldier turned his head and stared curiously at Alex as he passed by. Alex thought he looked vaguely familiar. Their eyes locked for a brief instant and then the soldier turned his head to the front and marched on. *That was my grandfather!* Tears welled in his eyes, and he was tempted to pull the soldier out of the formation, but he stood quietly and watched him pass through the opening in the chevaux-de-frise.

Alex stood transfixed as the column pivoted then passed from left to right directly across his line of vision. It was a grand and unforgettable sight. His chest swelled with pride, and tears again welled in his eyes. "Look at them!" he whispered. "Oh God! Just look at them!"

Furled about its staff, the battle flag suddenly sprang to life and waved wonderfully brilliant in the rays of the sunrise. The column ground to a halt and on command faced left. At the top of the slope the enemy waited—an endless line, two ranks deep.

The Union troops gazed down in silent admiration at the show of defiance from an enemy so few in number but so great in resolve.

While the two sides stared at each other, Major Jonas and his color bearer strode to the front and center of the Confederate line.

Despite the rattle of musketry and hammering of artillery around Fort Stedman, Alex was surprised how clearly he could hear Jonas' commands. At *Quick time, March!* the double lines of Confederate infantry were set into motion, up the slope toward the waiting rifles and cannon of the Union regiment.

When they had closed within three hundred yards of the enemy, Jonas shouted—*Double Quick Time, March!* The Confederate lines promptly surged forward.

Alex anticipated the Union artillery opening up at any moment, and when it did, the concussion nearly toppled him. The battery's two sections fired in unison. Geysers of red earth suddenly spewed along the whole length of the advancing infantry creating ragged holes in their ranks.

Despite the whir and whine of Confederate Minié balls and the occasional gasp or moan of a comrade pitching forward or backward, the Union infantry continued to hold their fire. Instinctively, Alex knew they were seasoned veterans who wouldn't be stampeded into firing prematurely.

The thin Confederate lines suddenly leaped forward as they made their final charge. From every throat the high quavering banshee wail of the Rebel Yell carried across the battlefield. A chill shot up Alex's spine as the mountain men surged toward the waiting enemy infantry.

A wall of dark gray smoke suddenly spewed from the whole length of the Union line followed by successive clouds of white smoke from the cannon. Alex reeled backward, stunned by the combined effect of blast and sound.

For a full, brief minute the battle raged.

Alex scanned the battlefield with his field glasses, but the pall of smoke hanging over the slope obscured his view.

As abruptly as it had begun, the firing stopped. An uneasy stillness fell over the battlefield as the smoke began drifting away from the higher elevation, helped along by a light northerly breeze.

Alex again held the binoculars to his eyes. The Stars and Stripes gradually appeared, fluttering from its staff above the haze. As he swept the field through the lenses, sunlight suddenly bathed the crest of the slope revealing the solid blue phalanx of Union infantry standing firm. The front rank knelt with rifles aimed while, behind them, the second rank stood with rifles primed and ready. The gunners stood beside their brass cannons, lanyards in hand, ready to resume the deadly rain of shell and canister. Silently they waited as they contemplated the eerie stillness that lay over the smoke-shrouded slope below them.

The northerly breeze gained strength, and the drifting shroud of smoke finally lifted from the lower slope revealing a frightful scene. Over the sights of their rifles the kneeling line of Union infantry stared in awe at the carnage.

Below them, the entire Confederate detachment lay in perfect order as though cut down by a scythe passing through a wheat field. The combined effect of musketry and canister at close range had been devastating. In neat rows every soldier lay dead. Major Jonas lay on his back staring at the sky through sightless eyes, his sword still gripped tightly in his right hand. Beside him, his flag bearer laid face down still clutching his flag staff—the Confederate battle flag fluttered on the ground like a mortally wounded bird.

CHAPTER 23

The Battlefield

7:30 A.M., MARCH 25, 1865

Alex was appalled by the incredible slaughter. That so many lives could be snuffed out so quickly seemed inconceivable in an age lacking the weapon technology that existed all too abundantly in the world from which he had come. Sickened by the carnage, he wondered what had possessed him to pursue a military career. *There's nothing glorious about being blown to bits.*

With an effort, he pushed aside his thoughts and concentrated on the scene being played out before his eyes. The last wisps of smoke had barely vanished when a Union skirmish line began advancing down the slope. The long, single line of infantry stepped over and around the Confederate dead. Finding no survivors among the slain, the skirmish line moved on toward the camp at the base of the slope.

Mike and Steve followed Alex out through the gap in the chevaux-de-frise and stood in plain sight waiting for the approaching Union infantry. Alex untied the white scarf from around his neck and held it above his head. Reluctantly, Mike and Steve did the same.

As the Union troops drew closer, Alex studied their faces, seeing contempt on some, curiosity on others; most appeared impassive but alert.

A pudgy, pint-sized corporal stepped up to Steve and relieved him of his cap and ball revolver while four of his comrades stood guard over the other two prisoners. Seeing that Alex and Mike were unarmed, the soldier stepped back a few paces and squinted at the three men attired in Union officer uniforms.

"My! My! Ain't this somethin'?" he drawled sarcastically. "All safe and sound are we? Too bad the rest of your outfit didn't fare as well. I've known some cowards in my time, but this beats all!"

"Well, you know what they say," Mike scowled, "a man's known by the company he keeps."

"You pokin' fun at me, Mister?" snarled the little corporal, squinting at Mike and scrunching up his face like he'd just bitten into a sour lemon. "It won't seem so funny when we tie a noose around your neck!

Empty your pockets; then strip off them uniforms. Won't do to have anyone mistakin' you for brave men. Those dead men lyin' out there might object to you wearin' a Reb uniform too, so I guess you'll just have to walk to the prisoner collection point naked as a jaybird."

A murmur of assent went up from his companions.

"Now, let's see what's in your pockets," the corporal repeated.

The prisoners lowered their hands and reached into their pockets for their meager possessions.

Alex pulled the little notebook from his coat pocket and flashed the corporal a deprecating smile as he handed it to him. Hoping for something of monetary value, the corporal sneered in disgust and promptly threw it on the ground.

However, as Alex unbuttoned his coat, the glint of his gold watch chain transformed the corporal's frown of disappointment to a smile of avarice. "Let's have that watch and chain," he demanded, stepping forward to assert his claim.

Alex was reluctant to give up the beautifully engraved watch and heavy gold chain. He glowered at the little man wondering what would happen if he refused. He didn't have to wonder long. Alex felt the prick of a bayonet tip against his throat as the corporal held out an impatient hand.

Alex unfastened the watch fob from the buttonhole in his vest and dropped the watch and chain into the eager palm.

"What's going on here, Corporal?" a familiar voice behind Alex suddenly demanded.

Startled and too short to peer over Alex's shoulders, the corporal stepped to his right and found himself face to chest with a tall figure with gold eagle buttons on his coat and a set of captain's epaulets perched on his shoulders.

"We're searchin' these prisoners for weapons and intelligence material, sir," the little corporal stammered, "before we take'em to the prisoner collection point."

"That so?" the captain replied dubiously. "Seems to me the notebook you tossed on the ground would likely contain more intelligence than this man's gold watch and chain. Did you search him for weapons?"

"Yes, sir. He don't have none."

"You mean, he *doesn't* have any," the officer corrected him.

"Yes, sir. Like I said, he don't have none," the corporal replied more loudly, figuring the captain had a hearing problem.

"I'm sorry to hear that, Corporal," the captain frowned, turning his attention to the prisoner. "Hello, Alex. Nice to find you alive and well. I was afraid you'd be up there on the slope with your friends. Incidentally, in case you are wondering, my men and I overpowered our guards and escaped. So here we are again."

"Hello, Matt," Alex replied, surprised and somewhat relieved to be in the company of Captain Matt Deveraux once again. This *is* unexpected, but I must admit I'm glad to see you. How about telling this corporal to return my watch and chain—it's a family heirloom."

"Perhaps," Deveraux smiled, savoring the change of fortune, "but as I remember, you have something of mine."

"You mean this?" Alex opened his unbuttoned coat exposing the handsome walnut and brass grip of the Manhattan Firearms cap and ball revolver stuck in his waistband.

Two of the corporal's cronies spied the weapon at the same instant as Deveraux and immediately swung their rifles up to their shoulders as if to fire.

"Hold on!" Deveraux ordered as he stepped protectively in front of Alex.

The corporal stood slack-jawed, staring at the pistol in Alex's waistband.

"*He don't have none*, eh, Corporal?" Deveraux said derisively.

"I...I didn't think...." he stammered.

"That's right, you didn't think," Deveraux berated the crestfallen soldier. "You were more interested in getting your hands on his watch than making sure he was unarmed. That kind of carelessness may get you killed next time. Then you won't need a watch."

Alex was about to hand the pistol to Deveraux then changed his mind as he observed a soldier peering at him over the sights of his .58 caliber Springfield. He also noticed the nervous twitch in the man's eye and hoped the affliction didn't extend to his trigger finger.

Deveraux gave the corporal a disapproving frown as he snatched the watch and chain from his hand. The end of the chain with the watch fob slipped through his fingers and swung back and forth like a glittering pendulum. Coiling the length of chain around his fingers, Deveraux held up the last link and examined the impressive 24K gold fob as it spun brilliantly in the sunlight.

"I suggest you put this in your pocket and keep it out of sight before someone else tries to claim it as spoils of war," he said, handing the watch and chain to Alex with his left hand, while deftly plucking the revolver from Alex's waistband with his right.

"I guess I should be grateful your pistol doesn't have a hair trigger," Alex smiled wanly, "otherwise, the loss of my watch might have been the least of my worries."

Deveraux checked the percussion caps on the nipples of the revolver's cylinder then slid it into his empty holster. "No cause for concern; it'd be safe in a baby's hands. This is a single-action revolver, and I keep the hammer on an empty chamber." He hesitated, then as an after thought added, "It was a gift from my father."

"I understand," Alex nodded. "The watch and chain were gifts from my grandfather; the watch fob was presented to me by the Grand Lodge in Charleston when I left for the war." It was, in fact, a truthful statement, yet Alex had nearly bit his tongue when he realized how close he had come to saying *for the war in Europe.*

Deveraux extended his hand. "It's been a pleasure, Alex. I'll see to it you and your friends are well-treated."

As Alex shook his hand, Deveraux did an odd twist with his grip. Alex gave him a surprised look as he recognized at once the secret handshake of a brother Mason.

Deveraux shook his head, warning Alex to say nothing about the Brotherhood in the presence of others. "Just tell me one thing, Alex," he said casually. "Why did you and your companions stay behind?"

Alex sensed it was not just a rhetorical question, so he picked his words carefully. "We were assigned as guides—nothing more—for a raid on General Meade's headquarters. When the raid failed with no hope of escape, they chose martyrdom over surrender. We preferred a different future."

When Alex finished, Deveraux looked at him oddly. "But why end it this way? It was nothing short of suicide—" he stopped short, unable to comprehend what to his way of thinking had been utter madness. He turned instead to the corporal. "Take these prisoners to the prisoner collection point at Meade Station and turn them over to the officer in charge. Give'm this message." Deveraux hastily scribbled a note on a page torn from Alex's notebook and handed it to him. "From there the prisoners will be taken by train to the Bull Pen stockade at City Point for further disposition."

MASON WATCH FOB FOUND ON PETERSBURG AREA BATTLEFIELD

(Author's Collection)

*". . . the watch fob was presented to me by the Grand Lodge
in Charleston when I left for the war."*

Alex thought the last statement was meant for his ears rather than for the corporal who undoubtedly could care less what became of them after he was relieved of his responsibility.

"Oh, and one more thing, Corporal. I'll be going to Meade Station shortly, and I'll check to see if these gentlemen arrived safely and with all their personal possessions intact. Understand?"

"Yes, sir!"

"Very well! Move out!"

Deveraux returned the corporal's salute then turned to Alex. "I'll see you later, friend, after I attend to business here."

As Deveraux walked away to rejoin his regiment, the doughboys were herded in the opposite direction under the watchful eyes of the corporal and his four-man squad.

A pair of crows high in the tops of a stand of pines acknowledged their presence as they tramped wearily along the Prince George Courthouse Road that led to Meade Station. Their *cawing* was the prevailing sound of the morning, calling attention to the deathly stillness that had settled over the land. The rattle of musketry and the booming of cannon were no longer heard. The struggle for Fort Stedman had ended.

Alex didn't need to look at his watch to know it was now around 8:00 A.M. as they trudged by the station where groups of soldiers, civilian sutlers, railroad men, and Negro laborers stopped and gawked at the little procession of guarded prisoners. Had they been wearing Confederate uniforms or civilian clothing, they would have merited only casual interest. The marching of prisoners of war to the railroad station was a common occurrence; however, the sight of three dirty and weary-looking Union officers under close guard being marched to the rear was unprecedented, and the curious strained for a glimpse as they plodded past.

A familiar-looking man appeared on the railroad loading dock. Recalling their brief stop at this place the previous evening, Alex recognized him as the freightmaster who had arranged a ride for them. The man stood with arms folded and a pipe in his mouth, watching the procession file past. His expression bore no sign of recognition.

At Meade Station they were diverted onto another well-used

wagon road that continued north, parallel to the narrow-gauge tracks of the City Point & Military Railroad. Alex noted without comment that they were retracing their footsteps along this stretch of road from the previous evening. He also noticed in the distance, a steady stream of figures crossing the road—some mounted on horses. *They're moving from west to east,* Alex observed, puzzled. *If Grant is rushing reinforcements to Fort Stedman, they should be coming from the opposite direction.*

The mystery resolved itself as they drew nearer. The indistinct figures gradually materialized into a long column of dispirited and emaciated Confederate prisoners being herded to the Union rear under heavy guard. "Well," Alex said dolefully over his shoulder, "this pretty much confirms the outcome of Gordon's attack on Fort Stedman."

As he watched the Confederate prisoners filing past ahead of them, Mike replied bitterly, "Everything considered, I don't see that we accomplished anything. We'd have a hard time convincing those walking scarecrows that Providence was on their side today."

"I think we made a difference, Mike—just not the way we expected," Alex said. "What history will say about this battle may very well reflect the influence we had on it. Maybe we couldn't change past events because we were also woven into the fabric of history."

"You mean, what will be, will be because we're part of it?" Steve chimed in, mulling the idea over in his mind.

"Yeah," Alex nodded, "that's a good way to describe it."

"Give it a rest why don't you?" Mike suddenly snapped. "Of all the people to be marooned with in another time, I'm stuck with two philosophers! You two are real woozes! I could care less about *why* we're here; it's the *how* that matters. Do me a favor—work on that!"

"Touchy, touchy, this morning aren't we?" Alex replied over his shoulder. "Something must have disturbed your rest last night."

"Lack of sleep, wild goose chases in the middle of the night, being shot at, and being marched on an empty stomach to a prisoner of war camp tend to make one grumpy," Mike countered testily.

The pounding of hooves rapidly approaching from behind ended the discussion. The corporal, who had been up front, suddenly dropped back alongside his charges growling "Make way! Make way!"

Two of the guards began shoving the prisoners off to the side of the road with their rifle butts to make way for the oncoming horsemen.

As he waited on the side of the road for the riders to pass, Alex studied the distant column of Confederate prisoners being herded into a fallow field alongside the railroad. Nearly a thousand prisoners were either milling about like so many cattle or sitting in groups staring vacantly at the steady stream of new arrivals.

Alex paid no attention to the cavalcade coming up the road until it suddenly reined to a stop beside him.

"Deserters?" inquired a deep authoritative voice with an air of contempt in the utterance of that single word.

Annoyed, Alex's eyes shifted from the prisoners and settled on the man who had asked the question. He was a Union officer mounted on a dappled gray mare, and there were two stars on his shoulder epaulettes, identifying him as a Major General. Alex was immediately attentive. Behind the General were six uniformed horsemen and an open carriage bearing a coachman and four passengers—two women and two men.

"Uh, no, sir," the corporal answered, obviously rattled by the unexpected entourage, "these here are Rebel prisoners."

"Oh?" The General said, sounding surprised.

"Then why are they wearing Union officer uniforms?"

"I don't know, sir," the corporal shrugged. "We captured these Rebs at General Meade's headquarters this morning. They was the only live ones. Some of the dead Rebs were also wearing Union uniforms."

"Is that so?" the General said, reining his horse over for a closer look at the prisoners.

"You're all that survived?" he asked, looking down at Mike and Steve.

Mike and Steve nodded wearily.

Alex took a step forward. "That's right, General, as far as we know."

The General contemplated Alex for a moment then turned to the corporal. "Stay put," he ordered.

Tickling the mare's flanks with his spurs, the General rode back to the waiting carriage and spoke briefly to one of the male occupants. A moment later he returned with another officer in tow. "Corporal," he said, "you will disregard whatever orders you have concerning the disposition of these prisoners." Then he pointed to the officer beside him. "This is Captain Warwick, my aide. Until he no longer requires your services, you and your men work for him. Turn these prisoners around and take them back to Meade Station. Captain Warwick will go with you. See to it that they are fed, bathed, and given a change of clothing. Then put them aboard the private coach at the end of the train parked on the station siding. They will remain there under guard until I return. Do you understand all that?"

"Yes, sir!" the totally confused corporal answered as he rendered a snappy salute.

The General turned to his aide. "They're all yours, Captain Warwick. I'll see you at the train."

"Yes, sir." Warwick saluted, but the General was already riding away.

The little cavalcade quickly turned around and rode off in the opposite direction while the corporal promptly obeyed his new orders.

Captain Warwick rode alongside the prisoners as the guards herded them back to Meade Station.

"Captain," Alex said, trying to engage him in conversation, "mind telling me what this is all about?"

Warwick peered down at him with cool analytical eyes. "You really an officer?" he asked, ignoring Alex's question.

Alex nodded, "I'm Captain Alex Wright."

"Well, Captain Wright, you'll find out—but not from me." Warwick spurred his horse, quickly outdistancing himself from Alex.

On a rail siding at Meade Station amid mountainous stacks of wooden crates and barrels sat a locomotive, its tender, one boxcar, and two passenger cars. Only the top of the locomotive's enormous balloon stack was visible behind the stacks of supplies. The train had escaped Alex's attention when they passed by the station earlier. He stared at the train liked a shipwrecked sailor on a raft eyeing an unknown shore, wondering what awaited him there.

CHAPTER 24

Meade Station, Prince George County
1:00 P.M., MARCH 25, 1865

The supply depot at Meade Station operated an immense dining hall that fed the army of laborers working in the sprawling complex, plus a continuous flow of transiting railroad employees, teamsters, and visitors. Upon their arrival, Captain Warwick treated his charges to their best meal in two days, which they washed down with fresh roasted coffee. The daily menu posted on a chalkboard outside the mess hall entrance implied that the cooks had access to an assortment of delicacies unheard of in the Confederate army. Quantity and variety notwithstanding, the prisoners listened attentively to the diners around them, noting with surprise that the shortage of eggs, milk, cheese, and other fresh produce was the primary topic of dinner conversation with barely a mention of the battle or Lincoln's visit.

When they had finished eating, Warwick took them, still under guard, to a ramshackle structure that had been hurriedly thrown up. Someone with a sense of humor had nailed a sign to the front door that read: *The Winter Home of the Quartermaster Department and Other Vermin.* Warwick pushed the door open. Two clerks sitting behind a counter looked up from their checkerboard looking resentful at the intrusion. Warwick walked casually up to the counter and handed a document to one of the clerks. "These three men," he said, pointing to Alex, Mike and Steve, "are to be issued new uniforms as stated on this form. You will note that this directive reads *by order of General Parke.*

In no time at all, they received a gratis set of new clothing, which per Warwick's instructions—and much to their chagrin—turned out to be Union enlisted men's uniforms.

Alex immediately voiced his objections. "If you can't accord us the courtesy and respect due our rank, then we'll just keep what we're wearing. Thank you very much!"

"I'm afraid not, Captain Wright," Warwick said icily, making it clear that the matter wasn't open for negotiation. "For one thing, the U.S. Quartermaster Department doesn't stock Confederate officer uniforms, and for another, we can't permit you to continue masquerading as a Union officer."

Disconsolately, but with their enlisted uniforms tucked under their arms, they left the Quartermaster Department and followed the corporal to one of the railroad bunkhouses behind which stood a makeshift shower. As filthy as they were, the prospects of an outdoor shower in the month of March was not an experience to be relished; Mike swore there were chunks of ice floating in the wooden cask mounted on the shower scaffolding. Alex ducked under the stream of ice-cold water, scrubbed quickly with a cake of lye soap, then rinsed off. They were all shivering as they dried off, their wet bodies steaming in the frigid air; however, there were no more complaints about their new uniforms as they hurriedly dressed.

His hands shackled in front of him, Alex stood in the doorway of the private railroad car looking gloomily up the tracks to the open field where Union infantry were rounding up and loading the last of the Confederate prisoners. A steam engine hauling a string of weathered boxcars had arrived at noon to transport the prisoners to the Bull Pen at City Point.

The sudden clatter of hooves on the corduroy road alongside the tracks roused Alex from his melancholy. Through one of the coach windows he caught sight of the cavalcade they had encountered earlier as it halted beside the train; however, the imperfections in the window glass distorted the images of the people outside. For a better view, Alex stepped out on the private car's rear platform where two guards eyed him warily. Leaning over the railing, his eyes followed the twin ribbons of steel emerging from under the coach to the sharp curve where the siding joined the main line beyond the storage area. From his vantage point the curving tracks allowed him to glimpse the entire length of the train. The locomotive pulling the rail cars was a graceful example of engineering beauty. The City Point & Military Railroad had lavished care upon her, and soldiers and laborers gathered to marvel at her sleek and powerful design. From headlamp and cowcatcher to the coupling on her tender, she gleamed in the afternoon sun, and Alex could clearly make out her identifying number *156* stenciled on her boiler and the bold *U.S. Military Railroad* emblazoned on the side of the tender. Festooned for the occasion, the Stars and Stripes fluttered grandly from a staff mounted on the right side of the cowcatcher. A plume of black smoke poured from the great balloon stack as the crew fired up her boiler to get underway.

A freshly painted boxcar, converted to accommodate horses, was coupled behind the tender, and through its open door Alex noted that each horse stall contained a small opening in the exterior wall for ventilation. Several grooms were busy with the cavalcade's horses, leading them up the ramp into the boxcar, unsaddling them, putting them in their stalls, and stowing the saddles and bridles in the tack room.

An elegant open-end passenger car was sandwiched between the boxcar and the private coach on which Alex stood. Through windows adorned with red velvet drapes, he glimpsed its plush and spacious interior of upholstered bench seats and polished mahogany paneling. *Obviously intended for the use of visiting dignitaries, high-ranking officers, and their personal staffs.*

The private coach remained as much an enigma to Alex now as when he first saw it. He had not been permitted beyond the luxurious lounge at the end of the car with its partition of rich mahogany bookshelves and paneled door that separated it from one or more compartments. Similarly shackled, Mike and Steve stood in the middle of the lounge admiring the fine workmanship and expensive

ENGINE NO. 156, U.S. MILITARY R.R.

(Courtesy of National Archives)

From headlamp and cowcatcher to the coupling on her tender,
she gleamed in the afternoon sun . . .

décor and speculating in low undertones about the identity of the car's occupant or occupants.

Alex didn't share their curiosity. He already knew the answer, and that knowledge made him very much ill at ease. Having been without sleep for more than twenty-four hours, his tired mind groped to find a plausible explanation for their present circumstance. *Of all the prisoners they captured today, why have they singled us out?*

Returning to the lounge, Alex had just settled into a wicker chair when he heard the scraping of feet on the platform's ornate, wrought iron steps.

A guard on the platform barked, "Atten-shun!"

The corporal and two guards idling inside the lounge promptly snapped to attention.

Spontaneously, the three prisoners jumped to their feet and stood side by side facing the platform doorway.

Alex's mouth was dry and, for the first time since elementary school when his teacher made him sing a solo in front of the class, his knees and hands shook.

A commanding figure stepped through the open doorway, acknowledging everyone in the lounge with a dour, cursory nod.

The two stars on each of his shoulder epaulettes and the war-time photographs Alex had seen of him in the Academy's library left no doubt in his mind that this Union officer was none other than Major General George G. Meade, Commander of the Army of the Potomac. Alex wondered if their presence accounted for his sour expression— understandable considering they had just sacked his headquarters. *He doesn't look the type to forgive and forget either.*

Another general followed Meade into the lounge. Alex recognized him from the cavalcade that morning. Captain Warwick had invoked his name, preceded by the prepositional phrase *by order of,* in arranging to have them fed and clothed. *So, this is Major General John G. Parke, Commander of the Ninth Corps, Army of the Potomac.* Alex studied the man briefly, remembering from what he had read that, although they wore the same rank, Parke was actually Meade's subordinate.

Parke had distinguished himself today and had become the man of the hour. When the Confederates attacked Fort Stedman in the pre-dawn hours, Parke was allegedly awakened and informed that Meade was at City Point. As the senior ranking officer on the field, he assumed the responsibility for organizing the defense and repelling the enemy assault. Parke committed reinforcements to blunt and stall the Confederate attack while he established a rear line of defense to contain the penetration. By 8:00 A.M. he had successfully beaten back the Confederate onslaught, recaptured Fort Stedman, and killed or captured 2,700 of the attackers.

At least that was the official version Alex remembered reading on the subject. Based on his own observations, he suspected there was more to the story than was ever released to the public or made it into the history books.

Parke appeared pleasant—undoubtedly pleased with himself. *As well as he should be*, Alex mused.

Seeing the three prisoners in their new privates' uniforms, Parke smiled congenially. "It appears you gentlemen have been demoted since we last met."

"I feel a bit naked without any rank on my shoulders, General," Mike grinned benignly. "I don't suppose you'd loan me a set of your epaulettes?"

Parke laughed heartily, his eyes crinkling at the corners with genuine amusement. "And if I did, you would probably get away with it too! You pulled off your little charade as Union Army officers very effectively."

Parke turned half way around, gestured toward the lounge's exterior door, and hailed in a deep booming voice, "Privates Mason, Goebels, Crawford, and Duncan! Front and center!"

There was a brief shuffling out on the platform; then four soldiers trooped single file into the lounge.

Alex recognized Mason and Goebels as the two sentries he had encountered at Fort Stedman, the ones with a taste for liquor. That their wrists were shackled didn't surprise him.

Crawford and Duncan were the off-duty sentries that Alex had befriended in the mess tent near Meade's headquarters. He hadn't known their names until now. He was pleased to see neither of them shackled, since by his way of thinking, they weren't guilty of any wrongdoing.

The four soldiers lined up in a row facing the three Confederate prisoners. Alex noted that Mason and Goebels looked frightened while the other two appeared understandably nervous.

Parke, smiling, his arms folded across his barrel-like chest, casually paced back and forth between the two rows of soldiers. "Do any of you recognize these three gentlemen?" he asked, nodding at the Confederate prisoners.

"Yes, sir," Mason and Goebels said. Both raised their shackled hands and pointed at Alex.

Taking a few moments to study each of the faces, Crawford and Duncan glanced at each other in silent agreement, then pointed at Alex.

"You're sure this is the same man you saw last night?" Parke pressed.

"Yes, sir," they all answered, nodding emphatically. Crawford, the one who had drawn the map of the headquarters encampment in Alex's notebook went on to add, "That's him for sure, except he was wearing a muddy lieutenant's uniform with a couple of buttons missing from his coat when we saw him."

"Thank you, that will be all," Parke said, dismissing the men.

Mason and Goebels cast Alex a smirk as they turned and filed out the door onto the platform with the corporal and two other guards following close behind.

Captain Warwick closed the door after them but remained outside on the platform.

"Please forgive my little interrogation," Parke continued pleasantly, looking at Alex all the while. "I just needed to…well, it doesn't matter," he hedged, apparently deciding he didn't owe the prisoner an explanation. "I'm sure you're wondering what this is all about. You'll have your answer in a few minutes," he added cryptically.

Parke glanced at General Meade seated at a small writing desk in a corner of the lounge. "While we're waiting, I'll introduce this officer and myself," he said, nodding at Meade. "This is Major General Meade, Commanding General, Army of the Potomac."

Meade merely acknowledged Parke's introduction with a curt nod; his sullen expression never changed.

"And, I'm Major General Parke, Commander of the Ninth Corps."

Then with only the briefest pause, he threw them a questioning smile. "And you gentlemen are...?"

Alex introduced himself and Mike by their real rank and names but thought it prudent to introduce Steve by his Confederate rank and alias.

Meade unexpectedly rose from his seat and crossed the room to greet them—if that was the proper term. Alex felt like a cornered mouse being scrutinized by a hungry cat as the man came toward them. His greeting was cold and perfunctory as he shook their hands.

Meade's contemporaries described him as quick tempered and exacting; however, to Alex, he appeared to be a man on the verge of total physical and mental collapse. Judging from the dark circles under his eyes and the pasty pallor of his skin, the war was taking its toll on his health.

Meade shook Steve's hand last, then stepped back and gave them an odd look as though he was trying to make up his mind about something. Finally he said quietly, "Someone of considerable importance has expressed an interest in meeting you."

Without further elaboration, Meade opened a paneled door leading from the lounge into the forward compartment, then disappeared into the narrow corridor beyond.

From inside the forward compartment, Alex heard the shrill, plaintive voice of a woman. "The nerve of that hussy! I saw her making eyes at you! But, of course, you pretend you didn't notice! She's scandalous, and she will bring you scandal if she can. You must avoid her, or she will be your ruin...and mine!"

"Yes, Mary," a tired-sounding male voice replied.

Alex blinked in wide-eyed amazement while Mike arched his eyebrows and scrunched up his face in sympathy for the henpecked guy receiving the wicked tongue-lashing.

Steve rolled his eyes and struggled to keep a straight face.

Parke flushed with embarrassment as he listened to the persistent female tirade coming from the compartment.

Beyond the open doorway a knuckle rapped hesitantly on a wooden door. The shrill voice suddenly stopped. A moment later the listeners heard the click of an interior door opening and a surprised

GENERAL GEORGE G. MEADE, U.S.A.

(Courtesy of Library of Congress)

. . . to Alex, he appeared to be a man on the verge of total physical and mental collapse.

inhalation followed by a sweetly melodious exclamation, "Why General Meade! How nice of you to call on us! I wanted to thank you again for taking time from your important duties to show us this morning's battlefield and for arranging such a magnificent review. I fear we have come at an awkward time and have inconvenienced you dreadfully. You do look a might peaked, General. Are you not well?"

"I assure you, Ma'am," replied the soft courteous resonance of Meade's voice, "that your visit is most timely, and the pleasure of your company has been wonderfully refreshing. As for my health, it's never been better, but I appreciate your concern."

"General, you're always so gallant," the woman prattled on; "however, I mustn't take any more of your time. I'm sure you and my husband have important matters to discuss."

"Ahh! General Meade! Welcome, sir!" A third voice inserted itself into the conversation, and all ears in the lounge listened attentively. "We were just about to indulge in some fine liquid refreshments that your staff so thoughtfully provided. Would you care to join us?"

"Thank you, sir, but I'm afraid I must hope for another invitation at some future time. Nor do I wish to intrude on your privacy; however, I thought you would like to know that the prisoners you inquired about are waiting at your leisure in the lounge."

"Well then, let's not keep them waiting," Lincoln chortled, relieved to have an excuse to leave Mary until her jealous rage abated. He was certain Meade and everyone else on their private car had overheard her outbursts. *A scalded cat would have made less noise. Well, it's not like this is the first time,* he fumed inwardly. He had casually suggested a few weeks earlier, after her last such violent episode, that she might consider seeking some professional help. Her reaction had been instant cataclysmic fury. He feared she might suffer a stroke and decided then and there to avoid the subject in the future.

Lincoln followed Meade through the car's narrow corridor, past a row of open windows on his right, a stateroom door on his left, then instinctively ducked his six-foot, four-inch frame under the doorway at the end of the corridor.

Reaching the lounge first, Meade stood beside the doorway and announced, "Gentlemen, the President of the United States of

202

America, Abraham Lincoln."

A hush settled over the room.

As he stepped through the open doorway Lincoln's gaze immediately settled on the three young men standing near General Parke's familiar rotund figure. Judging from their expressions, his sudden appearance was a complete surprise. But as he studied their faces, something seemed wrong. *No, it's more than that,* he thought, doing a mental reassessment, for he was good at reading faces. *Why are they looking at me like that? They look as though they've seen a ghost! How odd!*

The President strode toward the young men, oblivious to Meade as he passed him. *Considering the mission they were sent on maybe they're expecting retribution. And since only God Almighty outranks me in deciding their future, I suppose that might be a little unsettling.* He stopped beside General Parke, noting the sudden sadness written on the face of the prisoner closest to him. *Curious. How glum he looks, as if I had announced a death sentence.*

Lincoln spoke softly, breaking the silence in the room. "Please be seated, gentlemen," he smiled kindly as he gestured to them to take a seat on a richly carved walnut Victorian sofa adorned with dark red wine velvet upholstery and just wide enough to accommodate three people. "I observed you on the road this morning as you were being escorted to the prisoner collection point. When I discovered who you were, I asked General Meade to have you brought here so we could speak somewhat privately. I..."

The sudden nerve-numbing screech of metal scraping against metal turned every head in the room as the door leading out to the platform suddenly opened.

Lincoln paused as he recognized the short, stocky figure standing in the doorway. "Ahh, General Grant! Your arrival is most opportune, sir—good of you to come! This discussion may answer some questions that we have been pondering."

He motioned to Grant, Meade and Parke to pull up a chair, obviously trying to make the gathering as relaxed and casual as possible. Lincoln eased his long, thin body onto a cane-bottomed chair, then turned back to the prisoners who were seated about as comfortably as a Victorian-era horsehair sofa would permit.

For the moment, all eyes were riveted on Grant as he closed the door, found a chair, and dragged it over to where Lincoln was sitting.

Unaccustomed to such informality, Meade and Parke distanced themselves somewhat from their Commander-in-chief and Grant and shared a small settee slightly off to one side.

Grant gazed about the room with a frown as he took his seat. "Mr. President, it appears your safety has been overlooked. Why haven't security guards been posted in the lounge? After all, these men *are* prisoners of war." Grant shot Meade an admonishing glare. "If you will excuse me, sir, I'll summon a few guards from outside." Without waiting for an answer, Grant started to rise from his chair to tend to the matter.

"That won't be necessary, General Grant," Lincoln said, placing a restraining hand on his arm. "What we're about to discuss, I don't want heard or repeated outside this room. As for my safety, I've probably never been safer. The last thing these gentlemen want is to see me harmed—isn't that right?" he asked, giving them a perceptive smile.

"Yes, sir," Alex nodded, his voice sounding flat and lifeless.

"Which brings us to why we're here." Lincoln lowered his voice conspiratorially as he leaned forward in his chair and rested his pointed elbows on his bony knees. "I assume you recognize everyone here?"

"Yes, sir," the prisoners nodded.

"Then you have me at a disadvantage," Lincoln smiled, "perhaps you'll be kind enough to introduce yourselves."

"Please allow me, Mr. President," Parke interjected, half-rising from the settee, unsure whether he should be sitting or standing.

Lincoln nodded his approval.

While Parke made the introductions, Grant shifted uncomfortably in his chair, crossing, then re-crossing one booted leg over the other, wondering what this gathering was all about. It certainly wasn't part of the plan that he and the President had discussed privately that morning.

Introductions completed, Lincoln leaned back in his chair, rested his black-sleeved elbows on the wooden arms, and pressed his index finger against his lips thoughtfully like a lawyer pondering his closing argument to the jury.

Alex watched, mesmerized, until the finger dropped away from his lips.

"Not to belabor the obvious," Lincoln began, "I suppose you gentlemen would like to know what this is all about."

"Well...yeah!" Mike blurted without thinking.

Alex elbowed him in the ribs to shut him up, but it was too late—every eye in the room glared at Mike, repulsed by his coarseness.

That is everyone except Lincoln; his eyes betrayed a bemused twinkle.

Scowls turned to grins as the generals heard the President chuckle.

"Four long years of war have taken a toll on the resolve of my administration," he continued, his smile quickly fading, "and on the American people who have steadfastly supported the Union cause. My greatest fear has been that the country may choose to abandon their resolve, which has sustained us through so much, before we can bring the war to a satisfactory conclusion. As you probably know, there is a growing ground swell of support in the North for an end to the war on the basis of giving the so-called Confederacy the independence we have so long opposed. It's only a matter of time before the force of arms quashes this rebellion, but it's also apparent that *time* is now in the South's favor. It's inconceivable to me that a people whose land has been laid waste, whose cities are in ruins, and whose army is so decimated and deprived of food that its soldiers are starving in the trenches may yet win this conflict simply because their resolve is stronger than ours."

The room was silent as Lincoln paused to let the significance sink in.

"Although depleted through desertion and attrition, General Lee's army continued to demonstrate resiliency and the capacity to inflict heavy losses from well-prepared and stoutly defended positions. To order a general assault against the Rebel defenses around

Petersburg was an unacceptable risk. We could ill-afford another Fredricksburg, Chancellorsville, or Cold Harbor. The public mood in the North would not accept another such disappointment. The only alternative was to lure General Lee out of his trenches and invite him to attack us instead. And for him to do that, we knew he would be compelled to strip or abandon significant portions of his twenty-two miles of defenses. Accordingly, if we repulsed Lee's attack and then followed-up with a general assault along the entire length of his line, the Richmond-Petersburg defenses would probably crumble. But the trick was, how to entice Lee out of his trenches—and *soon*.

A month ago I met secretly with General Grant and laid out a desperate proposal for ending the long stalemate at Petersburg and bringing the war to a swift conclusion. My plan was quite sound with just one slight hitch;" Lincoln paused and smiled for effect, "success depended on helping Lee decide *where* and *when* he should attack. General Meade and General Parke were given the task of setting a trap by picking the weakest link from the chain of forts in the Ninth Corps' section of the Union siege line. Fort Stedman was found to be in a serious state of deterioration because of its close proximity to the enemy's Colquitt's Salient. To make Fort Stedman even more tempting to General Lee and General Gordon, we garrisoned the fort and the picket line in front of it with the dregs of the army. Alcoholics, mental incompetents, the lame and lazy, and disciplinary misfits were gleaned without complaint from every regiment and sent to garrison Fort Stedman. All of this, of course, was done covertly.

It wasn't long before your General Gordon detected the weakness in our lines and began sniffing at the bait. We were satisfied from the sudden shuffle of various brigades and divisions in the area of the Salient that a buildup was underway. What we didn't know was *when* the attack would occur. Quite frankly, we were stymied for quite awhile trying to devise a scheme that would prompt Gordon to attack sooner rather than later—preferably at a time of our choosing.

The answer came to me when General Grant invited me to visit his headquarters at City Point. We were, of course, aware that Rebel agents were tapping into the telegraph line along the James River below City Point and suspected that his message inviting me to visit him had been intercepted. General Grant became concerned for my safety and suggested in a message sent by courier that I consider delaying my visit until the following month. I, on the other hand, saw my visit as the answer to the dilemma of how to persuade Gordon to attack according to our timetable. A flurry of classified dispatches and telegraph messages was sent to various commanders in the field detailing my itinerary, which included an overnight stay at General Meade's headquarters on March 24th. By dangling myself as bait, I hoped Gordon would come after me and time his attack on Fort Stedman with my overnight visit with General Meade. As you well know, it's only a mile from Stedman to General Meade's headquarters."

"I suppose that's where we come in?" Alex interjected. It sounded as much a statement of fact as it did a question.

"More than you realize," Lincoln acknowledged with a smile. "Until you appeared in front of Fort Stedman last night, we didn't know for sure whether Lee or Gordon had swallowed the bait."

Alex tried not to look surprised, but he was pretty certain Lincoln had noticed Mike nudging him with his elbow.

"That's right," Lincoln nodded. "You were spotted the minute you crawled through the rail obstruction in front of the fort and stood up. The garrison's commanding officer had orders from General Parke not to interfere with any scouting parties the Rebels sent over. Unfortunately, two sentries challenged you before he had time to intervene, but you succeeded in talking your way past them. Normally they would have been charged with dereliction of duty and summarily shot; however, General Parke has not yet decided how to dispose of their case."

Alex had a feeling that Lincoln had tossed out this last tidbit to see his reaction. By confessing he had duped the two sentries into believing they were Union officers on official business, they could all be charged with spying. On the other hand, two lives hung in the balance, depending on what he decided to do.

Lincoln paused, shaking his head somberly.

"Mr. President," Alex interrupted, "I'm responsible for what happened. I passed myself off as a Union officer on business for the Inspector General to inspect the defenses of Fort Stedman. My companions were too far away to overhear what was said. The two sentries were not at fault and shouldn't be punished." Alex saw no reason to mention that he had caught them drinking and were more or less intoxicated.

Lincoln glanced at Parke.

Parke nodded, seemingly satisfied with Alex's explanation.

Alex was aware that by coming to the soldiers' rescue, he had probably put the noose around his own neck.

Lincoln's face softened, as if he were reading Alex's thoughts. "I don't see how it would serve any purpose to try you for spying, Captain Wright, although that's precisely what you were sent to do."

"I disagree, Mr. President," Alex replied. "We weren't spying. We were conducting a tactical reconnaissance of the area in and around General Meade's headquarters as part of the overall plan to breach the Union lines by capturing Fort Stedman."

"Why?" Grant asked.

"Why, what, sir?" Alex asked, failing to understand the question.

"General Meade's headquarters is at least a mile from Fort Stedman, so why were you conducting a *tactical reconnaissance*, as you call it, so far behind our lines?"

Alex considered where this line of questioning might be heading before answering. "After capturing Fort Stedman, Gordon planned to roll up the Union flank on either side of the fort, which is to say that he wanted to roll up the left flank all the way to the Appomattox River. He also intended to penetrate deep into the Union rear and cut your military railroad, main roads, telegraph lines, and destroy your supply depots. Capturing the Headquarters, Army of the Potomac and severing your lines of communication would have disrupted your command and control for a long time. The Army of the Potomac would have been fighting blind without effective leadership at the helm. Our mission was to reconnoiter the security in and around General Meade's headquarters and determine how to penetrate it."

"And who commanded the force that attacked my headquarters?" Meade interjected.

"Major Jonas commanded that detachment, sir. Another force commanded by Brigadier General Lewis was assigned the task of capturing three small forts in the rear of Fort Stedman."

"So, now we come to the heart of the matter and the reason I wanted to meet with you," Lincoln confided. "Soon, I must make a difficult decision concerning the treatment of the Rebel leadership when the war ends. How you answer my next two questions may influence that decision, so choose your words carefully."

Alex looked at Lincoln warily.

Lincoln leaned forward, his deep-set eyes under thick bushy eyebrows bored into Alex's. "First, what were Major Jonas' orders concerning me? Secondly, who issued those orders?"

Alex's eyes never wavered from Lincoln's as he considered the implications of his response. Before answering, he glanced at Mike and Steve. They stared back at him with blank, poker-player faces—telling him that how he chose to respond was entirely up to him.

With an acquiescent shrug, Alex turned back to Lincoln who seemed to be studying him with a mixture of anticipation and curiosity. "Major Jonas' orders—" Alex exhaled, then took a deep breath as he continued,"—were to seize General Meade's headquarters. Any women found inside the encampment were to be treated with the utmost chivalrous respect until arrangements were made to return them to the Union lines. The detachment was to hold the headquarters under the guise of being Union troops until Confederate reinforcements arrived..."

"Yes! Yes!" Lincoln pressed impatiently. "But what were his orders concerning me personally?"

A puzzled frown passed over Alex's face. "I'm not sure I follow you, Mr. President. Are you implying that you were at General Meade's headquarters last night? And that General Lee and President Davis may have been aware of it? If such is the case, we have no knowledge of it," Alex replied truthfully, throwing in a dumbfounded expression for good measure. So far as he knew, only Gordon had knowledge of Lincoln's overnight whereabouts.

Then with a smile Alex added: "If you were there, Mr. President, we're *sorry to have missed you.*"

Lincoln leaned back in his chair and gave Alex a long, knowing look. An unspoken communication had passed between them. Lincoln nodded slightly, and a hint of a smile appeared on his lips.

He understood.

"Well then," Lincoln said in a dismissive tone, "I suppose there's nothing further to be learned here, and we *do* have a war to get on with." He looked squarely at Alex. "Thank you, gentlemen, for your indulgence."

"The pleasure has been ours, sir," Alex said, looking first at Lincoln then at each of the three generals trying to etch their images into his memory.

Lincoln stood and shook their hands as he prepared to depart.

Alex was last to shake his hand. "Mr. President, it's rumored that Mrs. Lincoln is a patron of the arts, particularly the theatre."

The off-handed comment caught Lincoln by surprise. "Well, yes, I suppose that's a true statement."

Alex smiled, but retained his grip on the president's hand to hold his attention. "I understand the performance of *Our American Cousin* will be staged at Ford's Theater next month. I'm informed by reliable sources that it's simply awful. I anticipate the reviews will reflect a similar view. If Mrs. Lincoln entertains an interest in seeing it, I recommend you find an excuse to avoid going as if your life depended on it."

Lincoln stepped back and disengaged his hand from Alex's grip. He remembered his promise to Mary bribing her, as it were, to accompany him on this trip to City Point.

"Are you married, Captain?" he asked.

"No, sir, I'm not."

"I didn't think so. Well, some day when you are, and if you have been properly house broken, you will view things differently. When your wife asks you if you would like to go to the theatre, then sir, you would be wise to express agreement!"

There were chuckles, and one of the generals chortled, "Amen to that, Mr. President!"

Lincoln placed a fatherly hand on Alex's shoulder for a brief second, smiled with a hint of sadness in his eyes, then turned and left the room through the doorway by which he had entered.

Alex watched the president as he left the lounge. With a sinking heart he knew his second attempt to save Lincoln's life by thwarting his appointment with tragedy at Ford's Theater had also failed. He had never put much stock in the religious doctrine of predestination or *what will be will be*, but he was now having second thoughts about it. *Was our return to the past also predestined?* he wondered. *If so, for what reason, and how will it end?*

Glumly, Alex turned around in time to see Grant and Meade conversing in whispers by the rear platform door. Meade stood with his back to Alex, and Grant's hand rested on the door handle as they spoke. Grant's eyes kept darting at him coldly over Meade's shoulder, giving Alex a disquieting feeling about what they were discussing.

With a parting nod to Parke, Grant opened the door and stepped out on the platform. He paused briefly to speak to Captain Warwick who was waiting outside with the guards, then descended the three wrought iron steps onto the siding where his aide-de-camp waited with his horse.

As Grant rode away, Captain Warwick entered the lounge with three guards trailing close behind him and reported to General Parke. "General Grant instructed me to remove the prisoners from the train immediately, sir."

Parke looked at Meade.

Meade simply waved his hand in dismissal, indicating that the disposition of the prisoners was Parke's decision.

Parke noted the apprehension on their faces. "Until the war is over, gentlemen, I regret that you must remain guests of the United States Army. Captain Warwick will see to it that you are on the next train to City Point."

"Transportation has already been arranged, sir," Captain Warwick interjected. "A captain with a guard detail is waiting on the station platform to escort the prisoners to the holding pen at City Point."

"So soon?" Parke appeared surprised at this unexpected initiative. "Then I suppose it's time to bid farewell to these young gentlemen."

Parke gave them a fatherly smile as the prisoners filed past him. "Good luck. I hope this war ends soon so you can return home to your families."

Alex felt his sincerity. "Home would be good," he replied wistfully. "Thank you, sir, for the generous treatment we have received, and good luck to you as well."

A small detail of armed troops stood on the platform as Alex stepped off the private rail car. Exhausted and dejected, he didn't notice the officer-in-charge stepping forward to report to Captain Warwick.

"Captain Deveraux reporting with a detail to take charge of the prisoners."

Alex was startled to hear the familiar voice.

Captain Warwick returned the other officer's salute, then looked skeptically at the three men lined up behind him. "This is a pretty skimpy detail, Captain. Do you think four of you are enough?"

"Four armed Union soldiers against three unarmed Rebs?" Deveraux said, casting a disdainful glance at the prisoners. "Yeah, I've all the men I need to herd these few to City Point."

"Don't be too cocky, Captain," Warwick cautioned. "These aren't your run-of-the-mill Rebs. You better keep a close eye on them, or you may live to regret it."

Deveraux smiled indulgently. "I hand picked this guard detail; they're all sharpshooters."

Captain Warwick looked impressed. "Okay," he sighed resignedly. "I guess you know what you're doing. They're all yours."

The two men exchanged salutes; then Warwick led his own five-man guard detail to the far side of the station platform where he dismissed them.

The corporal who had tried to separate Alex from his pocket watch lingered behind for a moment. He scratched his scraggly beard as he reflected on his earlier encounter with Deveraux, wondering why the captain was continuing to take so much interest in these prisoners. Finally, he shrugged his shoulders and moved on.

Deveraux's men marched their prisoners along the siding to its junction with the main rail line then turned in the direction of the loading dock at Meade Station.

Sitting astride a wooden crate, two soldiers looked up from a chessboard set up between them and contemplated what appeared to be Union prisoners being herded toward the loading dock. Noting the shackles and the minimal-size guard detail accompanying the prisoners, the chess players dismissed the miscreants as mere low-life deserters or thieves and returned to their game.

Deveraux halted the guard detail at the far end of the loading dock where they could talk without being overheard while they waited for the train. In case someone might be watching, he slowly paced back and forth with his hands clasped behind his back for several minutes. His men stood at a vigilant distance from their prisoners.

"What gives, Matt?" Alex finally asked as Deveraux passed in front of him for the tenth time.

"Didn't I say I would see you later?" Deveraux answered. "Well, I'm here—supposedly to load you on the next train to City Point where you will be confined in a stockade called the Bull Pen. From there, you will be shipped to the prisoner of war camp at Point Lookout, Maryland."

Deveraux spoke with his back turned to Alex. He peered down the track as if looking for the next train.

"We expected that, Matt, but why are you in charge of this guard detail? Is this your way of getting even?"

"Quite the contrary, Alex," a smile flickered across Deveraux's face, "we're here to help you escape."

Alex started to say something—maybe express his appreciation, then closed his mouth.

"Why would you do that?" he finally asked.

"Well, it's more for you than for your friends," Deveraux replied matter-of-factly as he resumed pacing.

"That doesn't answer my question," Alex pressed.

"You're a Mason, Alex. Do you remember the oath you swore to uphold when you were inducted into the Brotherhood: To come to the aid of your brothers in time of need or danger?"

"Yes, of course, but this is war, Matt. What about your oath to defend the United States against all enemies, foreign or domestic, when you were commissioned?"

"Unless I'm badly mistaken you took the same oath," Deveraux tossed the words over his shoulder, "but that didn't prevent you from going over to the Confederacy. Like so many families divided by this conflict, our fellow Masons are no less divided; however, we here firmly believe the long-term interests of Freemasonry lay in preserving the Union."

"We?" Alex cocked his head to one side, a puzzled look in his eyes.

Deveraux nodded at his guard detail. "We're all Masons, Alex."

He stopped pacing and regarded Alex thoughtfully for a moment. "If we help you escape, will you swear to return to your home and never take up arms against the United States again? And will you swear it for your two companions here as well?"

"We would happily return to our homes this very second, Matt; however, the prospects of that happening aren't very promising at the moment."

"I understand," Matt nodded, remembering the newspaper accounts he had read of the widespread devastation the war had wrought in the South.

"As for the rest of it," Alex continued, "I solemnly swear never to take up arms against the United States of America, and I pledge my allegiance to the same."

"And as a Mason, do you swear it?" Deveraux demanded, looking Alex squarely in the eye.

Alex paused. *This is definitely an oath not to be taken lightly.*

"I swear it!" he firmly replied.

"And for your companions?" Deveraux demanded.

Alex gave Mike and Steve a questioning look.

"Don't know much about Masons and such," Mike shrugged, "but I'll give you my solemn oath as a soldier, as an officer, and as a gentleman never to take up arms against the government of the United States of America for as long as I live."

"And I swear it as well," Steve chimed in.

Alex looked at Deveraux. "Yes, I swear it for them." Then added for Mike and Steve's benefit the seriousness of his promise. "If they break their oaths I will take their lives or forfeit my own."

Alex heard Steve's low whistle registering his surprise at the price of oath-breaking in this outfit.

Apparently satisfied, Deveraux resumed his slow pacing. "After we board the train, the second stop will be Cedar Level Station about a mile or two from here. It's a commissary supply depot, so there's always a crowd getting on or off there. When the train stops, get off, then catch the next one going in the opposite direction. Stay on it to the end of the line. With luck, it'll take you all the way to Globe Tavern near the Weldon Railroad south of Petersburg. I doubt anyone will stop you, but just in case, I'll give you some forged passes. Tell anyone who asks that you're returning to your regiment—96th New York Volunteer Infantry—after being hospitalized at City Point for measles or dysentery. It happens a lot and explains why you're traveling unarmed. When you get off the train, I suggest you head south or west. Either direction will take you back into Rebel territory. You'll find a lot of Union troops, trench lines, and fortifications between the Weldon Railroad and the Boydton Plank Road further west. Getting past them won't be easy, but it can be done."

"How will you explain our escaping?" Alex asked.

"I'll just say you jumped from the train as it pulled away from Cedar Level Station, and you escaped. What's the worse they can do," Deveraux grinned, "put us in the infantry and send us to Petersburg?"

Ten minutes later, a locomotive hauling a string of empty flatcars, plus two boxcars tacked onto the end, pulled into the station on its return trip to City Point. Amid hissing clouds of steam, the engine slowed to a stop, and Deveraux and his men herded their prisoners onto the first flatcar behind the tender. The small crowd of passengers waiting on the platform avoided the flatcar on which the prisoners and their armed guards were boarding in favor of one with less villainous-looking company.

The three prisoners plopped down in the middle of the flatcar while Deveraux and his men took up positions close by. A few minutes later the engine's bell clanged and the string of cars lurched forward one by one until the entire train was in motion.

The President's private car still sat on the siding as they rolled past. Leaning against the railing on the rear platform, General Parke gazed at them.

PRESIDENT LINCOLN'S PRIVATE CAR AT CITY POINT

(Courtesy of National Archives)

The President's private car still sat on the siding as they rolled past.

CHAPTER 25

Cedar Level Station, U.S. Military Railroad
4:00 P.M., MARCH 25, 1865

Having removed the prisoners' shackles before reaching Cedar Level Station, Captain Deveraux watched the soldiers and civilian laborers begin streaming off the train. On his signal, the prisoners and their guards stepped from the flatcar onto the station platform and into the crowd of bystanders milling about. Deveraux quickly shook Alex's hand. "Good luck! I hope you make it!"

"We just might! Thanks, Matt!" Alex yelled over the din of voices and the sound of escaping steam from the locomotive.

A moment later the slow, melancholy ring of the locomotive's bell signaled the train's imminent departure.

Deveraux and his fellow Masons elbowed and shoved their way through the crowd and quickly re-boarded the train, finding a place to sit on the rough, splintered deck of one of the dilapidated flatcars. With a sudden series of neck-wrenching jerks and stops, the ancient, overworked engine began moving and gradually picked up speed as it pulled away from the station. Deveraux searched among the faces flashing by, then spotted Alex standing on the edge of the platform. Matt grinned and, briefly touching his hand to the brim of his cap, tossed Alex a salute.

Alex smiled and returned the acknowledgment with a *thumbs up*.

Before the train had even disappeared from view, the former prisoners set into motion a rudimentary plan to avoid drawing attention to themselves by blending in with the military work details at the station.

Steve found a broom and started sweeping spilled grain and accumulated litter from the platform onto the tracks below.

Alex and Mike wandered over to a loading dock where work details were busily engaged in loading and unloading a half-dozen canvas-topped freight wagons lined up hub to hub. On the platform, stacks of crates rapidly grew or diminished in size. In the roadway beyond

CEDAR LEVEL STATION, CITY POINT AND ARMY LINE

(Courtesy of Library of Congress)

*On the platform, stacks of crates
rapidly grew or diminished in size.*

the dock, another half-dozen wagons waited in line—the wagon teamsters dozing or playing cards as they waited their turn to move up to the loading dock. Along the road leading away from the station, clouds of chalky dust rose from behind the wheels and hooves of an endless stream of wagons moving to and from an enormous supply storage area. From where Alex stood, the distant workers looked like ants crawling on and around mounds of barrels and boxes. As witnesses to the scarcity of virtually everything on the Confederate side of the lines, the doughboys were awed by the boundless assortment of Union supplies stored at the Cedar Level depot.

Mike took from his coat pocket the little notebook and pencil that Alex had given him earlier. Their captors had found nothing of importance in it and allowed him to keep it after he explained that he took pages from it to write letters home to his ailing widowed mother and his eight younger brothers and sisters.

Alex had difficulty keeping a straight face when he heard Mike spin this heart-rending tale. Far from being the sole support for his impoverished family, Mike came from a wealthy background—his father was a successful banker, and his mother was a socialite who loved parties and had left the raising of their three children to a nanny.

With pencil in one hand and notebook in the other, Mike appeared to be listing the contents of each crate while Alex counted the quantity in each stack as if taking inventory.

Alex knew Deveraux would delay reporting their escape to the Provost Marshal at City Point for as long as he could. But eventually the authorities along the railroad would be telegraphed to be on the lookout for three-escaped Rebel prisoners disguised as Union soldiers. For the next half-hour, Alex kept an anxious eye on the two-story white frame house located a scant fifty yards from the station. The telegraph line running from one of the poles beside the railroad track into a downstairs window in back of the house, several horses tethered to a hitching post by the front steps, and the constant flow of visitors told him that the structure was probably the depot headquarters. Any moment he expected to see someone rush out the door and alert the sentries who were idly sitting around the station.

After an hour had elapsed, Alex began to wonder if they might be better off giving up on the train and striking out on foot. He was just about to discuss the idea with Mike and Steve when he heard a long whistle blast coming from the direction of City Point.

"About time!" Mike grumbled.

Curious onlookers crowded the edge of the station platform to catch a glimpse of the approaching train.

Like some great lumbering prehistoric beast, the steam engine suddenly appeared from around a curve. As the mass of iron and steel bore down on the watchers standing on the platform, dense black smoke belched skyward from its outlandish balloon-shaped stack, and sunlight reflected brightly off the glass of the square lantern perched high above the pointed prow of the cowcatcher. A white shroud of superheated steam enveloped the engine as it slowed to make its stop at the station. Alex frowned as a passenger car and a dozen boxcars materialized behind the tender. He had just assumed the train would make a brief stop then move on; he hadn't considered the possibility of a lengthy stopover to unload or uncouple some of the boxcars on the station's siding. *Something else to worry about,* he told himself.

A moment later the immense engine rolled past the siding switch and slowed to a stop beside the platform. *Clang! Clang!* The slow and melancholy tolling of its bell was sweet music to Alex's ears.

Alex grabbed the handrail of the open-end passenger coach coupled to the tender and swung onto the steps. Out of the corner of his eye he glimpsed Mike and Steve boarding the opposite end of the coach. As he opened the door and stepped inside his euphoria abruptly dissipated. The coach was full of Union soldiers!

He stood hesitantly in the doorway for several long seconds trying to decide whether to stay or turn around and leave; the latter, he decided, was no longer an option. Some of the men seated about the coach cast curious glances at him as he stared self-consciously at them. Marshalling his courage, he took a deep breath and managed a weak smile. He gazed around the car, digesting this strange new environment like some being from another world—which he was.

Most of the soldiers lounging about appeared to be veterans with a sprinkling of young recruits, conspicuous in their new uniforms. *The newbies are probably on their way to join their regiments.*

There were few empty seats. Alex looked on enviously as Mike and Steve took the last two seats on either side of the aisle at the far end of the coach. Finally, midway down the aisle, he wedged himself into what was questionably the last vacant seat between two over-weight sergeants who grudgingly made room for him. Pressed like a sardine against his smelly, unwashed travel companions without the benefit of circulating air, Alex began to sweat profusely in the oppressive heat.

The toe-tapping strains of a harmonica and the off-key harmony of a dozen voices belting out the refrain of the *Battle Hymn of the Republic* flowed from the back of the coach.

Obviously heat and discomfort don't appear to be a problem where Mike and Steve are sitting.

The string of cars suddenly jerked forward as the train got under-way, jostling the passengers roughly back and forth. Alex grimaced as he suddenly got a double-whiff of pungent armpits on either side of him. *Give me a break!*

A few minutes later, the train pulled into Pitkin Station, and the singing faded away.

Grateful for the silence, Alex leaned forward and peered out the windows on the station-platform side of the coach. Like a bad dream, he saw a squad of Union infantry waiting on the platform to board the coach. *Uh-oh! I have a hunch the Provost Marshal at City Point has been notified of our escape.* The warm sweat trickling down Alex's forehead suddenly turned cold.

The moment the train lurched to a stop, the infantry squad boarded the coach in two groups, one at either end. Five soldiers, with a tall baby-faced lieutenant in charge, entered the forward door and positioned themselves, rifles at the ready, facing the passengers. Alex couldn't see the rest of the soldiers, but he heard the second group coming down the aisle behind him as they began checking the passengers for orders and furlough passes. Those who couldn't produce the requested documents were promptly removed from the coach and placed under guard on the station platform.

A young private suddenly appeared in the aisle at the end of Alex's row of seats. Without waiting to be asked, the sergeants sitting on either side of Alex promptly handed him their papers. The soldier quickly glanced at the documents, returned them, then wiggled his fingers impatiently in front of Alex's nose demanding his papers.

Alex fumbled in his coat pocket, found the forged pass Deveraux had given him, then held his breath as he handed it to the soldier.

The private stared at Alex suspiciously as he unfolded the paper. He was a blue-eyed kid with peach fuzz on his cheeks. *Not even old enough to shave yet.* Curly blond hair cascaded down over his forehead from under the new regulation kepi pushed back on his head. He chewed his bottom lip thoughtfully as he studied Alex's pass.

Alex tensed as a frown appeared on the soldier's face, as if he had detected something not quite right. The young man looked Alex straight in the eye as he slowly, almost reluctantly it seemed, handed the unfolded pass back to him, then moved on to the next row of seats.

Alex exhaled softly as he refolded the pass and stuffed it back in his pocket. Then it suddenly dawned on him: *He couldn't read!* The kid had been holding Alex's pass upside down when he examined it!

After the lieutenant and his squad departed and the train pulled out, Alex moved to a seat next to an open window vacated by one of the unlucky passengers detained for questioning.

Meade Station was the next stop. Alex grew apprehensive that someone might recognize them when they arrived.

Not unexpectedly, a squad of infantry stood on the platform when the train reached the station. Alex pulled the brim of his cap down over his eyes, feigning sleep, as the soldiers entered the coach and began conducting their inspection. None of the faces looked familiar. A hand shook his shoulder roughly. Keeping his cap down over his face, Alex pulled the pass from his pocket and held it up for whoever wanted to see it. He breathed easier as a corporal cast a cursory glance at it then moved up the aisle to the next row of passengers.

For thirty minutes they remained at Meade Station while the

crew switched some of the boxcars onto the siding where Lincoln's private train had been earlier.

Impatient to get underway, Alex sat up and looked around to see what Mike and Steve were doing. Mike's head bobbed up and down as he dozed in a corner seat on the last row; Steve was reading a New York newspaper he had borrowed from a sleeping neighbor.

With a violent jolt, the locomotive returned and coupled-up to the waiting string of cars. In the fading daylight Alex slowly relaxed as the train began to roll away from the station. Lack of sleep was beginning to take its toll. He gazed drowsily out at the platform. His eyes glazed and fixed on the groups of workers engaged in lifting and hauling the stacks of freight. The faces of occasional passersby slipped past; Alex saw the faces with far-away, dreamy detachment. With an effort, Alex shook his head and blinked his eyes, forcing himself to stay awake just a little longer.

A face suddenly appeared in the window—it looked vaguely familiar. Alex focused on the blurry image as it kept pace with the moving train. Suddenly, his eyes popped open. *The freightmaster!* Alex slumped lower in his seat, hoping the window ledge would hide his face, but it was too late.

The freightmaster took the short clay pipe from his mouth and squinted at Alex through the coach window. Recognition had been mutual.

Uh-oh, Alex grimaced. *He recognized me.* Wide-awake now, he stood up and lurched from side-to-side as he moved down the aisle holding on to the backs of seats for support. When he reached the rear of the coach, he stepped over the outstretched legs of a sleeping soldier and slipped into a vacant seat across from where Mike was dozing. Alex leaned forward, pretending to look at the passing landscape out the window, then kicked Mike's outstretched foot.

Mike made an annoyed face but continued snoring.

Alex aimed the toe of his boot at Mike's ankle and kicked again.

Mike jerked awake, scowling. "It's going to hurt when I throw your butt out that window," he muttered irritably.

"You don't have time to sleep," Alex said. "We're in trouble."

"Oh yeah?" Mike grunted, pulling down the bill of his kepi over his eyes. "You're just now figuring that out?"

"Wake up, Mike! This is serious. Remember the freightmaster we met last night at Meade Station?"

"Yeah, so?"

"Well, he was on the platform just now when the train pulled away. He saw me through the window, and I'm pretty sure he recognized me. If he did and reports it, there will be a welcoming committee waiting for us at the next stop. We need to get off the train *now*."

"And how do we do that?" Mike said, keeping his voice low. "It's almost dark and the train's moving at a fast clip."

"I'll think of something. You and Steve meet me out on the platform at the rear of the coach."

Alex stood and again stepped over the outstretched legs of the snoring soldier sprawled on the seat next to Mike then headed for the door leading to the coach's rear platform. As he reached the door, he spotted Steve two rows back looking at him questioningly over the top of a newspaper. Alex nodded for him to follow.

Alex leaned over the platform railing watching the rails and railroad ties rushing from beneath the coach like the wake of a ship. *Jumping off the train at this speed would be a sure cure for the problem of growing old*, he mused cheerlessly. *Even if it slows down for a curve, jumping off in the dark would still be risky.*

One at a time Mike and Steve joined him on the platform. Alex explained the situation and his idea for getting off the train.

Steve winced and whistled through his teeth. "Well, if that's how we're getting off, I suggest jumping from the outside curve of the track. Centrifugal force will propel us away from the train's wheels."

"Yeah," Mike nodded sagely. "Sounds like good advice. I like that a lot better than Horn's 'Die well, my brothers.'"

Alex and Steve grinned.

"Well, let's get'er done," Alex said with a sigh. "Since it's my idea, I'll jump first."

Mike and Steve stood on opposite sides of the platform and leaned over the railing watching the tracks ahead in the fading light.

"There's a curve coming up," Steve called out. "Get ready to jump from Mike's side."

Alex and Mike clung to the hand railing on either side of the platform steps with Steve right behind them, ready to jump. Trees and foliage whipped past. The ground lay hidden in the train's shadow.

Alex felt the train slowing as the engine entered the sharp curve. "Get ready!" he yelled over the monotonous *clackety clack* sound of the coach's steel wheels striking the rail connecting joints.

"Go!"

Alex leaped from the passenger car but something almost instantly snagged the back of his coat collar. Like a cat held by the scruff of the neck, he dangled in the air flapping and kicking his arms and legs to no avail.

"Stop struggling," he heard Steve gasp, "unless you want me to drop you!"

Alex glanced down—and gasped too—thirty feet below him was a deep ravine dotted with tree stumps. It dawned on him that when he jumped, the train had just started across one of the trestles that spanned the numerous ravines and creeks along the Military Railroad. He blindly reached behind him until his fingers brushed against the handrail on the platform steps. Sensing Steve's grip on his collar beginning to weaken, Alex again thrust out his arm; this time his fingers closed around the handrail. Keeping a tight grip, he reached out with his foot and gingerly touched the bottom step. A second later he shifted the bulk of his weight to the step then latched onto the handrail with his other hand.

Mike and Steve each grabbed an arm and pulled him up onto the platform.

Alex leaned weakly against the railing. "Thanks!" he said gasping for air. "That was close!"

"I caught a glimpse of the trestle just as you jumped," Steve said. "I was lucky to catch you in time."

"And the only reason I'm not impaled on one of those stumps," Mike said, pointing into the ravine, "is because I hesitated—wanted to be sure I didn't land on top of you. Steve grabbed you just as I was about to jump. So I probably owe him my life as well."

225

STATION AND TRESTLE ON U.S.M.R.R.

(Courtesy of National Archives)

. . . the train had just started across one of the trestles that spanned the numerous ravines and creeks along the Military Railroad.

"I'm not keeping score," Steve shrugged humbly. "If we're going to stay alive, we need to pull together."

"Well so much for jumping off the train," Alex said. "I think we should reconsider taking our chances with the Union Army."

"No argument there," Mike seconded.

Steve nodded in agreement as the train crossed another trestle above a deep ravine.

At dusk the train pulled into Hancock Station, the first stop after Meade Station. Tired and dejected, the doughboys remained in their seats as the brass bell on the engine *clanged* monotonously, announcing their arrival.

The wheels of the coach squealed to a stop alongside the station platform.

Alex expected to see another squad of Union infantry waiting to board the car to arrest them, but the platform appeared deserted. Except for the mournful tolling of the bell and the sporadic hiss of steam escaping from the engine's boiler, there were no sounds of alarm.

Two lines of soldier-passengers formed in the aisle to exit the car by either the forward or rear door.

One of the two overweight sergeants Alex had sat between earlier waited last in line to exit the rear door. He eyed them with sidelong glances, trying not to appear obvious but not succeeding either. As the sergeant shuffled toward the door, he paused and leaned on the back of Mike's seat. "You boys look like you could use a hot meal an' some sleep," he said, noting their exhausted condition. "This is as far as the train goes tonight—too dangerous to run at night beyond this station. So you might just as well get off an' get yourselves a meal at one of the sutler tents or taverns. You can always come back an' sleep on the train if you can't find anything better, but I know a sutler who offers a meal, hot bath, an' a bunk for *two bits* a night. Does a thriving business from folks like us lying over for the night at the station—even changes the bath water every day!"

"Say that does sound pretty good," Alex smiled appreciatively, getting to his feet and stepping into the aisle. "A hot meal and a drink might be just the thing."

As he and Steve got in line behind Alex, Mike poked Alex in the back to get his attention. "A meal sounds good, but how do we pay for it?" he whispered. "We don't have a cent between us."

"I thought we might do a little bartering," Alex replied.

Before Mike could ask the obvious question, Steve cheerfully piped up. "I have a better idea—one that doesn't involve bartering family heirlooms to pay for dinner."

"I'm all ears," Alex said, raising a dubious eyebrow. "How do you plan to pay for dinner?"

"With the coin of the realm, of course!" Steve grinned. "Just so happens, I've got a bit hidden away."

"I may be sorry I asked," Mike frowned, "but by any chance is the money you have tucked away minted *after* 1865?"

"Of course not! I'm not a total twit, you know!" Steve said, rolling his eyes.

⬤━━━

The sergeant had moved ahead and was waiting for them when they stepped off the coach onto the station platform. "My name's Applewhite," he smiled, extending his hand. "I'm takin' the train to Warren Station in the mornin', but tonight I'm goin' to visit that sutler I told you about. You boys are welcome to come along if you want."

"We'll take you up on that offer, Sergeant Applewhite," Alex smiled as he shook his hand and introduced himself and his companions. "A hot meal would be real good!"

"It's called *Dicken's Tavern*. It's a short ways back up the tracks, close to where the train crossed the Jerusalem Plank Road. Dicken, the owner, picked a good spot an' gets a lot of business. Jus' follow me—it's easier an' faster if we stick to the railroad tracks. There's a road of sorts that runs alongside the tracks, but what with the rain we've had, the low spots an' potholes are full of water. Without a lantern you'd trip an' fall on your face before you saw the hole."

Applewhite shuffled carefully from one cross tie to the next, making the quarter mile walk to the Jerusalem Plank Road a slow torture that taxed the patience of his more nimble companions. When they reached the plank road, Applewhite stopped and pointed to a large ramshackle, open-sided structure looming ahead of them in the dark on the side of the road. A framework of misshapen six-inch poles supported a flat roof of pine boughs. From a pole by the roadside entrance hung a sign fashioned from a weathered cracker box lid. Bold white lettering, obviously applied with a paintbrush and a shaky hand, proclaimed the establishment to be *DICKEN'S TAVERN, Est. 1864.* Swaying lanterns suspended from the roof's support beams illuminated an odd-assortment of tables, benches, and chairs scattered about on a floor of pine needles. Conspicuous by its elegance and size, a brass and mahogany reception desk that had formerly graced the lobby of a regal hotel in some distant city served as a bar for the crudely-constructed tavern.

Although it was still early evening, the tavern was already crowded with attendants hustling about with trays of food and drink. As to be expected, the customers were mostly soldiers. Rowdy, drunken laughter and the clapping of hands to the accompaniment of a plunking banjo greeted them as they walked up to the entrance. Inside, the place was filled to overflowing with soldiers noisily eating, drinking, talking, and singing.

"Management obviously doesn't exert itself helping customers find a place to sit," Alex said plaintively, unimpressed. Two drunken Irish soldiers danced a jig to the tune of the banjo on a tabletop while those around them whooped and clapped and shouted encouragement.

"It's like this every night," Applewhite nodded at the crowd as if reading Alex's thoughts. "C'mon," he grunted, pushing his huge bulk between the crowded tables toward a table in a distant corner where two soldiers lay sprawled across it sleeping off an over-indulgence of whiskey, the house specialty.

Applewhite's enormous paunch cleared a path to the table which he unceremoniously tipped over, dumping its tenants on the floor. Neither man made a sound as they struck the hard packed earth.

"Two of you boys hold this table while the other comes with me. We hafta pay for our meals in advance over there," he said, pointing at the bar where a scruffy, villainous-looking bartender busily poured whiskey into customers' glasses.

Steve went with Sergeant Applewhite while Alex and Mike guarded the table and appropriated two more chairs from nearby tables vacated by their occupants who had stepped outside to relieve themselves.

Two brawny, dour-faced attendants shoved their way through the crowd to where Alex and Mike were sitting. Alex tensed, expecting trouble; however, the two bouncers paid them no heed as they snatched the two inebriated bodies on the floor by the ankles and dragged them out into the woods behind the tavern. No one seemed to notice.

Beginning to relax, Alex gazed at the noisy, smoke-filled pavilion. A crowd had gathered around the table nearest them where sat a muscular Irishman and his two cronies. The Irishman had stripped off his shirt and was boisterously challenging all comers to an arm-wrestling match. His cronies were busy taking wagers and collecting money from the previous losers. Alex and Mike watched as the Irishman beat two challengers in quick succession, after which the crowd's interest began to wane.

Eager to drum up business, one of the Irishman's pals, a snaggle-toothed runt of a man, looked over at them. He squinted for a moment, obviously sizing them up. "You lads look in fair shape. Maybe you'd like to try your luck against Paddy O'Riley here?" he solicited in a thick Irish brogue. "Those other blokes were mere babes compared to the likes of you. One dollar will get you four if either of you can beat O'Riley."

Applewhite and Steve returned to the table just in time to over-hear the offered wager. "While my friends are mullin' it over, why not start with me?" Applewhite offered innocuously. "I kinda like those odds. Besides, there's nothin' I enjoy more than whippin' a mere Irishman, unless maybe it be two or three of 'em at the same time, jes' to make it a fair fight." He smiled confidently, as though it would be a simple matter, like putting the cat out.

Snaggle-tooth's solicitous grin promptly transformed into a scowl.

Alex knew Irish temperament. Maligning their heritage was a sure fire way of starting a brawl. He wished he had stayed on the train.

Snaggle-tooth's left hand crept down to his waist belt where Alex suspected a weapon lay concealed.

The big Irishman clamped a restraining hand on Snaggle-tooth's arm as he flashed Applewhite a humorless smile. "I'll arm wrestle anyone, even an old tub o' lard like ya, if the wager's right. Why don't we make it more interestin'? I'll pay five ta one if ya can whip me."

Applewhite's eyes narrowed and took on a hard, flinty quality. "*An old tub of lard*, huh? Okay, Paddy, you're on."

Applewhite shuffled his three hundred pound bulk between the tables, then eased himself onto a stool at the Irishman's table.

From behind the bar, a waiter approached, weaving in and out among the tables and customers. On his shoulder he balanced a tray containing four brimming bowls of stew, a loaf of bread on a trencher, and four stoneware bottles of beer. He sensed trouble from the tone of the voices and quickly retreated back to the bar after depositing the food and drinks on Alex's table.

Alex nodded to Mike and Steve to begin eating and not to wait for Applewhite. They hungrily attacked the stew, wolfing it down and sopping up the broth with chunks of bread torn from the loaf on the trencher. They could smell trouble brewing and hoped to leave ahead of it with full stomachs.

The Irishman smiled confidently at the on-lookers standing around the table.

Applewhite shoved his extended belly up against the table and placed his right elbow on the tabletop next to O'Riley's. His hands were huge, and his forearms resembled country hams that dwarfed the Irishman's muscular arms. Sweat trickled down Applewhite's temples and jowls and dripped onto the table.

O'Riley's other crony, a skinny, squirrel-faced man, sat on a stool next to Applewhite and officiated the match. He checked to ensure the opponents' wrists were straight and their elbows were firmly placed in the center of the table. Then he explained *the rules*, of which there were few. "Keep your backside planted on your stool an' keep one hand behind your back." He looked at Applewhite as if he were explaining the rules just for him. "There will be three matches. Two wins out of three determines the winner. If your knuckles touch the tabletop, you lose!

D' ya understand the rules?" squirrel-face asked with a smirk on his face.

Applewhite nodded.

"All right then; let's see the color of your money."

Applewhite tossed a small wad of Federal fractional currency onto the table. Squirrel-face unfolded the bills and counted out a dollar in fractional denominations.

The big Irishman reached into a money belt hidden inside his waistband and pulled out a five-dollar gold piece. He smiled broadly, revealing a set of very white and even teeth, as he tossed the gold coin on top of Applewhite's pile of paper fractional currency. "You're sweatin' awful hard, Sarge," he said. "I wouldn't want ta be the one ta cause ya ta have a heart attack. On me sainted Mother's grave, I wouldn't, God Bless 'er. Ya still have time ta forfeit an' walk away if ya like, Sarge. There'd be no hard feelin's from me an' the lads here if ya do."

Applewhite smiled, but there was no friendliness in his eyes. "If you're plannin' to talk me to death, you're doin' a great job. If you wanna arm-wrestle, let's get on with it."

The two men glared at each other.

"Okay now," Squirrel-face said officiously, "you'll start when I count to three."

Each man tightened his grip on the other's hand.

"*One!*"

"*Two!*"

Alex raised his bowl to his lips and quickly drained the remaining stew before getting on his feet to peer over the shoulders of the crowd that had suddenly converged from the other tables.

"*Three!*" Squirrel-face shouted over the clamor of excited voices cheering and jeering.

The two opponents' hands immediately clenched in bone-crushing grips; their arm muscles bulged as each strained to gain an early advantage.

The Irishman gritted his teeth and twisted his hand and wrist back and forth, trying to weaken Applewhite's grip.

If Applewhite had a wrist, it was invisible to those observing the match. His huge hand appeared to be merely an extension of his meaty forearm.

As the seconds ticked away, O'Riley's bulging muscles and unyielding grip appeared to be wearing his opponent down. Gradually, he bent Applewhite's hand and forearm back until the knuckles of his hand were only an inch above the tabletop. The match lasted another four or five seconds until the Irishman called on his inner reserves of strength and slammed Applewhite's knuckles painfully against the stained tabletop.

"The winnah of the first match!" Squirrel-face shouted, pointing at the Irishman.

Applewhite drew back from the table and massaged his shoulder. "Must be my off day," he muttered, looking chagrined.

O'Riley took a swig from a stoneware bottle of beer that Snaggle-tooth handed him. He smiled, his face glowing triumphantly as he glanced around at the growing crowd. His eyes eventually came to rest on Applewhite. "Well, ya still have two more chances. Maybe your luck will change. Ya have a fine, strong arm, friend, so why don't we raise the wager ta make it really interestin'? How about ten ta two—my ten dollars against your two—winner takes all?" he smiled, setting the bottle on the table and offering his hand to seal the wager. "What d'ya say, pal?"

Applewhite reached across the table, ignoring O'Riley's out-stretched hand, and snatched his unfinished beer instead. He wiped the lip of the bottle with his sleeve, then tilted his head back and took a long pull. Foamy white rivulets cascaded from the corners of his mouth down his beard as he gulped the warm liquid.

When he finished, Applewhite set the bottle on the table, belched loudly, then wiped his graying beard with the back of his hand. As if still contemplating the Irishman's offer, he nodded. "Okay, you're on, but I'm a bit short of cash at the moment."

Applewhite looked around at the faces in the crowd. He smiled as his gaze came to rest on Steve. He crooked a finger at Steve who responded with a startled *Who? Me?* expression. Applewhite nodded and beckoned to him again with his crooked finger.

Steve wore a worried frown as he nudged his way through the crowd. A moment later he was standing behind Applewhite. "What d'ya want?" he asked.

"Lend me a dollar," Applewhite said, as if Steve were a life-long friend from whom he was accustomed to borrowing money.

Steve hesitated, not wanting to get involved.

Applewhite wagged a finger, motioning for Steve to come closer so they could talk privately over the den of the crowd.

Steve leaned over Applewhite's shoulder to hear what he had to say.

"Don't let me down, Johnny Reb," Applewhite whispered. "You owe me, an' I don't think you want to discuss the matter in present company. Trust me—your money's safe."

The threat in his voice was unmistakable; Steve quickly fished a silver dollar out of his pocket and handed it to him.

Applewhite tossed the dollar on top of the previous wager then looked at O'Riley. "There! Now it's your turn to ante up."

The Irishman nudged Snaggle-tooth with his elbow. Snaggle-tooth grimaced as he reluctantly pulled two small gold coins from his vest pocket and tossed them onto the growing pile of money.

Word quickly spread about the sizable wager. Most of the customers and tavern employees gathered around the participants to watch and make wagers themselves on the probable outcome.

Applewhite took another swig from the bottle, set it down, then leaned forward and rested his right elbow in the middle of the table.

O'Riley looked around at the sea of faces and smiled his confident smile, pleased at having attracted such a large following of supporters. He leaned over the table, placed his right elbow next to Applewhite's, and firmly gripped his hand.

The official again counted to three, smacking his right hand on the tabletop as he called each count. On the count of *three*, the two opponents' arms strained one against the other.

Almost from the outset, O'Riley appeared to be winning. His biceps bulged, and he gritted his teeth as he slowly but steadily pushed Applewhite's arm and hand back to within an inch of the table's surface. Sensing victory, the Irishman again called on his inner store of strength. Ropes of muscle coiled in his back and shoulders, and sweat trickled off his chin as he applied every ounce of strength to vanquish his opponent. His hand and arm quivered from the effort, but still the old man's hand refused to bend further. Feeling his strength starting to ebb, he glanced up into Applewhite's face.

The old man seemed unaffected. His eyes casually wandered

about the tavern observing the customers with detached interest. Like a big dog tiring of being pestered by a little dog, the old man slowly turned his head and focused on O'Riley, his lips curling into a malignant smile.

Inch by inch the old man forced O'Riley's arm back to the starting point, then rapidly pushed the Irishman's arm and hand back until his knuckles touched the tabletop.

"The winner of the second match!" Squirrel-face announced, showing little enthusiasm as he pointed at Applewhite.

"It appears the score is even," Applewhite said, a glimmer of satisfaction in his eyes. "Want to raise the ante again?"

His confidence shaken, O'Riley shook his head then angrily snatched Snaggle-tooth's beer from his hand and took a long swig. Finishing the bottle, he tossed it to Snaggle-tooth then looked at Applewhite curiously as he massaged his biceps in anticipation of the final round.

Packed around the table, the crowd buzzed with excitement, and money quickly changed hands as wagers were given and taken.

Swilling the last of his beer, Applewhite set the stoneware bottle down and leaned across the table placing his *left* elbow in the middle of it. He nodded at Paddy O'Riley, his yellow tobacco-stained teeth forming a hideous Cheshire grin between his bushy beard and his mustache. The old man's grin had an unsettling effect on the Irishman; a wary look appeared in his eyes.

O'Riley leaned forward to place his right elbow next to his opponent's, then hesitated as he noticed Applewhite's left elbow on the table. O'Riley frowned, confused. "What're ya doin'?" he demanded.

"Well, Paddy, you're right-handed, an' we played the first two matches your way. I think it's only fair that we make the final match a left-handed contest on account that I'm left-handed."

The crowd fell silent as they digested the implications of Applewhite's revelation. A murmur began, which swiftly grew to a ground swell of agreement and dissent. The *fairness* and *legality* of switching arms during the course of an arm-wrestling event became a matter of fierce debate as the spectators stubbornly defended their moral positions—and their wagers.

O'Riley was stunned to learn that he had been arm-wrestling

a left-handed opponent. He sat with his arms folded, refusing to continue with the match until the crowd resolved the issue. From the way tempers were flaring, it seemed to him that a general brawl was imminent—in which event, he would just grab the money off the table and run. The Irishman smirked at Applewhite as the debate intensified and the atmosphere grew more heated.

Just when tempers threatened to boil over, a deafening blast shook the tavern drowning out the uproar. An uneasy hush settled over the crowd as the chill of fear cooled impassioned tempers.

Richard Dicken, the tavern proprietor, stood on the bar with a double-barreled shotgun leveled at the crowd. He stared into the upturned faces. "I own this establishment, so it seems to me that I ought to be the one to set the house gaming rules." Dicken cocked the hammer on the unfired barrel of his shotgun. "Anyone got a problem with that?"

A nervous murmur of assent rose from the crowd, particularly from those who were closest to the bar.

"All right then!" Dicken said with a cheesy smile, which with the wild look in his eyes, made him appear more than a little demented. "These are the rules for arm-wrestling in this tavern: Prior to the start of any contest, both parties must agree which arm will be used for all matches. It can be the right arm or it can be the left, but no one will be permitted to switch from one to the other unless both parties agree."

The crowd greeted the new rules with an assortment of approving cheers and howls of disappointment.

"Quiet!" Dicken shouted, waving the muzzle of his shotgun menacingly to get their attention.

The tavern was immediately graveyard still.

"I said," Dicken continued, "from *now on* these rules will apply. However, the present match started before the fact, so in fairness to these two men and those of you who have already placed your bets, I have another way of settling this matter..." Dicken reached into his coat pocket and held up a big Liberty head penny. "I'll toss this coin. If it lands *heads* up, you'll finish the game as you began, that is, using your right arm. If it lands *tails* up, then you'll finish the game with your left arm. Anyone have a problem with that?"

Dicken demanded, brandishing his shotgun once more.

This time the crowd roared its approval, drowning out the meek objections of the few malcontents.

Dicken flipped the penny into the air and let it drop onto the top of the bar where it spun on its edge in a circle for a few seconds before rolling to a stop.

Before anyone had a chance to see how it landed, Dicken put his foot on it and called to O'Reilly and Applewhite: "Do either of you gentlemen want to see this for yourselves, or do you trust me to call it out to you?"

Applewhite and O'Reiley sensed the proprietor's impartiality.

"You call it," Applewhite said.

Reluctantly, the Irishman nodded his concurrence.

Dicken lifted his foot.

"Tails!" he announced. "So that settles it! Get on with the game!"

Alex noted the glimmer in Applewhite's eye as the crestfallen Irishman leaned across the table and placed his left arm and elbow next to his.

"Cheer up, Paddy," Applewhite smiled. "Maybe I was lyin' about being left-handed. Maybe I just wanted to make you sweat!"

O'Riley squinted at Applewhite, wondering if he really was bluffing.

Squirrel-face, the self-appointed official, strutted slowly around the table like a peacock confirming that both opponents were complying with the generally recognized rules for arm-wrestling. He rapped the knuckles of O'Riley's right hand as they surreptitiously grabbed hold of the rung on the back of his chair for support. The Irishman winced and glared at Squirrel-face. *I'll deal with you later* read the unmistakable message in his eyes.

Squirrel-face immediately regretted his error in judgment. Sporting a worried frown, he promptly returned to his seat next to Applewhite.

A hush fell over the crowd as Squirrel-face began the count.

On the count of *"One!"* the opponents tensed and tightened their grip on each other's hand.

On *"Two!"* they leaned against the edge of the table. It was not in violation of the rules.

On *"Three!"* O'Riley's back and shoulder muscles bulged. His whole left arm knotted and coiled as ropes of muscle strained against Applewhite's grip.

A distinct *crack* resounded through the tavern followed by a scream of anguish as Applewhite, in one lightening quick motion, jerked O'Riley's forearm and hand backwards to the tabletop. The Irishman slumped to the floor moaning in pain and clutching his dislocated shoulder.

Applewhite peered thoughtfully at the figure writhing on the floor. "Then again," he smiled as he reached across the table to collect his winnings, "maybe I wasn't bluffin' at all. I really wish you hadn't called me an *old tub of lard*. That hurt my feelin's."

Out of the corner of his eye, Applewhite suddenly glimpsed Squirrel-face lunging at him with a stiletto in his hand. With cat-like reflexes he deflected the blade with his arm but not before the tip plunged through two inches of fat and came to rest against a rib.

Applewhite grabbed the neck of the beer bottle and brought it crashing down on Squirrel-face's head— the knife dropped from his fingers. As Squirrel-face toppled over onto the floor, Applewhite rose unsteadily to his feet, pocketed his winnings, and backed away from the table. But he hadn't noticed Snaggle-tooth slipping away from the table at the end of the match, nor seen him sneaking through the crowd, and of course, he wasn't aware that the little runt was now standing behind him.

Snaggle-tooth reached inside his waist belt and pulled out a wicked-looking Bowie-knife with an eight-inch blade. He slipped it inside his sleeve and waited in anticipation as Applewhite tottered backwards toward him.

Snaggle-tooth's furtive maneuvering, however, had not gone unnoticed. Mike figured he was up to no good. Looking around for a weapon, he grabbed the closest thing at hand and shoved his way through a rank of spectators to stand behind the wily little Irishman.

Applewhite shuffled backward clutching his right side where a widening crimson circle oozed through his coat. His attention was now focused on O'Riley who had regained his feet and was wildly lunging toward him, swinging his good right arm.

Snaggle-tooth took advantage of the distraction. He lunged at Applewhite's exposed back with the long-bladed knife, but before he could drive the blade home, a ceramic bowl of hot stew came crashing down on his head.

Howling in pain Snaggle-tooth wandered in circles, slashing out blindly with his knife, until some bystanders wrestled him to the floor and disarmed him.

Unaware of the commotion behind him, Applewhite ducked a wild swing as O'Riley closed in, then grabbed his assailant around the chest in a bear hug and squeezed. The Irishman yelped in pain as his dislocated shoulder popped under Applewhite's anaconda grip. Frantically, he struggled to break free from the old man's crushing embrace, but Applewhite steadily squeezed the Irishman's chest until he heard the telltale sound of cracking ribs. O'Riley suddenly went limp in his arms. Applewhite released his grip and allowed his victim to slide to the floor like a rag doll.

Alex shouldered his way through the milling crowd and gently placed a hand on Applewhite's shoulder. "Let's leave, friend. Things are getting out of hand here."

"Leave?" Applewhite bellowed as if Alex was out of his mind. "Why this is the most fun I've had in months! The night's still young; the best is yet to come! Hey! That kinda rhymes, doesn't it? Bet you didn't know I was a poet?"

"If we don't stop that bleeding, you may be a dead one," Alex insisted, gently nudging him toward the tavern's entrance. "Let's get you out of here and have a doctor look at that wound."

"Oh, all right," Applewhite snorted in grudging acquiescence, "but I never got to eat my stew that I paid good money for."

"Don't worry, Sarge," Mike smiled, "I put it to good use. You got your money's worth. We'll get you something to eat after we find a doctor."

At the tavern entrance the proprietor stepped out in front of them blocking their path. Alex noted worriedly that Dicken was still toting his double-barrel shotgun.

"No need to rush off, boys. I just sent a man to fetch an ambulance.

239

The Army has an aid station up the road near Fort Davis. Looks like you need some doctoring, Sergeant," Dicken said.

"Ain't much. I'll mend," Applewhite chuckled, glossing over the seriousness of his injury.

"That so?" Dicken grunted, eyeing Applewhite's blood-soaked uniform and the steady spattering of blood on the brick walk. "That man you hit with the beer bottle will need some stitches. His friend got scalded from a bowl of hot stew that someone dumped on his head, then to add to his misery, a couple of the boys made a punching bag out of him. I don't suppose you'd know anything about that?" Dicken said, cocking his head inquiringly at Mike.

Mike didn't answer, just shrugged and smiled. Obviously, Dicken kept a close eye on his patrons.

Dicken nodded, smiled knowingly, then continued. "That big Irishman has a busted shoulder and possibly a couple of cracked ribs. The aid station will probably send him to one of the field hospitals."

"Sorry about the ruckus in there," Applewhite said, sounding genuinely contrite.

"Wasn't your fault from what I saw," Dicken shrugged, seemingly unconcerned. "I've seen worse nights than this. I wrote a letter to the Army some time ago suggesting they move the medical aid station across the road from my tavern—never got an answer. I wouldn't be at all surprised if there aren't more casualties here every night than on the front line at Fort Davis." Cradling his shotgun in the crook of his arm, Dicken stepped aside. "Don't you boys get careless out there. Hear? Come back and have a drink sometime."

Dicken had just turned away when they heard the sound of pounding hooves out on the road, then suddenly an ambulance wagon careened out of the darkness and rolled to a stop in front of the tavern, its team of horses lathered and breathing hard. Two medics jumped down from the wagon seat, pulled a couple of canvas stretchers from the rear of the wagon, and ran past them as they hurried inside.

"Wait," Applewhite said, shrugging Alex's steadying hand off his arm. "I gotta see this."

A minute later, assisted by some of the patrons, the medics reemerged from the tavern carrying two loaded stretchers. Then Squirrel-face emerged in his blood-soaked uniform, dragging his feet and clutching his head with both hands. Moaning in harmony with his two chums on the stretchers, he climbed painfully into the back of the ambulance.

With help from the medics, Alex and Steve hoisted Applewhite into the back of the wagon. "Are you going to be okay riding with these three?" Alex asked, concerned.

"Sure," Applewhite grinned. "If they give me any trouble, I'll finish the job." He winked at Squirrel-face who sat across from him then flashed him a lurid psychopathic smile.

His pain momentarily forgotten, Squirrel-face slid as far from Applewhite as the ambulance's confined space allowed.

"I'll see you boys when the doc' gets through with me," Applewhite said as the wagon lurched forward.

"How will you get back to the station?" Mike shouted.

"No problem," Applewhite yelled back. "I'll hitch a ride on an ambulance carryin' sick an' wounded to the station. The wounded, sick, an' lame are put on the trains haulin' empty cars back to City Point. There's a big hospital there."

Applewhite had been a welcome distraction, and for a brief time had taken their minds off their plight. A feeling of despair settled over them now as they watched the ambulance turn around then disappear up the Plank Road toward the desultory sounds of rifle and artillery fire. *We're so lost, not even God can find us,* Alex thought glumly.

CHAPTER 26

Hancock Station, U.S. Military Railroad
6:00 A.M., MARCH 26, 1865

Something struck his foot. Alex wasn't sure whether he actually felt it or dreamed it. Sleepily, he cracked open an eye and through the slit of his eyelids saw a ceiling with peeling paint that he didn't recognize. Then gradually, like replaying a bad dream, it came back to him: Sergeant Applewhite, Dicken's Tavern, and trudging back to Hancock Station to find a place to sleep.

Alex opened his other eye. *Must be the ceiling of the passenger car,* he told himself.

Again, something struck his foot, harder this time. Annoyed, he lifted his head off the seat and looked around. Where his feet dangled off the end of the seat, a shadowy figure stood in the aisle looking at him.

"You boys gonna sleep all day? You're burning daylight!" a grating voice chided them.

It was still too dark for Alex to see his face, but the voice sounded familiar.

"Hey! It's me—Applewhite! Wakey! Wakey!"

"Uh-huh. Any minute now," Alex croaked, still half-asleep.

From across the aisle Mike groaned, "My kingdom! My kingdom for a cup of coffee!"

Somewhere nearby, Steve murmured drowsily, "What year is this?"

Alex sat up. "You don't wanna know. It won't make your day any better."

"I can't offer you boys any coffee, but I've got somethin' almost as good," Applewhite chuckled, holding up a jar for them to see. "C'mon outside for some breakfast. It's also time you an' me had a little powwow."

Applewhite shuffled from the passenger car onto the station platform, found a bench, and waited.

Alex managed to get off the wooden bench seat and stumble stiffly down the aisle. Steve and Mike yawned as they shuffled after him. At the open doorway, Steve tapped Alex on the shoulder and whispered, "I didn't mention it last night, but I think Applewhite is on to us. He called me *Johnny Reb* when he borrowed that dollar from me at the tavern—said we owed him."

"Hmm? Interesting," Alex grunted. "Guess maybe we *do* need to have a little talk with him."

As they stepped off the passenger car, dawn revealed the remnants of last night's clouds racing to the east. The day promised to be sunny and warm.

242

Applewhite smiled pleasantly as they approached. He picked up a glass jar, unscrewed the lid, held it under his nose, and sniffed the contents. "Lordy, that smells good! Pull up a seat, boys; you're gonna love this!"

"What is it?" Steve asked, eyeing the jar skeptically.

"Pickled sausages, friend—the best you ever ate." Applewhite handed him the jar.

"Well you're right about that," Steve said, cautiously sniffing the contents.

"Help yourself," Applewhite said cheerily, "then pass them around."

Scarcely concealing his repugnance, Steve dipped his thumb and forefinger into the mouth of the jar and fished for one of the slippery delicacies bobbing about inside. After several unsuccessful attempts, he finally latched onto a fat four-inch-long sausage and pulled it out and waved it triumphantly. He handed the jar to Mike then plopped down on the bench next to Applewhite and stared at the rubbery morsel.

Applewhite chuckled; his rotund belly jiggled as he watched Mike holding the jar in front of his face trying to snag one of the elusive sausages with his stubby fingers.

When Mike ultimately snared one, he held it to inspect, sniffed it, then wrinkled his nose. "Gross! You really eat this, Sarge?"

"Well, not like that!" he snorted. "You're missin' the best part!"

"There's more?" Steve asked, queasily.

"You betcha!" Applewhite laughed, pulling a small beautifully molded bottle from his coat pocket. He pried the lid off with his pocketknife and handed the bottle to Steve.

Steve sniffed the mouth of the bottle and winced. Tears welled in his eyes. "Good Gawd!" he swore. "What is this stuff?"

"That, my boy, will put pep in your step an' pride in your stride!" Applewhite confided conspiratorially. "That's one hundred percent, unadulterated, pure horseradish! I hear they put it in that so-called *cathedral* bottle with the gothic arches because you'll swear you're about to meet your Maker when that first spoonful slides down your gullet."

Steve nodded weakly. "I imagine there's some truth in that."

"Go ahead! Give'er a try!" Applewhite coaxed. "Then pass the bottle around."

Alex, meanwhile, had found an empty keg to sit on; Mike passed the jar of sausages to him before taking a seat on the bench next to Steve.

Alex tilted the jar until one of the sausages floated to within easy reach, then plucked it out, barely wetting the tips of his fingers.

"Show off," Mike said, disgusted.

Alex handed the jar to Applewhite who promptly speared a sausage with the blade of his pocketknife with practiced ease. He leaned over and deftly dipped an end of the skewered porker in the bottle of horseradish that Steve held in his hand and was still contemplating with uncertainty.

Applewhite bit off the end smeared with horseradish and rolled his eyes appreciatively as he savored the tangy morsel. He smiled blissfully as he swallowed then delicately blotted his moustache with a folded handkerchief. "Umm," he purred, "that's just heavenly."

Mike followed Applewhite's lead, but before taking the plunge, he tentatively nibbled at the end of the sausage smeared with a hint of horseradish. He arched his eyebrows, regarded the delicacy for a moment, then awarding it his personal seal of approval, dipped it deeply into the horseradish and bit off a chunk. He nodded with relish as he chewed.

Alex moved closer to Steve and dipped his sausage in the horseradish as well. He sniffed it, seemed pleased with the aroma, then bit off an end of the sausage. "Umm! That's tasty!" Alex mumbled with his mouth full. Turning to Steve, he casually asked, "Do they serve anything like this in England?"

"Not even remotely," Steve sniffed disdainfully.

"If you're not going to eat your sausage," Mike said, "mind if I have it?"

"I didn't say I wouldn't eat it. I just have to convince myself that it's going to stay down." Steve dipped an end of the sausage in the horseradish, then took a bite and began to chew.

"Atta boy!" Applewhite chuckled, slapping him on the back.

Steve choked, then coughed violently. As the horseradish worked its way up into his sinuses, his eyes bulged and his face flushed.

244

He slid off the bench and sank to his knees struggling for breath. Beads of sweat popped out on his forehead and ran down his nose merging with the tears flowing down his cheeks as he doubled-over, moaning on the platform.

"Good, huh?" Applewhite grinned, peering down at him.

Alex and Mike guffawed.

Steve wiped his face on his sleeve and glowered at them. "Go ahead and laugh, but I could've died from that!"

Alex and Mike roared even harder. Applewhite joined in, bellowing so loudly that the train crew and a few passengers waiting around the station turned and stared at them.

Finally catching his breath, Alex figured now might be a good time to have that *little powwow* Applewhite mentioned. "How's your knife wound?" he asked, exchanging his smile for an expression of concern.

"Good!" Applewhite shrugged apathetically, as if it had been no more serious than an ingrown toenail, then added: "It's just a bit sore an' stiff is all. The blade scraped one of my ribs but didn't do any serious damage. I'll mend."

"You're lucky to be alive," Alex replied, refusing to be taken in by the old man's bravado.

"Maybe," Applewhite shrugged again, like it was no big deal. For a brief second he absently fingered the one-inch slit in the waist of his tunic.

Alex noticed for the first time that Applewhite's coat no longer bore any trace of the bright crimson stain from the night before, and he was wearing a fresh shirt. He marveled at the old soldier's resilience.

"In any event," Applewhite continued, "the doc put the kibosh on any more arm wrestlin' for the next couple of weeks. Speakin' of which," he said, turning to Steve who by now had gotten his color back, "I owe you some money." He reached into his coat pocket, pulled out a dollar in paper currency and a five-dollar gold piece and offered the money to Steve.

Steve shook his head, declining the offer. "I'll take only the dollar," he said. "You earned the rest of that money, and it nearly cost you your life. You keep it."

"Take it!" Applewhite insisted. "You grubstaked me in that game. If I'd lost, you would've been out your buck. As it is, you're entitled to an equal share of my winnin's. That's the code I've lived by all my life, an' I'm too old to change my ways. You don't wanna get on my bad side, sonny, so take the money!"

Holding the gold piece between his thumb and forefinger Applewhite tapped it hard against Steve's chest.

Steve acquiesced. "I've seen what happens to people who get on your bad side. I'll take it. Thanks!"

Applewhite nodded, satisfied, as he took a toothpick from his pocket and thrust it in his mouth. "Now, there's somethin' else we need to talk about…" He paused to work at a piece of gristle wedged between his teeth, then spat it out. "What're you Johnny Rebs doin' on this side of the lines? If our boys catch you in those blue uniforms, they'll string you up sure as God made little green apples—y'know that, don't you?"

Mike and Steve kept their mouths shut, deciding to let Alex handle this.

Alex mulled over his answer. He didn't see any point denying what Applewhite clearly knew, but on the other hand, he saw no reason to confide in him. "So, what gave us away?" he said evasively.

Applewhite snorted contemptuously. "You look an' smell like men on the run. With those soldiers searchin' the passenger car at each station for three escaped Confederate prisoners, it wasn't hard to figure out it was you they were after."

Applewhite was quiet for a moment, sucking thoughtfully on his toothpick. "Did you wonder why they didn't search the train again when you arrived here?"

"Yeah," Alex nodded. "That *had* crossed my mind."

"Well, that's because I cut the telegraph line back there at Meade Station."

Alex arched his eyebrows—surprised. Mike and Steve appeared equally dumbfounded.

"And just why did you do that?" Alex asked.

"Let's just say I've got a weakness for underdogs," Applewhite smiled. "The way I see it, you boys are definitely at the bottom of the totem pole. Lots of Grant's boys are probably searchin' for you this very minute. You're unarmed. You're on the run tryin' to escape. An' you—like the South—are just about used up. The war will be over soon. I guess you know that?"

"Yeah—we know. All we want is go home," Alex said truthfully.

"I thought as much," Applewhite nodded. "I figured you could use a little help."

"Not many Yankees share your point of view, Sergeant Applewhite, but we've been fortunate to meet a few, and we're most grateful. Thank you."

"Not necessary," Applewhite said, summarily dismissing it with a wave of his hand, "but you're welcome."

"What did you do before the war?" Alex asked, suddenly curious.

"Hard labor."

"Well, yeah," Alex smiled, assuming this was just more of Applewhite's homespun humor, "but what line of work *exactly*?"

"I was a convict—" Applewhite pulled the toothpick out of his mouth and pointed it at Alex—"exactly." He might have added, *Is that clear enough?* But he didn't. Their surprised expressions must have been answer enough.

"Oh," Alex managed to say; an awkward silence followed. "Well, what did you do?" he finally asked, shaking off his embarrassment. "That is, if you don't mind me asking?"

"Killed a man. I'm not proud of it, but I'm not ashamed either." Applewhite snorted and pointed at the stripes on his sleeve. "I got these for killin' good men, but for the one who really deserved killin', I got twenty years at hard labor. Y'know what hard labor is?" he asked, gazing from one blank face to the next. "No, I don't expect you do. In prison back in Pennsylvania we made little rocks outta big rocks by swingin' a sledge hammer from sunup to sundown, day in an' day out for twenty years—that, my boy, is hard labor."

Applewhite must have seen the skepticism in Alex's eyes. "And you're wonderin' how I got so sloppy fat after all that exercise—eh? Well, for a fact I didn't look this way four years ago when I was released. One thing that kept me goin' all those years on the rock pile was dreamin' about all the good food waitin' for me when I got out. Prison food was so bad even the rats wouldn't eat it!"

Applewhite's eyes had a faraway look in them. "But I survived. Some ex-cons go on drinkin' binges after they're released from prison. Not me, I went on an eatin' binge—gained 150 pounds in the past four years!

But I've strayed off course from the tellin' of my story an' why I helped you. I paid my debt to society," he smiled bitterly, "an' that's a laugh. I ridded society of a foul, blood-suckin' parasite, an' they rewarded me by lockin' me up for it. Where's the justice in that? Society is just another name for a herd of sheep that does whatever a few imbecile herders tell'em to do. While I sweated on the rock pile, I decided I wasn't goin' to be a sheep any longer; I would keep my own counsel an' live accordin' to my conscience about what's right an' what ain't."

"And that's why you helped us?" Alex interjected.

"Yeah," he nodded. "Seemed like the right thing to do."

Applewhite's face clouded. "Let's talk about something else," he said, shaking his head as if to clear away unpleasant memories. "How do you boys plan to get back to the Rebel lines? After that whippin' Bobby Lee got at Fort Stedman yesterday, Grant an' Meade will be probin' the Petersburg defenses. It won't be easy gettin' through."

Alex nodded in agreement. "If you were in our shoes, what would you do?"

Applewhite gazed thoughtfully at the morning sunrise breaking over the treetops. "Depends on where you wanna go. If you just wanna get away from Petersburg, I'd take the next train goin' south from here on the Gregg Branch line. I'd take it to Crawford Station, then go on foot through the Union rear lines into Rebel territory. But even if you make it, your troubles won't be over. If you're caught skulkin' 'round the countryside in those uniforms, it won't matter who catches you. U.S. Grant's boys will hang you as deserters an' Bobby Lee's boys will hang you as thievin' scalawags—either way you'll find yourselves dancin' at the end of a rope."

"How far is it to the Boydton Plank Road?" Alex asked, feeling less hopeful.

Applewhite chewed on his toothpick and squinted for a moment, figuring the distance. "A helluva long way," he frowned. "If that's where you're headin', I'd suggest you stay on this train to Warren

248

Station. When you get there, find out its final destination. If it goes west to Patrick Station, get off at Warren Station an' wait for another train."

"What's wrong with going to Patrick Station?" Alex queried. "That would get us closer to the Boydton Plank Road, wouldn't it?"

"Yeah," Applewhite nodded. "But there's a string of forts an' lots of Union troops 'round Patrick Station. Trust me. You don't wanna go there, 'cause you'll never get past the Union lines."

"What then?" Alex asked, his tone deflated.

"If this train, or a later train, takes the southwesterly line from Warren Station, you wanna be on it. It'll take you to either Humphrey or Griffin Station. Griffin Station's better 'cause it's the terminus for that line, an' it's a bit closer to the Plank Road, but Humphrey Station is where most of the trains stop an' turn around. Either is better than goin' to Patrick Station, an' either one will put you just as close to the Plank Road with a lot less danger. Understand?"

Alex nodded.

"From either Humphrey or Griffin Station," Applewhite continued, "work your way south past the Union rear defense line for at least three miles, then angle west until you meet up with the Boydton Plank Road near Diwiddie Court House. The area will be crawlin' with picket lines an' patrols from both sides, so keep your eyes peeled an' don't get careless. Anyway, that's what I'd do if I were in your shoes."

"Sounds like good advice," Alex nodded gratefully. "Mike, Steve—got any questions?"

"Just one," Mike replied. "How far will you be going with us, Sarge?"

"As far as Warren Station. I'm a commissary sergeant for an engineer company that builds an' repairs trestles for the railroad. I traded my rifle for a camp stove last year after I took a bullet through my leg in the Wilderness. I must admit though that I'm happier bein' in the food business. I'm returning from City Point with a shipment of rations—have to keep an eye on'em, otherwise they up an' disappear along the way.

You boys will need food an' drink. You won't find much to eat where you're headin'. I'll make you a deal—give me a hand unloadin'

249

my rations when we get to Warren Station, an' I'll give you enough to feed you for a few days. I'll even throw in a couple of canteens."

"Deal," Alex said without hesitation.

CHAPTER 27

Near Warren Station, U.S. Military Railroad
8:00 A.M., MARCH 26, 1865

"Grant an' Meade aren't wastin' any time."

Alex vaguely heard Applewhite's comment. He'd been dozing since the train pulled away from Hancock Station, and it took a moment for the words to register. Alex shook himself awake and sat up just as the train slowed then finally shuddered to a stop where the tracks crossed the Halifax Road.

He suddenly tensed in alarm, underscoring Applewhite's words, as he peered out the passenger car window. Columns of blue-clad infantry were hurrying north on the Halifax Road toward Petersburg.

For twenty minutes the long, dusty procession crossed the tracks while the train's crew and passengers waited patiently and watched.

"That's the Sixth Corps goin' someplace in a big hurry," Applewhite said to no one in particular. "Being a gamblin' man, I'll wager they're goin' to try to punch through the Petersburg defenses somewhere up that road."

Alex gazed through the window at the scene. "Great," he grunted, seemingly unimpressed. But his heart beat faster as he contemplated the events that were now unfolding.

Their train had stopped where the tracks formed a Y-junction, and Alex noticed another train stopped on the intersecting railroad spur. The familiar number *156* stenciled on the locomotive's boiler caught his attention. *That's President Lincoln's train!* Two figures stood on the private car's rear platform saluting and cheering on the passing troops—*Lincoln and Meade.*

After the last column had crossed the tracks, Alex's train lurched forward, crawling the last few hundred yards to Warren Station where it again shuddered to a stop.

Excitement ran high at the station as Applewhite stepped onto the platform with his three companions trailing nervously behind him. As quickly as his bulk allowed, he shuffled along the station platform toward the head of the train. He passed four boxcars before stopping beside the fifth where he took a brass key from his pocket, unlocked the heavy heart-shaped padlock that secured the boxcar's sliding door, then leaned his weight against the door and pushed. With squeaks of rusty rollers, the door slid open. Inside, stacks of wooden boxes filled the dark interior.

At that moment an Army Major and a civilian, apparently a railroad employee, happened to stroll past. The pair stopped, then turned and gazed suspiciously at the four soldiers gathered around the boxcar's open door.

Applewhite hoisted a fifty-pound box of Army bread from the stack nearest the open doorway and carried it out onto the platform. He was aware of the officer and the civilian watching them, but he ignored them as he set the box down in the middle of the station platform. "Okay, boys," he called over his shoulder, "get busy and start unloading! This is where I want those boxes stacked. I'll be back to check on you."

Pretending to be Applewhite's work detail, Alex, Mike and Steve immediately got to work moving the stacks of foodstuff from the boxcar to the loading dock.

Applewhite hobbled along the platform toward the Union officer and the civilian. "Excuse me, Major," Applewhite saluted and smiled as if he had just noticed him. "I wonder if you would know if this is the final stop for this train, or does it go to the end of the line? I need to deliver some rations to a bunch of engineers working on a trestle near Humphrey Station. If this train goes there, my work detail won't have to unload all the rations from that boxcar and then load them again on a later train. They can just stay on board this train and unload the rest of the rations at Humphrey Station."

The Major listened politely until Applewhite finished. "I'm Major Stokes, the Army liaison between General Meade's headquarters and the City Point & Military Railroad. I can't answer your question, but Mr. Dawes here is the Station Master—I'm sure he would know."

Dawes pulled a sheet of paper from a folder he was carrying and studied it for a moment. "You're in luck, Sergeant," he smiled affably, "this train does stop at Humphrey Station, and then goes on to Griffin Station which is, of course, the end of the line. That should save your men some work loading and unloading boxes."

"My boys will be glad of that!" Applewhite beamed. "They're pretty much worn to a frazzle. We're obliged—thank you." he said, giving Major Stokes a parting salute.

"Not at all, Sergeant," Stokes said, returning his salute; then he and Dawes turned away.

Applewhite watched them until they disappeared into the crowd milling about the station, then returned to the Rebel escapees and shared what he had learned from Dawes.

"Continue unloadin' this end of the boxcar, boys, while I go find some teamster friends who haul freight from the station to the camps. Help yourselves to any food in those boxes you have a cravin' for. It won't be missed because I'm the one who signed for it," Applewhite grinned as he reached into the haversack slung over his shoulder and handed Alex a small crowbar. "You'll need this to get into those boxes," he said, turning on his heel and disappearing into the crowd on the station platform.

The *doughboys* continued hauling boxes from the boxcar and stacking them on the platform, stopping only long enough to open an occasional box whenever the stenciled contents suggested something particularly tasty.

Steve came upon a box with the lid pried off suggesting that someone had already helped himself to the contents. He held the lid up to better read the bold lettering in the sunlight that shone through the boxcar's open door—**SAUSAGES, PICKLED 12 EACH JARS**. On top of an adjacent stack, a smaller box revealed similar signs of tampering. The stenciling on its side read—**HORSERADISH 24 EACH BOTTLES**. The bile rose in his throat as the memory of Applewhite's breakfast fare resurrected itself. Glancing furtively at

252

Alex and Mike to make sure they were busy elsewhere, Steve hastily replaced the lids, tucked one box under each arm, and lugged them out onto the platform where he quickly hid them among the growing stack of boxes. "If the Union fed its soldiers stuff like that, it's a wonder they won the war," Steve muttered to himself.

Mike picked up a crate and studied the words on the lid for a moment, then giving Alex a sly grin, he shoved the heavy crate over to the boxcar's open door. "When Applewhite comes back, I'll try to talk him out of a bottle of this."

"What is it?" Alex asked, his curiosity piqued.

"A case of Drakes 1860 Plantation Bitters."

"Booze?" Alex arched a quizzical eyebrow.

"Yep!" Mike nodded. "Just the thing for snake bite."

"Oh sure," Alex laughed, "like there's lots of snakes around in March—got to be careful where you step in the snow!"

"Well, all the same" Mike shrugged, "it'd be a shame to go back South without something to show for our troubles."

"I'm happy for you," Alex said indulgently as he lifted another box and carried it out onto the station platform.

The boxcar was almost unloaded by the time Applewhite returned carrying a bulging burlap bag slung over his shoulder. "Got some stuff for you," he said, looking over his shoulder to see if anyone was watching. "Inside," he hissed, then disappeared into the shadows inside the boxcar.

The doughboys followed him.

The heavy bag thudded as Applewhite dropped it on the floor. "Thanks to some friends, I have just about everything you boys will need for several days." He reached into the bag and pulled out two round Union Army-issue canteens. "Sorry, lads, they're filled with water," he smiled apologetically. "Tried to get brandy and cognac to put in them but those are in short supply these days."

"That's okay," Mike said as he took the canteens from Applewhite, "we can make do with water." He put a foot against the crate of Drake's 1860 Plantation Bitters and shoved it into the shadows.

Applewhite reached into the bag again and withdrew three India rubber blankets and an equal number of wool blankets. "The nights are cold, as you know," he smiled. "You'll be glad you have these blankets when you bed down in the woods. The India rubber blankets will keep the ground moisture off you." He tossed them to Steve, then holding the bag upside down, dumped out the rest of the contents.

A candle, a box of fulminate matches, a pocketknife, three spoons, and a brass pocket watch spilled out onto the floor.

Applewhite retrieved the pocket watch and opened the cover. Inside floated a magnetic dial; what they thought was a watch was actually a compass!

Next, Applewhite inspected the assortment of canned and bottled foodstuffs they had selected from the boxes, then paused to rummage around inside his haversack. "One more thing, you'll find handy... This!" he grinned, holding up a can opener like a prized trophy, before adding it to the pile of equipment. "Wrap those bottles, cans, an' these other things in your blankets so they don't break or rattle; then put everything in this burlap bag."

When they finished Applewhite nodded, seemingly satisfied, then smiled at them with a touch of sadness in his eyes. "I guess this is where we part company, boys. The train will be pullin' out in a few minutes. Stay in the boxcar 'til you reach Griffin Station. That's the end of the line; you'll be on foot after that. Head south from the station. Be careful, an' God bless!"

They each shook the old sergeant's hand. Alex was last. "We can't thank you enough for your friendship and for the risks you have taken for us. We're deeply indebted to you."

"No you aren't," Applewhite replied, "the pleasure was all mine. What a great story I'll have to tell my grandchildren some day!"

"You have a wife and kids?" Steve asked, surprised.

Applewhite laughed. "Well, sonny, as hard as it may be to believe, I do! Been married thirty years an' have six kids. Of course, much of that time I was in prison, but my little woman waited for me, worked, an' kept the children clothed an' fed. She brought them to see me every Sunday." Applewhite's eyes had a wistful, far away look in them.

"If you don't mind my asking, who did you kill and why?" Mike asked, unable to restrain his curiosity.

Applewhite's smile faded, and his eyes turned cold and flinty. He didn't answer right away as he gave Mike a long, appraising look.

Mike flushed with embarrassment and was about to apologize for prying.

"Well, you might as well know," Applewhite sighed. "He was an abusive, morally corrupt drunkard who habitually beat his wife an' kids. He was also my father-in-law, an' the town constable. One evenin' I stopped by their home to visit an' caught him beatin' his wife. He was in a drunken rage, so I rushed inside an' tried to make him stop. But he took a swing at me instead. My temper was already at a boil, so I started swingin' too an' struck him hard on the side of his head. The blow fractured his skull, an' he was probably dead before he hit the floor. But worst luck—my father-in-law, the trial judge, and most of the men serving on the jury were members of a secret society called the Freemasons. You might have heard of them. Since I didn't belong, the guilty verdict at my trial didn't come as any great surprise. The Masons always look out for their own, y'know."

Alex shifted his feet uncomfortably as Applewhite recounted his experience at the hands of the Masons. Embarrassed, he avoided making eye contact with Mike or Steve.

Suddenly, the boxcar lurched backward then forward. The slow, monotonous ringing of the locomotive's bell signaled the train's imminent departure.

As the train started to roll away from the station, Applewhite quickly stepped onto the station platform, then turned and looked surprised as Mike leaped onto the platform behind him lugging a box. "Wait, Sarge! This belongs to you!" Mike placed the heavy box of bitters in Applewhite's hands, then turned and sprang for the boxcar's open door.

"Hope you kept a bottle for yourself!" Applewhite shouted.

Mike leaned out the door and waved. "No, sir—I kept *two*! Thank you!"

Applewhite chuckled as he waved goodbye to his Rebel friends.

DRAKE'S 1860 PLANTATION BITTERS BOTTLE

(Author's Collection)

"Hope you kept a bottle for yourself!" Applewhite shouted.

CHAPTER 28

Griffin Station, U.S. Military Railroad

11:00 A.M., MARCH 26,1865

They sat in the doorway of the boxcar with their legs dangling above the rails. The wind whipped less strongly through the open doors as the train slowed to a crawl.

Looking out over the landscape of barren earth, stumps, and slashed brush and timber, Alex couldn't envision a moonscape more depressing or more devoid of life than this. He glanced over his shoulder and surveyed through the boxcar's other door the passing scenery on the opposite side of the train. The land appeared much the same—devastated.

He stood, then leaned far out the door glimpsing the locomotive and the reason it was stopping. A log barricade, marking the terminus of the line, lay across the tracks a few hundred feet ahead of the engine's cowcatcher. Alex crossed to the other side of the boxcar and peered out the door expecting to see a station platform or some other structure. There wasn't any. *I guess Griffin Station is merely a name they gave to the rail line terminus*, he surmised, disappointed. *From what I remember of my history, I think we're in the vicinity of the Union Army's 5th Corps.*

The moment the train stopped, Mike grabbed the burlap bag and jumped from the boxcar with Alex right behind him. Over half of the cars had been uncoupled from the train at previous stops so by the time they reached Griffin Station, only five boxcars, theirs being the last one, were still attached.

A light breeze carried the dense black smoke that poured from the locomotive's stack back over the whole length of the train, obscuring Alex's vision. Through the haze, he occasionally glimpsed the ghostly apparitions of soldiers, mules, and wagons drawing closer as, one by one, they unloaded the boxcars ahead of them. He knew it was just a matter of time before someone noticed them and started asking questions.

"Let's get out of here before the smoke clears," Alex said, pointing to a trestle over a stream the train had crossed moments earlier.

They followed the tracks away from the train, laughing and making idle conversation whenever they encountered someone coming toward them. It soon became apparent that their little charade was a waste of time. Like moths drawn to light, the few soldiers they met hurried on scarcely noticing them. It was obvious that the train's infrequent arrival was a much-anticipated event that provided, for a few minutes at least, a welcome respite from the daily monotony of camp life.

When the trio reached the trestle, they quickly slid down the embankment. At the bottom of the ravine they took refuge in a wilderness of vines, cattails, and elephant ears growing along the sluggish stream. Being careful to stay out of sight, they followed the meandering stream southward away from the trestle; only occasionally did the sounds of voices or axes felling trees reach them from the bluffs overlooking the creek.

All afternoon they moved silently, the hours passing uneventfully, until they blundered into a squad of Union infantry on a trail connecting two camps located on either side of the creek. As point man, Mike was making good progress following the stream bank until, swatting at a deer fly that had developed an annoying fetish for the back of his neck, he suddenly emerged from the protective foliage onto the trail, nearly colliding with one of the soldiers.

Alex and Steve caught a glimpse of the soldiers and quickly ducked into the tangle of wild grapevines.

The surprised soldiers stared slack-jawed at Mike.

Before they could react, Mike hitched up his trousers and pretended to fasten his suspender straps. "Sorry," he muttered apologetically to the soldier he had bumped into. "Bad place to relieve oneself; the damned deer flies and mosquitoes are ferocious!" Mike turned and walked away.

The squad leader watched Mike disappear up the trail behind them, then looked at his men, shook his head and grinned. The squad continued single-file, in the opposite direction.

As soon as the soldiers were out of sight, Mike doubled-back to where he had left Alex and Steve. "All clear! You can come out now," he whispered, sensing Alex and Steve were somewhere close by.

A wall of wild grapevines parted, and Alex stepped onto the trail. A few feet away, Steve stuck his head out of the foliage and looked up and down the trail like a cat coming out of hiding.

"That was a fine fix you almost got us into, Mike," Alex said, exasperated.

"Thought you could use some excitement in your lives," Mike shrugged.

"That's exciting all right," Steve nodded, still looking nervously up and down the trail. "It's going to be even more exciting when they slip a rope around our necks for being spies or deserters. Let's get off this trail before someone else sees us."

As they ducked into the thicket on the opposite side of the trail, Alex took the lead.

By nightfall they had come three or four miles. Although not out of danger, they were at least more comfortable with their surroundings. The despoiled landscape seen earlier from the train had been replaced with lush evergreen holly and budding dogwoods under the spreading boughs of a seemingly endless forest of towering hardwood trees.

At sunset they made camp in a wooded ravine at the base of a bluff where a spring, bubbling from a fissure, cascaded in a series of miniature waterfalls before spilling into the stream they had been following. Beneath a rock overhang near the spring, they built a small fire then shed their wet uniforms and hung them to dry on cut saplings by the flames. Alex took two blankets from the burlap bag and handed them to Mike and Steve who were already shivering from the falling temperature.

Alex resumed his fumbling inside the bag, this time producing three cans of beans and a can opener. He opened the cans, leaving the lids attached as handles, then set them in the fire's glowing embers.

For the next few minutes they sat around the fire staring into the dancing flames, each immersed in his own thoughts.

"I suppose you have a good reason for wanting to reach the Boydton Plank Road," Steve said, breaking the silence as he shifted his gaze to Alex. "I mean, sure we don't want to end up in a prisoner of war camp, so I understand the need to put some distance between us and the Union Army, but then what? We swore an oath to Captain Deveraux that we wouldn't take up arms again. Do we honor it, or do we return to the Confederate Army?"

Mike looked at Alex, curious to hear his answer.

Alex continued to stare into the flames for a long time, as if he hadn't heard the question. Finally he said, "Yes, I do have a plan. And yes, I do intend to honor my oath to Deveraux."

"Splendid!" Steve smiled approvingly, reverting to his English accent. "I just assumed you had acquired a passion for slithering about in the woods and sleeping in the buff in the frigid cold! You *do* intend to share your plan with us, don't you?"

"Well, I know where we're going," Alex replied reassuringly. "It's the part about what we're going to do when we get there that I'm still working on."

Alex pulled the cans of beans out of the coals, stuck a spoon in each one, and passed two of them to Mike and Steve. He dipped a spoonful from his own, blew on it, then cautiously put it in his mouth. "Good!" he mumbled, despite finding the beans still too hot to swallow.

"I think the reason we're here," Alex said, taking a sip of water from one of the canteens, "has something to do with that knoll. I've been thinking a lot about it since we met you, Steve. It's the one link we have in common." He stopped and smiled. "Maybe it's also the answer to our getting home again."

Mike nodded as he swallowed a spoonful of beans. "We wanted to go off to a distant war, and we got our wish—just not the way we expected."

"Maybe that thunderstorm somehow penetrated the fabric of time," Alex theorized. "Or maybe that old grove of trees is magical like the ones the ancient Druids worshipped. I don't know how to explain it," he shrugged, "but there's something drawing me back to that knoll in Dinwiddie County."

Steve gave Mike a quizzical look.

"Okay by me," Mike shrugged agreeably, wiping his chin on his blanket. "It's not like I've got somewhere else to rush off to."

CHAPTER 29

Near Hatcher's Run,
Dinwiddie County, Virginia
7:00 A.M., MARCH 27, 1865

At daylight they set off again, planning to cross the muddy stream that by Alex's guesstimate was Hatcher's Run. But it had rained during the night, and the stream had risen, making it too deep to wade across. They followed the steep bank upstream until they came to a place where in ages past a large oak had toppled over, its trunk spanning the run from bank to bank. A foot thick at its narrowest part, it seemed to offer, at first glance, a safe way across.

"Uh-uh," Alex grunted negatively, assessing the log's severely rotted condition and the damp, green mold sprouting from its decaying bark. "Getting across may not be so easy after all. It looks ready to snap in half if you look at it wrong. And even if it doesn't, it's wet and slippery—a bad spot to take a spill with the stream running so full and fast. On the other hand, I don't see any alternative. Since I'm probably the heaviest, I'll go first. If the log supports my weight, it should support you as well."

Chunks of bright green moss and decaying wood tumbled eight feet into the dark swirling water as Alex cautiously worked his way to the middle of the log. Keeping his arms outstretched for balance, he took short, tentative steps, testing for solid footing. Finally beyond the last hazardous slippery spot, he stepped off the end of the log onto solid ground on the opposite bank.

"Okay, next!" he said somewhat breathlessly, glad to be across.

Being the lightest of the three, Mike went next with the burlap bag tied to his waist. Wiry and coordinated—and much to Alex's chagrin—he literally raced across the log without a single misstep.

Then it was Steve's turn.

He had almost made it across when his feet suddenly flew out from under him. Arms flailing, he landed hard, face down on the muddy bank. In danger of being carried away by the swirling floodwater tugging at his legs, Steve clawed desperately at the crumbling earth, blindly searching for something to hang onto.

Alex and Mike leaned over the eroding bank, trying futilely to grab hold of him.

Alex suddenly had an idea. "Hang onto my ankles!" he told Mike.

Mike did as he was told and gripped his ankles tightly with both hands.

Alex slipped off his belt and leaned over the edge of the bank. He stretched his arms as far as they could reach and dangled the end of his belt in front of Steve's nose.

Steve glanced up at Alex, despair in his eyes as he slid deeper and deeper into the rushing torrent.

"Grab my belt!" Alex yelled, stretching his arms until his shoulders hurt from the effort. He waved the tip of his belt back and forth in front of Steve's face, urging him to take hold of it.

The only thing keeping Steve from being swept away was a half-inch-thick root protruding from the bank that he clutched with a two-handed death grip. He kept looking back and forth from the root to Alex's belt.

"Take it!" Alex snapped angrily, trying to shake Steve out of his torpor.

It had the desired effect. Steve turned loose of the root and lunged for Alex's belt.

"Okay! I've got'im!" Alex gasped, struggling to keep from being pulled over the edge of the embankment. "Let's pull'im up!"

Digging their toes and elbows into the earth, Alex and Mike inched backward, pulling Steve out of the water and up onto the muddy stream bank.

Slipping and sliding as he gripped Alex's belt tightly with both hands, Steve dug his knees into the mud and more or less crawled to the top of the bank where he collapsed wearily on dry ground.

Alex sat with his knees drawn up against his chest catching his breath. He glanced at Steve stretched out on the ground on his back, totally spent. "That makes us even," he wheezed.

"What?" Steve's eyes blinked open. "I'd hardly equate a two-foot spill down a creek bank to a forty-foot plunge from a railroad trestle. Not that I'm keeping score, mind you."

"Yep! He's okay," Alex grinned at Mike.

Hatcher's Run flowed in a westerly direction. Alex knew that if they followed it upstream they would soon encounter Union or Confederate troops, so he picked a safer route, one that would take them south, away from the stream and toward higher ground.

At mid-morning, Mike heard it first—the pounding of horses hooves coming toward them. Remembering when he and Sergeant Hill had been caught out in the open by the two Union couriers, he didn't repeat that mistake.

"Psst," Mike hissed. "Riders coming!"

Like a covey of quail they scattered, each taking cover behind or under whatever was readily available.

Alex dove behind a log, then peered cautiously over the top trying to catch a glimpse of the horsemen.

None appeared, and the sound seemed to be fading.

Alex sprang to his feet, leaped over the log, then sprinted a few short yards to a holly tree. The dense, bright green foliage offered the perfect concealment, not that it really mattered. As he pushed aside a prickly bough, he caught only the briefest glimpse of a small body of horsemen disappearing down a woodland track.

A moment later Mike and Steve joined him from wherever they had been hiding.

"Did you get a look at them?" Steve asked.

Alex shook his head. "Too far away to see their uniforms, but—" he paused, pointing to the trail where he had seen the riders, "—according to our map and compass this should be the Quaker Road. Although it shows the lay of the land fifty years in the future, the terrain features and most of the major roads haven't changed much. And if this is the Quaker Road, it should intersect the Boydton

Plank Road somewhere off to our right."

"Great!" Mike said. "That's where we want to go, so let's follow it."

"Maybe not so great as you think." Alex squinted sourly at the map. "It might also lead us smack into elements of the Army of the Potomac. The Union 2nd and 5th Corps occupy this area; it'd be safer if we head south for another five or six miles, *then* swing west to the Boydton Plank Road." Alex glanced at Mike. "Don't read too much into our reaching the Plank Road. That isn't our goal. It's just an identifiable feature. When we get to it, we'll continue west for a couple of miles, then turn north toward Dinwiddie Courthouse. It isn't shown on our map, but I'm guessing the knoll is a few miles north of the courthouse. The compass Applewhite gave us should help us locate it."

"I remember seeing woods and some abandoned fields near that knoll," Steve added, "but not much in the way of recognizable terrain. How can you be so sure we'll find it?"

"North of Dinwiddie Courthouse there's a narrow dirt lane, known locally as the White Oak Road. It runs generally east to west between Burgess Mill Pond on the Boydton Plank Road and a road junction called Five Forks. Our knoll with its grove of trees is located somewhere in the inverted triangle formed by the courthouse, Five Forks, and Burgess Mill Pond."

"How long will it take us to get there?" Mike asked.

"We have to be there no later than tomorrow," Alex answered, a worried frown creasing his face. "If we don't, it's going to get very dicey the following day—March 29th."

Mike rolled his eyes as he digested this bit of news. "I'm so glad you stayed awake through this part of your military history class, Alex. Just how *dicey* is it going to get?"

Alex hesitated for a moment as he mentally assembled all the facts he could remember. "Very!" he said finally. "For starters, the weather will turn nasty early in the morning on March 29th , and it will rain non-stop for two days. Streams will overflow their banks, and the land will become an absolute *sea of mud*, as some of the veterans described it. Roads will become impassable, and the Union Army will have to corduroy them with logs in order to supply their troops in and around Dinwiddie Courthouse."

"Seems to me," Steve mused aloud, "the bad weather ought to work in our favor—we'll be less visible."

"There's more," Alex replied, holding up a restraining hand.

"Oh, good!" Mike grimaced.

"I saved the best for last," Alex continued. "The day after tomorrow, General Phillip Sheridan will occupy Dinwiddie Courthouse with three divisions of Union cavalry. His orders from General Grant will be to feel out the extreme right of General Lee's defenses. If he can move around the Confederate right flank—which he will—he is to get astride the South Side Railroad and hold it. That will cut the last major supply line to Petersburg and the Confederate capital.

However, Grant and Sheridan don't know that Lee has dispatched General Pickett with a large force of infantry and cavalry to Five Forks. Pickett has been tasked to find Grant's left flank and foil any intentions he has of seizing the South Side Railroad.

When these two forces make contact, it will initiate two or three days of intense fighting between Dinwiddie Courthouse and Five Forks. And that's the part that worries me most. General Warren's Fifth Corps will be detached from Meade's Army of the Potomac and placed under the operational command of General Sheridan in support of his push toward Five Forks. From the accounts I've read, some of the troop movements and engagements took place in the vicinity of our knoll. That's why we have to get there tomorrow. We need time to unravel this mystery."

CHAPTER 30

Three Miles North of Dinwiddie Courthouse
11:00 A.M., MARCH 28, 1865

When they reached Dinwiddie Courthouse the previous evening, they found a force of Confederate cavalry camped in the sleepy little hamlet. Not wanting to risk bumping into a skirmish line in the dark, they made camp on a low ridge overlooking a wooded creek bottom a mile south of the courthouse.

At daylight they skirted around the tiny community without incident then continued northward.

By mid-morning it had become unseasonably warm and humid. "Got any idea where we are?" Mike asked, plopping down beside Alex on the crest of a steep ridge to take a breather. He was puffing and sweating from the climb up the slope.

"Not a clue," Alex rasped, shaking his head.

For a few moments the two men sat quietly, catching their breath as they watched Steve struggle up the precipitous slope toward them.

"We're lost?" Mike asked. It sounded to Alex more like a statement than a question.

"Nah," he wheezed. "We're here. It's the lousy knoll that's lost!"

Mike smiled and shook his head as he gulped the warm, damp air.

Gasping for breath, Steve crawled the last dozen feet to the crest on his hands and knees before flopping face down at Alex's feet.

Alex stood up, seemingly unaware of Steve's groans. "Okay! If everyone's rested, let's get moving. We've no time for dawdling."

Sucking down great mouthfuls of air, Steve lifted his head off the ground and glowered at Alex.

"Mike," Alex grinned, "have you ever noticed how soft and sickly they get after you take them off the farm and make aviators out of them?"

Steve rose to the bait.

"Let's go, wimps! I'm ready if you are," he replied indignantly as he staggered to his feet.

"My! My! A bit testy this morning, are we?" Alex chuckled.

"I'll take the lead," Steve grunted, setting off through the woods with long quick strides. "Try and keep up, won't you?"

Exchanging grins, Alex and Mike followed.

Midway across the ridge Steve suddenly stopped.

Alex and Mike stopped too, their grins fading.

"This looks familiar," Alex said as he turned in a 360-degree circle.

Mike pointed to an anomaly on the ridge where the ground sloped steeply upwards. "Yeah!" he said "This is it!"

Steve was already running toward the slope. "It's the knoll!" he shouted, forgetting in his excitement how far a voice carries in the woods.

As Steve scrambled up the slope, the ancient trail leading to the summit grew rapidly steeper forcing him to slow down and catch his breath. Moments later, Alex and Mike raced past him and disappeared into the foliage further up the trail.

Alex stared up at them in awe. The ancient trees were more magnificent than he remembered. Their gnarled trunks spiraled upward and outward in bizarre shapes and toward dizzying heights. Ropes of green moss hung from enormous lichen-covered limbs, while stray rays of sunlight filtered through the dense canopy bathing the grove in perpetual twilight and bestowing on it an aura of mystery and great antiquity. Wisps of mist floated in and about the trees, adding to their surreal appearance.

He sensed the presence of life primordial, of intelligence—old and wise as time itself. With a growing uneasiness, he remembered sleeping under these trees that first night. The grove seemed haunted, as though someone or something unseen was watching him. He could actually *feel* the hostility, like he was an intruder, unwelcome and encroaching where he didn't belong.

Mike broke the silence. "Well, we're here. Now what?"

Alex didn't answer. Instead, he walked deeper into the grove.

Looking up at the immense canopy high above his head, Alex sensed—*something, a presence*. He didn't know what it was, but he felt certain they were not alone. As his vision adjusted to the light, he moved on, comforted in the knowledge that Mike and Steve were close behind. All his senses were alert as he searched for clues that might solve the mystery of the grove and whatever resided within it.

When they reached the middle of the grove, Alex suddenly stopped and pointed. Through the swirling mist the outlines of two wall tents emerged.

Alex cautiously approached the nearest tent. As the mist dissipated, he recognized it as the one he had occupied a week earlier—*or was it half a century later?*—before his life turned upside down.

Pushing the tent flap aside, Alex peered inside—it was just as he had left it. Nothing appeared disturbed. He let the flap drop and watched Mike and Steve as they checked the other tent.

"These are our tents," Mike said, offering the explanation for Steve's benefit, "and it was here that our journey back in time began." He looked inside the tent with Steve peering over his shoulder, then glanced in Alex's direction and shrugged, communicating that everything in his tent appeared as he had left it.

"The key to this mystery has to be here," Alex said as he stood with his hands on his hips surveying the grove and the area around the tents. "Let's spread out and examine every inch of this knoll. I have no idea what we're looking for, but make a note of anything unusual—*anything*, manmade or natural. We'll divide the knoll into three pie-shaped sections with my tent being the center of the circle. Work from here to the edge of the grove then down the slope to the base of the knoll. When you finish your search, come back here and we'll compare notes."

By late afternoon Alex had reached the base of the knoll. The search of his self-assigned area had produced *zilch, nada, nothing.* Wearily, he treaded back up the boulder-strewn slope to the summit. Mike and Steve had already returned and were sitting beside his tent, relaxing. From their cheerless expressions, he knew they hadn't turned up anything either. Tired and hungry, he slumped to the ground, propping his aching back and shoulders against the trunk of one of the giant oaks.

"Find anything?" Steve asked dully, already knowing the answer.

Alex shook his head. He tilted his head back against the tree and gazed up at the overhead foliage. Through a small opening high above he glimpsed a graphite-colored sky. "The weather's about to change," he said matter-of-factly, his voice sounding as drawn and tired as he felt. "Be glad we have tents tonight."

Mike dumped out the last of their rations from the burlap bag: three cans of beans and two bottles of Drakes 1860 Plantation Bitters—the latter he had carefully wrapped in pieces of discarded canvas to keep them from breaking. "Another cold meal I suppose?" he said, opening one of the cans and handing it to Alex.

Alex nodded, drew a deep breath then let it out, communicating his own distaste for cold beans for a second straight night. "Can't risk a fire," he said. "The smoke would be seen for miles. Possibly as early as this evening, but tomorrow for sure, this area will be crawling with Confederate and Union troops. One or the other could stumble upon us at any time."

"So, what do we do tomorrow?" Steve asked, wrinkling his nose repugnantly as he shoveled a spoonful of cold beans in his mouth.

"The same thing we did today," Alex replied. "We keep looking. There's something here that we're not seeing."

"What's there to see?" Mike grumbled. "It's the same hill and the same trees we saw in 1918!"

"There's more to it than that, "Alex countered. "There has to be—I can feel it. All of the evidence points to this place."

Setting his spoon and empty can aside, Alex got to his feet and strode over to his tent. He pushed the canvas flap aside and disappeared into the dark interior. A moment later he reappeared carrying a black leather boot in one hand and a canteen in the other. The canteen resembled the round, bulls-eye-shaped ones Sergeant Applewhite had given them.

Alex dropped them in Mike's lap. "*These* are why we came back here. Sergeant Pratt showed them to us in the mess tent one morning—remember?

Mike nodded as he re-examined the relics before handing them to Steve.

"Pratt told us that he found them up here in the grove," Alex continued. "They obviously date from the Civil War, but as you can see, they look almost new. So how could these fifty-year-old battlefield relics turn up in this condition in 1918? The answer is: the same way we traveled back in time to 1865—through a time warp or something like that. If we can just figure out how it happened, then maybe we can return to the future the same way."

Steve ran his fingers over the supple leather and examined the shiny steel tap on the boot heel. Setting the boot aside, he held up the canteen and studied it, noting that it was identical in size and shape to the one that hung from his shoulder. As his gaze strayed beyond the canteen to the overhead tree canopy, an idea suddenly occurred to him. "Maybe we've been looking in the wrong places for the unusual, Alex. Look at those overhead tree limbs. See anything odd about them?"

Alex looked up and gazed at the limbs and foliage for a long time. Finally, he gave up and shook his head. "You must see something I don't. All I see are big limbs, hanging moss, and thick green foliage."

"You can't see the trees for the forest," Steve smiled. "How old would you guess these trees are?"

"Hundreds of years at least," Alex sighed, giving the obvious answer and wishing Steve would get to the point.

"Uh-huh," Steve nodded. "Wouldn't you expect to see split and charred limbs from lightning strikes on trees as tall as these, especially if they're perched on top of a knoll?"

Alex looked again, more closely this time.

"You're right, Steve," he conceded." There's not a mark on them, and what's more, there aren't any dead limbs on them or on the ground."

Mike yawned sleepily, obviously unimpressed. "Are you going somewhere with all this?" he asked, giving Steve a bored look.

"Yep! I'm going someplace with it all right," Steve grinned. "And it just may be our ticket home!"

Mike sat up, suddenly attentive.

Steve continued to pontificate, intentionally drawing it out, savoring his explanation. "The law of natural selection states that species that are incapable of adapting to change and threats to their environment are doomed to extinction. Trees have been adapting more or less successfully to environmental changes for eons. However, a few thousand years ago a new threat appeared on the scene—*Man*. Man has indiscriminately destroyed much of the earth's vast forests causing the extinction of many species of trees with others tottering on the brink. Evolution hasn't adapted fast enough to counter the human menace, so what defenses do trees have against the ax, saw, and manmade fires? The answer, of course, is *none*. But just suppose, hypothetically of course, that a unique species of tree has evolved

270

that possesses intelligence and the capacity to react to danger. If this tree can't flee or hide in the usual sense, then how else might it evade danger? I suspect this unique species has learned to flee or hide another way—through time displacement."

Steve paused to check their reactions. Alex was listening. Mike, however, was having difficulty keeping a straight face.

"So, you're suggesting that whenever these trees feel threatened, they escape danger by moving forward or backyard through time. Is that it?" Alex said as he thoughtfully rubbed his hand over the week-old beard on his chin.

"Exactly! The grove of trees on the knoll moves through time but not the knoll itself, of course," Steve said with growing conviction, not to mention his self-absorption in playing the role of *expert* regarding such matters.

"I hate to throw cold water on your theory, old boy; however, you will notice that we and our equipment were transported through time and we're not members of the tree family." Mike laughed, playing the role of devil's advocate. "Just how do you explain that?"

"True," Steve nodded reflectively, "however, the one common factor is the undeniable fact that we and our equipment were within the grove when it displaced to a different time. The boot and canteen may simply have served as catalysts that enabled it to return to the year 1865."

Alex's eyes widened with sudden realization. "You may have just hit the nail on the head, Steve!" he said excitedly. "We were in our tents during the night of the thunderstorm. The boot and canteen were lying on top of my field table, and I distinctly remember seeing them glowing and pulsating with brilliant light during the height of the storm. At the time, I didn't know what was causing it—maybe *now* I do."

Continuing to play the devil's advocate, Mike countered with another compelling observation. "Well, if you're saying the grove brought us back to 1865, then how long had it been sitting there when we stumbled across it in 1918? For that matter, is there a time beyond 1918 to and from which the grove can travel? Does it travel back and forth to specific time periods like a homing pigeon coming home to roost?"

Steve shook his head. "I wish I knew the answer to those questions, but I don't. Maybe the past and present are the limits to the grove's time travel. If so, maybe it spends most of its time in the present until threatened; then it retreats into the past as a temporary refuge until the danger in the present passes."

Mike's forehead wrinkled in deep contemplation. "Then why wouldn't the reverse be true as well? Assuming you're right about this particular place in time being a temporary refuge, then maybe all we have to do to get back home is to make these trees feel threatened."

"It might be as simple as that," Steve shrugged, "or maybe something that poses a danger to the entire grove. I really don't know—it's all hypothetical."

"Then why not put it to the test?" Mike shrugged, imitating Steve. He got up off the ground and began searching among the leaves. "Ahh! This should do the trick!"

Mike hefted a rock that must have weighed close to two pounds.

"Hold on, Mike!" Alex said, placing a restraining hand on his arm. "Let's think this through before going off half-cocked."

"What's there to think through?" Mike replied. "As Steve says, it's all theory. And frankly, I'm not sold on it. The day when trees can think and travel through time will be the day pigs can fly!"

Before Alex could stop him, Mike hurled the rock at the largest tree in the grove.

It struck the massive trunk with a loud *thwock*, then fell to the ground and rolled a few feet. Even before the rock stopped rolling, an angry *hum* filled the grove—low at first; then louder as if a swarm of a million bees had been disturbed. The ground vibrated beneath their feet, like standing on a ship's deck and feeling the throb of its powerful engines underneath.

"Look!" Alex pointed at the tents. They were glowing with an eerie, pulsating light. Then he stared at his extended hand. It, too, glowed, as did his whole body.

Alex glanced at Mike and Steve to view their reaction, only to find them staring at their own glowing bodies.

Rudely awakened from its slumber, something within the tree had stirred, or so it seemed to Alex. It had sounded an alarm, warning

272

the grove of imminent danger, then testing the air and finding the threat gone, or of little consequence, the hum and the pulsing glow gradually diminished then faded away entirely.

For several moments the doughboys stood rooted in place, overwhelmed by what they had heard and seen.

"I think *that* was your answer," Alex said softly, breaking the silence that followed.

"Or at least a hint of it," Steve agreed. "Whatever that thing is, Mike definitely got its attention."

Mike hastily backed away from the tree. "Well, that's that, I suppose," he said, brushing the dirt off his hands.

Alex and Steve exchanged glances and shook their heads.

"If these trees are the doorway to our time, we need to figure out what makes them react and behave the way they do," Alex mused aloud. "Did you notice that the tents and our bodies glowed with that pulsing light, but nothing we have from the Civil War-era glowed, including our uniforms and that boot and canteen? I wonder if the grove's time travel is linked to artifacts from specific time periods brought to or discarded on or near the knoll."

"If artifacts *are* the key to the grove traveling forward and backward through time," Steve interjected, "the boot and canteen your sergeant found could have been left behind by the Union deserters I saw here in November 1864."

"Yeah, that fits," Alex nodded. "That could account for why we arrived here several months after you did, instead of on the same day. The artifacts may be homing devices that enable the grove to evade danger by returning back in time to a particular artifact's arrival.

"To a time when the danger didn't exist," Mike chimed in.

"Precisely," Steve said. "Danger being tornadoes, hurricanes, severe thunderstorms, and the presence of humans, too, I suppose."

"I would think so," Alex agreed.

"Any theories on how the grove connects with the artifacts?" Mike asked.

"I'll venture a wild guess," Alex replied. "Just as tree rings mark the growth of trees from year to year, these trees may have evolved a means of recording or remembering specific events affecting the entire grove. Whenever a foreign object or animal intrudes on this knoll, the trees record the event. If the object remains on the knoll, the trees plot the specific time it first appeared. I think that's why the tents and our bodies were glowing. When Mike struck the tree with the rock, the grove initiated some level of alert. If the level of alert continued to escalate, the grove might have been compelled to evade the danger—perhaps by returning to the year 1918."

"What you are implying is the tents or our bodies could be the homing mechanism, is that it?" Mike asked, digesting the idea.

"In theory, yes, possibly," Alex nodded. "Conversely, when the grove was threatened at different times by a tornado and by the severe thunderstorm, the canteen and boot may have been the catalyst that caused us to end up in the year 1865. I think the grove is aware of our presence, but for some reason it doesn't view our intrusion as sufficient danger to warrant escaping to a different time."

"Do you think it could escape into the future, beyond the year 1918?" Mike asked.

"I suppose," Alex shrugged, "but let's hope that the grove's time travel is limited to traveling only from the present to the past and back to the present again—and that it considers *the present* to be the year 1918."

CHAPTER 31

The Grove On The Knoll

8:00 A.M., MARCH 29, 1865

The day began dark and rainy. The night before the doughboys had developed a strategy. As they stepped from their tents armed with stout wooden clubs, they were ready to set it into motion.

"Ready?" Alex asked apprehensively as they gazed up at the grove's largest and most magnificent trees. From his Lilliputian perspective, the grand scheme they had devised under the cloak of darkness now seemed incredibly naïve and ludicrous in the light of day.

"Wish I had an ax," Mike said wistfully "—a big, double-headed ax."

"Yeah," Steve nodded as he gazed in awe at the nearest tree. "With an ax and a month of Sundays, you might actually do some serious damage to one of these trees."

"Well, we're here," Alex shrugged, "so let's get on with it and see what happens."

On Alex's signal, they commenced to pummel the tree trunks with their clubs.

The response was immediate.

The same menacing hum they had heard the previous evening resonated through the grove. The tents and their exposed flesh glowed intermittently—encouraging signs—but as the high-pitched quavering hum grew louder, it became excruciating painful, like someone driving nails through their skulls.

After two minutes of intense exertion, their breathing grew ragged, and the clubs they wielded grew heavier. The grove was not going to give up its secrets easily.

His chest heaving and his arms feeling heavy as lead, Alex lowered his club and gazed up at the towering giant. "What—?" he vented his frustration. "What do we have to do? You brought us here, so why won't you take us back?"

At the sound of Alex's voice, Mike paused in mid-swing and let his club drop to his side. Sweat dripped from the bridge of his nose. Noticing that the humming had begun to taper off, he studied the unscathed bark on the tree. "I wonder if I look as dumb as I feel smacking this tree with a club," he muttered. "Obviously, I'm not making much of an impression on it either."

Tiring of the seemingly pointless battering he was administering to a great live oak, Steve tossed his club aside. "It's got to be the largest and oldest in the grove," he said aloud as he gazed up at the towering giant and experienced a pang of guilt for his callous treatment of such an ancient and venerable living thing. But he also sensed he was being scrutinized as well. And he didn't like the feeling.

Steve's thoughts flashed back to those final moments inside the funnel cloud when he was spinning earthward in his biplane. Just as he was about to lose consciousness, a tree had appeared below him, a gnarled and immense thing, much like the one that now towered above him. An instant before a blinding burst of light suddenly engulfed him, he remembered thinking—*how odd that this should be the last thing I will ever see.*

How much time had passed he had no idea, but when he opened his eyes, the funnel cloud had vanished. The branches of the enormous tree he had seen were still there, clawing up toward him like the talons of a bird of prey. Having escaped being wrung to pieces and scattered across the landscape by a tornado, he now faced another, albeit inert, danger on the ground just as deadly. He jerked the control stick back toward his belly as far as it would go and heard the engine fairly scream as he pushed the throttle wide open. He held his breath as the *Jenny* pulled up sharply. The weight of centrifugal force pressed his body lower into the cockpit, and he expected any second to hear the biplane's wings ripping away from the fuselage. Something scraped against the machine's canvas covering beneath him as he banked the *Jenny* hard on its right side to avoid the tree's topmost branches. As the biplane climbed skyward, he shot a quick glance over his shoulder, catching a final glimpse of the giant tree disappearing from view behind him.

Alex venting his frustration brought Steve back to the present just as an idea began to germinate. He smiled for the first time that day.

A light rain was beginning to fall. Somewhere off to the east the rattle of musketry commenced and seemed to roll ominously closer.

Gathered around the small table inside Alex's tent, the threesome paused to listen.

The urgent notes of a bugle suddenly rang through the wooded ravines south of them, followed by a smattering of carbine fire.

They knew what it meant—Sheridan and his cavalry were on the move toward Dinwiddie Courthouse.

Steve turned to Mike. "Do you still have the bottles of hooch you got from Sergeant Applewhite?"

Mike arched an eyebrow, and a bemused grin creased his face. "Getting drunk isn't the answer…"

"Forget the booze," Steve said, shaking his head impatiently. "I need those bottles and all the canteens. I don't suppose there's any ammunition lying around?"

"Just some boxes of pistol ammo in my field safe," Alex replied. He looked at Steve curiously, wondering what this sudden interest in liquor bottles, canteens, and ammunition was all about. "Mike and I had the only weapons," he said, giving Steve an empty palms up gesture as a reminder that they had gotten rid of their pistols, "so why are you interested in ammunition?"

"I don't need pistols, or bullets, just the powder in the shell casings," Steve replied evasively.

"What are you up to?" Mike asked, fetching the two bottles of Drake's 1860 Plantation Bitters from the burlap bag stored under the table and unwrapping them from their protective scraps of canvas. Mike gave each bottle a parting kiss as he handed them to Steve.

"I just had a flash of inspiration," Steve replied. "We don't have much time before some of Sheridan or Pickett's boys drop in unannounced, so I'm going to need your help."

Hefting the two bottles, Steve sensed that one weighed less than the other. He held up the lighter one, eyed the contents, then looked accusingly at Mike.

"I just sampled a little last night to make sure it hadn't gone bad," he offered lamely.

Steve pulled the cork and sniffed the open spout. "Whew! I hope you weren't smoking when you sampled this! It's pure alcohol!"

Steve picked up an empty tin cup from the table, poured a thimbleful of the pungent liquid into it, then set it on the ground. Striking a match against the wooden table leg, he held it at arm's length and dropped it into the cup. An instantaneous two-foot-high flash of flame shot from the cup. Everyone jumped back.

"This'll do," Steve smiled with obvious satisfaction.

"*Do*, for what?" asked Mike, his curiosity piqued.

"Now I need your help with that ammunition," Steve said without answering as he carefully placed the two securely corked, amber-colored bitters bottles back inside the burlap bag.

For the next hour they sat around the table taking apart hundreds of pistol cartridges and emptying the gunpowder into two metal canteens which had been emptied of water and dried over a candle beforehand.

Alex brushed the gunpowder residue off his fingertips as he watched Steve plug the powder-filled canteens. "Mind telling us what you intend to do with those?"

Steve ignored the question for the moment as he eyed the kerosene lantern hanging from the ridgepole above the table. "I need that lantern too," he said, reaching up and jiggling the lantern to make sure it was full of kerosene.

"All right then," he smiled conspiratorially, "here's my idea..."

As Steve explained, he took the scraps of canvas the bottles had been wrapped in and tore them into long, one-inch strips.

When Steve finished laying out the details of his plan, Alex and Mike looked at each other incredulously.

"And that's your plan?" Mike asked, dumfounded.

Steve smiled and nodded.

"Are you and Alex related by any chance?" Mike asked. "That's the dumbest thing I've ever heard! You don't actually believe it will work, do you?"

Steve shrugged. "You have a better idea?"

It was Mike's turn to shrug.

"You're sure you can do it alone?" Alex asked, ignoring Mike's objections.

"Have to," Steve said, pushing away from the table and up on his feet. He draped the straps of the two canteens over his shoulder, then took the lantern down from the ridgepole. "If this works, you and Mike need to be here but in some better-protected shelter."

Steve frowned at the lead-colored overcast sky through the open tent flap. "Guess I'd better get going before it rains any harder." He wrapped a piece of canvas around the box of matches and stuffed it inside his uniform pocket. "See you chaps in 1918!" he grinned, giving them a British-style, palm outward salute. "Stiff upper lip!"

With the burlap bag in one hand and the lantern in the other, Steve ducked under the tent flap and disappeared into the gray mist that had settled over the grove.

Steve hoped for a lot of things as he slipped and slid on the wet leaves on the knoll's precipitous slope. Uppermost at the moment, he hoped he wouldn't lose his balance and tumble head over heels the rest of the way down. Beyond that, he hoped no one was out and about to hear or see him, that Alex's promise of heavier rain wouldn't come about for another hour or two, and that he was heading in the right direction. The mist worried him. Everything depended on his not getting lost.

Relying on the compass that Sergeant Applewhite had given them, he walked in a northwesterly direction for almost half-an-hour. Anxiety gnawed at him as he drew closer to the White Oak Road along which General Pickett's Confederate troops were deployed. Drizzle with light intermittent showers continued to fall from the leaden clouds soaking his uniform as the firing of artillery rumbled off to the east near the Boydton Plank Road. It seemed more intense—like a major engagement had commenced. Of more immediate concern from the south and west, the rapid popping of carbine fire crept worrisomely closer. Steve plunged ahead in the direction the compass pointed him, pushing aside the thought that a sharpshooter might be lining him up in his rifle sights.

He crossed a shallow bog that ran generally south to north. It looked familiar. His heart began to race as he hurried up a gradual slope through a thicket overrun with vines and brambles. He cursed quietly—a difficult thing to do—as the brambles snatched at his coat and trousers and scratched his face and hands. He quickly used up his extensive stock of profanity and had to create new expressions as he plowed headlong through the thicket using the weight and momentum of his body to clear a path.

At the top of the slope Steve suddenly broke free of the clinging fetters and stumbled out into a field overgrown with knee-high weeds. He looked around anxiously, half-expecting to see a line of Confederate infantry or a troop of Union cavalry swooping down on him. His heartbeat slowed as he studied the surrounding landscape. Except for an occasional bird flitting from bush to bush, he saw no other signs of life.

Deciding to risk being caught out in the open, he continued walking out into the field. Level and covering an area roughly six hundred yards long by four hundred yards wide, it was indistinguishable from a hundred other uncultivated fields dotting Dinwiddie County.

Steve was nearly halfway across, still following his compass heading, when he stopped and stared at the split-rail fence bordering the north end of the field. It was mostly tumbled-down, yet he noted something familiar about it. He walked faster across the middle of the field toward it, his eyes sweeping the ground in front of him in search of something.

Thirty yards farther on, he found them—the faint traces of wheel ruts. He knew what had made them.

The narrow ruts were visible for a few feet, disappeared for a few yards, then re-appeared again a short distance farther on.

I imagine these tracks would be baffling to anyone coming across them in 1865, Steve told himself as he followed the ruts through the weeds. The five-foot distance between them was suddenly bisected by a third indentation, as if something had been dragged behind the wheeled conveyance.

Near the north end of the field, the ruts abruptly disappeared. Steve wasn't surprised.

He waded through the boot-top high weeds closer to the split-rail fence. *That's too close,* he concluded, realizing his mistake. He backtracked, this time keeping to the edge of the field until he found a familiar notch in the tree line. Months earlier, he had camouflaged the *Jenny* with brush cut from the surrounding thickets. During the intervening months, a new growth of vegetation had grown over his latticework of saplings and vines making detection of the biplane virtually impossible. He had walked right past her hiding place the first time.

Steve stopped and scanned the tree line around the edge of the field. Satisfied he was in no immediate danger, he turned to the artificial barrier in front of him and began pulling away the foliage.

Within minutes he had removed from the *Jenny's* wings and fuselage the elaborate camouflage that had taken an entire morning to create. Steve stood for a moment gazing affectionately at the *Jenny*, noting that her surfaces no longer bore the glossy luster they had on that fateful day when he landed here. Months of exposure to the elements had taken their toll on her exterior paint. *I just hope they don't try to make me pay for it,* he chuckled, his spirits lifting at the sight of the *Jenny*.

Steve carefully inspected the engine and the flying surfaces, finding no damage beyond a little rust, after which he untied the canvas cockpit cover and peered inside. Spiders had been busy weaving webs within the interior, and a family of field mice had supplemented its diet from the leather pilot's seat. Sweeping the cobwebs aside, he climbed into the cockpit and settled onto what was left of the leather cushion. Somewhere he had lost his flying cap and gloves, but fortunately he had had the foresight to leave his goggles inside the cockpit.

As he slipped his goggles on, he noted they appeared unchewed. *Probably not as yummy as the seat cushion,* he guessed.

With the temperature dropping and the rain falling more heavily, Steve began to shiver uncomfortably—he was soaked to the skin. *Well, old boy, a spot of hot tea with a shot of brandy would be just the thing about now,* he thought as he checked the *Jenny's* instruments. His teeth chattered. A hard chill suddenly squeezed his heart and lungs. His hands were shaking so that flying the machine was out of the question, assuming of course, he could even start the engine.

Folding his arms across his chest for added warmth, he hunched forward, waiting for the chill to pass. His foot brushed against the burlap bag he had dropped on the floor of the cockpit.

"Salvation is at hand!" he smiled ecstatically.

He groped inside the bag until his hand closed around one of the amber, log cabin-shaped bottles of Drake's 1860 Plantation Bitters. He pulled the cork with trembling fingers and took a swig of the fiery liquid, feeling it burn deliciously as it progressed down his throat and pooled in his stomach. He suddenly felt warm all over. *I think this qualifies as drinking for medicinal purposes,* Steve rationalized, wiping his beard with the back of his hand. Corking the bottle, he set it aside, then reached in his coat pocket and pulled out the canvas-wrapped box of matches. His hands were steadier. Lifting the glass globe on the lantern, he struck a match and lit the wick. Minutes later, he was almost basking in the warmth that the tiny flame produced in the confined space of the cockpit.

Well let's see, Steve mused, *so far I've violated every regulation and flying field policy concerning drinking and flying and open flames around aviation fuel. Major Brown, the Langley Field commander, would be just a bit irked if he could see me now!*

The warm glow of the liquor coursed through his arteries. Steve grinned, then laughed—he was definitely getting a *buzz*. "All right, chum, let's see if you can get this crate off the ground!"

Chapter 32

Confederate Skirmish Line
Near White Oak Road, Dinwiddie County
11:00 A.M., March 29, 1865

Privates Leroy Skaggs and TJ Davidson of Company C, 24th Virginia Infantry, Kemper's Brigade, were on the extreme left of a skirmish line thrown out to act as the eyes and ears of a large force of infantry commanded by General Pickett. The Confederates had just seized Five Forks, an important road junction, and the skirmish line had been ordered to advance across White Oak Road toward Dinwiddie Courthouse. Their orders were brief and simple.

See what's out there, and if you see anything, report it.

Leroy and TJ were not aware of it, but they were alone. Soon after crossing the White Oak Road they had become separated from the rest of the skirmish line. As they scouted in a southeasterly direction through a long stretch of woods, the two men came to the edge of a fallow field overgrown with weeds. Instinctively they crouched out of sight at the edge of the tree line and studied the thicket on the far side of the field.

TJ heard it first—the sound of a man's laugh. He tapped Leroy on the shoulder to get his attention, then pointed at the distant thicket.

"My Gawd! What an awful laugh!" TJ whispered.

"As cold an' wet as it is, what could possibly be funny?" Leroy muttered sullenly.

"I didn't say he was laughing about something funny," TJ sighed resignedly, remembering that Leroy was a tad hard of hearing. "It was an evil sounding laugh, like he was about to cut someone's throat an' enjoy doing it."

"Uh-huh," Leroy grunted tersely, squinting through the rain that now poured in rivulets off the brim of his hat.

Suddenly a loud, unworldly coughing and sputtering noise came from within the thicket across the field.

Then silence.

Two more sputtering coughs.

Then a continuous deafening roar poured forth from the distant thicket.

Leroy and TJ crouched lower and exchanged bewildered looks.

"What the hell's that?" TJ whispered.

The awful noise drowned out TJ's voice as it rived up and down with varying levels of intensity.

More curious than afraid, TJ and Leroy hugged the ground, trying to figure out the source of the sound. Nothing moved on the far side of the field.

"Suppose you go check it out, and I'll cover you," TJ suggested.

"And suppose you go to hell!" Leroy grunted, giving TJ a *Just how dumb do you think I am?* glare out of the corner of his eye.

Two minutes ticked by. The noise had diminished to a low continuous rumbling, like a huge cat purring in the undergrowth.

TJ was about to offer another suggestion when he spotted movement on the other side of the field. "L-Look!" he stammered, grabbing a handful of Leroy's shoulder and shaking it roughly.

The rain let up momentarily, giving them both a clear view of what TJ was pointing at—a winged-nightmarish creature clawing its way out of the thicket opposite them.

TJ and Leroy stared in disbelief as the thing rumbled into the middle of the field. It lurched to a stop, seemed to sniff the air, then slowly spun around, pointing its whirling snout in their direction.

TJ just knew that whatever it was, it had caught their scent. Then sure enough, in the next instant, *the thing* leaped across the field toward them, snarling horribly as it came closer and closer.

"Jumping Jehoshaphat!" TJ yelled over the noise. "What is that thing?"

If Leroy heard, he didn't answer. His eyes had that fixed, cottontail rabbit stare about them. He didn't twitch a muscle, not even his nose.

To their utter amazement, *the thing* took a final leap, then sprang into the air like some great flying insect. As it soared over the spot where they were hiding, TJ heard again the maniacal laughter he had listened to earlier.

"It's the Devil himself!" TJ yelled fearfully.

Totally panicked, they jumped to their feet and ran, tossing aside their heavy rifles, and dashing blindly through the woods, tripping and falling. How long and how far they fled, neither TJ nor Leroy would later remember. But they stumbled on until they could run no farther; then, panting and wheezing, they took refuge under the foliage of a recently toppled tree. Even then, they peered fearfully through the branches overhead expecting to glimpse *the thing* riding the air currents in search of human prey.

"Are you goin' to report what we saw?" TJ gasped, struggling to control his emotions.

"And say what? That we saw a flying dragon? Humph!" Leroy snorted, derisively. "I don't think so!"

"But we *both* saw it, Leroy. They'd have to believe us."

"Saw what?" Leroy gave TJ a blank look. "I didn't *see* nothin'. And that's just what I'll say if you open your big mouth about this."

CHAPTER 33

Abandoned Tobacco Field
One Mile Northwest of the Knoll
11:00 A.M., MARCH 29, 1865

High on a rush of adrenaline—and alcohol, Steve laughed long and loud as the *Jenny* bounced off the ground for the second time, and then with only a few feet to spare, the little trainer cleared the treetops at the end of the field.

Steve tilted the bottle and took another snort to celebrate. "Whew! That's good stuff!" He licked his lips and basked in the warm glow he felt all over. He felt good, really good. And he was flying too! *Got this baby off the ground in the pouring rain from a muddy pasture. Not bad, if I say so myself. Even better, it's 1865, which puts me forty years ahead of the Wright brothers! I think that calls for a little toast.*"

Steve tipped the bottle in a mock salute. "To you, Orville and Wilbur! Eat your hearts out!" He took another long pull, then held the amber bottle up to see how much was left: *half-empty.*

"On the other hand, it's also half-full, which is better than half-empty, I think," he told himself, but it required more heavy reasoning than his muddled mind could sort out. "Well, whatever," he frowned drunkenly. "In either case I'd better save some of this for what I came up here to do."

Steve checked his cockpit compass. The *Jenny's* nose was pointed due west.

"Wrong direction," he chided himself. Easing back on the control stick, he climbed another 500 feet to a safer altitude, then put the *Jenny* into a hard bank until the compass indicated a southeast heading. He leaned over the edge of the cockpit and looked down, hoping to spot a familiar landmark, but he caught only brief glimpses of the ground flashing by through the low overcast, and nothing looked familiar.

Steve was no longer smiling or feeling all that good either. The mellow sensation in his stomach had suddenly turned rancid. *This is becoming a bit vexing. Alex and Mike are somewhere below me, and I can't communicate with them.*

He dropped down 450 feet; his altimeter registered 300 feet. *I sure hope I spot the knoll before I fly into something.*

Dark wisps of rain-laden mist flashed past between his upper and lower wings, momentarily obscuring the wing struts, and then he dropped below the cloud deck giving him his first good view of the ground.

The scene below was wet, gray, and dreary.

Steve didn't breathe any easier. A new problem had surfaced; moisture collecting on his goggles was hampering his vision. The only cloth available was his sleeve, but it was also wet, so he pulled the goggles off and let them hang around his neck.

Ahead of the *Jenny* the outline of a ridge gradually emerged through the mist. It looked like the right one, but the treetops along its crest were hidden by the low overcast. *That knoll has to be here somewhere, but it's hidden too.*

Steve approached the ridge, then banked to the east and flew parallel to it, not wanting to risk smacking into the knoll or the trees on its summit.

After flying back and forth twice with no success, he finally gave up and turned away from the ridge. *The weather isn't improving either,* he noted gloomily. *Hmm? Well, if flying under the cloud ceiling didn't work, maybe there's a chance I can get above it and see something.*

Steve nosed the *Jenny* upward. Within seconds the dark, moisture-laden cloud cover had swallowed him. He felt uneasy as he remembered his last encounter with dark gray clouds swirling around him. At 2000 feet he sensed the cloud cover beginning to thin. At 4000 feet a definite improvement, and when he reached 5000 feet, he broke out of the overcast.

But Steve felt little elation.

He was sandwiched between a low and an upper cloud deck with only a few hundred feet between the two layers. The cloud-free elevation could disappear at any moment. *At least the rain has stopped,* he told himself, trying to paint an optimistic picture on the situation.

For the next five minutes he flew a crisscross pattern over the area hoping a break in the lower cloud deck might give him a glimpse of the knoll or the tops of its towering trees. But the cloud cover stretched as a solid gray blanket to all points of the compass.

Steve frowned as he noticed the thin cloudless pane rapidly growing thinner. *I can't fly around up here in this soup forever,* he told himself. And then it hit him. He had been so focused on finding the *Jenny* and getting her off the ground that he hadn't given any thought to how and where he would land later.

Reviewing his options didn't take long. There weren't any. *If the ground gets socked in, I can't make a safe landing,* he told himself. *Then, too, with all this rain, the Jenny would sink up to her belly in the mud—or worse—if I landed in the same field I took off from. It would probably be the same story trying to land elsewhere. One thing's for certain, I'm coming down sooner or later. Like I used to tell my student pilots, 'I've never left anyone up here yet!'*

At first he thought it was just an anomaly in the otherwise immense flat surface of the lower cloud deck. He dismissed it and continued scanning the cloud cover in front of him from left to right. The next time he glanced at the anomaly, now a mile off his right wing tip, he noticed something odd. It had retained its shape.

Steve's heart skipped a beat.

Now that's really an anomaly! He smiled broadly as he banked the *Jenny* and headed toward it.

As he approached within a half-mile, it became readily apparent that the irregular shape was actually the top of an incredibly huge tree protruding above the low-lying cloud cover. Its misshapen limbs resembled those that he and the *Jenny* had narrowly missed on that fateful day five months earlier. More importantly, they belonged to the largest tree on the knoll.

"Okay. Let's take a spin around it and see if we can spot anything else down there," Steve grinned, talking to the *Jenny* like an old friend. "Hopefully, Alex and Mike heard the engine and are inside a protective shelter by now."

Steve remembered Alex's comment when he sprang his aerial bombing proposal, pointing out a possible flaw in his plan. "Let's say you spook the grove, and it decides to take refuge in 1918 while you're making bombing runs and loop the loops. What makes you so sure you and your flying machine will be invited to tag along?"

He had already thought of that and had an answer. "The grove took us back in time with it when my machine and I tumbled out of that twister in 1917. Dropping a few bombs just might persuade it to spring back to 1917 or 1918. Either year is good—I'm not picky."

Steve made a quick pass around the tree, but the knoll and the rest of the grove were still hidden under the cloud cover; worse, the upper cloud layer had begun to merge with the lower.

Steve frowned. *Time's running out!*

Banking the *Jenny* sharply, he turned for another pass at the tree. "Okay! Let's do it!" he cheered, the sound of his voice building his confidence. "We're going to upset this tree big time!"

Steve dropped the *Jenny's* nose into a shallow dive, then lifted the glass globe on the lantern dangling beside him in the cockpit. He struck a match and lit the strip of kerosene-soaked canvas that he had stuffed into the mouth of the second bitters bottle before take off. *This would be a lot easier and less risky if I hadn't lost my silver cigarette lighter way back when.*

Steve eased back on the stick. The *Jenny* pulled up out of its dive just above the tree's giant branches.

Rolling the biplane slightly onto its left side, he dropped the bottle and watched the spiraling orange tongue of flame disappear into the clouds below.

Twice more, he dive-bombed the tree. On each pass he dropped a canteen full of gunpowder with a flaming strip of kerosene-soaked canvas dangling from its spout.

As he completed his third pass, he thought he heard a muffled explosion, then an eerie humming. He wasn't sure. *Could have been the wind whistling through the cockpit or the engine backfiring.*

He retrieved the half-full bitters bottle from under his seat cushion.

Hate to give this one up, but it's for a worthy cause. He pulled the cork out with his teeth, then stuffed a kerosene-soaked strip of canvas into the bottle.

Steve banked the *Jenny* for a final pass over the tree. Taking his eyes off it just long enough to light the canvas strip dangling from the bottle's lip, he didn't notice the dark cloud descending.

When he looked again through the windscreen, dark, moisture-laden mist was whipping past him with zero visibility. Vertigo immediately set in. Without a horizon to fix on, he couldn't tell if he was going up or down—he could be flying upside down for all he knew. Dizzy, he tossed the bottle over the side and watched the tiny flame disappear into the swirling mist.

Steve was literally flying blind, and he sensed danger looming ahead. He pulled back on the control stick and tried to climb. The gray shroud in front of the *Jenny* parted for an instant.

Directly ahead, the ghostly, gnarled branches of the enormous tree rushed toward him. With no time or room to maneuver, he threw up his arms to protect his face. The *Jenny's* upper wing tore away from the wing struts, and the wooden propeller suddenly exploded into jagged splinters.

CHAPTER 34

The Knoll

Dinwiddie County, Virginia

1:48 P.M., MARCH 29, 1865

Alex and Mike sat at the table in Alex's tent mulling over Steve's plan. The rain fell in a steady torrent, drumming against the canvas.

Alex hadn't shared Steve's optimism. His plan was full of *ifs* and riddled with flaws. And with the weather deteriorating, he had become even less optimistic.

Mike had similar misgivings.

As crazy as his idea sounded, Steve had persuaded them both that he could pull it off. "Not exactly a piece of cake," he had told them, "but entirely possible."

"It's been almost two hours," Alex frowned, looking at his pocket watch again for the umpteenth time. "Even if he found his flying machine in this downpour, he probably couldn't get it off the ground. Or if he did, then crashed, we would never know."

Mike nodded as he nervously drummed his fingers on the tabletop.

Alex was about to continue, then stopped and cocked an ear. Despite the pitter-patter of the rain against the canvas, he thought he heard something—a distinctive *humming*. He glanced at Mike.

Mike suddenly jerked upright in his chair. "I hear something!

Ignoring the torrential rain, they rushed outside and stood staring up at the tree canopy.

The humming came from within the grove, and it was growing louder.

Alex and Mike exchanged puzzled glances, wondering what was causing it.

As he listened, the cold rain trickled from Alex's matted hair, running down his face and neck. Then he heard another sound far away, so faint that he had trouble distinguishing it from the humming coming from the grove.

Seconds went by. Then he heard it again—more distinctive now—a drone, like a bluebottle fly buzzing against a windowpane.

Alex noticed the humming within the grove growing louder as the sound of this discordant note drew closer. The grove seemed to be listening and watching, alert for danger.

"It's Steve's flying machine!" Mike shouted above the noise. "I can't see him, but that's him up there all right. He did it!"

The distant droning became a loud rumble as Steve's biplane approached overhead, then circled the grove.

"Even if we don't see him, he obviously has a fix on us!" Alex shouted over the discordant tones of the biplane's rumbling engine and the grove's high-pitched *hum*.

Mike pointed at the tents, then clasped his hands over his ears as the *hum* suddenly rose to an ear-piercing crescendo.

Alex's eardrums throbbed painfully as he stared at the tents. They had suddenly taken on a luminescent quality. A brilliant white light flowed from them, pulsing in a slow rhythmic pattern as though they had become living and breathing jellyfish-like creatures. Even more startling, Mike's skin also began to glow.

Mike stood mutely, hands clasped over his ears, staring at Alex.

Alex felt a tingling sensation in his fingertips. He held up his hands and gaped at them, awed by their translucent appearance. Wiggling his fingers, he could see the bones moving under his flesh.

The ground suddenly quaked under Alex's feet. With an explosive roar, flames suddenly engulfed the base of the grove's largest tree.

Steve's first homemade bomb had found its mark.

Shaken out of his stupor, Alex grabbed Mike by the shoulder, nearly jerking him off his feet. "Get out of here! Run!" he shouted.

"Where?" Mike yelled. "We need to stay here!"

"No! It's too dangerous up here!" Alex said, running toward the edge of the grove. The high-pitched *hum* quavered like a siren. His ears hurt and his head throbbed. "We have to find cover before Steve makes his next bombing run. The most protected place is the rock overhang below the crest of the knoll where Sergeant Hill found shelter during the night of the thunderstorm.

At the edge of the grove the ground dropped away steeply. Alex and Mike never slowed. They leaped over the edge and rolled down the muddy slope. Below them a ten-foot-wide slab of rock appeared, jutting out perpendicular from the hillside. They dove under it just as the second bomb exploded in the grove above them. The concussion shook the knoll. Flakes of shale showered them, loosened from the rock slab above their heads.

"That must have been one of the canteen bombs," Mike remarked casually, as though he were critiquing a July 4th fireworks show.

"You think?" Alex said, brushing the debris out of his hair.

Moments later another explosion rocked the crest, followed by the sound of crashing limbs.

"Another canteen bomb," Mike announced authoritatively, "but I think it went off in the trees above the ground.

"Yeah," Alex nodded. "And listen to that wailing! Whatever is living in that grove didn't like it. Maybe it'll get fed up with all this abuse and decide to go someplace more peaceful."

"And take us along, we hope," Mike added.

The rumble of the biplane's engine seemed closer as Steve made his next bombing run.

"He's really coming in low this time," Alex said. "Hope he knows what he's doing."

The words were barely out of his mouth when they heard the sound of crumpling metal and splintering wood. The rumble of the biplane's engine suddenly stopped.

In the same instant the world around them exploded in a blinding flash of light.

Alex writhed and convulsed in pain, unable to breathe, as if an invisible cold hand had reached inside his chest and squeezed his heart and lungs. He screamed as the light absorbed his body...then he felt nothing as consciousness left him.

CHAPTER 35

U.S. Army Field Training Site
Dinwiddie County, Virginia
1:15 P.M., MARCH 23, 1918

"Are you all right, sir?" The voice sounded far away. Alex winced. His head felt like someone was tap dancing on the inside of his skull.

"Sir, can you hear me?" a deeper, concerned voice asked.

Hands tried to lift him.

Pain shot through his body, setting every nerve and fiber on fire. Alex screamed.

The hands promptly withdrew.

The pain gradually subsided.

Alex opened his eyes.

A boyish face peered down at him.

Alex tried to speak, but his mouth was sandpaper dry and rough. He swallowed, licked his lips, then tried again.

"Can you hear *me*?" he croaked, his voice barely audible.

"Yes, sir. I can." The young man leaned closer to hear.

"Good," Alex rasped. "Touch me again—I'll kill you!"

Alex closed his eyes. He felt dizzy, but at least the little guy tap dancing inside his skull had slowed down. As he drifted in and out of consciousness he heard another voice ask, "How about the Exec? Is he alive?"

There was a long pause.

Alex tensed.

"Yeah," someone finally answered. "He looks to be in about the same shape as the Captain."

Alex breathed easier. He slowly opened his eyes, letting them adjust to the light. Without moving his throbbing head, he looked around. He was still lying beneath the rock overhang.

The boyish face reappeared.

"What time is it?" Alex whispered.

"It's about one fifteen in the afternoon, sir."

"No," Alex squeezed his eyes shut, then opened them again. "I mean—what year is it?"

"Year, sir?" the young man appeared confused, unsure he understood the question.

"Yeah."

"It's 1918. March 23, 1918 to be exact, sir. Why d'ya wanna know that?"

Alex didn't answer—he just smiled. A tear rolled down his cheek. Then clenching his teeth against the pain, he rolled over onto his left side.

Mike lay sprawled on his back a few feet away, eyes open and focused.

"Mike, did you hear that?" Alex grinned. "We did it! We're back!"

Mike smiled weakly and held out a hand.

Alex grasped it. Both were laughing and crying at the same time.

The three Army medics hovering over them exchanged puzzled looks.

Alex sat up. A medic kneeled beside him and handed him a canteen cup of water. He gulped it down, then nodded for more. Mike, his head thrown back, guzzled water from a canteen.

Minutes later they emerged from the rock shelter, shaky but at least standing—the pain mostly gone. As they stepped into the sunshine, they suddenly stopped, startled to see a group of men from their company quietly gathered on the slope and on the crest of the knoll above them.

The men broke into loud cheers. However, these immediately died away, giving way to open stares.

Alex hadn't anticipated the reaction. He was suddenly conscious of his scraggly beard and the dirty, ragged clothing that had once been a Union Army uniform. He and Mike looked like fugitives from hell.

Silence settled over the assembled soldiers as a lone figure casually descended from the summit of the knoll. Men in his path stepped aside respectfully, giving him passage. He looked neither right nor left as he approached. His features were chiseled, rock-hard, as were his dark deep-set eyes. From a height of six feet, four inches he viewed the two officers distastefully for a moment before stopping in front of Alex and rendering a perfunctory salute. He didn't smile. That was not unusual; no one had ever seen him smile. His face remained expressionless as his eyes flicked coolly over the two officers. Among the men in the company *that* was generally viewed as a good thing, because no one wanted to be the object of his attention when he *was* wearing an expression. Everyone present knew, respected, and feared this stern giant of a man. He was First Sergeant Edmonds, or simply "First Sergeant." To Captain Wright, he was "Top."

"Afternoon, sir," Edmonds said, peering down at Alex. "We were concerned when you didn't show this morning. I trust you're okay?"

Alex knew Edmonds was studying every detail of their strange appearance, but he gave the impression of total indifference.

"Yes, quite okay. Thanks, Top," Alex said without elaborating.

"Sergeant Thomas Hill is also missing, sir," Edmonds continued. "Have you seen him?"

"Not recently," Alex answered, poker-faced.

Edmonds puckered his lips as if he were sucking a sour lemon. "You might want to consider changing into a more presentable uniform before the regimental commander arrives."

Colonel Phelps is coming here?" Alex asked, surprised.

"Yes, sir," Edmonds nodded. "Regrettably, I had to report your absence this morning, especially in light of the flying machine that inexplicably crashed into the grove of trees where your tents are pitched. Or rather I should say *were pitched*. Your tent was destroyed by some sort of explosion that left a small crater. A big limb fell on Lieutenant Dent's tent, crushing it. It's fortunate that you..."

"What happened to the pilot?" Alex asked, interrupting him.

"He hasn't turned up yet. I sent out search parties to scour the area when we discovered the wreckage. One of the search teams found you."

"Show us the wreckage," Alex said. "The Colonel's visit can wait for now."

Alex and Mike started up the steep slope, pulling themselves up hand over hand.

Edmonds followed behind.

Weakened by their ordeal, Alex and Mike ran out of steam as they neared the summit. Several soldiers standing on the crest gave them a helping hand up the last few feet.

Alex paused to catch his breath and stared at the chaotic scene within the grove. Tree limbs of every size littered the ground. Confirming Edmonds' report, only a shallow crater marked the site of Alex's tent. Mike's tent lay buried under several feet of fallen debris. Scorched and charred, the trunk of the largest tree bore testimony to the accuracy of Steve's firebombing. Shafts of sunlight reflected brightly off scattered bits and pieces of what was left of the biplane.

"Have you checked under all this debris, Top?" Alex asked as he surveyed the mounds of limbs blanketing the ground.

"Pretty much, sir," Edmonds nodded. "All we found were small pieces of wreckage."

Alex pressed his palm against the seared tree trunk; it came away blackened with soot. Wiping his hand on his tattered pants leg, he studied the debris field under the tree. Partially hidden beneath a huge fallen limb, he glimpsed a fragment of crumpled wing.

"Give me a hand with this," he said, soliciting Mike and Edmonds' help in pushing the limb aside. The three of them grabbed the limb and put their weight behind it, but it wouldn't budge.

Three soldiers searching through the debris nearby promptly pitched in to help. As they pushed the massive limb aside, its splintered end swung around and scraped against the scarred trunk of the ancient tree. A low hum arose from the giant oak, which was promptly imitated and magnified by the rest of the grove.

"What's that?" one of the soldiers asked, awed and a little spooked by the sound.

"Just the wind in the boughs," Alex smiled reassuringly. "It sometimes makes weird noises. If you don't believe me, try sleeping up here sometime."

The soldier looked dubiously at the huge limbs littering the ground and the crater where Alex's tent once stood. "Thanks, sir, but I'll pass."

Alex nodded—*smart kid*. He kneeled to examine the piece of wreckage they had uncovered. It appeared to be a chunk of the upper wing of Steve's biplane.

Alex frowned, then looked up at Edmonds. "So, where's the fuselage?"

Edmonds shrugged his shoulders. "We searched for it. It's not here."

Alex and Mike exchanged glances and each knew what the other was thinking. *Did Steve make it back too? If so, was he still alive?*

Alex studied the debris. He wouldn't allow himself to write Steve off—not yet.

A sudden stiff breeze rustled the foliage. Sunlight filtered through the canopy and reflected off a shiny object lying among the leaves where the limb had been.

Kicking the leaves away with the toe of his boot, Alex stooped and picked up a pair of flying goggles. He smiled as he dangled them in front of Mike's nose.

Mike imitated Steve's low whistle. "He has to be somewhere close by."

Alex looked at the blackened tree trunk again, letting his eyes wander up past the point where the charred bark stopped. The lowest limb was twenty feet above the ground, and he could see maybe forty or fifty feet up the trunk beyond that. But he knew the tree towered much higher than that. Beyond seventy feet, the foliage was so thick it shut out most of the sunlight.

"Everyone be quiet for a minute and listen," Alex said. On a hunch, he cupped his hands to his mouth and shouted: "Steve! It's Alex! Can you hear me?"

The echo of his voice rebounded within the grove for several seconds. The grove's natural acoustics surprised him, magnifying his voice almost ten-fold; it reminded him of the Charleston opera house, only this was better.

Suddenly an omnipresent voice with an English accent boomed high above them, "I say, chaps, whenever you can spare a few minutes, I'm afraid I'm in a bit of a fix up here."

Alex and Mike grinned as they peered up into the overhead canopy.

"Steve," Alex shouted, "we can't see you. Just where are you?"

"Pinned inside the fuselage about eighty or ninety feet above the ground. I'll toss something down; maybe that will help."

After a brief pause Steve yelled, "Here comes a burlap bag."

A moment later, Alex spotted the bag half-falling, half-floating to the ground. Scanning the foliage high above where it first appeared, Mike pointed to a dark mass lodged in the fork of a huge limb.

"Okay," Alex yelled. "We see you! We'll get you down! Are you hurt?"

"No! But I'm wedged inside the cockpit and can't get free!"

"Just hang on!" Alex said. "We'll get you some help!"

"I'll be here! I'm not going anywhere—I don't think."

Steve was quiet for a moment. "Alex?"

"Yeah?"

"Tell me something!"

"What?"

"What year is this?"

"What year would you like it to be?"

"How about 1918?"

"You got it!" Alex grinned.

"Really?"

"Yeah!"

"How come I still hear shooting, Alex?" Steve sounded dubious. "It's far off, but it sounds like it's coming from somewhere around Petersburg!"

"Trust me, Steve! The firing is from Camp Lee! It's really 1918, and I've got a bunch of soldiers with me dressed in olive drab uniforms who'll swear to it!"

"Great, Alex! I'm convinced, but hurry up on getting me down from here! I don't know which scares me more, a strong wind or another thunderstorm—if you get my drift!"

"Yeah, I get your drift, Steve! We'll hurry!"

"One more thing, Alex!"

"What?"

"Don't laugh, but I don't think this tree likes me! I think it's harboring a grudge!"

"Can't imagine why!" Alex laughed.

Alex was suddenly aware of at least thirty of his men standing around watching and listening. Most looked puzzled; others were whispering among themselves.

"Okay, boys," Alex said, springing into action, "I know the Exec and I look a bit strange, and some weird stuff has happened today, but just put it aside for the time being. We have an emergency. A man's life is in danger. I need volunteers, especially anyone with experience working in high places. You know—lumberjacks, scaffold workers, pole climbers—jobs like those."

Four men promptly stepped forward.

"Maybe we're what you're looking for, Captain," said a tall, lanky corporal, obviously the group spokesman. "We worked for a New York City construction company before the war. Spent most of our time in high places, walking steel girders and scaffolding. We're also good with tools. We're willing to give it a shot if you can use us."

Two more men who had been whispering together stepped forward. One was small and wiry-looking; the other was average height but muscular.

The small wiry one spoke for the two of them. "We're loggers from Michigan, sir. We don't doubt for a second that these New York men are good at their trade, but we used to earn our bread and butter climbing and topping trees like this." He hesitated as he squinted up at the giant oak. "Well, maybe not *quite* like this. Our Michigan trees are a mite smaller. But just the same, anyone scaling a tree this size needs special footgear and tree climbing experience. Two men at the most ought to go up there. Any more, and you risk the whole *shebang* coming down the hard way, including the rescuers."

"What kind of tools and equipment would you need?" Alex asked.

"We can fabricate the climbing gear we need pretty easily. We'll need about three hundred feet of one-inch rope, a hand saw, some spikes, and a hammer. I imagine the fuselage is made of light material, so we can probably cut the aviator out of it using a hack saw to saw through metal bars and struts, a bolt cutter, and a tin-snip. All that stuff should be in the supply tent."

"Looks like you've got it pretty well worked out," Alex said.

After listening to the lumberjacks, the New Yorkers conceded that the Michigan men were probably better suited for this kind of work. Everyone smiled and shook hands.

"Okay then," Alex nodded, "you loggers have talked yourselves into a job!"

Steve suddenly called out, "Alex, how's it going down there?"

"I found two former lumberjacks from Michigan who have specialized in this type of rescue all their lives!" Alex answered with a grin, winking at the two lumberjacks for the slight exaggeration.

"That's great! What do they think of my situation?"

"They think you're going to die, but they'll enjoy the challenge!"

"I'm happy for them! Thanks for that bit of cheer!"

"Just hang on, Steve! They'll probably have you down within an hour!"

"Does that mean they're going to shake the tree 'til something tumbles out?"

"Maybe. In which case, just flap your arms; after all, you *are* a flyer!"

"Well, I'm just sorry I made bombs out of those bottles of Drake's 1860 Plantation Bitters. I could use one of them about now!"

The *Jenny's* fuselage lay wedged in the fork of one of the oak's largest limbs eighty feet above the ground.

In a matter of seconds, the two Michigan lumberjacks scaled the trunk with breathtaking agility and reached the limb.

Steve's would-be rescuers had intended to use one of the ropes to lower him to the ground. However, now that they had literally crawled out on a limb, they realized just how precarious the situation really was. It wouldn't take much—a gust of wind or a vibration—to dislodge the fuselage and send it plummeting. To have the aviator dangling on a rope beneath it no longer seemed like such a good idea.

A few snips with a bolt cutter was all it took to free Steve's pinned legs from the wreckage. The fuselage creaked ominously as one of the lumberjacks extended a hand to help pull him out of the cockpit.

As Steve worked his shoulders clear of the wreckage, his grip on the logger's sweaty hand suddenly slipped. He fell back into his seat, the sudden jar caused the fuselage to shift. It slid half way out of the fork, then teetered back and forth as if waiting for the next breath of air to upset its balance and send it crashing to earth.

From this new vantage point Steve had an unobstructed view of the ground and the tiny figures looking up at him. All at once he felt cold and clammy, and he was rapidly developing an abnormal fear of heights. *Acrophobia,* he told himself, *is not a trait the Army Air Service likes to see in its aviators.*

Larson, the little wiry lumberjack, tossed Steve the end of a rope with a loop attached. Steve slowly and carefully slipped his hands and arms through the loop and settled it snugly under his armpits.

Larson tied his end of the rope around the limb, then signaled to Steve that the next move was up to him. The lumberjack didn't want to risk shaking the limb by trying to help.

Hand over hand, Steve gripped the taut rope and pulled. Then inch by inch, he gradually worked his body out of the cockpit.

Larson coached him, telling him exactly where to place each hand and foot as he crawled from the teetering fuselage out onto the limb. Steve's arms weren't long enough to reach all the way around the huge limb, so he dug his fingernails into the bark and gripped the limb with his knees. Like a giant inchworm, he slid along the limb toward the trunk of the tree. It was only fifteen feet away, but to Steve it looked a mile.

Slupinski, the heavier, muscular lumberjack, led the way toward the trunk, walking confidently and easily along the limb in front of Steve. In similar fashion, Larson walked upright behind Steve, continuing to offer encouragement and advice.

When Slupinski reached the trunk, Steve looked up to see how much further he had to go—then froze, horrified.

Before Steve could shout a warning, the hammer in Slupinski's hand was already swinging downward to strike the head of the big eyebolt he was holding against the tree trunk.

"Nooo!" Steve yelled, just as the metallic ring of steel striking steel rang through the grove.

Intent on what he was doing, the lumberjack gave the eyebolt another solid *whack,* before casting a curious glance at Steve.

Steve's warning had come too late.

A high-pitched *hum* emanated from the stricken tree. In a matter of seconds, the rest of towering giants in the grove were echoing the alarm.

Puzzled, the two lumberjacks gazed around from their lofty perch for the source of the sound. Slupinski suddenly shouted a warning as the limb under his feet began to vibrate.

Steve looked over his shoulder just in time to see the fuselage slide from its perch and disappear into the void below. There were warning shouts from men on the ground followed a moment later by a faint thump like someone had dropped a cardboard box.

Steve clung to the vibrating limb, trying to keep from being dislodged, as he inched toward Slupinski who by now had dropped his hammer and was straddling the limb with his back pressed against the trunk of the tree. He appeared surprisingly calm as he tied an end of a rope around the limb, then dropped the remainder of its hundred-foot length.

"Ever done any body rappelling?" he shouted, his voice vibrating.

"Some, when I was a kid," Steve nodded, trying not to look down.

"Well, it's not what we planned, but it's the quickest way down—if you don't count jumping or falling! Just in case you've forgotten the basics, I'll talk you through it. Do you remember how to wrap the rope around your body?"

Steve nodded.

"Let me see you do it!"

Steve wrapped the rope around his body while the lumberjack watched.

"Good! That's the way. A couple of things to remember: You're going to walk down the trunk of this tree, so keep your body perpendicular to the trunk. Keep your feet shoulder high, any higher than that, and you'll lose your footing and end up dangling upside down. Remember to brake with your right hand and to feed out the rope to descend with your left hand. Most important, remember this: If you lose your balance, bring your right hard against your chest. You may end up dangling upside down, but there's no way you're going to fall out of the rope. Understand?"

"Got it," Steve nodded.

"Any questions?"

Steve shook his head.

"Good! I'll go first and demonstrate how it's done. Just do like I do. You'll soon get the hang of it. It's better than jumping, trust me!" He grinned and gave Steve an encouraging slap on the shoulder.

The lumberjack stood up on the vibrating limb, tied the end of a second coil of rope around the oak's trunk, then tossed the rest of the coil out into space and watched it fall out of sight below. After wrapping the rope around his body and between his legs, he casually kicked away from the limb he was standing on. He walked down the trunk for ten feet leaning straight out away from the trunk, then paused and waited for Steve.

More slowly and with a bit of awkwardness, Steve performed a reasonable imitation. He found Slupinski smiling confidently, obviously in his element, as he rappelled down alongside him.

"You're doing great. Keep your feet up a little higher.... No, sir!

Don't look down! That won't help!"

Side by side they descended another thirty feet.

Steve was quickly gaining confidence.

"We're halfway there!" Slupinski said. "The rest is a piece of cake!"

Against his better judgment and Slupinski's warning, Steve couldn't resist looking down. He turned his head and eyes to drink in the view. It was his undoing. In a flash, his feet went up in the air, and he found himself dangling upside down forty feet above the ground. Remembering Slupinski's final guidance, he brought his right hand holding the rope hard against his chest. As he slowly spun around, upside down with the blood rushing to his head, the relentless humming of the trees did nothing to calm his frayed nerves.

"You're okay!" Slupinski shouted. "Don't panic! You can either try to turn yourself right side up and pick up where you left off, or just feed yourself some slack rope with your left hand and keep going down the way you are."

His confidence shaken, Steve decided to make the best of his predicament and finish the rappel upside down.

Gracefully executing a series of six-foot leaps, Slupinski reached the ground first where, with Alex and Mike's assistance, he helped Steve untangle himself from the rope and land on his feet instead of on his head.

Perched on the limb eighty feet above them, Larson watched Slupinski and Steve's descent. When Steve and the others were clear of the tree, he stood up, wrapped the rope around his body, and pushed away from the limb. He was incredibly agile and made the descent in a series of ten-foot leaps that delivered him safely to the ground in seconds.

As soon as they were on the ground, Alex and Mike herded Steve and the lumberjacks toward the edge of the grove at a dead run. Everyone else was gone.

"Sorry fellas," Alex puffed as they plunged headlong down the trail, "there's no time for congratulations, pats on the back, or explanations. We've got to get off this knoll *now!*"

The nightmare wasn't over. Alex recognized the danger when the *humming* in the grove reached that ominous wailing pitch. He had ordered everyone off the knoll and back to camp on the lower ridge.

First Sergeant Edmonds with a half-dozen armed men stood at the foot of the path leading up to the knoll as Alex and the others emerged into view. "I've seen a truckload of weird shit in this Army," he muttered to himself, "but it's diddly squat compared to what I've seen today!"

At the base of the knoll, Alex glanced up at the summit. Even from this distance he heard the ominous swarm-like *humming*.

Swarm-like? Alex closed his eyes and listened again. Commingled with the *hum* was a new sound—a low rumbling off to the north.

As the seconds ticked away, it gradually grew louder.

Steve and First Sergeant Edmonds stood beside him, listening.

"Whatever it is, it's coming this way," Alex said.

"Military flying machines," Steve concluded, cocking his head to one side as he listened. "Sounds like several."

Suddenly three biplanes appeared a mile distant skimming low above the woods. As if sensing their presence, the formation turned toward them, then climbed rapidly to clear the ridge.

"They're flying unusually low," Steve commented, assuming an air of authority. "'Looks like they're searching for something."

"Probably you," Edmonds replied, gazing at the last machine as it shot past the ridge a close quarter-mile away.

"Me?" Steve said, surprised.

"Am I mistaken?" Edmonds said, affecting a smile. "Or is there *another* crashed flyer around here?"

Steve was momentarily at a loss for words.

"No?" Edmonds asked, arching an eyebrow. "I suppose not. But I was obliged to report the crash of your machine when we discovered the wreckage this morning. I gave our regimental headquarters the map coordinates of the crash site which, it appears, they forwarded through channels."

The rumbling of the search planes' engines grew louder as they circled for another fly-over of the area. But now something else held Alex's attention. The *humming* from the grove had suddenly become acutely louder and angrier-sounding.

The biplanes appeared on the horizon, approaching the ridge on a line that would take them directly over the knoll.

The flashes of pulsating light on the summit apparently caught the attention of the patrol leader. The lead machine suddenly dipped toward the knoll for a closer look.

Alex groaned as the *humming* rose to a quavering pitch. "The grove thinks it's under attack!"

Edmonds and the two lumberjacks looked at him strangely. Alex didn't care. He already had so much to explain, *what's a little more?*

The two trailing pilots had followed their leader and were just pulling out of their dives when the summit appeared to explode in a blinding flash of light.

Alex shielded his eyes with his hands. When he looked again, the three search planes were circling the ridge at a respectful distance, but its appearance had changed.

The ridge's most prominent feature—the knoll—had vanished!

CHAPTER 36

U.S. Army Field Training Site

DINWIDDIE COUNTY, VIRGINIA
3:00 P.M., MARCH 23, 1918

Colonel Dudley A. Phelps, Regimental Commander, arrived a half-hour later.

Slightly built with slicked back hair and a pencil-thin mustache, Phelps wore, as he always did, a tailored wool uniform, polished knee-length riding boots, leather Sam-Brown belt, riding crop, and a campaign hat tipped jauntily to the side.

Conversely, Alex and Mike—with Steve tagging along for moral support—reported to him wearing scruffy beards and ragged Union Army uniforms. Not that they had any choice; it was all they had. Being a meticulous, by-the-regulation type of leader, Phelps was not impressed, at least not favorably.

Seated at a table in the seclusion of the company supply tent, Phelps wrote in the little notebook he always carried as he questioned Alex and Mike about *certain irregularities* that had come to his attention.

Alex and Mike made no mention of their recent experiences: nothing about the grove on the knoll, going back in time to the year 1865, joining the Confederate army, General Gordon's secret plan to capture President Lincoln, Lincoln's own secret plan for ending the war, or how they returned to the year 1918.

Probably just as well we didn't bring that up, Alex mused as he watched Colonel Phelps scribbling notes, *I doubt Phelps has room for all of it in his little notebook.*

At the conclusion of his interrogation, Phelps put down his pen and picked up his notebook. He leafed through it for a moment.

"Let's see if I have all this right: You can't account for why you're wearing Civil War-era uniforms or how you came to be found in a shelter cave this afternoon. You claim that the loss of numerous items of United States Army equipment, including two pistols with holsters and belts, ammunition, and tents, etc. was a result of a thunderstorm. You have no recollection of the Army Air Service machine crashing last night. And lastly, the whereabouts of Sergeant Thomas Hill is unknown. Is that a fair summary?"

"Yes, sir," Alex nodded.

Phelps frowned as he closed his notebook and slipped it into the breast pocket of his tunic. "Well, you sure haven't told me much. And it's pretty obvious you're holding something back." He eyed them coldly for a moment. "Is there anything else you care to add?"

"No, sir," they replied one after the other.

"Well, its been quite a day," Phelps sighed, seeing that he wasn't going to get anything more out of them. "I'm sure you're looking forward to getting back to post and a hot shower."

"Yes, sir. We are," Alex smiled, happy to see the Old Man leaving. "The trucks are already here. It shouldn't take long to load everything and then it's good riddance to Dinwiddie County!"

Pausing at the door of the tent, Phelps gave Alex a curious look. "That must have been some storm last night."

"Yes, sir," Alex nodded. "It was pretty incredible all right."

"I got that impression," Phelps said, thumping his notebook. "And having a flying machine crash almost on top of you, too... well, that's really something!"

Phelps looked at Steve. "You're lucky to be alive, young man."

"Just a bit, sir," Steve replied, preferring to say as little as possible.

"We'll arrange transportation to get you back to Langley Field. Your unit is very anxious about you. I'm sure it was just the poor telephone connection, but it sounded to me like your Major said that you and your flying machine have been missing for five months. I suppose you would have some explaining to do, if that were the case." A glint of humor appeared in Phelps's eyes. "I see you're wearing a rather unique uniform, too, Lieutenant. Is that standard issue for Army Air Service flyers these days?"

Before Steve could reply, Phelps dismissed him with a curt nod then turned back to Alex. "I've no choice but to convene an investigation to look into Sergeant Hill's disappearance. I suggest you consider very carefully what you're going to say to the investigating board," he said pointedly. Phelps walked to the tent's opening, turned and gave them an impromptu salute with his riding crop before stepping outside in search of his driver.

Alex reached into his coat pocket and pulled out the gold ring Sergeant Tom Hill had asked him to give to his wife. He held it in his hand and stared at it.

Mike and Steve stood on either side of him not saying anything but sensing his pain. They, too, shared the burden weighing on his conscience.

Mike cleared his throat to get Alex's attention. "I don't know what we're going to tell an investigating board, Alex. I can't see us telling them the truth and expecting them to believe it. But what are you going to tell Tom Hill's wife and kids? And what will you tell Marian?"

Alex didn't answer right away. He studied the ring for a moment more, then closed his hand around it. There was a profound sadness in his eyes—the same sadness that Mike had seen before in the eyes of someone else in another time.

"What would *you* tell them?" Alex asked.

A long moment of silence followed, until First Sergeant Edmonds entered the tent. "The Regimental Commander just drove away," he said to Alex, "thought you'd like to know. Also, you have a visitor. Do you want to see him?"

"Who is it?" Alex shrugged, obviously not in a welcoming mood.

"An old man. He just showed up. Says you know each other."

Curiosity piqued, Alex nodded. "Okay. Send him in."

A few seconds later a well-dressed, elderly gentleman with a mane of white hair and a neatly trimmed beard and mustache entered. A sleeve on his coat hung empty—its cuff turned up and pinned at the shoulder.

Alex smiled and started forward to shake his hand. *The old man's face does appear vaguely familiar...*

Alex suddenly stopped and did a double take.

"Hello, Captain," the old gentleman smiled. "Nice to see y'all again. It's been a while."

"Gawd Almighty!" Mike stared in awe. "It's Sergeant Tom Hill!"

EPILOGUE

The notes I took while Alex Wright recited his story at the nursing home end here. Of course I had to indulge my curiosity—or maybe it was my fantasy—and I attempted to pick up the ninety-year-old trail where Alex's tale left off.

Surely, I reasoned, there must be a record of the investigation into Sergeant Tom Hill's disappearance and his inexplicable reappearance as an old man. My inquiries turned up nothing, and I almost gave up the search, until one day in April, 2006, I came across a mysterious reference to Sergeant Tom Hill in a loose, one-page declassified SECRET document from the former War Department files. It merely stated that the board of inquiry convened at Camp Lee, Virginia, September 18, 1918 was subsequently adjourned because Sergeant Tom Hill, the principal party in the foregoing investigation (file not found), had died October 4, 1918 before giving testimony. Whatever occurred at Camp Lee involving Sergeant Hill that prompted the U.S. Army to convene a board of inquiry and classify its proceedings as SECRET must have been extraordinary.

I did manage to locate Tom Hill's grandson, Colonel Charles Ambrose Hill, U.S. Army retired, living in Durango, Colorado. After a long drive from Texas to Colorado, I met him for lunch at a quiet Mom and Pop restaurant in Durango. A tall, gray-haired, militarily trim man in his late fifties, he was quite cordial but understandably curious vis-à-vis my interest in his long-deceased grandfather. On the pretext that I was researching his grandfather's World War I unit, I explained that I had uncovered some puzzling questions about Sergeant Tom Hill's military service. For obvious reasons, I didn't mention Alex Wright's Civil War dementia-ward tale; however, I did show him a copy of the declassified SECRET document I had found in the Department of the Army's archives. After he read it, I asked him if he knew anything about the board of inquiry or the substance of his grandfather's testimony.

"I've no idea," he said, shaking his head. "This is the first I've even heard of it."

He read the document again, then handed it back to me.

"Sorry, I can't help you with this," he smiled apologetically.

"Is your father still living?"

"Nope. He died about five years ago. Heart attack. Mom's dead too—died before Dad."

"I guess I don't need to ask if your grandmother Hill is still living."

"If she were she'd be about a hundred and twenty years old by now," he chuckled. "She was born in 1891 and died way back in 1955; I was in high school at the time. She was a grand lady, and I have a lot of great memories of her. She practically worshipped my grandfather, and although she was still relatively young when he died, she never remarried."

"Did she ever talk about him—about his military service, I mean?"

"Hmmm," Colonel Hill grunted meditatively, staring off into space. "Not much that I remember. One thing I do remember—and that's because it made such an impression on me at a tender young age—she said that he wasn't in the Army all that long, but when he came home from the war he wasn't the same man. He had aged terribly—both physically and mentally—like he had been gone for years, had lost an arm in the war, was haunted by nightmares, and often talked about the war in his sleep. I remember her leaning over and whispering in my ear, so no one else would hear. What she said, or maybe it was the way she said it, sent chills up my spine: 'He wasn't fighting the Germans in his dreams,' she said. 'It was a different, god awful war. Your granddaddy wouldn't talk about it when he was awake, but there was no mistaking where he was when he talked in his sleep.' She pressed her fingers to her lips and looked like she had seen a ghost. 'And that's the last I better say about that' she said, 'or you'll think I've totally lost my mind.'" Colonel Hill paused as if to collect his thoughts, then continued. "Grandfather Hill died in the 1918 influenza epidemic before being discharged from

310

the Army. Grandmother did say he had a problem getting medical disability from the Army because they couldn't find any mention of a combat-related injury or treatment in his medical records. But as soon as he died, she had no problem getting her widow's pension. She got it almost immediately, like the Army couldn't do enough for her, even sent an officer to help her fill out the paperwork."

Perhaps as an afterthought, Colonel Hill suddenly pointed at the gold ring on his right hand. "This belonged to my grandfather, Sergeant Tom Hill. My grandmother used to wear it around her neck on a gold chain. Just before she died she gave it to my dad, telling him it was a Hill family heirloom that had been passed down from father to eldest son for generations. She apologized for not giving it to him sooner, but it was one of the few keepsakes left by her husband, and she just couldn't part with it. Years later on his deathbed, my father gave it to me." His expression saddened as he reflected on the memory; then he abruptly changed the subject.

"Y'know something? A year or so after my dad died, I wrote to the National Archives for a copy of my grandfather's service records." He paused and looked me squarely in the eye. "Have you seen them?"

"I have," I nodded, already anticipating where he was going with this.

"Then you know."

"Yeah, I know," I said. "According to his military service records, your grandfather never saw combat. For that matter, he never went overseas."

"That's right," Colonel Hill nodded. "So how did he lose his arm, and why did Grandmother Hill insist that he had lost it in the war?"

"I hoped you would be able to tell me," I said, disappointed. "By any chance, do the names Captain Alex Wright and Lieutenant Michael Dent ring any bells in connection with your grandfather?" I asked the question aware that it was a long-shot but still worth a try.

Hill shook his head, no. "Who're they?"

"Your grandfather's company commander and company executive officer when he was stationed at Camp Lee. I was hoping he might have mentioned them in a diary or personal letters."

"If my grandfather kept a diary, I never saw it. We were a close-knit family in those days. Grandmother Hill lived with us during her last years, and I'm pretty sure I'd have heard about any diary or letters she might have had. There weren't any."

It was readily apparent Colonel Hill had nothing more to offer which might shed light on his grandfather's military service or his association with either Captain Alex Wright or Lieutenant Michael Dent. I thanked him for his time, shook his hand as we left the restaurant, then climbed into my Toyota FJ Cruiser for the long drive back to Texas. The trip produced nothing substantial, just more questions with no answers.

Tracking down First Lieutenant Steven Clarke, 22nd Aero Pursuit Squadron, United States Air Service (aka Lieutenant Nevill Anderson, 24th Virginia Infantry, Kemper's Brigade, Pickett's Division, Longstreet's Corps, Army of Northern Virginia, Confederate States Army) proved relatively easy. On the other hand, his trail came to an abrupt and regrettable end. Steven Clarke, the intrepid aviator and a principal character in Alex Wright's saga, joined the American Expeditionary Force in France in the summer of 1918. Unfortunately for both him and my research, his was one of approximately sixty Allied aircraft lost during the Battle of Saint-Mihiel during the period September 12-15, 1918. Although no Allied pilots reported witnessing the downing of his aircraft, and no remains were ever recovered, he was presumed killed in action on September 15, 1918.

I didn't have to search very hard to find First Lieutenant Michael R. Dent, U.S. Army. According to his service records, he was promoted to Captain, Infantry, May 1, 1918, and died from wounds received during the Battle of Belleau Wood on June 15, 1918 while serving with the 3rd Infantry Division. I thought it was odd that both his service records and those of Captain Alex Wright were missing pages pertinent to the first six months of 1918 and their duty assignment at Camp Lee, Virginia.

Since this narrative begins with Alex Wright, it seems only fitting that it should end with him. When I returned to the nursing home in Temple, Texas where we met, fifteen years had come and gone and the nursing home had long ago shredded all his records. I assumed that his nephew, whatever his name was, was probably deceased or in a nursing home himself. I hadn't written his name down but I did recall that his last name wasn't Wright—not much to go on. As a last resort, in April 2008, I made plane reservations and flew from Austin, Texas to Richmond, Virginia where I rented a car and drove to Petersburg. At the Prince George County Courthouse I found what I had come to find—a marriage license issued by the Clerk of the Circuit Court of Prince George County, State of Virginia, dated the 18th day of June, 1918 to Alexander Buford Wright and Marian Herritick Gilliam. Verifying that part of Alex's story gave me a glimmer of hope that Marian might still be alive. But alas, she had predeceased her husband by eight years, and they had no children. Back in Texas, I went to the genealogy section of my local library and found Alex and Marian in the 1920 Federal Census. They came to Texas in 1919 and settled in Goliad County where they made a living from ranching and farming. After Marian's death (pneumonia) in 1986, Alex gave up the ranch and moved to Georgetown, Texas where he lived with his nephew until he was admitted to a nursing home in 1993.

Months of exhaustive research failed to produce a single shred of hard evidence substantiating Alex Wrights' version of events he claimed to have witnessed during the siege of Petersburg in March 1865. The only rational conclusion, of course, was that the story was a total fabrication created by a brilliant but delusional mind incapable of distinguishing reality from fantasy.

One evening I sat in my den dejected and lamenting the time and effort I had expended researching Alex Wright' fable. I slowly leafed through my unfinished manuscript, then with a sigh, dropped it in the waste basket. I sat and stared at the ream of paper lying in the bottom of the basket until, little by little, an idea occurred to me.

With renewed optimism, I retrieved my manuscript from the

trash. The next day I boarded a plane to Richmond, Virginia, then drove a rental car to Fort Lee, an Army post located next door to the Petersburg National Battlefield. Hoping I wouldn't be arrested, I spent a week surreptitiously probing and digging in and around the densely wooded 1865 site of General Meade's headquarters which today is located on the post.

Tonight as I sit at my desk writing the last lines of this story, I gaze at the two rusted Colt Model 1911, .45 caliber pistols that I brought back, and then I think of Alex Wright and his dementia ward yarn and—y'know—I still can't help but wonder....

List of Photographs

WORK CITED

The War of the Rebellion: A Compilation of the Official Records of the Union and Confederate Armies. Published Under the Direction of The Hon. Daniel S. Lamont, Secretary of War, by Maj. George B. Davis, U.S.A., Mr. Leslie J. Perry, Mr. Joseph W. Kirkley, Board of Publication. Series I-Volume XLVI- In Three Parts. Part III-Correspondence, Etc., Washington: Government Printing Office. 1894. Republished by The National Historical Society, Gettysburg, PA 17325, Copyright 1972. Pages 50 and 86.

www.ingramcontent.com/pod-product-compliance
Lightning Source LLC
Chambersburg PA
CBHW070221260626

47160CB00002B/629